# THE
# Corpse
## WITH
## THE
# Crystal
# Skull

## CATHY ACE

FOUR TAILS PUBLISHING LTD.

For Gemma and Kevin,
with love and thanks

## Breakfast and a Body

The conversation around the breakfast table was understandably muted; we'd all had a late night, and I, for one, was feeling the effects of a few too many G and Ts. My darling husband, Bud, surveyed the food arranged on the mahogany sideboard with bleary eyes. His more-salt-than-pepper hair was still damp from the shower, but he was already sweating through his shirt; May in Jamaica can be exhaustingly humid.

"Anybody want another mango? Or this last piece of banana bread?" Bud's tone lacked enthusiasm.

John Silver shook his head above his coffee cup, then scrunched his eyes, suggesting he wished he hadn't made such a rash move. "Thanks, no," he croaked, with a polite smile I read as a grimace.

He looked tired; wiped out, in fact. I'd first met him when he'd helped out with a family matter in Amsterdam that Bud and I had been looking into, less than a year earlier; back then he'd looked vigorous, and in his prime. Now? He'd aged. A lot. I wondered why. Maybe it was work-related; I'm still not entirely sure what he does – he somehow provides coordination between a number of secret service operations around the world…lots of opportunities there for stress, I'd have thought. He looked as though he needed the week-long break he was just beginning with us.

"Anyone fancy a Caesar?" Bud's other ex-colleague, Jack White, forced a smile; they'd served together in the Vancouver Police Department for years, forging a friendship that had endured beyond their respective retirements. Jack glanced at his wife with a wink, rubbed a hand through his rapidly thinning hair, and groaned.

Sheila tutted and wagged a friendly finger at her husband. "No alcohol for you for a while, I think, dear."

I sighed. "I might never drink again."

A subdued chorus echoed my sentiment.

I gulped some juice. Sadly, it was far from cold; even at nine in the morning the dining room was already stifling, and the ice in my glass had melted quickly. Overall, I was enjoying the faded grandeur of the big house at the heart of the private estate we'd rented; the colonial style building was a symphony of white walls, dark hardwood floors and beams, and furnishings upholstered in scrambled egg-hued chintz patterned with bottle-green palm fronds.

Occasionally, breezes wafted through the openings in the walls which housed dark-wood jalousies with slats that could be shuttered against the weather. However, I yearned for the luxury of air conditioning; the two large ceiling fans above the dining table were turning as fast as they could, but the result was about as refreshing as using a hairdryer in a sauna. Luckily, our private bungalows on the estate were so compact they had better through-draughts than the main house.

Bud came to sit at the end of the gleaming mahogany table beside me. I closed my eyes as his chair scraped across the floor. It didn't help.

"Will Lottie be joining us?" Bud sounded almost cheery.

Every bloodshot eye in the room turned, slowly, toward John Silver, who replied, "She was taking a shower when I left." He checked his watch. "A long shower, by the looks of it. I dare say she'll be along in a bit."

"I suspect she'll be in better shape than any of us," I ventured.

"Good morning all. What a beautiful day. It looks as though it's going to be sunny, at last." Charlotte Fortescue – Lottie to her friends – waltzed into the dining room in a swirl of periwinkle silk chiffon, bouncing blonde curls, and a waft of fruity perfume. She looked irritatingly fresh, which I put down to her being about thirty, whereas I'd turned fifty a couple of weeks earlier – hence the festivities the previous night.

Of course, that hadn't been the original plan at all. Initially, Bud and I were supposed to be alone at the Captain's Lookout Estate, on the northern coast of Jamaica, for an entire month. Then Bud had somehow managed to invite Jack and Sheila to join us for a fortnight, then he'd also gone and asked John and his "plus one" to come along for our final week.

Fortunately, I'd been alone with my husband for My Big Day; that had been my choice, and Bud had understood. At least, he'd *said* he understood. The fact that one specific day or date makes a difference to a person's life is something I'm happy to acknowledge to myself, and even to Bud. But to have to party to order? No. Not for me. Really. Besides, I knew that fifty was a significant age, and I hadn't been looking forward to becoming it at all; once you hit fifty it's almost impossible to convince yourself there's more of your life ahead of you than behind, and that's a difficult pill to swallow.

Jack and Sheila White had arrived about a week ago, and they'd busied themselves with all the standard tourist trips: marvelling at the sandy beaches; ogling magnificent waterfalls; being punted along a winding river, and wondering at all the watersports that seem to enthrall so many. I have no idea what's so inviting about being bounced across the ocean on a giant banana, but – apparently – it's all the rage.

It had been agreed that we'd wait until John and Lottie had completed our party to…well, party. Last night's belated birthday celebration had left me feeling crumpled and haggard, bleakly realizing that the passing years make a heck of a difference when it comes to recovering from a long night of over-indulgence.

A feeble chorus of "Good mornings" acknowledged Lottie's arrival; she kissed John on the top of his slightly balding head, then all-but skipped to the buffet dishes. I focused on my juice, so I didn't have to see her gratingly lithe back wriggling about beside the fruit plates.

When the wailing reached our ears, we all turned toward the French doors. Amelia LaBadie rushed into the dining room from the lush tropical garden beyond. She held onto the door frame to support herself as she caught her breath. Usually smiling above her immaculate, cobalt-and-white striped dress, the woman who had been our cook, cleaner, and server during our stay was surprisingly dishevelled; sweat was trickling down her face, and her braided hair had tumbled from its topknot.

Bud, Jack, and John were all out of their seats in seconds. I put down the last bit of my banana bread, and felt the energy in the room shift. Seismically.

"What's wrong, Amelia?" asked Bud.

"Mr. Freddie. Him on the floor, up in the tower. I see him through the keyhole. There be a lot of blood. I think him…him…"

She collapsed into John's arms.

"Oh, I say!" was all Lottie Fortescue could manage.

Sheila White's "Damn it!" was more succinct.

## A Tower Full of Trouble

Following a moment of stunned silence, Bud and John managed to get Amelia to a chair. I rushed to her side with a glass of juice, which the poor woman took from me with a shaking hand; she spilled a fair bit, but managed to get some of it down.

Sheila arrived with a napkin to wipe Amelia's eyes, and Lottie hovered with Jack, neither of them seeming to know how to help. When the housekeeper had finally managed to compose herself a little, Bud, Jack, and John exchanged a glance. Bud spoke.

"Now, tell us again, Amelia. What did you see, exactly?"

Amelia wiped a fat tear from her cheek. Her chin puckered. "Mr. Freddie. On the floor. There was…so much blood." She sobbed into the napkin, shuddering. The poor woman looked completely traumatized.

"And this was where, precisely?" pressed John.

Amelia waved an arm. "Top floor of him tower. Lookout room."

Bud's jaw flinched. "I tell you what, Amelia, you stay here – Sheila, Cait, and Lottie will look after you – while we go take a look."

I glared at Bud. He returned my glance with a sheepish smile; he's well aware of how I view assumptions about traditional male and female roles.

"You can't get into him room. It be locked. Mr. Freddie, him have the only key," sobbed Amelia.

Bud glanced at his two ex-colleagues again. "Maybe, between us, we could break down the door?"

He looked as uncertain as I felt. Bud was the only one of the three under sixty – just – and none of the men were at what one might call "peak fitness" levels.

"I'm going. Who's coming?" I snapped. "Freddie might not be dead at the moment – but he could be by the time you lot faff about."

I strode out into the garden and along the winding, crushed-shell pathway that led from the shared house and pool area, past our private bungalows, toward the tower atop which was our host, Freddie Burkinshaw's, favored eyrie. I could hear footsteps crunching behind me and saw that everyone, except Lottie, was following. Of course someone had to stay with Amelia, and I was glad it was Lottie; she could flutter her eyelashes at someone other than my husband, or Sheila's, for a while, and do something more useful than being merely decorative.

I sighed away my annoyance at Lottie as I focused on the matter in hand. The door to the stumpy, square building that formed the base of the round, castellated structure was wide open – left that way by Amelia, I assumed. It took a few seconds for my eyes to adjust to the gloomy interior – all the jalousie window shutters were closed. I began to walk up a stone staircase, which wound around inside the tower to a room on the first upper level. This room was brighter, because all the shutters were open, and was set up as a sitting room. Everything looked undisturbed to my eyes, though I'd never been in the place before, so had nothing to go on by way of a comparison. The stairs led up again, and once more opened into another room, this time slightly smaller, because the tower diminished in size as it rose. The fact that there was a massive four-poster bed in the middle of the room told me this was

Freddie's bedchamber. I took a breath or two and waited for Bud to catch up, then allowed him to mount the final set of steps ahead of me.

After we'd climbed for what I judged to be almost the full circumference of the building, we encountered a door blocking our path. It was set into the stone walls in a wide wooden frame; both it and its frame looked ancient – maybe even original to the tower, which had been built around 1680 by Sir Henry Morgan, allegedly for a mistress, so Freddie had told us.

Bud hammered on the door, with no response, then waggled the large iron handle, but the door wouldn't open.

"Amelia said she saw him through the keyhole," I offered.

"Peep through the keyhole, go on," urged John, who'd just joined us on the topmost steps.

Bud kneeled and pressed his face against the elaborate blacked-iron plate which housed the massive lock. Jack joined us, and I heard Sheila behind him, panting even more loudly than me. We must have looked quite the sight – all sweaty, pink in the face, still hungover, and listening for the slightest sound.

"He's down alright," announced Bud, "and there's blood. And a gun. I can see his eyes. He's…there's no need for urgency. His eyes are open. Fixed. He's definitely deceased." Bud's use of the formal term told me he'd automatically clicked back into cop-mode; he does that when there's any sort of critical situation to deal with. I find it incredibly comforting.

"He might be looking over at the door, unable to speak, but hoping for help," said Sheila quietly.

Bud stood, shaking his head. "I'm afraid not, Sheila. If he were alive, he'd be blinking away the flies."

That seemed to settle everything, other than my stomach. I swallowed hard. "We'd better phone the police. You can apologize to them for messing up their scene, Bud, flapping your hands about all over the handle," I quipped as I turned.

Sometimes people find my levity inappropriate, but I knew that none of us huddled there on the staircase was a stranger to sudden death – well, with the exception of Sheila, who's been spared that sort of encounter on a regular basis. Bud, Jack, and John have all put in decades of service in law enforcement, and I seem to trip over dead bodies wherever I go. But Sheila? Lovely, unassuming, homebody Sheila would probably be more upset by this discovery than the rest of us.

I waited for everyone to turn so we could all make our way downstairs, and they did, shoulders drooping. A sudden death impacts even those who've experienced many such incidents in ways that differ for each individual. For Bud? He was back in cop-mode already, so he reacted within that role.

"I don't think it's a crime scene, Cait," he said a bit snappishly.

"I said scene, not crime scene," I replied coolly. Bud nodded, and we all finally began our descent. I lowered my voice so only Bud could hear, "Shot in the head?"

Bud shrugged. "Not as far as I could see," he whispered back, "though there could have been trauma hidden at the back of the skull, or on the right side of his face. Maybe through the mouth? I couldn't see everything. The blood seemed to be more around his midsection than at his head."

I couldn't resist. "Oh, come off it, Bud, who commits suicide by shooting themself in the stomach? That's just bonkers." As I spoke, I realized I couldn't *not* take a look at the scene for myself, so I pushed past Bud and rushed up the few steps we'd already descended to peep through the keyhole, even though Bud tried to stop me.

Everything Bud had described was accurate; Freddie Burkinshaw was on his side, his dead eyes looking toward the door, his arms outstretched, with his entire body lying at a forty-five-degree angle to the entryway. Beyond him was a massive dark-wood desk, and beyond that was a pair of doors, wide open. I knew from the exterior view of the building – with which I was familiar – that the doors led to a walkway that encircled the tower around which Freddie would march every morning at sunrise, and every evening at sunset, singing "God Save the Queen" through an antique megaphone.

When he'd welcomed Bud and me to his private estate a few weeks earlier, he'd told us how proud he was to have performed this ritual every day since he'd moved into the property in 1962. His little routine had provided a bit of a rude awakening each day of our visit, and it was only then I realized I hadn't heard his horribly tuneless rendition that morning.

"He's been dead for some hours," I observed as Bud joined me at the impressive door. He helped me to rise from my uncomfortable kneeling position.

Bud smiled. "And why do you say that? Is that your non-existent set of medical qualifications kicking in?"

We started down the stairs again. "What time was sunrise this morning?" I asked. Bud shrugged. "Never mind, we'll Google it later. I reckon it was about half five. My point is, if Freddie had been alive at dawn he'd have sung, and I don't think any of us could have slept through that. We certainly haven't managed to miss it even once since we arrived here."

Bud glanced up at me over his shoulder as he descended below me. "Oh, come on, Cait, we were probably all still comatose at dawn. I reckon I could have slept through an entire performance of the 1812 overture, canons and all, and not heard a thing. Besides, the local coroner, or ME, or whatever they have here, will determine time of death when the local PD shows up. It's not going to make any difference when he died, is it? The poor guy's gone, and that's that."

"But what if it *does* matter, Bud? What if he didn't shoot himself – in the *stomach*?" I put a fair bit of emphasis on that last point.

We were in the sitting room of the late, and probably soon-to-be-lamented, Freddie Burkinshaw's tower when Bud turned to face me, his expression serious. "Cait, stop it. This is some poor guy who chose to take his own life. It just so happens he chose to do it when we were renting the bungalows on his estate. You heard what Amelia said – there was only one key to that tower room, and he had it. He's obviously locked himself in there and shot himself. We both saw the gun. That's the only explanation that makes any sense of the facts."

I allowed my mind to wander, then focus. I stepped closer to the window and managed to catch a slight breeze, which was a relief. The view was fabulous – the never-ending turquoise sea peeping through the palm trees, with a sideways view to the estate's lush gardens, and the glorious beaches beyond. It was the sort of view that would make a person happy.

I didn't turn around as I spoke. "Well, for one thing we don't know for certain that Freddie had the key with him, in that room. It's equally plausible that he was up there with someone else, they killed him, took the key and locked the door behind them, taking the key when they left."

Bud's chin rested on my shoulder, and he snuggled my back as he replied, "But why on earth would anyone want to kill Freddie Burkinshaw? I mean, I know the guy was more than a little eccentric, but he's – what – eighty-ish, perfectly harmless, and the way he told it he hadn't left the island since he arrived in the 1960s. So why on earth would anyone want to kill *him*?"

I turned and looked into the piercing blue eyes of the man I so enjoy calling Husband. Despite the fact we'd slathered ourselves with SPF 50 for the better part of a month we'd both developed quite a tan – his deeper than mine. That, combined with his sun-bleached silvery hair – which had grown quite a bit longer than usual in the past few weeks – and his increasingly silvered eyebrows, made him look even more heart-meltingly handsome than usual, in my book. He was making what I knew he believed to be his "appealing little boy" face, which doesn't wash with me, except when I want it to.

I kissed him gently. "Bud, it's all wrong. Can you honestly say, with your hand on your heart – not to mention using the experience from all your years in law enforcement and detection – that the man with whom we sat dining then drinking until just before midnight last night, who hugged us all goodnight, then left our jolly soirée with a big smile on his face…that *that* man decided to do himself in just a few hours later? The psychology of it isn't right. He wasn't a man on the edge of a cliff of despair – he was thoroughly enjoying himself, dancing, chatting, and telling tall tales, as usual. Yet you want me to believe that maybe five or six hours later he shot himself to death? No. I don't buy it. This wasn't a suicide. It couldn't have been."

Bud held me tight and sighed. "Oh Cait, whatever am I going to do with you?"

# The Constabulary Takes Control

"It couldn't have been anything but suicide," said Sergeant Eggbert Swabey with authority. Constable Cassandra Lewis nodded beside him.

There was an audience of eight in the lounge of the main house for this pronouncement – we six guests, plus Amelia LaBadie and her grandson Tarone Thomas, with whom she shared a little bungalow tucked away in the part of the estate closest to the road.

I'd come to know Tarone because he was the one who drove us around in the estate's Suburban to wherever we wanted to go on the island, by arrangement. He was a cheery boy of eighteen who split his time between working on the estate as a sort of general factotum, and training to be what he referred to as "the new Usain". I knew he was a hard worker on the estate but had no idea about his prowess as an athlete. He certainly looked the part, but that was all the evidence I had to go on.

Amelia hadn't stopped crying since she'd started about five hours earlier, and Tarone had been summoned from his training session at the local gym to attend to his grandmother. Thankfully, she seemed to be calmed by his presence. I had no idea at all about why the grandmother and grandson lived together, nor where Tarone's parents might be. It had never come up, and I'm really *not* a naturally nosey person. Not under normal circumstances, anyway.

"Did you find the key to the lookout room?" I asked the sergeant.

Bud glared at me.

The policeman's face broke into a broad smile. "Ah, Mrs. Anderson. I didn't quite hear you. Could you repeat your question, please?"

I'd seen the man taking notes earlier on, and he'd been speaking to Jack at the time; I assumed Jack had given him Bud's name and had referred to me as Bud's wife.

"The name's Cait, C-A-I-T, Morgan," I replied, "and I asked if you'd found Mr. Burkinshaw's key to his tower lookout room on his person, or in the room with him."

Sergeant Swabey looked confused, but I couldn't be sure if it was me telling him my name or my asking him about the key that had thrown him. He flicked through his notepad, and whispered something to his subordinate, who shook her head in response.

Swabey looked at me earnestly; he appeared to be only in his late twenties, but had the bearing of a man who felt he had already made something of himself. "When we gained access to the scene – which took some time, as you all know, due to the fact we had to summon help to open the door in question – we discovered that Mr. Burkinshaw had the only known key to the room in the pocket of his trousers. This is one of the reasons we have no doubt that he took his own life. It is sad, but it is also not a police matter. The coroner will be involved, of course, but I have no doubt she will concur with our conclusions. It was a suicide."

Amelia sobbed afresh, and an appropriate murmur of sympathetic noises passed around the room. It was clear that everyone felt uncomfortable; we'd only known Freddie Burkinshaw for a short time, as our host and the owner of the estate we'd rented, whereas I understood from conversations we'd shared through various mealtimes that Amelia had been working for him for several decades, with Tarone having been born on the estate. They were the ones I felt sorry for – they'd both lost someone significant, and would possibly be out of their jobs, and their home, in the not too-distant future. I focused on wondering about inheritance and their tenure in an effort to buoy myself up.

The truth of it was that I felt utterly deflated; I'd been so certain that Freddie couldn't have wanted to end his own life that the news he had the only key to the tower room in his pocket had taken me aback. Bud, who was nestled next to me on the spacious sofa, rubbed my back; I've seen him do much the same to Marty, our lovely – but slightly overweight – black Lab, when he's denied him a treat. I wriggled under his kindly hand.

"Are you certain there were no other keys to the place?" I asked Amelia. "Maybe someone got a copy made?"

The poor woman didn't stop sobbing, instead Tarone answered me. He looked surprised. "You seen the key? Man, it huge. I don't know how Mr. Freddie could even fit it in him pocket. Him usually swing it about on a big chain like him got some kind of weapon. It got to be about six inches long, and real fat, and heavy. No one could copy that thing. It a real antique – as old as him tower."

I wondered why a man like Freddie who, in life, had prided himself on his immaculate and dapper appearance, would have wanted to have such a large, weighty object stuffed into his pocket as he ended his life.

*Just one more thing that makes no sense,* I thought to myself.

Having watched our brief back and forth with some bemusement, Sergeant Swabey and Constable Lewis departed, saying they would inform us when we were alone on the estate – which I thought was a delightfully polite way of telling us they'd let us know when the body had been removed.

Almost immediately after they left, the heavens opened; it turns out that short deluges are not uncommon in Jamaica in

May – which might have been one reason why the rates for the rental of the Captain's Lookout estate had been so reasonable. Stripping off soaked clothing and towelling ourselves dry was something Bud and I had become accustomed to since our arrival; of course, on the days when the rain swept in to spoil our time lounging by the pool there was no issue, because we were undressed and wet already, so it hardly mattered. But on this day? On this day we could have done with no rain, a lot less heat, and the chance to all return to our own hidey-holes, rather than feeling trapped by the weather in a room with two people who really needed to grieve.

None of us had eaten lunch – there'd been such a lot going on in terms of official vehicles arriving, explanations to be given, details to be checked, and so forth, that the opportunity hadn't arisen. Now it was past two, and I was feeling more than a little peckish. Why is it that after a hangover has passed, I feel like tucking into vast quantities of stodgy, or greasy foods, and even a drink or two?

I stood and waggled my hand at Sheila in an attempt to attract her attention. "Just popping to the loo," I announced to the room – surprisingly, if Bud's expression was anything to go by. I rolled my eyes at Sheila, hoping she'd follow me. Instead she looked puzzled.

"You okay, Cait?" she asked, standing.

I took my chance, grabbed her hand and headed toward the bathroom. Bless her, she scuttled along behind me like a trooper and didn't even bat an eyelid when I dragged her into the powder room with me and locked the door.

Her expression told me she wasn't alarmed. "What's up?"

I spoke my piece. "Look, in all honesty, I'm starving. But I don't think we can really expect Amelia, or even Tarone, to cater to our needs – given the circumstances. The trouble is, I think if I ask Amelia if we can have access to the kitchen and supplies and so forth, so we can look after ourselves, she might insist on carrying out her duties. She's that sort of woman — proud, a perfectionist, and with an overwhelming sense of duty. She and Tarone need some time to themselves. They should go home. Will you back me up when I put this to Amelia?"

Sheila looked relieved. "Oh yes, of course." She grinned sheepishly and squeezed my hand. "For a minute there I thought you were going to tell me you were convinced Freddie couldn't have killed himself and that someone got into that tower room and murdered him, somehow — because I know that's the way your mind works and…well…no…nothing." She patted my arm. "I'm just glad you wanted to talk about Amelia. And of course, you're right; we can all look after ourselves just fine."

I gave my reply some thought. I like Sheila; I met her because she's Jack's wife, and Jack was something of a mentor to Bud when he joined the Vancouver Police Department. She loves dogs, works hard in her kitchen garden, and is a devil to get hold of when it's jam-making or pickling time. She's a generous soul, if a little over-fussy, on occasion; whenever we visit the Whites, we seem to leave with a collection of mason jars stuffed with various things they've grown on their acreage. Sheila's a decade older than me, a head taller, and someone I enjoy spending time with. She dresses simply, presenting a no-nonsense, make-up-free face to the world and has decided to allow her neatly bobbed hair to change color naturally. She is who she is. A real Prairies girl. There's no spite in her. But I have to admit I don't know the "inner Sheila" very well; Bud makes a good point when he says I don't get close to people, and while I instinctively like the woman, she's not really forthcoming.

With all that in mind I decided that: "So what do *you* think about Freddie's death?" was the best thing to say.

Sheila hesitated before she replied. She hooked her hair behind her ears, straightened her slightly wrinkled, floral cotton top over her flat tummy, then said, "He didn't seem suicidal at dinner last night, did he?" I shook my head and raised an eyebrow by way of encouragement. "I thought he was in fine form, to be honest," she added. "That story about the belly dancer staying at Noël Coward's neighbor's house back in the 1960s? That's the second time he's told that one since we arrived, but it was still hilarious. That bit when he did Coward's voice? Too funny. For Freddie to shoot himself just hours later? I can't see it."

"Me neither," I admitted.

Sheila nibbled the corner of her lip. "The cops seemed pretty sure he did it, though. He even had that key in his pocket," she whispered.

I nodded. "Him stuffing such a huge thing into his pocket before he killed himself? Odd. And, if he did kill himself, then why lock himself in that room at all? Every opportunity he had, he told us he believed the tower was a critically important part of Jamaica's history, so why would he do something that would necessarily mean damaging a part of it? Locking himself in that room, then killing himself, would have meant that someone, somehow, would have to damage the door, or at least that old lock, to get to him."

"It's puzzling, for sure," said Sheila.

"It is."

We both jumped when there was a knock at the door.

"You two gals alright in there?" It was Jack.

"Fine," shouted Sheila. "We're just tidying ourselves up." We looked at each other, both a bit dishevelled and sweating because of the humidity of the day – and the fact we'd been in the tiny washroom for a while – and giggled. "With you in a minute," she added, and we both fiddled about with our hair as cover, before rejoining the rest of the group in the sitting room.

I put our plan into action, encouraging Amelia and Tarone to leave us to look after ourselves at least for the next few days, and I was pleased when everyone chorused their support of the idea. Amelia finally relented, promising that she'd let Tarone take her back to their home once she'd shown us where everything was in the kitchen. I dragged Bud along with me to find out how we might be able to pull together a meal for half a dozen peckish people.

# Dining and Dishing

Half an hour later, the six of us were at the dining table tucking into slices of thick, mixed-veggie frittata, accompanied by a giant bowl of salad from which we served ourselves; it was all Bud and I could manage to pull together in a pinch. Most of the ingredients Amelia had in the store cupboard and fridge were pretty useless as far as I was concerned, because I'm not a dab hand at grilling a lobster or preparing jerk chicken.

I threw some bread rolls into a basket, filled a jug with juice, plonked everything on the table, and hoped for the best. No one complained, though the conversation was far from sparkling – even the irritatingly bubbly Lottie seemed subdued. Which I suspected might be a good thing.

"Maybe we could go out to a restaurant for dinner tonight," suggested Jack.

I chose to take this comment as not being related in any way to the food Bud and I had just prepared.

"Good idea," replied Bud swiftly. "Most of the stuff in that kitchen needs hours of preparation, and a decent knowledge of local ingredients. I've been happy to eat everything Amelia has put in front of us while we've been here, however novel it's been to my admittedly limited palate, but the relationship between all the knobbly fruits and vegetables she's got in the pantry and what's ended up on our plates is a bit beyond me."

"Me too," I agreed. I'm not a bad cook – anyone who enjoys eating as much as I do ends up being able to produce some pretty decent meals – but I haven't a clue how to make salt fish edible, nor how to make rice and beans taste the way Amelia did.

"We'll sort something," offered Jack. "When Sheila and I toured the coast towards Negril we spotted a couple of pretty decent-looking places."

We all nodded our thanks.

"It was a good idea to get Amelia to leave us to our own devices," piped up Lottie. "She was a bit down in the dumps, wasn't she?"

I managed a sideways glance at Bud just as I felt the pressure of his hand on my knee; a warning to not say what he doubtless guessed I was thinking – *how well he knows me.*

I was pleased that John responded – he was the one who'd invited the woman none of us had ever met before as his plus one, after all. "To be honest, Lottie dear, Amelia's hardly likely to be dancing a merry jig, is she? She'd just discovered the corpse of someone who meant a great deal to her. She's likely to be out of a job, and maybe homeless too, in the not too distant future."

The room fell silent. Everyone was immediately finding the food on their plate to be incredibly interesting.

"Good points, John dear," replied Lottie lightly, and I felt the atmosphere shift a little.

"So," said Sheila, "are we staying on here, or do we think we should be looking for hotel rooms, or something?"

There was a general rumbling about "having just settled in" from John and Lottie who, to be fair, had only arrived a couple of days earlier and who'd barely had the chance to rest their backsides on a lounge chair. Jack and Sheila had at least been able to enjoy a week at the estate – much of it a great deal less rainy than the past couple of days had been.

"To be honest," Bud replied, "it hadn't even occurred to me that we wouldn't stay here for the remainder of our planned visit. We've paid up front, and – other than the fact we'll have to fend for ourselves – I can't see any reason why we should leave. The police didn't seem to think our being here was a problem."

"But *they* believe he killed himself," said Lottie, surprising us all.

John looked most taken aback. "Do you think he didn't?"

This time we all ignored what was on our plates and stared at Lottie, who leaned back in her chair. "Well, I suppose he *might* have done, but Amelia said he wouldn't have dreamed of it. He was pretty much a Catholic, she said. They tend not to. Kill themselves. Terrible for them in the afterlife if they do, I understand."

"And when did you glean this snippet of insight about the late Freddie Burkinshaw's religious persuasion?" enquired John as he mirrored Lottie's movement, also sitting back in his seat.

"When you lot were all off at the tower, of course," she replied calmly. "Amelia was blubbing, but quite chatty – all things considered. She said Freddie was a man who believed in many things, Catholicism being his choice of the Christian religions, but that he also thought a number of aspects of other religions were good ideas too. She was telling me how she hoped he was now finally able to answer the question he'd always pondered – which version of God was the right one. She also wondered what type of funeral he'll have. He'd told her that all the arrangements were detailed in a document he gave to his lawyer when he turned eighty, some years ago. Which surprised me, because I rather thought they'd have solicitors and barristers here, like we have in England, because their legal system is based on ours and answers to the Privy Council, in London. But maybe they don't; maybe they just have lawyers. Amelia said she's hoping it's nothing weird. His funeral, that is. And she's pretty sure he'll have written something in said document about preventing some obnoxious Italian neighbor of his from showing her face at whatever does happen. Though Amelia said the woman would probably want to attend, just to make sure he's really dead. By the way, she's an Anglican. Amelia, not the neighbor. I don't suppose many Italians are Anglicans, are they? Likes the old hymns, does Amelia, not the new ones. Did you know that some people say Jamaica has more churches per capita than anywhere else in the world? They aren't all Christian churches, of course, and I have no idea who 'they' are in this instance, so maybe it's all complete twaddle. But I do believe you'd take an awfully long time to count them all. We saw quite a lot just being driven here from the airport, didn't we, John?"

I was amazed at Lottie's lung capacity – she'd hardly drawn breath as she spoke. The expressions around the table varied from bemused to stunned as Lottie ripped apart a bread roll and expounded. I was one of the bemused ones.

"Wow," said Sheila before stuffing a last forkful of omelette into her mouth.

"Sounds as though you and Amelia had a good chat while we were all at the tower," Bud managed to hide almost every trace of sarcasm in his voice.

Lottie nodded vigorously. "As I said, she was quite chatty. Considering. She told me lots of other stuff too. About the Italian neighbor, and the realtor who's helping said Italian to fight Freddie for the land he owns, but which she says is really hers. It all sounds fascinating. Lots of skulduggery, Amelia said. I bet you'd fit in rather nicely on the island –" she nodded at John – "you too, Bud. And Jack. I mean, I know you're all 'retired' now – though when you disappear off to goodness knows where for days at a time, John, I do wonder if you're *really* out of it all. But, whether you're out or still in, you've all done your bit for law enforcement over the years, with a fair amount of secret squirrel stuff on the side, haven't you." It wasn't a question.

Bud and Jack swivelled their heads to stare at John, who scratched his ear, slowly. "Well, we've all been cops, or coppers in our day, Lottie, you know that, yes. But as for representing any other services—"

Lottie laughed, tossing back her head. "Oh, come off it. Just look at you. All three of you. And you, Sheila, Cait – you two, as well. The looks on all your faces? Goodness knows how you ever managed to get away with any undercover work, boys. Besides, you know very well that's how we met, John."

John looked genuinely confused. "We met at a dinner at the House of Lords." He sounded as puzzled as he looked. "What do you mean, exactly?"

Lottie sounded triumphant. "And who was hosting the dinner?"

We all looked at John as he gave the matter some thought. "Lord Buckford, was it? Or Lady Dillworth?"

It amused me to realize John was invited to dinner at the House of Lords so frequently that he couldn't recall which particular titled person had invited him on any specific occasion.

"No, it was Sir Roger Rustingham, John. My Uncle Rusty," replied Lottie. "Not that he's really my uncle, you understand, but I have known him my entire life," she added, addressing the rest of us. "You know, the chap who's head of your cloak and dagger lot, dear. Don't you remember me telling you how Daddy used to do some work for him? We discussed it, terribly discretely, of course, before the port was passed."

"And who exactly is 'Daddy'?" asked Jack, wriggling with discomfort.

Lottie looked surprised. "Who's my father? Sir Tarquin Fortescue. Everything he did for Queen and Country in his day was terribly hush-hush, of course, but why do you think he got his knighthood? On Her Majesty's secret service, and all that sort of thing. Not that anyone knew the exact nature of the services involved. Except Mummy. Mummy knew, I think, but she's dead now, and he won't say a word about it. But that's why Uncle Rusty invites Daddy to those dinners all the time, with me on his arm; it's the way Rusty brings in the young chaps to meet the old guard. But you know all this, John." She sounded sure of herself.

This wasn't turning out to be the luncheon conversation I'd been expecting, but it was fascinating, nonetheless. And a little unsettling.

I knew all about Bud's illustrious career first with the RCMP, then with the Vancouver Police Department, because he'd hired me as a sometime-consultant on cases needing the expertise of my victim profiling skills. As a professor of criminal psychology I'd been able to put my theories into practice, and to play a tiny part in him becoming so successful in his role overseeing the integrated homicide investigation team that he'd been invited to hand-pick a group to work under him to liaise with international law enforcement tackling the scourge of gangs and organized crime. Then he'd retired, because of his wife's murder.

That's still difficult for us to tackle, head on; if she hadn't died, Bud and I would never have become a couple. Never. I'd enjoyed working with him, but he and Jan had been so happy together that it would never have crossed his mind to stray. Nor would it have crossed mine to invite him to do so. But…here we are, together. However, we're always so dreadfully aware that our happiness grew from her death that we still struggle with trying to focus on the positive aspects of that. What we most certainly enjoy is the fact that he's now retired, and his time is his own.

However, even with that knowledge of his professional life, it had taken a near-disaster in Mexico, followed by months of labored questioning, for me to get *anything* out of Bud about the work he'd done for the Canadian Security Intelligence Service, and associated international bodies. He'd flatly refused to divulge any specific details about what he'd got up to on their behalf throughout his career. Nor would he tell me what work Jack had done for CSIS. Nor John, for whatever bodies he'd worked for. At. All. Bud was awfully good at saying nothing.

All I really knew for certain was that if it hadn't been for the fact that Jack and Bud had attended some of the same training courses as each other, Bud and I would have been in a right pickle because of that poor, murdered woman in Mexico. And if John hadn't intervened in Budapest, I might be…well, let's just say that the past few months of physical and mental recuperation haven't been a bed of roses for me, and leave it there.

I suspected Sheila knew a great deal more about what Jack had done for CSIS than I knew about Bud's exploits, and that – because of the dynamic between the three men – John had by far the most experience in such matters, the greatest number of connections around the globe, and most certainly had *not* been retired when he'd rushed to our aid in Hungary less than six months earlier.

Sheila and I exchanged a glance as Lottie's comments hung in the heavy air, then we looked at our respective husbands. They, in turn, were glaring at John, who'd puffed out his cheeks, snapped his napkin onto the table, and pushed away his plate.

He said, "Right-ho, this obviously needs to be addressed. Lottie dear, you don't *know* anything about any operations that Bud, Jack, or I may, or may not, have been party to. Cait and

Sheila are married to two wonderful men who've put in their years for Canadian law enforcement and have both now retired from that life. I, as you know, have a desk job. Yes, I work in Whitehall, and, yes, I have to travel within my role, on occasion. But I can guarantee you that – if I ever *had* been involved in that sort of undertaking – I would now be well past the age when I would be called upon to carry out any 'secret squirrel' work, as you so quaintly described it. I know that Rusty, Sir Roger Rustingham, is professionally involved with a particular branch of British security in a senior role, but he *does* have friends and acquaintances from other areas of his life too. I got to know him when we worked together on a couple of charity committees. Where I also met your father, I might add. It's all totally innocent, and above board."

"Well, that's a pity," replied Lottie with a wry smile, "because when I spoke to Daddy on the phone earlier today he said he'd known of Freddie Burkinshaw, and had always wondered if he'd been dispatched to Jamaica to 'keep an eye on a few local chaps'. Apparently, Freddie arrived here just around the time independence was granted, and was pretty close with Ian Fleming – and we all know what sort of a war *he* had, and what he got up to after it, don't we, children?" She rose, and swooshed her chiffon scarf around her firm, young throat. "I'm off for a shower now. It's so dreadfully humid. The rain's stopped at last, I see. Thank you for a delicious…egg thingy, Cait, Bud. See you in a bit, John. Maybe someone will be kind enough to let me know what sort of place we're dining at tonight, when you've made the arrangements, so I can dress accordingly. Bye-ee."

And she was gone. Leaving us all a bit flummoxed, and – in my case anyway – fixated on the fact that I'd just heard several potential reasons why someone might want Freddie Burkinshaw dead. It seemed he might not have been the innocent octogenarian without an enemy in the world we'd all thought him to be, after all.

# Discovering Deceit

An unsurprising silence followed Lottie's departure, though I could almost hear the ice crackling in the stares Bud and Jack were directing toward John.

John's the tallest of the three men by far – worthy of all the inevitable *Long John Silver* jokes – but he never usually stoops the way some tall men do. Now he was slouched in his chair; wishing it would eat him up, no doubt. He was fiddling with the buttons on his navy, open-necked shirt and I could hear the rubber sole of his canary-yellow deck shoe slapping against the hardwood floor as his knee bounced. Sweat trickled from his receding hairline.

Bud's expression was grim. "I've never had anything but the greatest respect for you, John, as you know, and I will forever be in your debt – for so many reasons," he began – which is never a good start to a speech, because there's always an inevitable "but" on the horizon – "but Lottie seems to believe she knows quite a lot about our careers. Have you succumbed to pillow talk, eh? At your age? With your years of experience?"

John didn't look up. He shook his head. "I swear, I haven't said a thing. Not a dickie bird. She's just…inferring."

"Well, she's sure managed to infer a lot, and pretty accurately," said Jack quietly.

Sheila nodded and patted her husband on the leg. "She doesn't really *know* anything, Jack. You can tell."

I looked at Bud, whose ears were red, something which doesn't happen often, but which tells me he's incredibly angry. I instinctively reached to touch his arm. I didn't like it when he pulled it away to waggle his finger at John. "You need to have a word with her." Bud's tone was alien to me. It made my tummy clench.

For once I thought it best to say nothing and I literally bit my tongue. *It helps.*

"Come on, chaps," said John, rallying, "Lottie's just chattering on, the way she does. You must have worked out she does that, by now. It's part of her charm, in a funny way. She's really a good deal more intelligent than most folks give her credit for. Her entire family is peppered with bright sparks who many people think are potty; they aren't, they're just not terribly good at expressing themselves, that's all."

Bud tutted. He doesn't usually tut. I'm the tutter in the family. Well, me and his mother; sometimes we have tutting duets. At Bud's expense.

"You might think it's nothing to be concerned about, John, but if she rattles on like that all the time, she could easily say the wrong thing to the wrong person," said Bud, still sounding weird. His tone made me wonder just how much about his past CSIS-associated undertakings I still didn't know.

"Exactly. Especially here, now," added Jack.

I had no idea what he meant, and my tongue was starting to get sore, so I finally blurted out, "Okay, that's enough. What the heck is going on? Bud, I know you always shut me down with 'I can't talk about it, I swore an oath,' and I've accepted that since I first stumbled upon your top-secret activities. And I know Jack's done his bit for various agencies. John too. But what do you mean by 'here, now', Jack? Why are you so angry, Bud? And who on earth is this flaming Lottie person anyway, John? I mean we're all too polite to say it, but I bet we're all thinking she has to be the best part of thirty years your junior, and an extremely attractive young woman – so what's she doing with *you*? I truly enjoy your company, John – something

I can't say about many people – and I know how supportive you've been of Bud and me…but just how long have you two been a couple? How did you ever *become* a couple? I mean, really? You and her? You're such an unlikely pair. Come on, I want to know what's going on – everything. It's just us here, in private – everybody, out with the truth, now."

This time the silence vibrated with its own frequency. Not even Sheila met my gaze. *Fishy.*

John spoke first. "In my defense, Lottie's just happier going out with an older chap. We've been seeing each other for a couple of months, now. As I said, she's sharper than she appears and she's a popular person to socialize with. I enjoy her company a great deal. And she's older than you might think. Almost thirty-five, so there's not quite thirty years between us. Not so unusual." He looked cowed, and I felt guilty about how nasty I'd been.

I covered my embarrassment by saying, "Well, I trust you're both very happy then, John," and managed a genuine-looking smile, I hoped. But I wasn't going to let Bud and Jack off the hook. "So come on then, Jack – what *did* you mean by 'here, now' exactly? Bud, I thought you'd retired, fully, even from your secret stuff. And I believed we'd come here so I could round off my recuperation from all that mess in Hungary with a bit of time in the sun, being waited on hand and foot. What aren't you telling me?"

Bud sighed.

Sheila wriggled.

"You know too, don't you?" I snapped. Sheila had the good grace to nibble her lips and blush.

Bud sighed again, then turned, and took both my hands in his. *Not good.* His tone was earnest, his loving gaze direct. "The reason we got such a great deal on this place for a month's rental was that I was asked to come here by Freddie himself.

Indirectly. In fact –" he paused and glanced at John, then Jack – "we're only paying what we are to act as a cover; I'm reporting back to someone about something that might have happened here over half a century ago."

"Bud…" warned John.

Bud shrugged and said, "Sorry, guys. And sorry, Cait. You know I love you, and I'd have told you if I could. I can't even tell you everything now, but I can tell you this much – something was lost…or misplaced…over fifty years ago, and it's become important that it's retrieved, soon. I was tasked with coming here to gather information from Freddie Burkinshaw about events back then. As Lottie seems to have gathered from her father – who really should have known better than to say anything at all about this – Freddie wasn't just a man who'd retired to the sun at an enviably young age. There were…papers…that found their way here in the early 1960s; for a long time those papers were forgotten about – they didn't matter. Now things have changed in the world, and it's critically important that the papers are located. Honestly, I can't say more than that. Indeed, as Jack and John know, I've already said more than I should have done."

I could feel my insides churn, and it wasn't because of what I'd eaten at lunch. My eyes began to sting. *I will not cry, here, now.*

"So, this trip was never about my fiftieth birthday. Nothing to do with my recuperation. It wasn't about us having time together in the sun, as a couple. I thought we were going to have a month alone, then you conned me – yes, conned me – into sharing our time here with other people. It was all an elaborate cover for some sort of operation." The first hot, angry tears rolled down my cheek. Bud's face was a blur, but I could see enough to know he was hurting too. I wiped my eyes with my napkin and stood. "I'm going back to our bungalow now. You lot can clear up. But try not to talk too happily about how you all managed to pull the wool over my eyes, will you? Thanks. See you all later."

I stomped out of the room trying to hold back sobs. I didn't want to show them how horribly they'd all wounded me. And how angry I was at myself that I hadn't suspected a thing. I'm supposed to be good at reading people – it's what I do. It's my whole career, my life. I'm a professor of criminal psychology, for goodness sake. I profile people. I write research papers about profiling people. I apply my years of academic and real-life experience to profiling people. I can usually work out what people are thinking, and why they do what they do. I'm no good at anything else. It is who I am.

And I had just found out that my husband, the man I love and trust completely, *and* my closest friends – okay then, my *only* friends – had all been lying to me. For ages. And I hadn't suspected a thing. *I am an idiot.*

## Of Love and Lies

I'd dragged myself out of bed that morning expecting nothing more than a stinking hangover – which I knew I deserved – and a day of gradually nursing myself through it. Instead, there I was, curled into a ball on the bed crying my heart out, and wondering if I'd ever be able to come to terms with the fact that my husband had lied to me. Worse, I'd had my nose well and truly rubbed in the fact that he would probably never be able to be completely open and honest with me about his covert missions.

I told myself it wasn't as though I'd found out he'd been cheating on me.

Then I reasoned that he was only lying about work, not life…not the stuff that really mattered.

*So what* if this whole trip had been planned to allow him to fulfil some sort of orders? He had a duty to our country, and he was doing what he had sworn he would.

But why couldn't he have trusted me with the facts?

Clearly Jack had told Sheila; why hadn't Bud told me?

I went back and forth, listening to the voices in my head arguing it out. They were loud, and neither was going to give up easily. But the longer I lay there – the shutters closed, the room oppressively hot – the more I was drawn to the conclusion that I simply had to ask Bud why he hadn't told me what was going on.

Because *that* was my real concern. The only concern worth having.

When I finally managed to stop sobbing, and sat up to dry my eyes and blow my nose, I could hear noises in the sitting room. The jalousie doors between the bedroom and the sitting area of the little bungalow meant it was difficult to not be aware of the fact Bud was pacing about just beyond them. I spent a few minutes in the bathroom, trying to cool off by running water over my wrists, then I steeled myself to face him.

I pulled open the bi-fold double doors, and Bud spun round.

He looked flushed, and blurted out, "I couldn't tell you, Cait, because I was specifically ordered to *not* tell you. I can't believe Jack told Sheila…he said she wormed it out of him. Which I have to say is a worry, though I reckon Sheila's able to be discreet. Which isn't to say I don't think you can be. Oh heck, this is all coming out wrong. Look, I'm so sorry, Cait. I love you. I trust you. I wouldn't have told you what I have, now, if I didn't. And I need you to trust me. Please don't let this come between us? I have a duty. Orders. There are lines I just can't cross. And I'm always terrified that you knowing something you're not supposed to might end in disaster, somehow. I never want you to be in danger because of my work. That's why Jan…you know…it's why Jan died. Because of my work."

I knew.

And in that moment, I understood with absolute clarity how difficult it must have been for Bud to make the decisions he'd made. And why he'd done what he'd done. I reached out to him, held him, and told him so. We both cried in each others' arms for a few moments, then we just swayed, clinging together in the middle of the room – until we both acknowledged that we needed to break apart to be able to blow our noses.

Despite the heat, and our general dishevelment and sweatiness, we snuggled on the wicker sofa, as best we could.

I finally said, "You're really good at lying, Bud. I didn't notice that anything was even a little bit off. You're so much better at deception than I had any idea you could be."

Bud squeezed me. "Thank you. I think."

"Look, I get it that there's a lot you can't tell me, but I have to say that when I imagined you doing work for CSIS, and whatever other organizations you've liaised with over the years, I'd pictured you in a sort of strategic planning role, you know – working out how intelligence could be gathered, how resources should be used, that sort of thing. A bit like *M* in the Bond films…not the Ralph Fiennes *M* in the new ones, but the original *M*s, when Connery and Moore were Bond. But you haven't been doing *just* that, have you? You've been using skills on me that you've honed through training and experience in operations where you've had to hide things from people – maybe even hiding who you really are." Bud didn't respond. At all. So I pressed on. "And that's a revelation to me. I know how you're motivated by justice, how you're fantastic at command and control operations – but I hadn't realized you were also capable of such deception. It's going to take me a while to come to terms with that."

"I wish I could say I've never been less than truthful with you, Cait, but you know I have. That said, I promise I've only done it with regard to work, and on orders. Which is something that doesn't touch the core of me – of *us*. I have to compartmentalize. I've always had to. You understand that, don't you?"

I nodded, struggling with the concept. It's not something I've ever been good at. I'm very much an all-or-nothing kind of person. Which has been a bit of a problem, on occasion. "I do, Bud. I do understand," I said, trying to.

We sat in silence for a while, and – to shut up those annoying voices in my head – I focused on Freddie Burkinshaw again.

Bud looked surprised when I asked, "So do you think your secret reason for being here is connected in some way with Freddie's death?"

He shifted on the sofa, looked deep into my eyes. "Are you sure this is really what you want to talk about, Cait?" I nodded. He sighed. "Okay then, yes, I do. But I don't know how, exactly. I fear it's too much of a coincidence for there to be no connection at all."

I recalled what he'd said when we'd seen the body. "You questioned why on earth anyone would want to kill a harmless octogenarian, Bud. Well, clearly Freddie's more than I thought he was – he's linked, somehow, to these sensitive papers. So, can you be open with me about the manner of his death, at least? Tell me what you honestly think?"

Bud nodded. "When you left us all in the dining room just now, I explained to Jack and John that I was going to continue to be as open with you about our mission as possible – without divulging any classified information. You'll have to trust me to tread that line, my darling. I'll tell you as much as I can. Sheila will be in the same position. But we've all agreed that Lottie can't be brought into our circle of trust. Which'll make for some difficult situations. We're basically asking you and Sheila to be as deceitful as we three are, but without the benefit of all the training we've been given, and all the experience we've had."

I managed a half-chuckle. "Sheila's a natural. It wasn't until Jack let the cat out of the bag that I could see she knew what was going on. She's good. And I can be, too. I promise. I haven't warmed to Lottie, as you know, so won't feel compelled to share anything with her you don't want me to. Just be clear about what I can and can't divulge, and I'll stick to your rules." Bud's eyebrows rose. I shoved him. Playfully.

"Don't do that. I *can* follow rules. I know it's not one of my natural strengths, but I can apply myself."

Bud kissed me.

"Right then," I continued, feeling a little better, "do you *really* think Freddie killed himself, or do you believe he was murdered?"

The genuine smile that spread across Bud's face warmed my heart. "Honestly, I wish I had a proper answer to that one for you. See, I'm concerned that our presence here, the sensitivity of the situation, and the…ambiguity…of Freddie's connection with it, might have led him to take his own life for some reason. But I'm equally concerned that an unknown party could have got wind of what's going on and might have taken action to prevent what we see as a successful outcome. I've already heard through channels that the autopsy will be rushed through, and we'll be given sight of the findings. That might clarify matters. But, while we wait for that, Jack, John, and I must press on, hoping our mission isn't compromised."

I gave some thought to his words. "You know I don't think it was suicide, but now that idea seems less…well 'appealing' isn't the right word, but you know what I'm trying to say. Despite that giant key being found in his pocket, I'm still not convinced Freddie was suicidal. But what do I know? I'm really beginning to question the belief I've always had in my ability to judge people; if I was wrong about all of you, maybe I was wrong about Freddie, too." I had to say the words out loud, not just hear them banging about inside my head.

Bud's brow furrowed. "I knew that was where you'd be with this, Cait, and I need you to understand that your skills are still the best I've ever seen. It's not that you failed at something, you just didn't try. You didn't see our deception because you weren't looking for it. But know this – when you *are* looking for it, you always hit the nail on the head. And I agree with your observations and instincts about Freddie. When we were at the scene, I had to try to manage the situation until John, Jack, and I had a chance to confer. *Whatever* you'd said on that staircase, I would have taken the opposite point of view, just so there was a balance being struck whenever the topic was raised in front of other people – including the cops. But, in all honesty, I'm with you; I suspect that someone, somehow managed to kill Freddie then lock him into that room, making it look like suicide."

I felt relieved. "And, if that's the case, do you think the motive for his murder was connected to your situation?"

Bud shrugged. "That I don't know. I *hope* not, because that could mean…well, a lot of things I don't want to be true. But…" I waited. "I think it unlikely there'd be anyone beyond those interested in our situation who'd want to kill him. It just seems like…"

"…too much of a coincidence," I said. We shared a smile. I felt a little spark of excitement. "I could be of real help to you all, couldn't I? I could work on this as though I know nothing about your secret case. I could do what I do – profile the victim to try to work out how he might have become a victim."

"If he really *was* a victim," said Bud warily.

"Rather than hang about and wait for the autopsy results – which might be completely inconclusive in any case – I could start now, and assume murder."

Bud smiled. "Yes, Wife, you could do that. By all means. And maybe Sheila could lend a hand."

"Maybe even Lottie, if she wants. Because that would keep her out of your hair, wouldn't it?"

"It would. Just so long as you treat our mission as completely off limits, as far as Lottie's concerned."

"And you 'boys' could get on with your search for these mysterious papers, regardless of Freddie's death."

"We could indeed."

"Do you have any idea at all where they might be? How did Freddie come to be connected with them?" I could tell by Bud's expression that he was calculating what he could and couldn't tell me. I didn't want him to worry so jumped in with: "Okay, let's not start there – let's start with what you can tell me about Freddie…his life and so forth. Or can you point me in a direction where I could find out?"

"Now that I can do, and I'm happy to do it to the extent I'm able. But how about we do this as a group – Lottie included. She might even have picked up on some insights we men don't have – for example, I've no idea what she was talking about when she mentioned that Italian neighbor and some sort of land ownership dispute. That might turn out to be something we can look into, while you also use it as a focus for your investigation. Maybe we three guys can come up with some way of introducing what we know about Freddie into the group conversation, and I can always fill you in once Lottie believes she's being included. But let's make sure it's a private conversation, not something we do in a public place. I tell you what – I'm guessing a shower and clean-up is in your future, so why don't you get going with all that? I'll sort out a few things with the two J's; it's kind of a pain the two of them being named Jack and John, but they don't get to use their real names all the time, so it's nice when they can do it, you know?"

I didn't know, and I felt I didn't really *want* to know. Instead, the idea of having clean, non-sweaty, not-lank hair beckoned, and I gave myself over to the luxury of a long, hot shower with 10CC singing *Dreadlock Holiday* in my head.

## Dinner and a Few Deaths

Sheila had proved she possessed superpowers by arranging for a restaurant situated just along the coast to deliver food to the Captain's Lookout estate, so we could all eat in the dining room to talk about Freddie Burkinshaw's death in private. Lottie was the only one not terribly impressed by this arrangement, but she had little choice but to put up with the majority's decision. I didn't feel at all guilty that we were keeping her in the dark about our real reasons for not wanting to have our discussions in a restaurant. To be fair to her, as she helped me set the table, she told me she recognized it might be insensitive to discuss the death of a well-known local resident in a public eatery.

Sheila had ordered a pretty wide variety of dishes, and we all managed to fill our plates with something we fancied. After my earlier upset, I felt the need for comfort food, so was especially delighted that there were some spicy patties, mounds of rice and beans, plus some goat curry; the three foods I feared I'd become addicted to over the previous few weeks, though I suspected they would never taste the same anywhere else in the world.

We raided the stock of wine and beer in the sideboard and fridge, and we all sat eating for a while, trying to have a normal conversation. The topic of the weather was front and center, of course, and I think we managed to describe rain in about fifty different ways, before Lottie raised the inevitable issue of Freddie Burkinshaw. I was glad she was the one who did it, because it saved me a job.

"Has anyone heard any more about Freddie's death?" she asked, innocently enough.

All five of us seemed to inhale at the same time, but it was Jack who answered.

"I don't think we can expect to hear much more from the authorities; we're just visitors here. I guess they'd be in touch with Amelia, if anyone at all. Did Freddie mention family to anyone? He loved his little habit of cornering one person for a while and monopolizing them, Lottie," he explained, "though he didn't do much of that last night, because he had two new audience members for what I reckon were his standard stories. I know I heard him tell you guys a few he also told Sheila and myself on our first night with him. Had you and Cait heard everything three times, Bud?"

Bud and I exchanged a knowing glance. "You betcha," said Bud. "His 'How I Used to Party with Ian Fleming and Noël Coward' stories were the first he told us. You guys, too –" he nodded toward Jack and Sheila – "and you guys last night, I know." He winked at John. "But he didn't mention family to me at all. Did he to you, Cait?"

I shook my head. "He said he'd never married, so I assumed no children – though that's not necessarily the case. I don't recall any mention of siblings."

"Well he can't have said anything about siblings then," said Lottie, picking at a lobster claw, "because you wouldn't have forgotten – not with that memory thing you do."

I glared at John; he was the only one who could have told Lottie about my eidetic memory. I was aware that everyone else at the table knew, but Lottie? I prefer to choose for myself who to tell, because as soon as anyone finds out about it they're tempted to treat me like some sort of performing animal, which annoys the heck out of me.

"Don't worry, Cait," said Lottie, "I'm not going to test you by asking what day of the week it was on the fifteenth of July 1927, or anything like that. I know you don't like people discovering you have a photographic memory – John told me – but I do think it must be a bit weird to be able to do all that stuff."

"It's not weird at all," I snapped, "I'm just able to recollect things I've read, or heard, or experienced in some way or another. I can't 'do' dates, nor count how many matches you might hurl across the floor. Not my skill set." I knew I sounded grumpy – because I was. I poked a piece of spicy beef patty into my mouth and almost choked – I should have taken a small bite, not gone for the whole thing.

By the time I'd recovered, and Bud had retaken his seat after bringing me water and telling me to "breathe through your nose" goodness knows how many times, Lottie had demolished her lobster and was eyeing up the box containing the patties. I knew I couldn't eat another, but that didn't stop me from taking one before she could get her mitts on it. She helped herself to some of the fragrant goat curry instead, and we all fell back into silent eating-mode.

"Freddie wasn't short of female companionship, by all accounts," volunteered Sheila. "Amelia and I spoke about it at breakfast one morning, though she didn't mention any children."

"I wonder who'll get this place, then," said Lottie – something I knew we were all thinking. "Maybe the documents he lodged with his legal representative included a last will and testament. If he'd gone as far as writing up his wishes for his funeral, as Amelia said he did, it follows that he'd have written a will, don't you think?"

We all nodded our agreement.

"I hope he leaves something for Amelia and Tarone," said Sheila, sounding sad. "They could do with something to help them in the future. Tarone was telling me that he needs all the money he earns here to help him afford the costs associated with his athletic endeavors."

"That can't be very much," snorted John. "I mean, shoes and stuff like that, but what other costs can there be?"

"Training costs, gym fees," said Bud.

"Transport to venues here, and maybe on other Caribbean islands," offered Jack.

"Physiotherapy? Other medical treatments," I said.

"Maybe a nutritionist?" volunteered Lottie.

John raised his hands in submission. "Okay, okay, I clearly know nothing about such things. I get it. Both he and Amelia will need something to tide them over until they can replace this source of income, and somehow fund a place to live, too. Yes, I agree, I hope Freddie left them something – and I hope his affairs were in order, so probate doesn't take forever."

"That's what happened with Sheila's sister," said Jack.

Sheila's lips clamped into a thin line at her husband's comment, and I was puzzled.

"I didn't know you had a sister, Sheila," I said. "And I had no idea you'd lost one. I'm so sorry. Was that recent?"

Sheila smiled – too brightly. "Oh no, don't worry about it. It's all so far behind me now. Yes, I had a sister, but she died – oh, how many years is it now? Time passes so quickly, doesn't it? It was 1989, a long time ago. Lots of water under lots of bridges since then." She was gabbling. Not like Sheila; Sheila is the personification of common sense.

"She was here for Christmas. That's when it happened," said Jack, sadly. "Not *here*, here…she was staying in Montego Bay, wasn't she, Sheila?"

Sheila nodded silently. For all that she'd said the loss was far from fresh, I could tell she wasn't seeing the food she was looking at on her plate.

"Terrible thing," continued Jack, "scooter accident. Never even made it to the hospital." He reached for his wife's hand.

Sheila sighed. "Yes. Dreadful." She sighed again, then dragged her attention away from her deep-fried okra. "As Jack said, there was a real mess with Wendy's estate. Hadn't thought of writing a will, of course, because she was only in her twenties. I did what I could."

"I guess Wendy thought she was too young to plan for that sort of thing," said Jack quietly, smiling at Sheila as he patted her hand. "It was a nightmare just getting the body repatriated, wasn't it?" Sheila nodded. "That's the only other time Sheila's been to this island, and she had to come alone because I couldn't get away from work, so I'm glad we're here together, now. Though, of course, Freddie's death isn't…ideal."

"I suppose at something over eighty, Freddie realized he'd need to make his wishes for his final arrangements, and his estate, known. I bet I'm not the only one at this table who's sorted out his will," said John. He winked at Lottie. "Though there's a lot of life left in this old boy yet."

I hadn't foreseen our conversation taking this route, and I hoped that the grunting by Bud and me that we'd sorted out our wills, and by Jack and Sheila to the same effect, would bring the topic to a natural conclusion. But Lottie didn't let it go.

She laughed, then said, "Daddy's made sure I've reviewed my will every year since I turned twenty-one. That's when I got my inheritance from my late mother. It had been in trust until then, but the minute one actually owns it all, one simply *has* to pay attention to what's going to happen to the lolly, as well as the houses, after one's gone."

She might as well have chucked a bucket of water at me; beautiful, bright, young, *and* wealthy? *Of course.*

"Lolly?" queried Sheila.

"Money," whispered Jack.

"I can't imagine what it must be like to be rich," said Sheila; there wasn't a hint of envy in her tone, just an innocent wonderment.

"It's rather odd, at first," replied Lottie earnestly. "Daddy had been incredibly strict about my allowance, then – overnight – I had all this loot sloshing about in my bank account. It was so tempting to rush about spending it willy nilly, but Daddy was terribly sensible and packed me off on a series of financial management courses. They were deadly dull, of course, but I got the gist of it; you can only spend money once, so spend it wisely. Invest when one can, do one's research and due diligence thoroughly, and know that if something sounds too good to be true, it usually is. I haven't experienced any major disasters so far, though I must admit it's awfully tiresome to be constantly told about 'fabulous opportunities' by all and sundry at dinner parties, and so forth. That's one of the reasons I enjoy being with John – he doesn't have the slightest interest in markets and start-ups and all that sort of thing."

She beamed at John, who returned her smile sheepishly, and I began to understand what he'd meant about Lottie – she was bright alright, and probably a lot of people underestimated her…possibly to their cost.

Then she upended my generous thoughts by saying, "I'd like to see Montego Bay again, John. I came to Jamaica sometimes with Daddy, just for short breaks, you know, and I loved the song before I ever saw the place. Haven't been there for almost twenty years. How about it? I know you might not be too keen, because it's where you spent your first honeymoon, wasn't it? But I really would love to see it again. I'm sure it will have changed a great deal since I last saw it, but so have I. I could face it again, now."

Several questions flashed through my brain, seemingly all at once: couldn't Lottie recognize that talking about the place where Sheila's sister had died so tragically was just a bit inconsiderate?; why didn't I know that John had once been married?; what did Lottie mean by his "first" honeymoon…how many had he had?; and why could Lottie "face" Montego Bay again, now…what had happened there to make her not want to face it previously?

"You honeymooned in Jamaica with Sascha?" asked Bud. *He knew John had been married? And knew his wife's name?*

John shook his head. "No, not Sascha, she was number two. We went to Klosters. Winter wedding. Emily and I came here. It was fun, until it wasn't. Beginning of the end there and then."

"Ah, Emily," chorused Jack and Bud. *They both knew about more than one of John's wives?*

I couldn't resist. "How many wives have you had, John?"

"Only three," he replied, sounding grim.

"That must mean a good deal of alimony," I dared.

Bud kicked me under the table – he actually *kicked* me. Well, it was more of a nudge with his foot, I suppose, but it was enough.

"Not really." John's voice was heavy. "Sascha remarried within months of our divorce, and Suzie did likewise. But Emily died. By her own hand. It knocked me for six at the time. Don't mind admitting it. And all over a stupid affair she had. More of a fling, really. I kicked up a fuss about it. We were young. My first time to believe I was going to spend the rest of my life with someone. But I pushed her away when she needed me most. Didn't know it at the time, of course. Bad show, all round." He seemed to be talking to himself, not us.

I understood the warning I'd received from Bud, though I thought the kick was a bit much; I decided I'd have a word with him about that later…after this less-than-ideal dinner was done and dusted. For a group of people who'd all agreed to meet to discuss a specific topic – Freddie Burkinshaw – we weren't doing very well at keeping on track.

"I got them to deliver some coconut ice cream for dessert," said Sheila. "We could tidy up while it become less brick-like."

The spell was broken, and we worked as a team to clear the detritus from the table, sort out the washing up, and find some more alcohol; it seemed we'd been drinking rather a lot as we'd been chatting about the brevity of life, and most of us felt the need for a least a nightcap to round off the evening.

The rain had finally stopped, the warm air had dried all the outdoor furnishings, and the almost-full moon was peeping from behind the ragged remnants of the clouds. We agreed to have brandies at the small tables beside the pool, to be able to make the most of the less-humid night air. The three men and Lottie all lit large cigars, while I stuck to my usual tiny cigarettes. Sheila sat close to Jack, inhaling as much of his cigar smoke as possible; ex-smokers do that quite a bit, I've noticed. To be fair, it was a delightfully aromatic cigar.

After the Budapest incident, Bud and I had agreed I'd give up smoking – again! – as a part of my physical recovery. But, as usual, I'd struggled with it, and he'd capitulated when we'd arrived in Jamaica, on the basis that I could only smoke outside; I'd agreed, and promised I'd try to keep my intake low. Then Freddie joined us for dinner on our second evening at the place, and Bud had shocked me by accepting a cigar from him afterwards, along with a fancy brandy. Both had now become a regular thing for him, which I didn't mind at all because it stopped him nagging me about my smoking, though it was strange to see him puffing away, and using the cigar as an extension of his hand – a bit like an orchestra conductor's baton – as he chatted. We'd both agreed we'd get back to normal when we got home…for Marty's sake, as well as our own, because he's getting on a bit and we don't want to force our poor, old dog to smoke.

The nocturnal insects, and other invisible wildlife, filled the air with a soothing cacophony, and our voices were mellowed by the tropical planting and the glowing water in the pool. It was idyllic. The only problem was that I knew it wasn't really an escape to paradise, but a covert mission for some, and a necessarily duplicitous investigation into a suspicious death for the rest of us.

With that in mind, I knew I had to give us the chance to begin the conversations we so desperately needed to have so that I could get on with trying to profile the late Freddie Burkinshaw.

"I know none of us want as late a night as last night," I began – four heads nodded in agreement, while Lottie looked puzzled, "so I just wanted to say that I'd like to take the initiative, and maybe find out a bit more about Freddie; we've all had long chats with him, some more than others, and I'd like to hear everything he told each one of you about himself. We might be able to discover someone who wanted him out of the way."

"Other than his Italian neighbor, and her realtor, you mean," said Lottie.

"Yes, what about them?" I replied. "Did Amelia tell you any more than what you mentioned earlier today, Lottie? Did Freddie mention this Italian woman to anyone else?"

Bud and I had agreed this was the best way for all of us to appear to be throwing ourselves into investigating Freddie's demise, so I looked toward him with some hope. But his expression told me he knew nothing. As did every other face, except Lottie's; her eyes were gleaming with excitement even though the only real illumination came from the lights beneath the pale turquoise waters of the swimming pool.

"John had forty winks earlier on, and I did a bit of research," she began. "Amelia mentioned the Italian woman's name, and I tracked her down online. Now bear with me, because I don't have your memory, Cait, but I do know more now than I did this afternoon. The woman's name is Nina Mazzo, and she was a starlet at the Cinecittà Studios in Italy, back in the 1950s. Came here in the 1960s with her husband, who built the house on the estate next to this one. It's called *Caro Mio*. That's 'My Dear' in English, so maybe he named it for her. Anyway, the man she married – Luca Mazzo – was extremely wealthy. Apparently, he had buckets of cash at his disposal right after the second world war – which suggests he made it by dodgy means, if you ask me, because crooks are the only sort of people who have pots of money after a war. He was a good deal older than her. I found pictures of her online, but not him. She was stunning. Very much the same sort of stamp as Sophia Loren. All curves and pouty lips. She had a few small bit-parts in some of those sandal-and-toga things they were making at the studios in Italy at the time, but packed it in when she married. Spent the rest of her life here. Her husband popped his clogs in the 1980s. She never remarried. In her eighties now."

Bud looked impressed, and John was positively glowing.

Lottie allowed herself a little smile when she noticed John's expression, then continued, "It seems there was a landslide in the earthquake of 1993 that affected the access road to her house, and she's been 'negotiating' with Freddie over a strip of land that would make life easier for her ever since then. They've been in and out of court for years, according to some articles I read in the *Jamaica Gleaner*, where it also says she's going to file some paperwork which proves she's actually owned said bit of land all along, and that Freddie has no right to it at all."

I was beginning to realize Lottie might have her uses; her information-gathering seemed thorough, and her reporting of it succinct.

"That sounds interesting," said Bud. We all nodded our agreement.

"I downloaded some photos of her in her heyday," added Lottie, fishing her phone from her evening bag and scrolling.

The device reached me last, and I could see why everyone's eyebrows had shot up when they'd seen the woman in question; Nina Mazzo had been a real stunner. An hourglass would have been jealous of her curves, and she had that fabulously haughty look one sees on the faces of women who know just how attractive they are.

"That was taken in 1957. She was seventeen. She married Mazzo the next year," said Lottie as I returned her phone.

I was gobsmacked. "Seventeen? Good grief, when I think how I looked when I was that age, I shudder. Her? She looks so mature. I don't mean just her clothes, accessories, hair and make-up, which I bet she learned about at the movie studios, but her entire presentation of herself to the world. It's quite something. Amazing."

"There are lots more photos of her online, right up until her husband died, then there's almost nothing," chirped Lottie. "She'd have been in her mid-forties when he died. Young enough to have remarried, but she didn't. I dare say you'd find that strange, wouldn't you, John?" Lottie grinned playfully.

"I'm just an eternal optimist," countered John. "Maybe she'd had the perfect marriage and couldn't imagine replacing her dearly departed husband."

"Or maybe she was just happier living alone, spending her late-husband's money," I countered.

"Ouch!" John grinned. "Is she always this cynical, Bud?"

"Part of her charm," quipped Bud.

"I'm sitting right here, you know. I am not a chattel," I said. Not too earnestly, I hoped.

"And perfectly capable of speaking for yourself, yes, I know, Wife," said Bud. "Maybe there's something in this battle between Freddie and Nina over land rights, but can you really see an eighty-year-old woman shooting a man a few years her senior just so she can enlarge her driveway? Seems a bit unlikely to me."

"She uses a man named Niall Jackson to represent her. Irish blood, and known as a bit of a rottweiler in court, apparently. Quite high profile locally. Likes cases with lots of newspaper coverage," said Lottie.

"You've really dug into this," observed Sheila.

Lottie laughed. "Well, maybe John had more like eighty winks than forty. And –" her voice took on a different tone – "I wanted to be helpful. I like to be helpful when I can be. Especially when I meet a new group of people as lovely as you all are."

I responded with: "You've been incredibly helpful, Lottie. Now all we need to do is work out how we might be able to find out a bit more, and we *could* be onto something."

"Nina Mazzo has invited us for coffee, tomorrow morning, just us three girls. Would that be a good start?" Lottie beamed.

"How did you manage that?" asked Bud.

"I dug around until I found a number for her, then phoned and told her what had happened this morning. She was agog. The invitation was instant. I think she wants all the gory details." Lottie glowed as she spoke.

# Death Scene Do Over

"It looks like Lottie's keen to help," said Bud as we turned in. "That could be useful. If she's busy with you and Sheila, investigating possible reasons for Freddie being murdered, it'll keep her out of our way so we can try to track down what we're looking for."

I plumped my pillow. "What you mean is that we girls can do busy-work so you boys can get the important job done, isn't it?"

Bud sighed. "No, that's not what I meant at all. I meant what I said. It's important that we – as a group – find out if there are any real leads to a possible killer. We need to tackle that issue, as well as finding the items we need to secure. Both jobs need doing. And the sooner we understand why Freddie was killed – assuming he was – the easier I'll sleep, because we still don't know if his death means that someone was onto him, and therefore might be onto us."

The exquisite, cool, cotton pillowcase felt good against my cheek when I snuggled down. "I know," I admitted. "Just playing."

"Sometimes it's hard to tell how serious you are," said Bud quietly.

"Good," I replied, smirking. "Now, let's get some sleep. John and Lottie are on breakfast duty in the morning, but I'd like to lend a hand too. Then I can make myself presentable to meet a movie star."

"Sweet dreams, Wife," said Bud.

"Sweet dreams, Husband." I closed my eyes and allowed my entire body to relax into the sumptuous mattress.

I gave it about half an hour, but sleep eluded me, the sneaky way it does when you know you have to get up early. Bud's snoring was in steam-train mode when I got up and padded to the little seating area outside our bungalow. I lit a cigarette and watched the smoke wreathe in the moonlight. I could hear the surf in the distance and the occasional rustle of a creature in the darkness surrounding me. It was blissfully cool – I'd sweated enough in the past few weeks to last a lifetime.

I allowed my mind to tiptoe through the events of the day, noting volumes of body language, and the expressions on the faces of my fellow guests as we'd discussed some surprising topics. I'd learned quite a bit about two people, John and Sheila, who'd been known to me for some time. I pressed the stub of my cigarette into the ashtray as I realized that, although I'd spent a fair amount of time with both of them, I didn't really know them at all.

Sheila was Jack White's supportive, homemaker wife – that was that; John Silver was something high-up in some sort of international secret service thingy, and had worked on cases with Bud in the past – something about which neither of them could speak openly. Siblings and ex-wives had never entered any of my conversations with either of them, and I challenged myself to wonder why that was the case. I answered myself that it was probably because I'd never asked them any personal questions. I rationalized that there was a pretty good reason for me not to have done that in John's case because he was more of a "business" acquaintance. But Sheila? Did I really not care at all about a friend's personal circumstances? I admitted, silently, that I didn't. People don't interest me a great deal, unless I need to try to work out why they are the way they are, or why they do what they do.

I care about Bud. How he feels matters to me. But my interest in anyone else is…marginal. Yes, human beings are fascinating, but in an academic way. I've always felt the same, even before psychological profiling became my profession.

I told myself that was *my* normal, and to stop wasting time metaphorically contemplating my belly button. It's pointless; I've just turned fifty, so I'm not going to change now.

I shook myself, the way Marty does after he's been rolling about in the grass, and told myself to focus. To be practical. I decided I'd take the rare opportunity of being completely alone to recollect the scene of Freddie's death; I reckoned that would help sort out my befuddlement.

I closed my eyes to the point where everything goes fuzzy and hummed, quietly. That's what I find helps me recollect my experiences better than anything else.

I'm walking toward the place Freddie Burkinshaw called home. He doesn't live in the main house on the estate; that's made available to paying guests. Instead, he's set himself up in a tower built in the late 1600s by Sir Henry Morgan, when he was lieutenant governor of Jamaica. Freddie has told me this, and I have viewed the tower from afar; it's impossible to miss seeing the walkway around its topmost level from almost anywhere on the estate. I quite like the building. It's quirky. It's not as elegant, slim, or tall, as the lighthouse at Negril, but it has its own appeal. There's a squat, square building at the base, above which there are three floors of a round tower.

I know I'm going to the scene of an unexpected death, and I can feel the excitement and anticipation in my tummy. I'm also quite pleased to have the chance to explore Freddie's private domain.

It's dark inside because all the shutters are closed and I give myself a moment to let my eyes adjust, shoving my sunglasses onto the top of my head. The furniture in the room suggests this is a workroom: there's a rudimentary kitchen area with a counter; there are three blenders and a chopping board on it; there's also a worktable; a stone sink, beneath which there's a collection of buckets and bowls heaped on the floor; and there's a pile of wood. It looks as though it's ready to make a fire in the stone fireplace. A fire? In Jamaica, in May? Is that normal? Beside the sink there's an old dark green brocade curtain that hangs from the wooden ceiling rafters to the flagstone floor. It's hooked half open – I see a bathroom. Freddie didn't need fancy fittings, it seems.

I hear Bud entering the large, square, ground-floor room behind me. I know the others will soon follow. I set off up the stone staircase which curves around inside the tower in a languorous semi-circle, my sandals slapping as I walk, my hand running along the roughhewn rocks of the outer wall that has been lime-mortared – probably many, many times over the centuries. There's no handrail; Freddie was surprisingly good on his feet, nimble even, despite his age, so this isn't a surprise. Tiny, slit-like windows have been pierced into the outer wall of the tower allowing some light to illuminate the climb, but it's not the safest footing on the stones which have been worn to a slight shine.

The staircase opens into a light-filled room that's obviously furnished for lounging, and for eating. A somewhat worn mahogany table and one chair sit in front of a vast opening in the wall that looks toward the sea, a view partially blocked by waving palm trees. There's a good breeze. I see similar openings set into the curve of the wall opposite the sea – all the dark-wood jalousie shutters thrown wide. There's an armchair, its upholstery worn, but I can tell it would once have been jewel-toned. The place has a hint of cigar tobacco about it. There are ashtrays on the hardwood floor, with stubs in them. There's a collection of drinks in decanters atop a long, low mahogany sideboard obviously built to hug the curve of that specific wall. It looks ancient, but well cared for, clean.

On the table there's a large glass standing in an earthenware bowl that's half-filled with water. The glass has an inch or so of orangey sludge in it. My tummy clenches. Yuk.

I mount the next staircase, which again curves around the wall of the turret. The walls are angled inwards. I know before I get there that the room on the next level will be smaller than the one I have just left. It is.

There's an intricately carved, mahogany four-poster bed set up so that it gives a view out through another vast opening over the tops of the palm trees, toward the sea and the horizon, visible once the sleeper sits up. Wardrobes, curved to fit against the walls, sit between more windows around the rest of the room. There's a little stool beside the bed with an oil lamp on it, but there are no tables, just a curved antique dresser beside the next set of steps.

I ponder the architecture of the tower as Bud joins me. Wouldn't it have been better to design it with rooms that took up each entire floor, then connect them with internal wooden stairs, rather than using a crescent of the entire floorplan to make the stone steps?

I see Bud mount the next set of steps ahead of me, I can hear Jack and Sheila chatting to John. I want to get to the top before them, so follow Bud.

As I look down the stairs behind me, with Bud peering through the keyhole of the door, I see three upturned faces. John is closest to me, I can smell his aftershave, or cologne. It's a beachy smell, and fits with our location perfectly. He's glistening with sweat. Is it really that hot? I can feel a slight breeze pushing through the slits in the wall. It's a good feeling.

Jack is one step lower than John, and Sheila's behind him. Each one of them has a look of anticipation on their face, but each differs a little: John looks worried but focused; Sheila's eyes are glowing with...what is it? Is that anger I see? *Why?*; Jack's chewing his bottom lip, his eyes fixed on Bud's kneeling figure.

Knowing what I do now about the men's mission, their expressions make sense. Sheila's doesn't. I recall that when Amelia broke the news of Freddie's death, Sheila seemed annoyed, not shocked. "Damn it!" she had said. *That doesn't seem right.*

I make my silly quip about Bud having impacted the integrity of the scene. I look down and see those faces again. John's bemused, Jack too. Sheila's...relieved. *Why?*

Sheila stares at Bud for a few more seconds, then turns, then she, Jack, and John walk down the steps.

Now I'm slipping past Bud to have a look into the room myself. I kneel on the cold, hard stone, and push my right eye against the massive keyhole; there's a large round hole and a widening gash descending from it – just the way a child might draw a keyhole. I let my eye take in the whole scene. There's Freddie, his mouth closed, eyes wide open. His chin is touching the floor, the right side of his face obscured. His arms, hands, and fingers are extended, his legs at odd angles. The keyhole is at about waist height, so I am kneeling up, and the hole is so big I can bob my head about to get a slightly different view of the room from different angles.

Right in front of me there's Freddie's body. Can I see anything else about it, or on it, that might help me deduce if he killed himself? No. As Bud had noted, there's no visible gunshot wound, but there is blood. The blood isn't on the floor in the area nearest his head, it's near his midsection, but the angle of his body means I cannot see his torso. There's a fair bit of blood, and it's pooling on the uneven surface of the wooden floor. Maybe more has found its way into the floorboards, and between them.

There's a gun. It's on the floor beside the body. Its barrel is facing me, and it's at an angle that means I can't make out what type of gun it is; I reason that, even if I could see it more clearly, I wouldn't be able to identify the model or type in any case.

I make a mental note to ask Bud about the gun; he knows guns.

I also make a mental note to ask everyone if they heard a gunshot; I haven't done that yet, and I cannot at this moment imagine why not.

I take some time to recollect everything else I saw of the room. There's a desk between the body and the window, beside which are the doors to the walkway. I can see that both the window shutters and the doors are open. The desk seems to be covered with items, but they are difficult to make out because of my viewing angle. I see something tallish, that seems to be made of brass; a cylinder of some sort? Maybe a telescope. I see some papers in a bundle. They look old – the edges are well worn – but it's not a book, it's definitely a bundle. There's something on top of them – probably a paperweight – but all I can see is that it's made of clear glass…the sun is reflecting off it. There's a pot full of pens and pencils…but that's all I can identify, other than something that looks like a large roll of sheets of paper, tied with a blue ribbon; the sheets look as though they are very big, because the scroll looks quite long.

I move my head and see shelves set against the wall. It's a bookcase, curved like the furniture in the sitting room below, but it's not only being used for books. I can't see it all, but can see enough of it to make out that this is the room where Freddie has chosen to house his knick-knacks, which include a large butterfly, displayed behind glass, in a frame. There's a big ball that looks to be made of knobbly, old iron – maybe an ancient cannon ball? There are lots of books; they look old, and they're all lying down, heaped higgledy-piggledy. There's a bunch of feathers, stuffed into what looks like an antique ink well.

I stretch my neck, which is aching. I can't see anything else. Bud helps me up, and we take our leave, talking quietly as we descend, then we pause in the sitting room, and I recall again how absolutely certain I was at the time that the man we'd dined with the previous evening wasn't in the frame of mind to end his own life.

I open my eyes, and I still believe that to be the case.

"Couldn't you get to sleep?" Bud sounded barely half awake when he sat up in bed.

"No, but maybe I'll be able to now."

"Good. It's late."

After a trip to the bathroom I joined Bud in bed. He hadn't started to snore. "Do you know what sort of gun it was? In the tower." I asked him.

"What?" Bud sounded puzzled, groggy.

"The gun on the floor beside Freddie's body. Could you identify it?" I tried to not sound impatient.

Bud gave me a muffled, "No idea. Couldn't see it properly," he sighed, then added, "please try to sleep, Wife. We've got to get up in a few hours."

"Night, night, Husband."

No reply.

## Breakfast and a Bombshell

Lottie's idea of breakfast was to put bowls of fruit on the table beside jugs of juice and let us all have at it. Fortunately, John was a man who understood the need for gallons of coffee first thing in the morning, and he kept pots of it coming. It was another thing I'd miss when I left Jamaica – the taste of fresh Blue Mountain coffee; it's exquisite: rich, yet not bitter. I glugged it down, then peeled a banana as I raised the question of how Sheila, Lottie, and I were to get to the *Caro Mio* estate to meet Nina Mazzo in a couple of hours' time.

"Can't we just walk?" asked Sheila. "It's only next door."

"That could be quite an undertaking, given we don't know how large her property is, nor how circuitous the road through it to her house might be," I replied. "And it's already hot." I suspect I sounded grumpy; I love the heat, but only if I don't have to exert myself…and walking along a dusty Jamaican road in the humidity of May most certainly counts as exertion.

"I don't think we should ask Tarone to drive us; we should let him stay with his grandmother. But we could borrow the vehicle," said Lottie, who was happily slicing into a mango. "I'll pop over to their bungalow to ask for the keys, if you like."

What I thought was, *I hate people who are bright and bouncy first thing in the morning*, but I replied, "Great idea," hoping Lottie would shut up so I could come to properly.

"With you girls going off to meet La Mazzo," said Bud, "we thought we might go fishing for the day." He sounded cheerful. I glared at him. *So this is the plan they have to be able to disappear?*

Lottie put down her knife. "When did you all decide this?" she asked John. "I thought we could enjoy some time together by the pool when I get back. Or maybe pop over to Montego Bay. We've hardly spent any time at all relaxing properly, or sightseeing, and I thought that was why we'd come."

I could understand why she sounded annoyed; she had no idea about the mission the men were on, so she must have imagined John was trying to avoid her. Not nice, when you've been looking forward to a bit of time with your boyfriend…though I struggled with the concept of John Silver being anyone's "boyfriend".

"Maybe we could do that tomorrow?" replied John. "Jack heard about a chap with a boat who swears he knows the best place for us to catch something we might be able to have for dinner. Fish doesn't come much fresher than that."

Lottie sounded sulky as she stabbed at her defenseless mango. "Does Jack also know someone who'll clean and prepare said fish, so we don't have to?"

"The guy who owns the boat might do it," volunteered Jack. "We'll probably walk away with fillets ready for the grill."

Sheila smiled. "You've got to love their confidence," she said, winking at Lottie. "Sounds to me as though they've as good as caught it already."

"If there's too much for us to cope with, we could pop it into the freezer here," continued Jack, "or maybe even give some to Amelia and Tarone."

"Well, just make sure you catch something," said Lottie still sounding annoyed. "And not bonefish. I don't like bonefish."

"Okay," said John. "No bonefish."

It sounded as though bonefish had made quite an impression on Lottie when she'd holidayed on Jamaica. I'd finally managed to pour enough coffee into me to remember what I'd wanted to ask everyone. "Did anyone hear a shot yesterday morning...or Freddie singing the national anthem?"

Five puzzled faces took on an expression of thoughtfulness.

"Didn't hear either," said John.

"Me neither," agreed Lottie. They exchanged a glance, nostrils flared, eyes glittering with mischief. *Otherwise occupied?*

"You know I'd have mentioned it if I had," said Bud.

"Me too," added Jack.

"I heard something," said Sheila.

We all looked at her. She didn't add anything.

"What did you hear?" asked Jack, trying to sound patient.

Sheila put down the orange she was segmenting and furrowed her brow. "I was going to the bathroom. Don't know what time it was. It was still dark, I know that much. I heard something that sounded like...oh, I don't know...like when a big dragonfly gets caught against a windowpane in the summer, and it just flutters and flutters, you know? I was a bit scared for a moment, thinking it might be one of those huge, black witch moths – they call them duppy bats around here, and they're almost big enough to be bats. Of course, we have a lot of bats flying about at night at home, and they don't bother me at all. But those moths – they make my skin crawl. So maybe that's what it was, I don't know. But I do know that it definitely wasn't a gunshot, I'd have recognized that."

"Have you heard a lot of gunshots, then?" Lottie's tone suggested she thought it unlikely.

Jack leapt to his wife's defense. "Sheila was a good cop, she'd know a gunshot. If she says she's sure it wasn't one, it wasn't."

I was gobsmacked. I had no idea Sheila had served.

"When were you in the police?" was out of my mouth before I could stop it.

Sheila didn't look at all fazed. "The CBC broadcast the Royal Canadian Mounted Police swearing-in ceremony for the first ever female Mounties when I was a teen. It was September 1974 – I'll never forget it. They swore in a whole bunch of them all at the exact same time, across the country, so no one would ever have to be 'the first'. Troop 17. The RCMP college is in Regina, close to where I'm from –" she seemed to be explaining all this to Lottie, but I was also taking it in – "so I guess I also felt some pride that it was in my province. I wanted to join the RCMP more than anything else in the world – and I managed it. I thought I'd made it for life."

Sheila sighed, and laced her fingers. "I could tell you so many stories from that time, but I won't. Let's just say that while there were women who were ready to join the RCMP, the RCMP wasn't necessarily ready to cope with female officers. It was difficult."

Jack added, "We met when Sheila was transferred to the Burnaby detachment of the RCMP in British Columbia, before I'd even thought of joining the VPD. We married and, shortly afterwards, she fell pregnant with our son. At the time, the RCMP was still grappling with how to deal with officers marrying each other, let alone them being pregnant. Remember all the fuss about your sidearm, love?" Sheila nodded.

I blurted out, "Pregnant? With your son?" I didn't know Jack and Sheila had any children. Indeed, I'd always been convinced they were quite happily childless. I noticed Bud squeezing his eyes closed and wondered if I'd put my foot in my mouth, again. *At least he didn't kick me.*

"He was born very prematurely. Too early to survive," said Sheila quietly. "It happened just a couple of months after my sister had died. It was a terrible time. I left the RCMP soon afterwards, and…well, I never managed a full-term pregnancy after that."

I didn't know what to say, and I wasn't alone. The silence was broken only by the hum of the ceiling fans, one of which had developed a definite clicking sound.

"Dear God, that's awful," said Lottie.

"I'm so sorry," I said.

The men didn't comment.

The revelations I'd just heard puzzled me even more – why didn't I know *any* of this? Why hadn't Bud told me?

By the time we'd cleared away the breakfast – which really didn't take much effort – we all seemed to be as "back to normal" as was possible, given the circumstances. Sheila and Jack seemed to be a bit over-jolly, if anything.

As the conversation in the kitchen returned to the fishing trip, and our visit to see Nina Mazzo, what amazed me about Sheila – almost as much as the news I'd just heard about her past – was the ease with which she was dealing with the men's cover story about their "day out", chattering brightly about the lovely time the men were about to have.

I kept having to remind myself I had to act as though it were all real, because Bud's always telling me I'm a terrible liar, and I have to admit he has a point. Under normal circumstances, I think being a poor liar is generally a good thing, but – given our agreement to keep certain parts of our joint activities a secret from Lottie – I realized it might prove problematic. Sheila, on the other hand, seemed to be taking to the situation like a duck to water. *So, she can hide her true emotions when she needs to. Interesting.*

Later, while I was choosing what to wear to visit a hermit-like, now-aged Italian starlet, Bud informed me he was off, and that Lottie would meet Sheila and me at the front of the big house in half an hour. I settled on what had been a loose cotton top a few weeks earlier; now all I could say about it was that it pulled across my tummy a bit less than any of my other tops. Big zig-zag patterns in green and turquoise did a pretty good job of hiding that fact, and toned nicely with my aqua-colored capris, I thought. I felt as well put-together as possible when I headed off to meet my co-investigators. Sheila had opted for another inevitable floral frock, and Lottie looked annoyingly good in wide-legged white linen pants and a little vest. The brim of her pink straw hat kept the sun off her face and made her complexion glow. Me? I tried to stop my sunglasses from sliding down my sweaty nose every thirty seconds.

# *Viva la Dolce Vita*

When we left, we turned onto the little private track that followed the line of the coast. *Caro Mio* was the only thing beyond the Captain's Lookout estate, so I hadn't ventured in that direction before. The public road ran on higher ground to our right; it was busy with cars and trucks, most of which appeared to be whizzing along at an alarming rate, with drivers seeming to feel the need to regularly check if their horns still worked.

The single-lane route ahead of us was rutted and littered with rocks and potholes. We lurched along, each of us making little noises as we were shaken about.

"I can see why she'd want to widen this road," said Lottie, hanging onto the bucking steering wheel.

"Is it this bit that's in dispute?" asked Sheila, gripping the dashboard.

"Yes. Her estate used to have its own access road, but because of the landslide she has to use this one." Lottie paused as we approached a particularly large boulder. "Oh, I see. That must have been her old access route."

Between us and the main road was a sort of promontory, which meant the track we were on had to take a sharp left, up a rising gradient. You could see the gap in the hillside from where the soil had let loose; I suspected a slip lane to *Caro Mio*, like the one we'd used to exit the main road to Freddie's property, had been engulfed by the landslide. Now, anyone wanting to get to Nina Mazzo's home would have to use this poor excuse for a track. I wondered if the discomfort of the trip might have something to do with a woman in her eighties choosing to rarely, if ever, leave her home. If so, that would suggest Freddie had been really rather mean; even if he hadn't wanted the woman to own the land, he could at least have put some effort into ensuring it was well maintained – at least as well maintained as the portion of it that led to his own property, which was in pretty good shape.

As we reached the top of the rise, the difference between the smooth ride on the *Caro Mio* estate's asphalt driveway and the grinding, shuddering trip we'd just endured was a delight. It also looked as though Nina Mazzo had tried to corner the market in bougainvillea; from magenta through the palest pinks to white, from the most vibrant orange to a variety of yellows, the colorful plants scrambled up, and cascaded from, every possible type of support along the driveway – stone walls, iron archways, and even hedges made of other plants. It was astonishing. But even that didn't prepare me for what we saw when we rounded the final arc of the driveway; there was the house – looking for all the world like something out of a Hollywood blockbuster – and then there was the view.

I'd seen the Caribbean Sea from so many angles, and in so many different types of weather, over the past few weeks that I had thought it held no more surprises for me. However, this peekaboo view, through the colonnaded breezeways between the white stuccoed central block of the house and each of the wings extending to the left and right, was unique. I reasoned it must have had something to do with the height of the land, or the angle of the sun, or maybe the fact that it looked as though grass was rolling right down to the sea; whatever the cause, the ocean was a host of colors I'd never before seen melded together that way. I was sure there wasn't a name for it – turquoisegreenbluenavycobaltopal probably isn't an actual colour. But I liked it. *Loved* it.

I dragged my eyes away from the sea and allowed myself to focus on the house. It was whitewashed, with a red tile roof. The central portion was entered through a triple-arched, colonnaded portico; the many windows were internally shuttered against the sun. It was a relatively plain-fronted building, with magnificent Italian cypresses growing up to the roofline, like black daggers against the gleaming white of the walls. A young man wearing a three-piece suit, beautifully tailored in a lightweight, dove-gray cloth, rushed down the wide steps from the massive wooden door, and helped us all out of the Suburban. Lottie cottoned on that he was going to park it for us and handed him the keys.

An older man with a fuzz of white hair, dressed in a similar uniform, descended the wide, stone steps and introduced himself in a rich voice, "I am Arnold, Signora Mazzo's butler. Allow me to take you to her." His Jamaican accent was strong, and his voice had a hint of Morgan Freeman about it, while his tone and expression as he uttered his employer's name made me believe he at least thought kindly of her; there was a tenderness there.

Lottie strode up the steps behind the butler, while Sheila and I rolled our eyes at each other, stifled a girlish giggle, and cantered to catch up. The entry hall was massive, and marbled; the slapping of our sandals on the ancient-looking tiled floor echoed in the atrium, within which there rose an impressive, sweeping staircase. The air was cool, and I could see straight through the entire building to the glint of a swimming pool, and the sea beyond. We were surrounded by imposing artworks and artifacts that looked authentic, and ruinously expensive. It was amazing. Clearly designed as a display of wealth, it did the job exceptionally well – the life-sized, patinated bronze statues of Julius Caesar and Nero either side of the arched entry were the icing on the cake, so to speak.

We followed Arnold as he led us through an equally grand sitting room, where chairs and settees were grouped around tables, suggesting elegance rather than coziness. I wondered just how much use the room would be to a woman who hadn't been seen in public for decades. Did she host wild parties here? Or merely ensure her staff kept it well dusted?

Almost the entire rear wall of the building was made of tall, wide, glass doors, set in pairs. They were all open, and we passed through the central set. The pool ahead of us was vast and infinity-edged; it incorporated several waterfalls and had two rows of spouts which sent water arcing through the air, all of which created a fabulous splashing sound. There was seating for about thirty people, in a variety of styles, and on one lounger, close to the steps which led into the pool itself, was a tiny female figure that appeared to be carved from a knotty, dark wood that had been oiled, then placed inside an amethyst-colored, one piece-swimsuit. As we approached, the figure rose, and Nina Mazzo pulled a glittering golden wrap about herself.

A wide-brimmed hat that exactly matched her swimsuit shaded a face that was largely covered by a pair of massive sunglasses; a wisp of snow-white hair lay on her dark neck, and she had suspiciously pouty, red lips. Nina Mazzo was thin to the point of emaciation, and the bits of her body I could see were wrinkled, crêpy, and tanned to a deep mahogany. Even in her amethyst kitten heels she was still a good few inches shorter than me, and I'm only five-four, on a tall day.

As Lottie shook her hand and introduced us by name, Nina removed her sunglasses; her facial skin was taut across cheekbones that were unusually angular. Despite the knots and ropey veins on her hands, her forehead was almost without a crease. To be fair, her surgeons deserved medals...but there had clearly only been so much they could do.

We accepted her invitation to sit at a table shaded by an acid yellow umbrella, and all agreed we'd call her Nina, as she'd asked.

I could see Arnold was standing just inside the sitting room directing a short, wide woman in a dove gray dress to bring a massive tray to the table we'd chosen. The server arrived and nimbly set down the tray on a side table; we were invited to select our refreshment of choice. Though our invitation had been for "coffee", none was offered. Instead, I had a Ting – a grapefruit-flavoured soda I've grown to love during my time on the island – Sheila had a fizzy water with lots of ice and lemon, and I thought Lottie was extremely brave to take a ginger beer, because it can be incredibly fiery in Jamaica, I've found. I was a bit peeved when Arnold himself arrived with a glass of champagne, on a silver tray, for Nina; had I known it was on offer I'd have taken that.

When the four of us were finally alone, and I was able to pay attention to the woman we'd come to visit, I still found myself distracted by the epic pool and the view beyond. This didn't seem to bother our hostess at all, and she was only too happy to give us an introduction to her fabulous estate.

"Don't you think it's beautiful here?" she asked simply. Her voice was surprisingly deep for such a small woman, and a little cracked with age. All three of us nodded and murmured our agreement.

"My late husband Luca was a man with great vision." She waved a twig-like arm toward the house. "He designed all this himself. It's the perfect place to entertain, and we have four guest houses, two at the end of each wing."

I allowed my eyes to dart about and fell in love with the delightful symmetry of the grand edifice.

"This was one of the first infinity pools in the world, and certainly the first on this island. Luca had an American come here to design and build it as the house was being constructed. They camped in tents as the work was being undertaken so they could both oversee every step of the construction. The way the land falls away to the sea here means it works very well." She sounded proud.

"It's so attractive, to have all those little tiles printed into the vinyl," I noted.

"Ah yes, this is very clever. This was done when I had it refinished. It has been here many years now." Nina shrugged as she spoke.

"There was a fabulous infinity pool in one of the Bond films," said Lottie. "I can't remember which one it was, but I expect it was some sort of set they built for the purpose."

I couldn't resist. "Actually, the scenes featuring the house where the villain Willard Whyte lived in *Diamonds Are Forever*, which is where you saw the infinity pool, were filmed at the Elrod House in Palm Springs, built by John Lautner. Beautiful place, built in 1968."

Lottie tutted. "How on earth do you know so much about so many things?" She sounded annoyed.

"I read a great deal," I said, trying not to sound as though I wanted to poke my tongue out at her.

Nina peered over her sunglasses and champagne. "Maybe it is the same man who built this pool. Though he built ours in 1963, so much earlier." This distinction seemed important to Nina.

Nina's accent still had an Italian cadence, but the sometimes-dramatic swoops Italians use in their speech patterns had been smoothed away. It was lovely to hear.

"I expect you've had some wonderful times here," I ventured.

Nina's mouth smiled a little, though the rest of her face didn't move very much at all. "Indeed. We had twenty or so good years here, before Luca died. So many wonderful parties, some lasting for days. Then, there were many interesting people who had homes on the island, or who would visit. Since then? It has not been the same. He has gone of course, and the people here? They are not as interesting. Now I live the life of a poor, old widow, waiting to die."

She dropped her head and clutched at her chest, but I caught a twitch of her lips, and suspected she was toying with us. She seemed perfectly pampered and content in her palace beside the sea. She certainly hadn't let her looks fade – she'd obviously done whatever she could to retain them. But for who? Not her staff, surely.

"You promised to tell me about Freddie," she said, steering the conversation to the topic I suspected most interested her. "Tell me how he died." She sounded excited, conspiratorial.

Lottie was the one who'd made our appointment, so it seemed fair that she should tell the story…which she did, up to the point where Nina interrupted with: "So you did not actually see his dead body?"

"Not personally," confessed Lottie.

"Did you, or you?" Nina sounded annoyed as she peered at Sheila and me.

We both nodded.

"And he was dead? Truly dead?"

We nodded again.

"Good," she replied.

There weren't many ways to take the conversation, but one, after that.

"You didn't like Freddie?" I asked.

"The man was a snake," hissed Nina. "He was a viper, slithering through the grass, hiding his poisonous nature," she added, dramatically. "When Luca was alive, we spent much time with him – and him always the big man, knowing everyone, moving in exalted circles. Then, when we had the earthquake in 1993, the road to my home was lost, but Freddie would not help me. All he had to do was let me take ownership of a small strip of land, and I could have kept my home easily accessible. You have seen what that tiny track is like. There is nothing that can be done to make a new access-way, because of the main road and the geology of the place. If he had maintained it, I would be happy. If he had sold me that land, I would be happy. But, no. He is so stubborn, that one. Greedy. He needed to own everything he desired to own. Now it is almost impassable. It was as though he was punishing me for something. Me! I am just a poor, old widow. I do not want much from this life, but a road so I can get to my home is one thing I need – and I wish it to be a good road. He was an evil, greedy man – but that sort of person always has to pay some price. Now he is dead. This is good news."

Nina was getting a bit worked up, and I thought it best to try to deescalate the situation as best I could, but – on the other hand – I wanted to work out if this woman had hated Freddie so much that she might have somehow managed to kill him. She certainly seemed to be headed in that direction – which was good, in a way.

"Had you tried legal action?" I asked, knowing the answer.

Nina raised her arms and shouted, "Niall is my lawyer, and he is a worker of miracles. He will take my papers to court and get that land for me, you'll see. He has been very clever and has photographs that will be evidence that what Freddie says is his was always mine."

"How's that?" I asked.

"Before we came to Jamaica a local man owned all the land that was once Henry Morgan's, here along the beach. He built the main house where you are staying, and he lived there. In the 1960s the man died, and the land was divided up. One part was called the Captain's Lookout estate. We bought this piece of the land, and Luca named it for me. We should have been given more when we bought it, but maybe Freddie cheated us then, and we did not know it. Now? Now it will be easier to get what I am sure is mine anyway."

"You mean now that Freddie's dead?" I pressed.

Nina put on her sunglasses and tilted her head. "I do not know if him being dead makes a difference."

"Well, he's gone, and the next owner of the estate might be more ready to do as you want," said Sheila sounding practical.

Nina put the tip of a sharply manicured thumbnail into her mouth, where she ran it along her perfect white teeth. "This is what I believe, and it is what Niall believes." She pulled down her glasses and peered at us. "I have spoken with Niall yesterday, on the telephone, as soon as I had news about Freddie being dead. Niall says this will be good for my case. 'It will clear the path,' he said – which is very funny, because it means two things, no? Niall is very clever this way, saying things that can be understood by different people in different ways. And we have the evidence, the photographs that prove this has always been my land. Now we can get it. At last. I am certain of this. Niall will arrange things. He is good at arranging things. But, for now, tell me how Freddie looked when he was dead. I want to know exactly."

All three of us shifted in our seats. I took a deep breath and began, telling Nina what she wanted to know. I gave her a brief version of events.

"Was the skull damaged?" she asked. It seemed, to me, to be an odd question.

I thought about my response. "He might have hit his head when he fell, I suppose. I couldn't see the right side of his skull at all, nor the back. The left side didn't appear to be damaged."

Nina looked puzzled. "Not *his* skull, *the* skull."

Sheila, Lottie, and I exchanged a look that suggested to me they didn't understand what Nina was talking about either.

I replied, "I'm sorry, Nina, we don't know what you mean. *The* skull? What skull, if not Freddie's?"

Nina stood, ripped off her glasses and stomped about on skin-and-bone legs. "The *crystal* skull. The thing that was his most prized possession. The skull he says Henry Morgan brought from Panama with him. The skull he tells everyone is a gift from the gods. The skull that is possessed of great power. *This* is the skull I mean." Her Italian accent thickened as she became more overwrought.

We all shook our heads. "We don't know anything about it," I said, on our behalf.

"Maybe it is gone! Stolen! Maybe, Freddie did not kill himself at all – it is not the sort of thing I think he would do anyway. He was too vain. Maybe someone killed him because they wanted the crystal skull for themselves, so they can have its power. Freddie used its power for many, many years. I wonder who it will make strong now. The stories about it say it is dangerous for a man to own it – that it changes a man. It corrupted Freddie. You must have heard these stories."

We all shook our heads.

Nina sat again. She moved with surprising ease for a woman in her eighties. She picked up a brass bell from the table beside her and rang it above her head. Arnold immediately appeared at the top of the steps leading from the house. It was a tiny bell, and I was surprised that the man had been able to hear it – which made me think of how sounds can bounce around in unexpected ways.

"I don't suppose you heard a gunshot in the early hours of yesterday morning, did you, Nina? Or anything at all out of the ordinary?" I ventured.

When Arnold arrived, Nina addressed him. "The ladies require their vehicle, and I want my telephone." She turned to me and said, "When I sleep, I hear nothing," then she held out her hand by way of telling us it was time to leave.

As we made our way to the car, I was aware of the fact Nina hadn't answered my direct, final question. But she had given me a lot of food for thought.

## Fishing and Floundering

Back at the estate, we all agreed to have a few minutes to ourselves, then to meet up beside the pool. I changed into my swimming skirt and tank top, then covered up with one of the lightweight flowy things I'd been all but living in prior to John and Lottie's arrival, which had coincided with more regular rain.

Sheila and Lottie were already enjoying cool drinks beneath the largest cobalt-and-white striped parasol when I joined them. Sheila's lean figure and short bob suited her canary yellow one-piece, while Lottie looked stunning in a white bikini that was barely there. I've never had the sort of flat tummy that allows a bikini to look good – well, not since I was about twelve, in any case – so I sat up as straight as I could when I joined them.

"Nina Mazzo is quite a character," said Lottie as we all sipped our drinks.

Shelia nodded. "You could feel the energy coming off her in waves."

"And still rather beautiful, even at her age," added Lottie.

"What did you think about the information she gave us?" I asked eagerly.

Sheila gulped her drink then said, "She didn't like Freddie, did she?"

Lottie laughed. "You're not kidding. Did you see the way her eyes lit up when you described how his body was lying on the floor, Cait?"

I nodded. "I think she'd developed a healthy dislike for Freddie, but maybe that's not so surprising if they'd been fighting over an access road for decades."

"It seems downright mean of him to not let her have a better road to her place," said Sheila. "I think it'll take a week for my neck to get over being bumped around on that awful track. I wonder why he wouldn't let her buy that piece of land from him so she could do a better job of it than he would."

"Maybe we can carry out some enquiries at the local newspaper," Lottie suggested. "They seem to have covered all the court proceedings over the years. I could track down one of the reporters, who might know a bit more than they actually published."

Having found Lottie's enthusiasm to be, initially, quite endearing, her constant volunteering to investigate was starting to grate on me. Yes, she was bright, but did she need to be quite so ebullient?

"Hello girls," boomed Jack as he emerged from the Whites' bungalow. "Had a good morning?"

Sheila popped up from her chair and gave her husband a peck on the cheek. "Fancy a drink, love?" she asked excitedly.

Jack squeezed his wife's waist. "John'll be along in a minute or two, I guess, and Bud had to do something with the fish, in the kitchen. We caught a good few – certainly enough for dinner for all of us – and decided to come back earlier than planned." Jack sounded triumphant. "Bud said he'd bring beers with him when he came through. That'll do me." He kissed Sheila and she smiled.

I smiled too as I thought to myself, *"They're such a smashing couple – I only hope Bud and I are as happy as them when we've been married as long as they have."*

"I'll catch John in our place, then," said Lottie, rising and heading toward their bungalow. "Won't be long." And she was gone.

Jack rolled his eyes. "Young love?"

Sheila sighed. "Well, she's young, alright. But John? Not so much. He's your age, isn't he, dear? Early sixties."

Jack took a seat and chuckled. "Hey, so you're saying I'm an old man? I think I have a few years on him, but Bud's the baby boy here. Still in his fifties, lucky guy. You too, now Cait, eh?"

I managed a smile. "*Just* fifty, thanks, Jack. Rub it in, why don't you."

Sheila patted my arm. "Well, you're lucky you made it at all, given what I understand happened in Budapest. Getting older isn't fun, but it's a lot better than the alternative."

"Hear, hear," said Jack, quickly followed by: "Good man!" when Bud approached with a collection of beer bottles poking out of an ice bucket.

"Fancy a cold one, Wife?" Bud asked as he dumped himself into the chair next to me. The wicker shook and creaked as he settled in.

"Why not?" I replied, noticing I'd already finished my Ting. Bud grabbed the long neck of a Red Stripe Melon beer from the bucket, snapped off the top and handed it to me. I would never have put money on me drinking a melon-flavored beer, which I initially thought sounded disgusting, but I shall miss it when we leave; they tell me you can't get it anywhere but Jamaica. Maybe it'll make it to Canada one day, then I can relive the wonderful memories I've had on the island by drinking beer – which is a pretty good idea as far as I'm concerned.

"So, what's she like, this old movie star?" asked Bud, having downed almost half a stubby Red Stripe himself.

Sheila and I recounted our impressions of, and time with, Nina Mazzo for Bud and Jack. They made the most of the fact that Lottie was out of earshot to pepper us with questions about whether we thought Nina might be capable of killing Freddie. We all agreed it was unlikely – especially since we couldn't work out how he could have been killed up in that tower, locked in, and all alone, in any case. Nina didn't look as though she could have scaled the tower to get into or out of the room where he was found.

"The land dispute thing might be relevant," concluded Bud. I told him about Lottie's energetic offer to gather more information on that matter, and we agreed between us it would be a useful way to give her something concrete to do while we all freed ourselves up to do whatever else was necessary for the men's mission.

By the time Lottie and John joined us, we were happy to move on to other topics, which was just as well because it transpired that Lottie had made a reservation for an early dinner for us at a place about an hour away that accepted fish you brought in yourself; they prepared and cooked it, then presented it with all the trimmings. We were due to hand over the catch of the day in a few hours' time, so I scuttled off to freshen up and change my clothes. Bud offered to help, and a round or two of ribald comments ensued.

Closing the door of the bungalow that gave access to the pool area, thereby gaining as much privacy as possible, I asked Bud the question I'd been desperate to know the answer to: "So, did you find the papers you're after?"

He laughed. "Calm down, Cait. Not yet, but we did finally get a concrete lead. We can follow up tonight."

"Tonight?"

"After dinner. Has to be done around midnight."

My interest was piqued. "Why around midnight?"

Bud sighed. "Can't say."

"You're so annoying."

"I know. Just trust me. It's nothing bad."

"Or dangerous?" I was immediately worried.

"Not at all. It's just we need to see someone who's easiest to locate around midnight."

I pottered about in the bathroom, feeling left out of things, then stuck my head back into the bedroom – so I didn't have to shout – and asked, "Can I come too?"

Bud shook his head. "No. Absolutely not. I don't want you in harm's way."

I grabbed my chance. "You said it wasn't dangerous. You've lied to me. Now you have to tell me the truth."

Bud sat on the edge of the bed. He was quiet for a moment, then replied, "We've tracked down a man who might know where what we're looking for was once kept safe. He might even know where it is now. His current circumstances mean the best time to have a confidential word with him is going to be around midnight. That's all."

"In what way would it be dangerous for me to come with you?" I pressed.

"Because only I am going, alone, so that I'm less conspicuous. Only one of us needs to talk to him."

I gave his words some thought. "And this chap knows where you can find what you need?"

"Maybe. Maybe not."

I felt frustrated. "Bud, can't you give me a straight answer?"

"No, because I don't have any answer other than that. Now, what about all this property ownership thing? Do you think it could be something to do with Freddie's death? That he was killed to make it easier for this woman to get her hands on the land, or something along those lines?"

"You're changing the subject. And I don't know. Nina Mazzo wants to own a strip of insignificant dirt so she can build an access road to her property. She seems convinced that'll be easier with Freddie gone, as does her lawyer, she said. But how could the desire to own one small piece of land lead to murder?" As I heard myself say the words, I realized how stupid they were and added, "I know – value is in the eye of the beholder, and if someone saw that strip of land as more important to them than Freddie Burkinshaw's life, then they'd kill him to get it. But she could have done that at any time. And she seemed convinced she now had some new evidence that would give her a watertight case. So why now? Why not before?"

Bud nodded slowly. "It's that aspect – the timing of his death – that bothers me. There's nothing from the coroner yet, about the autopsy. I checked with…people who would know. Any news on what's going to happen to the estate itself? If it's not about a small bit of land, could it be about ownership of the entire estate? Could someone have wanted Freddie dead so they could get their hands on the whole thing?"

I ducked into the bathroom, and started the water running in the shower. "That's much more likely. I could talk to Amelia to find out if she's any the wiser about the inheritance situation – she might know."

"When? We're off out soon."

I stepped into the shower rather than answering, because I don't like to waste water. As I soaped myself, I reckoned I could get over to Amelia's bungalow and back again before we needed to leave. Checking if we could use the Suburban again that evening would be good cover for a visit, and there was an outside chance someone might have been in touch with her about Freddie's wishes regarding the estate.

Bud's head appeared through the shower curtain. "Don't be too long – I need to get in there too, and shave. My hours of fishing have left me a bit grubby."

"I don't believe you went fishing at all – other than for information. Where did you get the fish we're taking with us tonight? Did you buy it down at the beach?"

Bud had gone and didn't answer.

## Morgan, Cait Morgan

I was approaching Amelia and Tarone's home when I heard raised voices; the grandmother and her grandson were arguing. Rather than interrupt, I crept toward an open set of jalousies as quietly as I could and listened. Even though they were almost shouting I couldn't catch everything; when interacting with us, they both used their best Jamaican-accented English, now they had reverted to the local patois. I'd taken every possible chance to listen to the wonderful Creole-based language as we'd traversed the island, but it's difficult to pick up on all the nuances, and to understand all the vocabulary. That said, I thought my comprehension skills weren't too shabby.

The gist of the heated conversation was that Tarone believed his grandmother should tell us all to leave the estate before our due date; that if she and he weren't going to be paid, they shouldn't have to look after us.

Amelia replied to the effect that Freddie's lawyer had already told her they would be paid in full for the time we were due to be at the estate, so they should continue with their duties. *So, Freddie's lawyer is in the picture. I wonder who she or he is, and what she or he might know.*

Amelia was pressing home her point that she and Tarone would have a safe future on the estate. I edged forward. *Why does she sound so sure of herself, even in the face of Tarone telling her she's talking rubbish?*

I crunched some shells on the edge of the path. The couple stopped shouting, and I had no choice but to call out, "Hello? Anyone there?"

Amelia came to the front door, which she opened. "Mrs. Cait, how are you? How may I be of service?" She sounded a little out of breath.

I smiled – probably too broadly – and flapped my arms about a bit. "I just wanted to check on how you're doing. Are you coming to terms with things at all? Tarone, too, of course…if he's in."

Tarone joined his grandmother in the doorway. "We both here, you see it," he said. His tone had an edge to it I'd never heard before.

"Good, it's wonderful to have family to rely upon at a time like this," I said, beaming. "And, well, we wondered if we could borrow the Suburban for the evening. Would that be okay? We'll drive ourselves, of course. You can stay with your grandmother, Tarone. We wouldn't dream of asking you to leave her."

"Of course you can. Not our Suburban. It for paying guests," he snapped.

Amelia smiled nervously. "My boy worry 'bout how things be here, now Mr. Freddie gone," she said quietly.

I took my chance. "But of course, you must both be concerned. Have you heard anything about what will happen to the estate itself? To you two?"

"We gonna always be here. This is our home," said Amelia with confidence. *Or was it bravado?*

"That's good," I replied. "Do you know that Freddie left provision for you, in his will?" I hoped I wasn't going too far.

Amelia continued to look nervous. "Mr. Freddie always tell me we be looked after when him gone. Him know this is our true home. Him make sure we be safe. Secure."

Tarone looked down at his grandmother with a glint in his dark eyes. "You don't know this, Granny. Him owe us nothing. Him gravalicious, too."

I wondered what Freddie had ever done to make Tarone think of him as greedy. "Why gravalicious, Tarone?" I asked.

Tarone sucked his teeth and turned away. "She know," was all he said as he loped inside.

I looked at Amelia, hoping I was radiating sweetness and light. "Mr. Freddie seemed to be quite a generous host," I opened.

Amelia smiled demurely. "Him always good with guests," she said, studying her toes.

"Maybe his lawyer will tell you what his will says sooner than you think," I said brightly.

"Him already tell me I's to come to him office tomorrow," said Amelia, still not making eye contact. She finally looked up. "If you don't be needing it at that time, we could use the vehicle. Maybe Tarone him drive me. Him can miss training for one day. Kingston a long way on the bus," she added.

I took my chance. "I'd be happy to drive you myself. I could do with one last visit to Kingston. We only have a few days left before we go home – there must be some bits and pieces I can pick up before I leave."

Amelia's eyes grew round. "Oh no, I couldn't be askin' you to drive me, Mrs. Cait. Tarone will do it for his old granny."

"Not at all, it's no bother. What time's your appointment?"

"Half nine. Sharp, him said."

I did a bit of calculating; the drive, parking, washroom before meeting. "How about we leave here at seven, then? That should do it. We can take the A1 highway pretty much all the way; that's the way Tarone took us when he drove us there a few weeks ago." Even as I said it, I was a bit horrified at the prospect of such an early start.

"You a kind woman, Mrs. Cait. Thank you. I bring the snacks and drinks."

I was alarmed that Amelia thought we were going on such a long journey that we'd need refreshments, but was delighted I'd managed to create a potential opportunity to hear about the contents of Freddie Burkinshaw's last will and testament as soon as possible. I felt rather proud of my underhandedness; Bud would be pleased at his non-CSIS-trained wife's natural abilities to gather intelligence.

"You all goin' off the estate tonight, then?" asked Amelia, sounding a little more like her usual cheery self.

I explained about the fishing trip – in all its fictional glory – and named the restaurant we'd been booked into by Lottie. Amelia sucked her teeth – something I had already learned meant, in her case, that she was thinking hard about something. I wondered why the restaurant's name had caused her to react this way, and was immediately concerned about hygienic food handling.

I had to ask. "Is there something wrong with the place we're eating? Is it not clean?"

Amelia looked me up and down, almost as though she were seeing me for the first time. "Not bad. You like it. Big plates. But I think it hard for Miss Lottie to go there. Her father had bad blood with the old man who ran it. Him son there now. Growed up with Miss Lottie back in the day him did. Might still be bad blood."

I tried to wrap my head around what Amelia had said. "Miss Lottie grew up here? In Jamaica?"

Amelia sucked her teeth again. "Mr. Freddie tell me I not to say I know her when she come, and I do as him tell me. I hear her talk to all you good people and she say she come here for holidays. Them some long holidays. She here for years. Go to that fancy private school for rich kids, along the way there. Her father, him come here sometimes, but her mother with her here all the time."

I wanted to make sure I'd understood. "Lottie and her mother lived here in Jamaica for years, and her father would visit?"

Amelia nodded.

"How old was she when she left?"

Amelia closed her eyes. "'Bout sixteen, I think. Look like a little kid, then. Not like now. Now she curvy. Then she straight."

I laughed it off. "I've only just met Lottie, so maybe I'll talk to her about her time here on the island this evening, at dinner. Though if you say there were problems between her father and the father of the man who runs the place where we're due to eat tonight, things could be a bit awkward. Do you know what the problem was?" *Please know!*

Amelia stepped toward me and leaned in. "Everyone know. Her father try to get the restaurant away from the man who own it. Irish man. Drank. The man dead now. Son a lawyer, and him own the restaurant these days."

"Is his name Niall Jackson, by any chance?" It was worth a try.

"You know him?" Amelia sounded surprised.

"I've heard his name mentioned. He's Nina Mazzo's lawyer, representing her to try to get that strip of land from Mr. Freddie. That's the one, right?"

Amelia nodded. "Him the man. Nasty like him father. But sharp, too. Never drinks. Much. That's the difference. If a man drink and him angry, him fight with him fists. If a man don't drink and him angry, him fight with him words. Niall fight with him words. Him and Mr. Freddie got history too. I think Mr. Niall try to make things good with Mr. Freddie lately – him even come see Mr. Freddie, and them talk together, alone in

Mr. Freddie's tower. Strange times. But I don't think them agree. Mr. Niall got history with a lot of folk; him father a drinker for many years, so bad blood all over the island."

"Granny, you ever comin' back in?" called Tarone sharply.

I looked at my watch. Where had the time gone? "I'd better run," I said, hating that I had to, but knowing Amelia and I would share a long journey the next day, when I could dig deeper. "I'll be here at seven in the morning. See you then." I waved as I hurried along the shell-strewn path.

I wondered if Mr. James Bond had ever felt quite as pleased with himself as I did at that moment. I couldn't wait to tell Bud everything I'd learned.

## The Catch, Caught

Everyone was waiting for me when I arrived at the main house. Sheila had taken the role as designated driver, which I acknowledged was kind of her, though my own early start the next morning meant I knew I had to be careful about how much alcohol I put away that night, too. Bud and I were squished together in the third row at the back of the Suburban and I managed to whisper most of my news to him as we made our way to the restaurant. He kissed me by way of congratulations for my stellar work, then suggested we could talk more after dinner. He asked me to hold off on sharing the information I'd gathered about Lottie – which annoyed me a bit because I'd been rather looking forward to confronting her about her lies.

"Leave it to me," he concluded as we arrived at our destination. "I'd like to check a few things with John before we open that particular can of worms, okay?"

All I had a chance to do was agree as I got out of the vehicle backwards – not an elegant exit, but the safest way to wriggle around the middle bench-seat and step down onto the ground without twisting an ankle.

I patted down my wrinkled clothes as I took in the restaurant. Seeing it made me wonder if the meaning of the word wasn't being stretched almost to breaking point; the place seemed to be not much more than a shack constructed from driftwood and gaudily painted corrugated iron sheets, bent and hammered into place. The color theme was – as often the case on the island – yellow, green, and black, with red trim, and there was a collection of what appeared to be randomly selected chairs and tables dotted across a dirt floor. My heart fell. Then I heard the music, and it fell even further. I never used to be averse to steel drums, but I'd heard enough of them in the past few weeks to last me a lifetime. Could I cope with yet another evening of them? It seemed I had no choice, so I slapped a smile on my face, and in we all trooped, with Bud, Jack, and John each carrying a bag full of fish.

Luckily, it turned out that the part of the restaurant you could see from the parking area was just the bar; the real eating area was beyond, arranged over a series of platforms that looked out over the ocean where the sun was beginning to head toward the horizon. Luckily, we hadn't missed the sunset, and our table was far enough away from the band for the steel drums to provide melodic background music, all of which was good. The place was a-buzz with tourists; I was impressed that Lottie had been able to get us a table for six people at short notice, and at what appeared to be a popular time. After what Amelia had told me, I was itching to quiz Lottie about her history on the island, but I respected Bud's wishes and didn't plan to raise the topic at all.

We quickly ordered beers, then enjoyed them with the best possible view in the world. Sunsets in the Caribbean aren't quite "blink and you'll miss it", but they aren't far off; yes, they are spectacular, but that golden ball sinks into the sea extremely quickly, then the colors in the sky deepen and shift rapidly until you're suddenly encased in another velvet, starlit night. The clouds that evening added to the drama of the sky's changing palette, and seemed to disappear as darkness fell, which was good, because it's not much fun to settle to dinner on an open deck if the rain chooses to sweep down from the mountains.

As the last light of the sun faded there was a palpable stillness in the air – the "doctor" winds coming from the sea stopped blowing and it was as though the island held its breath for a moment before the "undertaker" winds from the inland mountains began to rustle in the palms. And with that rustling the now-familiar chorus of the tree frogs started; when we'd arrived on the island it had driven me to distraction, now I wondered how I'd cope without it.

We ordered appetizers we could share while we waited for the kitchen to prepare and serve our fish, however, when all the dishes arrived, it looked like more than we'd bargained for. I picked at the flat-bread-like bammy, and the sliced jerk sausage, forgoing everything else because I hoped our fish course would fill me up.

Bammy is easy to eat, and another one of those things I'd never thought I'd take to, but did; the menu for this place had made a point of explaining that their bammy was handmade on the premises, and had a "secret" blend of spices added to the grated cassava and butter for the baking process, before it was soaked in coconut milk, and fried. I could feel my arteries harden with each bite, but it was delicious.

Inevitably our conversation turned to Freddie's death, and I told everyone about the plan for me to drive Amelia to Kingston the next morning, as Bud and I had hurriedly agreed I should.

"I'd love a run to Kingston," said Lottie enthusiastically. "I haven't been there for years."

I was so tempted to say something that the only thing I could do was shove a piece of sausage into my mouth to shut myself up. Bud rubbed my leg under the table the way he rubs Marty's head when he's being a good boy and not mooching for scraps.

A server brought another round of drinks – we were all selecting beers from the lengthy list they carried – then eventually our empty plates were cleared. We were informed that our fish was all-but ready, and the men were congratulated on their catch. I wondered if anyone in the kitchen would have spotted that the fish had been bought not caught, but the boys didn't seem to be too bothered, so I just chattered happily with Sheila about Tom, her nephew by marriage. Bud and I had met Tom White in Vegas, where he'd been a chef at the time. He'd now moved back to British Columbia and was due to open up his own place – one of those restaurants where they focus on farm-to-table dining. He was living with Jack and Sheila while he set up the business, so was able to look after their dogs and our beloved Marty, who enjoyed being a lodger with his doggie chums.

When the main course arrived, there was quite a performance; several servers writhed through the maze of tables to reach ours, each with a platter held high above their head. Side dishes of leafy, dark-green callaloo and fluffy rice dotted with emerald peas were placed for sharing, but a small portion of fish was served to each of us, individually.

As the last of the servers turned to leave, Bud said, "I thought there was more fish than this."

"There sure is, sir. We bringin' the biggest and the best one, last. Here it come, now."

A striking-looking, tall, red-haired, freckled man was approaching us. He was dressed in a lightweight suit and carried a huge platter above his head. "Make way for the catch of the day," he called in a strong Jamaican accent. As he drew closer, I knew I'd seen him somewhere before, but couldn't put my finger on where, or when – an eidetic memory is like that: it's all in there somewhere, but sometimes it doesn't want to reveal itself in a timely manner. I told myself to focus on the food, and to give the matter some thought when I had a moment.

He placed the plate on the table, filling the only remaining space. "Biggest fish we seen today," he announced, taking a bow as he stepped back. Having finished his theatrical performance, he smiled at each of us at the table in turn. I smiled back, of course, and was still looking straight at him when I saw his expression change. His smile shrank, and his mouth hung open, his eyes growing round.

"Hello, Niall," said Lottie, calmly.

"Hello, Charlotte," replied the shocked man.

We all looked at Lottie. "How are you?" she asked him, almost smiling.

We all looked at the man, who was swallowing hard. "Good," was all he managed. "You?"

We turned toward Lottie. "Just fine. Daddy sends his regards. I spoke with him this evening. Your father's dead now, I hear. What a shame." She reached out to help herself to a heaped spoonful of callaloo, concentrating on the vegetable, rather than the man.

He stood there, swaying, for a moment, then said, "I didn't know you were back."

Lottie didn't look up as she replied, "I'm not 'back'. Just here for a short visit with my beau," she indicated John, who was staring at her, wide-eyed. "You never left, I see."

"No. Jamaica's my home." The stunned-looking man finally dragged his eyes off Lottie and looked around the table at our faces, which must have all shown our surprise. "I...I am Niall Jackson, owner of the restaurant. Good evening to you all." He scurried off, heading to the bar, where I suspected he'd pour himself a stiff drink.

For about thirty, long seconds Lottie acted as though nothing out of the ordinary had happened and chattered on about how good the fish and vegetables looked, and how successful the men's fishing trip had been.

No one responded until John said, "You know Niall Jackson? Isn't he the lawyer who's representing that Italian woman – Nina Mazzo?"

"Yes, I do. And yes, he is," replied Lottie.

"You didn't think to mention knowing him when his name cropped up?" continued John. His voice had a harsh edge to it.

Bud placed his hand flat on my leg and pressed down.

Lottie finally looked at John. "I didn't think it mattered. I spent a good deal of time here in Jamaica when I was younger, as I told you. Mummy, Daddy, and I used to eat here. When Niall's father owned the place. Niall owns it now. They've always been good at fish here."

It was plain to me that Bud hadn't had a chance before dinner to tell John what I'd learned about Lottie's time in Jamaica; I felt sorry for John because he'd been blind-sided and wasn't taking it well.

Sheila said, "So Niall's father used to run the place, now he does? And he's also a lawyer? That's quite the workload, I'd have thought. Long hours."

Jack cleared his throat. "He seemed surprised to see you, Lottie."

Lottie laid down her cutlery. "You mean he looked shocked and horrified to see me, and I sounded heartless and cold, don't you?"

Jack fidgeted. "Well, he sure didn't seem pleased to see you – let's put it that way."

"Yes, let's," replied Lottie, with a hint of cruelty in her voice. "Daddy had a nasty run-in with Niall's father many moons ago; I was quite young at the time, and it made an impression on me. I didn't know Niall terribly well, because he's a bit older than me, but I'm of the opinion that the apple rarely falls far from the tree, and his father was a deeply unpleasant man. He made both Mummy and Daddy terribly unhappy, and he almost killed me, too."

That was everyone's cue to abandon any thought of their food.

John spluttered, "What do you mean Niall Jackson's father almost killed you? How?"

Lottie placed her hand on his. "It's not really as dreadful as it sounds, John. It was probably just a case of bad food poisoning – and possibly a complete accident. But Mummy and I were both terribly ill, and Daddy was convinced that Niall's father – Keith – had poisoned us intentionally." She sighed. "Looking back, it might just have been some poorly prepared ackee – which can be toxic, sometimes fatal. But Mummy and Daddy weren't getting along terribly well at the time and…well, I think Daddy suspected there was a bit of a thing between Mummy and Niall's father. I'd have been oblivious, of course. They worked us like slaves at that school."

"I thought you said you used to come here on vacation," said Sheila, sounding confused. "Why were you going to school during your vacation? Was it like a summer school?"

I was so glad Sheila was there, because she was great at asking all the right questions without sounding as though she wanted to point shiny lights at Lottie – which I suspect I'd have done.

Lottie sat back in her chair and stared at her plate. I took the chance to exchange a furtive glance with Bud, then I adopted the half-smiling, vacant expression I usually reserve for the faculty meetings I'm forced to attend at the University of Vancouver.

Finally, Lottie leaned forward and spoke quietly. "John, we really haven't known each other terribly long, and I've been brought up in a home where saying nothing is the best policy, largely because Daddy could never talk about his work, and Mummy barely spoke about anything beyond her blessed gardens. I don't talk about my past a great deal; it's private, and irrelevant to the person I am today. Of course you don't know everything about me – who could after just a couple of months? I certainly don't know all about you. And the rest of you?" She looked coolly at our faces. "Well, we've only just met. And we've all been rather preoccupied since Freddie died. I thought it would just complicate matters if you all knew that I used to live here, and had a history with the place. With Freddie too, truth be told."

"You knew Freddie Burkinshaw before this visit?" John sounded almost apoplectic. "What the...? Why didn't you tell me? The man's dead. You've been actively investigating his death. Why didn't you speak up?"

"Why didn't Freddie say something about knowing you when you arrived?" asked Sheila.

We all nodded, and stared at Lottie.

She flushed. "Daddy told him not to. And Daddy told me not to, too."

John slapped his napkin onto the table. "Your father did that?"

Lottie nodded, and poked at her fish.

John glared at Bud. "So, Tarquin Fortescue's up to his neck in this? Him and Roger, I bet." He turned his attention to Lottie. "Is that who's pulling your old man's strings? Roger Rustingham? Your good old 'Uncle Rusty'?"

Lottie chewed her lip. "I don't know. All I know is that Daddy keeps phoning me, asking questions, and telling me what to do, and what not to do. I think he's afraid that if you all find out what I know, it will look bad for me."

I was on the edge of my seat.

"And why would that be, Lottie, dear?" asked John, sounding frighteningly calm.

"It's about the treasure, you see." The tealights flickered on the table, and Lottie's eyes glittered. I suspected she was about to go off on one of her breathless diatribes again. I was right.

She settled herself. "The treasure is Captain Morgan's Panamanian cache, that he supposedly buried on this island. I know a lot about it. More than most. I found out about it when I was a girl here. And when Freddie showed me the crystal skull I was sure that meant he'd found the rest of the treasure too – because Morgan must have buried the skull with the rest of it, mustn't he? And if Freddie had that, then he must have found all of it. Daddy knows how big a part of my life the treasure has been. I track items being sold around the world that might have been part of it. Daddy didn't want me to come here at all. I thought that telling him I was coming with John would make him change his mind, but it didn't. He said John would be too busy doing his own thing to keep an eye on me, so he forbade it. I've no idea what he meant, other than that he must have suspected that John would prefer to spend time with his old friends than with me – which is true, as it turns out. But, as I told Daddy, I'm not a child, and I have my own money, so I came. It was just too good an opportunity for me to miss – to stay at Freddie's estate again, have a poke about. But when we got here, I found that Daddy had already spoken to Freddie about not letting me talk to him about the treasure, which Freddie has always poo-pooed in any case, even when I was young."

As I looked at this beautiful, still-young woman, with the face of a petulant child, I wanted to shake her. And still she hadn't finished.

"I first saw the crystal skull when I was about nine years old. It was the most beautiful thing I'd ever seen. I couldn't imagine how it had been made, it was so perfect, almost liquid…and yet made from something that was so difficult to carve. I thought it was magical then, and I still think that today – though I haven't set eyes on it for many years. It was just after I first saw it that I heard the rumors of a trove of treasure brought to Jamaica by Henry Morgan when he left Panama. Eventually, Charles II knighted him and made him Lieutenant Governor of Jamaica. But I bet Cait, at least, already knows all this; Morgan was Welsh – you two even share a name. There aren't a lot of Welsh people who've achieved what he did, and John's told me that you're still rabidly Welsh, despite the fact you ran away from the police to live in Canada."

All eyes swivelled toward me. I hadn't been expecting such a neat bit of character assassination as part of an explanation about why Lottie had lied to us all, so my response came from my heart and out through my mouth, without a great deal of editing along the way.

"You've got the cheek to cast aspersions on my character when you've been lying to us all this time?" I snapped. "Yes, I'm Welsh; always will be, though I don't think of that as some sort of disease, as you seem to, rather a birthright of which I am proud. And yes, I chose to leave my family, friends, and my home, because the English tabloids – not the *British* tabloids, they're all *English* – chose to hound me and make my life unbearable after I'd been released by the police – *released* I emphasize – having been completely cleared of any suspicion of having killed my abusive ex-boyfriend. But I'm not the one who's lying to everyone's face about my connections with both a man we just found dead, and one of the people possibly connected – somehow – with that death. *You* are. You've known Freddie since you were a girl. You used to live here, even attended school here. Were you in school with Niall Jackson? Is that how you knew him? *You're* the one who needs to tell us what's going on, not me. So, tell us, Lottie; don't change the subject with me as your scapegoat. You won't enjoy the results."

Bud whispered, "Try coming out singing, not swinging, eh, Cait?"

I glared at him, but knew he was trying to help, so I took a deep breath and a swig of beer to try to calm down.

Lottie had the cheek to roll her eyes before she said, "When Freddie and I met at dinner that night he died, he immediately told me that Daddy had forbidden him from acknowledging me, so I didn't mention it. I phoned Daddy and challenged him about what he'd done when John fell asleep that night, and Daddy said he'd done it so that the subject of the treasure didn't come up in public. Daddy always tells me I appear foolish when I talk about the treasure. He hates it. And then, when Freddie died, Daddy was afraid you might all think I'd killed him to get my hands on it. So he made me swear to not tell about knowing Freddie at all. He'll be furious when he finds out I've let the cat out of the bag."

"What leverage did your father use to get Freddie to keep quiet about knowing you?" asked Jack. The tone he used wasn't one with which I was familiar; usually Jack sounded jolly, or concerned, or enthusiastic…now he sounded disdainful. *Odd.*

Lottie sighed. "I gather Daddy knows a fair bit about what Freddie used to get up to with his flash friends here decades ago, when he indulged in more than fine brandies and cigars. And Freddie didn't want the stories about his peccadillos getting out and ruining his reputation as a respected and important man on the island." Lottie looked around, then leaned in even further. "I don't know any more."

I suspected she was lying.

John looked at his plate of fish. "This is cold, and I can't face it anyway." His eyes were glassy when he looked up at us. "If you all want to stay and eat, go ahead. I'll get a taxi back to the estate. In fact, please do all stay. Especially you, Lottie. I can't bear to look at you at the moment." He stood, angrily pushing back his chair. "Best I don't say anything I'll regret later. I'll sleep in the main house tonight, or beside the pool. Feel free to use the bungalow, Lottie dear. Goodnight."

He cut a swathe through the tables, and was gone.

# A Storm Strikes

The first heavy drops of rain beat a tattoo on the windshield as we all bundled into the Suburban and Sheila started the engine. We'd poked our food about on our plates for a while with Lottie sobbing quietly, but since no one wanted to comfort her except Sheila – who always did the honorable or kind thing in a crisis – the situation was so strained it had to end. Somehow. A distant rumble of thunder came to our collective rescue.

A silent return to the estate and a subdued leave-taking followed, before I found myself leaning against the closed door of our bungalow watching Bud sit on the edge of the bed and mutter, "People never cease to amaze me."

I couldn't help but laugh. Quietly. "I love you, Husband," I said, sitting beside him. "It's been quite a day. What do you make of it all?"

Bud stood. He stretched his arms above his head. "It's hard to know. You've had your day. I've had mine. And now? Well, mine's not over yet, as you know."

I looked at my watch. "It's only half past ten. How long will it take you to get to your midnight appointment?" I was still worried about the safety of his plan. "Even if you have to meet this bloke alone, can't Jack and John – or at least one of them – come with you, in case you need back-up of some sort?"

The corners of Bud's mouth crinkled into a smile. "I'll be fine. It's just a chat with a guy who's in his seventies. Nothing bad's going to happen. I've been in law enforcement my whole life. I know how to ask a few questions of a guy who's got nothing to hide. I just need to jog his memory, that's all."

I didn't like it one little bit, so decided I'd have another go. "But if Jack were to come with you, he could stay in the Suburban while you had your chat, so you could get away faster, if you needed to." I suddenly realized something important. "But Jack's been drinking – he can't drive. Nor should you."

Bud reached to stroke my hair. "You didn't notice I was drinking alcohol-free beer, did you?"

I cast my mind back to the bottles I'd seen him lifting at the dinner table. "Bitburger alcohol-free?" He nodded. I was relieved. "Good job, Husband. So, you could drive, but Jack could be there, in the Suburban. Waiting."

"Who says we need to drive at all?" Bud tried to raise just one eyebrow; it never works.

"Have you seen the weather? It's a downpour. You'll be soaked in minutes. Besides, it would take longer than that just to get off the estate's grounds. Where exactly are you going to meet this man?" I couldn't imagine.

"Can't say. But I'll find him."

I was getting a bit fidgety, so stood and paced. "Come off it, Bud. You can't just take off, alone, in the middle of a nasty tropical thunderstorm in the dead of night and expect me to be okay with the idea you're just going to wander about until you run into an old bloke who has information you need about some papers that disappeared decades ago. That's ridiculous. I want to say, 'I won't let you', which is equally ridiculous, but you know what I mean. You wouldn't let me do it, would you?"

Bud scratched his hand through his hair – always a sure sign of stress – and lifted one of the slats at the window. "The weather's not good, you're right, but you have to understand, Cait, this is what I am trained to do. This is my job."

That was it – I'd had enough. "No, Bud, this isn't your 'job'. You've retired. This is – what, a hobby now? Just because you've done work for CSIS in the past, they can keep calling upon you to do some undercover, and possibly underhand, work whenever they want? That's bonkers. This is real life – our life. Why you? Why not some young blade who's not usually at home tending to his ageing parents, or the acreage, or his dog? And don't say you can't tell me. That's not fair."

Bud pulled me into his arms. "Some young blade? You do make me laugh." Bud chuckled. "It's not fair, I know. What I will tell you is that the reason *I'm* doing this is because I know the man I need to meet. He'll trust me when he sees me. He'll tell me what he knows, if he knows anything at all, because of that trust. And that counts for a lot. We're under some pressure to achieve a positive outcome, Cait. His knowing me can save us valuable time. That's why me. Today we finally managed to find out where he'll be around midnight, so I must be there too. Jack and I have been trying to locate him for a week or more, and our tenacity has finally paid off. And I can't take a vehicle, because he lives on the beach, in a shack. Totally off the grid. He never gets there until midnight; the local cops give him some peace until sun-up, then he moves on again. We located the shack this morning. It's not far. Best way for me to get there from here is along the beach."

He stroked my hair. I tried to not think of him petting Marty. I felt a little less anxious, but still my tummy wouldn't unclench.

"But Jack could come with you, couldn't he?"

There was a gentle knock at the door. Bud's head snapped up.

"It's me, Jack."

"Come in." Bud unwrapped his arms.

Jack looked a bit sheepish. "Sheila says I'm to come with you. Won't take no for an answer. And I agree. Can't hurt to have me along, right? I'll stay in the shadows when I need to. Background support only."

I couldn't resist. "See?"

Bud raised his hands in submission. "Okay, okay, we'll go together. I guess we'd better tell John, or he'll sulk."

Another knock at the door.

"What's going on? Anything I should know about?" It was John. He was wet through. "Couldn't sleep. Saw Jack come over here from my vantage point on the couch in the big house. Thought I should check up on you chaps."

I knew when I wasn't needed. "I'm going over to your bungalow, Jack. I'll wait with Sheila. It might help if we share the stress. Each of you take care of the others, and make sure you let us know what's happening, when you can. If for any reason you can't come straight back here after your mysterious rendezvous, then you phone me, Bud. Promise?"

Bud kissed my forehead. "I promise."

"And Bud?"

"Yes."

"There's just one more thing," I said at the door. "You'll be soaked in seconds, so please use some of the plastic bags in the bathroom to keep your phones dry. You secret agent types never seem to think about the practicalities of life, do you?"

Bud nodded, smiling. "Plastic bags? Right."

## *Treasure Tales, and a Turn for the Worse*

Sheila opened the door to the Whites' bungalow half a millisecond after I knocked.

"Are they going together?" she asked, as she dragged me inside.

I wiped the rain off my face. "Yes, all three of them."

"Good. I'm glad about that. If they have to go at all, it's best they go together. Jack's not as young as he was, but has no idea that's the case."

I smiled. "Bud too. But, there again, do we?"

Sheila's brow unfurrowed, and she grinned. "I guess I don't, for sure, but then we're not the ones yomping about on the beach in the dead of night, trying to track down some old guy who upped and left a cushy job when the going got a little sticky."

Once again I felt a prickle of annoyance that Jack had clearly been more forthcoming with his wife than my husband had been with me. "Ah well, they'll keep each other safe," I said, trying to make myself believe it.

"They sure will," replied Sheila, sounding about as convinced of it as I was. "Fancy a drink?"

Usually my answer to that question would be "Yes", but on this occasion I wanted to remain fully alert, just in case. Just in case of *what*, I didn't care to imagine, but *Just In Case*. "You haven't got anything non-alcoholic, have you?"

Sheila checked the little fridge that sat between the bedroom and bathroom. "Only beer."

"We could run over to the big house. Wait for them there. I could smoke there, too," I suggested.

Sheila shrugged, then grabbed her phone. "Good idea." She waggled the phone at me. "Got yours?" I waggled mine at her. "Let's go then."

Running in flipflops in the rain is a pretty slippery undertaking, so as we crossed the area surrounding the pool, where there were lots of puddles, I slowed to a waking pace – I was already wet through to my undies, so there didn't seem to be any point in running and maybe having an accident. Just as I thought it, and not *because* I thought it, Sheila went skidding past me, toppled over and fell headlong onto a lounge chair. Despite the noise of the rain, the clattering of the furniture was loud, as was her ripe language.

I rushed to her side. She was caught in the chair – quite how she'd managed that I didn't know – so I had to pull her arm and leg free, then I tried to get her to her feet. She swore the whole time.

Lottie loomed out of the sheeting rain. "What happened?" she shouted.

I didn't think the situation needed an explanation, so didn't give one, but gestured that she should help me get Sheila into the big house. Sheila couldn't put weight on her right foot, so we did our best to shuffle-carry her until we were under the portico, where we plopped her onto another lounge chair – this one intact, and out of the rain which drummed on the roof above us.

Ten minutes later, we'd managed to get Sheila onto a proper sofa, with her foot elevated and wrapped in a compression bandage I'd found in the first aid kit in the bathroom. I made her take some painkillers I'd found, too. Lottie had gone to the kitchen to find something that might help reduce the swelling around the egg-like lump on Sheila's ankle. The bag she returned with was full of bits of something brown, of indeterminate source, but at least it was cold, and malleable, so it hugged Sheila's ankle quite nicely.

I brought each of us a large bath towel from the linen cupboard, and we managed to dry ourselves off a little. Lottie brought each of us a brandy – which suddenly seemed like a much better idea than a ginger beer – and we all settled as best we could. Sheila looked relatively comfy, for a woman who was obviously in pain, and insisted her constitution could cope with a small brandy as well as painkillers. She even reminded us, twice, that she hadn't had a drink at dinner.

By the time we'd done all that, the rain had eased a little and the wind had stopped gusting, which was a relief.

"You'll have to stay off that for a couple of days," I said, nodding at Sheila's ankle. "R.I.C.E. Rest, ice, compress, elevate. But maybe you should see a doctor tomorrow, to check it's only twisted."

"Maybe you should go to the hospital? Get an X-ray?" said Lottie quietly.

"It's a sprain, for sure," said Sheila forcefully. "I've had them before, I'll have them again. Once your ankle's gone this way, it'll go this way easier and easier forever more. Did it the first time falling off a barstool in Regina. Must have done it at least half a dozen times since."

Lottie looked puzzled. "Are you very clumsy? I've never sprained an ankle."

"With any luck you'll still be able to say that in twenty-five years' time," replied Sheila tartly, "when you're as old as me. And, no, I'm not clumsy, until I am. Such is life."

"Where are the men?" ventured Lottie.

Sheila and I exchanged a wide-eyed glance.

"Gone for a beer on the beach – some bar they heard about. Helping John drown his sorrows, and hoping the rain wouldn't drown them in the process," said Sheila.

Even I almost believed her.

"Oh," was all Lottie managed.

With Sheila in physical pain, and Lottie in what I expected was emotional turmoil, I knew it was my responsibility to put aside my worries about Bud's activities and somehow carry a conversation.

"So, do you really think there's buried treasure to be found somewhere hereabouts, Lottie?" I asked. I had a feeling that would be a useful opening gambit, and Lottie bit.

"Oh absolutely," she gushed. "I firmly believe Freddie discovered the treasure's original hiding place and was selling it off one piece at a time."

I had to admit, I was intrigued. There can't be many children who haven't been excited by the idea of an X on a map being held by a piratical figure contemplating his chests full of doubloons or pieces of eight. And I'd read enough Enid Blyton books in my formative years to believe that hidden treasure could sometimes be stumbled upon in the oddest of locations.

I sat forward and lit a cigarette. "Well, if we're going to wait here until the men have drunk their body weight in beer, why don't you take the chance to tell us why you think that, Lottie?"

Lottie smiled nervously. "I'd love to. But stop me if I go on a bit too much."

"We haven't yet," I quipped, but my barb was lost on her.

She cleared her throat and said, "How much do you both already know about Captain Henry Morgan?" she began.

I raised my multipurpose eyebrow. "Quite a lot, as it happens," I replied. She couldn't have known how entranced I'd been by the idea of my namesake since I was a child. "Born around 1635, possibly in Llanrumney near Cardiff, but definitely somewhere in Glamorgan, in south Wales – where I'm from. I prefer the idea of the Llanrumney roots, and I think it's supported by the fact Morgan named one of his plantations here after that town. He turned up in Jamaica, aged about twenty, most likely sent as an ensign by Cromwell to serve in the fight against the Spanish in Central America. He was known to have been involved in the disastrous campaign led by the Welshman Vice-Admiral Penn – whose eldest son, incidentally, founded Pennsylvania – which failed to capture Hispaniola. There's a letter of marque dated 1667 giving Morgan the right, as a captain, to seize vessels on behalf of King Charles II, so he must have had enough experience at sea by that time to make him worthy of such recognition. He quickly established a reputation as a ferocious and successful fighter – on sea and land – possibly earning him the nickname Bloody Morgan, though we cannot be sure that was a contemporaneous nickname; if it was, it suggests he didn't shy away from violence in pursuit of treasure for his king. He certainly amassed a great personal fortune by stripping Spanish wealth from ships, and towns."

"He was a violent man, but a great success," said Lottie, nodding.

I couldn't let that pass. "He probably wasn't the brute portrayed by Esquemeling, the disaffected Dutchman who sailed under him, who wrote a best-selling biography of Morgan, targeting readers from countries that were the enemies of the English crown. Did you know that Morgan won the first ever successful libel suit in history against the publishers of that book?"

Lottie shook her head. "I didn't know that. I can, however, say I know Morgan was never on a par with the infamous Welsh pirate, Black Bart Roberts. You Welsh seem to make good pirates. Roberts took more ships – four hundred – and probably more lives, than any other pirate, ever."

I was impressed. "Good for you for even knowing about Roberts," I said. "A lot of people don't."

"I didn't" said Sheila, looking bemused. Lottie poured her another brandy.

I pressed on. "Granted, it's true that Henry Morgan was in some trouble with Charles II in 1672, and was called to London, but instead of being prosecuted and possibly hanged, he ended up being knighted and returned to Jamaica as its lieutenant governor. Over the next decade or so he oversaw a programme of intense 'cleansing' of Jamaica's less palatable inhabitants, especially around the Port Royal area. He died an extremely rich man in 1688. He lived in hard, unforgiving times, and certainly did some dreadful things, such as ensuring that Jamaica was able to become a key port in the trafficking of slaves. There are so many lenses through which you can view his actions, but one thing's for certain, for a boy from rural Wales, he lived an extraordinary life."

Sheila looked impressed, as did Lottie. I felt somewhat gratified.

Lottie smiled. "I thought you'd know a bit about him. But it's his time in Panama that I've researched most deeply."

"He sacked Old Panama City in 1671, didn't he?"

"He did," said Lottie, her eyes glowing. "However, despite the fact he took the city with minimal loss of men on his side, and huge losses on the Panamanian side, the bounty for each man who fought with him – the share they got from the monies he captured – was small. From that time onward there have been tales about him hiding a great deal of treasure that he managed to sneak out of Panama and hide on a ship to come to Jamaica. He arrived in Port Royal, in the harbour opposite Kingston, in March 1671. The treasure *must* have come to

Jamaica with him, because this is the only place he landed after leaving Panama. Then, in April 1672 he was arrested here, and sent back to England, as you said, with the idea that he might stand trial for ignoring the Treaty of Madrid that had been signed between England and Spain just before he ransacked Panama. So, he *must* have hidden the treasure in that year before he was arrested."

"But you can't be sure there *was* any treasure," interrupted Sheila from her supine position.

"Yes, I can. I have good evidence – but I'll get to that in due course," snapped Lottie. She was sitting very upright on one of the dining-room chairs, and was at full alert, focussed on her tale. "When Captain Henry Morgan – as he then was – got to London, he didn't end up being tried for breaking the law at all, instead, Charles II knighted him, made him Lieutenant Governor of Jamaica, as you said, Cait, and sent him back here with the new governor, the Earl of Carbury, and the new chief justice, Colonel Sir Thomas Modyford, who'd been governor here from 1664 to 1670. All three men knew each other, and I've always thought that Charles II saw in them an excellent triumvirate with the right skill set to secure and rule Jamaica on his behalf. And the treasure? Well, that was why I think Morgan accepted a political role – he wanted to get back to it, here. He wasn't a politician, he was a fighter, and the life of a man who owned plantations, and had endless meetings with people about liaisons and agreements just doesn't seem to fit with the earlier years of his life."

"He might just have had enough of fighting," I suggested. "It's one thing to make your mark in your twenties and thirties, and quite another to have to keep going off to battle all the time in your forties and fifties," I added.

"Especially when you're rich," said Lottie, seizing on my point. "You see, although he was paid handsomely for his privateering, and for his official roles once he returned here, there's no way he could have afforded to buy everything he bought, and build everything he built, using just that wealth. *That's* where the treasure came in. I believe he used it, a bit at a time, to be able to do what he wanted. Building the tower here, for example. He married his cousin in 1666, but they had no children. In his will he left all his money to his two godchildren, with some for his sister. Can you imagine Jamaica in the 1600s, and a man like that – a hero, a vital man, the lieutenant governor – not having any female companions additional to his wife? I believe the stories that he built the tower for a mistress, or consort."

I sighed. "He might have just wanted to live in it himself, Lottie. It's close to the beach. He must have loved, and probably missed, the sea, having spent so much time sailing on it. It's also a building that would be pretty easy to defend, if he found himself in trouble again," I suggested.

"Stop it," snapped Lottie. "That's not the point. The point is he built it, owned the land upon which it stood – stands – and more surrounding it. The land he owned at the time was much greater than the size of this estate; it also encompassed what used to be a large plot to the west – which fell into the sea in the late seventeenth century – and it also included what is now the *Caro Mio* estate to the east. As Nina mentioned."

"And that's relevant because – what?" challenged Sheila.

"I think Freddie started looking for the Morgan treasure in the late 1950s and moved here, to this estate, in the early 1960s because he believed this was where it was hidden. He wanted the treasure to fund the lifestyle to which he hoped to become accustomed. And I think he did just that." Lottie looked smug.

I wasn't convinced. I challenged Lottie with a direct: "How can you say that? What proof do you have?"

"Have you ever read *Live and Let Die*?" she asked.

Sheila shook her head. "I've sure seen the movie though," she said. "Roger Moore, Jane Seymour. Filmed here, wasn't it? Well, you know, bits of it."

I said, "I read the book, a long time ago. Why? Oh, hang on…SMERSH is using seventeenth-century gold coins to finance its Soviet operations, and the coins are supposed to be a part of Henry Morgan's secret treasure, which they've discovered here, on Jamaica. Right?" Lottie nodded enthusiastically. "You do know that Ian Fleming wrote *fiction*, don't you?" I asked as pointedly as I dared. "He invented landscapes to meet the needs of his stories, and he didn't even do Henry Morgan's real story justice. He just wove bits of poorly-sourced history into fiction to tell a better tale."

"Ha, ha," said Lottie dourly. "Yes, I'm aware. But Fleming would have known the rumors about Morgan's Panamanian treasure, just like everyone who lived here did. He wrote that book in 1953, before Casino Royale was even published. He wrote it in Goldeneye, his house just a few miles from here. He knew this tower, and I bet you he even had a theory about where the treasure was 'really' buried, as opposed to what he made up for the book. Everyone else had their favorite theory back in those days; many still do, today. They'd probably talk about it as they drank their cocktails and smoked their cigars – possibly in this very room, when Freddie was giving his famous parties in the 1960s – swapping stories about the good old days of the war, and the hateful Ruskies threatening Western supremacy. Trust me, Daddy goes on and on…and on…about all that stuff. Not that he was here back then, of course, it was before his time, but he was told tales by people who were, and the whole thing becomes part of the canon of what makes Jamaica, Jamaica."

"Don't Jamaicans make Jamaica, Jamaica?" quipped Sheila.

"Maybe you shouldn't have had that second brandy, not with those painkillers," I observed. *Maybe she's just tired?*

Lottie looked confused. "No, Sheila, they don't – well, yes, of course they do. But there've been people using the island for their own ends since Columbus arrived here; the Spanish followed in numbers, almost wiped out the poor Arawak and Taíno peoples, then they shipped in slaves from West Africa to work on their plantations. Then came the British, the privateers…and so on, and so on. It's always been like that here; constant tension, for so many reasons."

I checked my watch. It was half past twelve. I hoped Bud and the boys would be heading back to the estate, and decided to press Lottie to get to the point where she told me something concrete.

"And Freddie and the treasure?" I asked. "What *evidence* do you have he ever found it? Other than possibly the crystal skull you mentioned."

Lottie studied her empty glass, placed it on a side table and spoke more quietly; she wasn't declaiming any longer, but remembering. "I first met Freddie Burkinshaw when I was a girl; Mummy and Daddy would bring me here when they met their chums, and I would sit with Freddie and he'd tell me stories to 'amuse' me. He told me about the Nazi's blitzing his home in 1941; he lived in Hull, which suffered more damage than any other British city or town from bombing during World War II. He grew up through rationing, and reconstruction, and always with the sea right there beside him. But it was a cold, unforgiving sea, not the sort of sea he read about in books. He told me about how the Bond novels captivated him. He laughed when he told me he hardly understood what they were about, but he loved them. He was just eighteen years old when he first came to Jamaica. It was his heart's desire to see the place, and he managed to get himself a job with a shipping firm in Hull that did business here, and got transferred. He would light up when he told me about that – so pleased with himself. And I think that's when he began his grand plan – to find the treasure he'd read and dreamed about."

*Freddie was part of her family's circle of friends back then,* I thought. What I said was: "How on earth did he expect to manage that?"

"Contacts," said Lottie. "He was good at making contacts. Although Daddy's never been terribly forthcoming, he did say that Freddie had a reputation for being able to get things for people. Unusual things. Probably some illegal things. Freddie built a network of contacts and used that to build a network of 'customers'. By 1962 he was sufficiently well-placed to be considered a valuable enough resource for the British government to want to have him here, and he'd amassed enough money that he could afford to buy this place. Daddy only hinted at it, but I think paying a low price for this estate might have been a prerequisite of him gathering and providing information for London."

I lit another cigarette and checked my watch, again. "It's a lovely story, Lottie, but what about the treasure?"

"We weren't here when the big earthquake happened in 1993, and we didn't come back for a year afterwards; the island sustained a great deal of damage. They have hundreds of quakes here every year. In 1692 there was a big one, too; that's when about a third of Henry Morgan's lands here fell into the ocean – as well as the cemetery in Port Royal where he was buried, his remains being claimed by the sea after all. Ironic, really. Freddie first showed me the crystal skull when we visited in 1994. I'll never forget seeing it for the first time—"

"As you told us at dinner," I interrupted. "But the rest of it?"

Lottie tutted. "I believe Freddie couldn't resist holding onto the skull for himself, but that he kept the rest of his find a secret, and sold it off a bit at a time. It wasn't until I turned twenty-one and got all of Mummy's money that I had the time and resources to dig a bit deeper and test my theories. It's marvellous to have cash, and not have to work. I put all my efforts into it. I found records of sales of items that could only have come from Panama in the 1670s, and some which were likely to have been there at the time. The sales took place all around the world from 1995 right up to the present day. Golden chargers embossed with contemporary designs, or chased with the crests of families living in Panama in those days; small caches of specific, traceable coins; items of jewelry seen in portraits, or described in records of the time; and a magnificent chalice known to have been looted from a Panamanian church during the sacking by Morgan – its body was covered with cabochon rubies, signifying the blood of Christ. Unique. All the transactions were kept pretty hush-hush; rather than being made through the big sale rooms, the auctions took place online, even in the 1990s. I found someone who was prepared to act as an intermediary, to track down such items on behalf of an anonymous 'collector', and I was able to see photographs of the items being offered for sale, and being sold. I kept the photos, of course. So, yes, I'm certain that Freddie had indeed found Henry Morgan's Panamanian treasure. I further believe that it must be located somewhere close to this estate – if not on it – because Freddie hasn't left the place overnight since 1962, as he never tired of telling even those who didn't want to know."

I gave some serious thought to everything Lottie had said. I had to admit she'd done her homework, and I felt more inclined to accept her theories about Freddie Burkinshaw's source of wealth than I had done at dinner. But was there a connection to his death?

Might Lottie herself have been desperate enough to discover the location of the treasure that she'd have killed Freddie during, or after, an attempt to get him to tell her where he'd secreted it? Or might someone else have also come to the same conclusions she had, and thereby ended up in a situation where his death resulted from some sort of interrogation?

I realized how much we stood to learn once we were notified of Freddie's autopsy results, and also wondered if – or when – the police might return the key to the tower room, so that I could get in there to have a proper look around.

As I thought of the key, and of being able to enter the room I'd only been able to peer into, I realized I'd been incredibly stupid: the cops had called in someone to somehow open the door to allow them to access the body. If they'd done that, then they probably hadn't been able to re-lock it. I could have got into the tower room any time I'd liked.

I swore, internally. *I really annoy myself, sometimes.*

"So, are you convinced?" asked Lottie, standing and smoothing down her still wet, and now exceedingly crumpled, dress. She tossed her long, damp hair as best she could.

I pushed aside my self-chastisement and was just about to reply when Bud and John ran through the French doors. They were both soaked through, their eyes wild, and both were struggling to catch their breath. Bud had a large pink-ish stain on his shirt.

My entire nervous system seized up – it looked like blood.

## Pool Party

Bud shouted, "Everybody get into the pool. In your clothes. Just jump in, quick!"

"Pardon?" said Lottie.

"What?" I said.

"Where's Jack?" shouted Sheila, hoisting herself up onto an elbow.

"He's right behind us, Sheila. Now come on, quick." He grabbed me out of the chair, then shooed me toward the open doors and the pool beyond.

"You're frightening me, Bud," I said, everything clenching. "Don't you dare push me into that pool. You know I can't swim. I'll get in for myself, at the shallow end." And I did, though I had no idea why. Bud launched himself into the deep end.

Lottie and John joined us – causing a mini-tsunami – just as Jack appeared from the direction of the beach. "Where's Sheila?" he screamed.

"She's on the sofa. Sprained ankle. Can't walk," I called at his scurrying figure.

As Jack disappeared into the house, Bud grabbed me and held me tight in the chest-high, undulating water. I tensed. "What's going on, Bud? Did I see blood on your shirt? Is it yours? Have you been hurt? Are you alright?" I sounded as panicked as I felt.

He held my face in his strong hands. "It's blood, but not mine. We found the guy I needed to see, but he'd been attacked before I got to his shack. Shot. Twice. Left for dead, I think.

Then we heard the cops coming. We ran for it. When they get here, we've all been messing about in and around the pool since getting back from dinner, okay? We've agreed that's our story. Stick to it."

I looked into his eyes and could see his focus, his determination. I nodded, and kissed him.

That was how the cops found us: Bud and me kissing in the pool like teenagers; John and Lottie shouting at each other, and splashing; Jack squished onto a sofa indoors, wrapped in towels, comforting his wife who had a sprained ankle. Just some idiotic tourists, doing idiotic touristy things, at a luxurious private estate in paradise.

The cops were patient as we four got out of the pool and dried off; they were concerned for Sheila when we explained how she'd hurt herself in the general frivolity; they were understanding when we explained how we weren't usually that rowdy, but that we'd been out for a lovely dinner and had probably enjoyed a few too many cocktails. It helped that one of the officers was Constable Cassandra Lewis, who'd met us all when she'd attended the scene of Freddie's death the day before.

When we enquired – as one would – about why they'd come onto the estate from the beach, their answers were less than forthcoming. They focussed instead on asking us all if we'd seen or heard anything out of the ordinary. When her superior left us beside the pool, to talk to Jack and Sheila in the lounge, I took the chance to press Constable Lewis about what was going on…as one would.

She seemed like a pleasant enough young woman, and she whispered, "An attack, on the beach, along the way a bit. Anonymous call came in. Old man, shot dead. Homeless. Harmless. Not a good thing to happen, but it does. We see a figure run off to the bush, behind the beach. Male, we think.

Think him come this way. Also think we see another figure, running. Gender indeterminate. Couple, maybe? Followed. Ended up here. You all say they didn't come this way."

"I suppose they could have got up onto the main road, or had a car waiting, or something," I said. Helpfully, I thought.

The officer tilted her head, thoughtfully. "Could be," she said. "Two old men dead in two days, less than a mile apart. Violent deaths."

"So sad," I said.

"And unusual," she replied.

"Really? You can't imagine that the deaths of Freddie Burkinshaw of the Captain's Lookout estate and some homeless chap in a shack on the beach are connected, surely? Freddie killed himself; this man was murdered. Completely different."

Her eyes narrowed. "I mention a shack?"

My insides sank. "I think your colleague said something about it." *Best recovery I can manage.*

"When you all leave?" she asked, jutting her chin toward me. *A challenge?*

"At the weekend," I replied, possibly too brightly. "Your sergeant said it was alright for us to stay on. It is, isn't it? Okay, I mean." I was trying to judge her inner thoughts, but her face wasn't giving anything away.

She sucked her teeth. "If him say so." She cocked her head and sauntered toward the doors to the dining room, to check her superior's wishes, I supposed. She turned, more somber-faced than before. "Sorry to spoil the party. Walk good."

I watched as both officers returned toward the beach, and shuddered with relief, then realized my whole body was vibrating. And not in a good way. I was a wreck.

What had happened to the woman who was able to focus in a crisis, wade in, take charge, and not blurt out a damning fact?

Had I kissed her goodbye when I blew out the single candle on my fiftieth birthday cake? Or had she gradually disappeared as I grew into my role as Bud's wife, a participant in a partnership rather than a single, independent person? I didn't know. But at that moment I was pretty sure she'd gone. *I miss her.*

All of us – Lottie included – knew better than to immediately talk about the situation, but when Bud suggested "one for the ditch" we all accepted a brandy without any disagreement. We flopped on various chairs and sofas in the lounge of the main house, probably looking like half a dozen freshly-caught fish tossed onto the beach – glassy eyed, mouths agape, and stunned.

We remained that way for at least a quarter of an hour, with very few words exchanged. Even when we all said our goodnights and made our way toward our respective bungalows, not one of us mentioned the evening's events. I judged we were all too shocked to discuss what had happened – and I was equally certain that each couple would be sitting up to dissect the tragedy before trying to snatch some sleep. I wondered how John would explain things to Lottie – at least Sheila and I had an inkling of what had been planned.

I tended to my needs in the bathroom and set an alarm for six in the morning; my phone helpfully informed me that was in just over four hours' time, which didn't lift my spirits.

When Bud finally eased himself into bed, I held him tight. "What can you tell me?" I asked. I thought that was the best way to put it, rather than demanding he tell me everything. He gets all stubborn when I do that, and clams up. *Gently, gently, catchee monkey.*

I felt him tense in my arms. "I arrived at the location, stayed in the shadows, saw a light inside the shack, and made a determination that the subject was already there. I approached the structure, entered through the front, and discovered the subject prone on the sand, groaning. I turned him onto his back. He'd been shot in the chest. Twice. I attempted to stop the bleeding, but his wounds were too extensive for me to be able to affect any remediation. Moments later he was deceased. I made a cursory search of the premises, but found nothing of any relevance to our needs. John was concealed at the rear of the structure. He alerted me to the imminent arrival of police officers who were approaching along the beach. I exited via the rear of the structure, following John into the bush behind the beach. Jack joined us as we made our way back here."

He couldn't have delivered a more Bud-like description of the events. I hugged him tighter. "I'm sorry, Husband. So sorry."

I felt Bud's head nod above mine.

"Were you able to get the information you needed?" I asked.

Bud sighed. "I asked him what I needed to. He answered as best he could. I'll need to pass on that information to find out if it's useful. It meant nothing to me."

"What did he say?" I had to know.

"'Cooper. Man. Male.' Maybe Cooper is a family name, and he meant a man, or male member of that family. Or maybe he meant mail – like mailing something to a man called Cooper. Don't know. I'll do my best to find out in the morning, when you're off to Kingston with Amelia. Which I know means you have to get up real early – so we'd better get some sleep."

Sleep? He was kidding. "I was terrified when I saw that bloodstain on your shirt. I thought it was your blood. It could have been your blood. You were lucky whoever did it wasn't still there." The thought made my tummy turn. "You didn't see anyone else there, did you?"

I could feel Bud shake his head. "No. The three of us split up to approach the structure. Standard operating procedure. Jack moved furthest along the beach, with John taking the central spot, and I remained on the flank nearest this estate. Agreement was to observe for ten minutes to establish the subject's presence, then I was to be the only one to approach via the front entrance, which faced the sea. I didn't see anyone enter or leave the structure during that observation period. Only thing I saw was the glow of a light – which turned out to be a propane lamp, burning low."

"Do you think whoever did it called the police? They must have done – who else knew? And why would they do that?"

Bud was silent for a moment. "I was thinking of that as we all sat in the lounge. I agree that only the killer could have known our man was dead. Maybe they wanted the crime discovered quickly, for some reason."

I gave it some thought. "Bud, you're too bright to have not thought it through. Someone knew you were supposed to be meeting that man, needed to shut him up, and wanted to set you up for his murder," I said quietly.

"No meeting had been agreed; it was simply a case of our discovering where the subject could be found and when – and planning to intercept him there and then."

"Please don't try to protect me by not telling me the truth, or all of what you're thinking. Not fair, Bud."

"Yes, you're right, not fair. Now try to get some sleep."

"Who else could have known about your clandestine meeting tonight? Who did you tell, Bud?"

"No one outside the operational unit. And that's a small group."

"Other than John and Jack, that would be…?" I allowed my question to hang in the night air.

I felt Bud half-chuckle. "Nice try, Wife. A very few people in a few off-island locations, that's all I can say. All in the know. All giving direction, and support. No one questionable."

"What was the dead man's name? I can't keep calling him 'the subject' or 'the victim'. The man must have had a name."

"He did, but I'm not sure I should tell you, Cait."

"He's dead. Who can it hurt now?"

Bud sighed. "His name was Wilson Thomas. Happy now?"

"Might *he* have told someone about the planned meeting?"

"Cait, you need to stop. And you need to get some sleep. And, no, as I said, he couldn't have told anyone, because he didn't know I was planning to go to his shack tonight. As far as I'm aware he didn't even know that I was trying to track him down. Please, sleep?"

I kissed him on the cheek, then turned and rolled into my usual fetal ball. On my left side, because I have a tendency to have night-time dyspepsia, and laying on your left side helps prevent it. Though the sourness of the brandy, the lack of a real meal, and the unsettling nature of the tragic death of Mr. Wilson Thomas meant I didn't hold out much hope of making it through the few hours I was going to be in bed without the aid of some Tums.

## Road Trip

I felt wretched when I woke. Bud was lovely; he made coffee while I got ready to face the day, and toasted and buttered some bagels he'd found in the freezer. He offered to come to Kingston with me, and even to drive. I assured him I would be perfectly capable of undertaking the journey and the interrogation of Amelia during our road trip, and to be alert enough to capitalize upon any opportunities that might present themselves to gain knowledge of the contents of the late Freddie Burkinshaw's will.

"You'll text me to let me know you've arrived safely?" he asked.

"I shall," I replied.

"You'll get in touch if there's anything you find out that I could do with knowing before you get back?" he pressed.

"I promise."

"And you'll…"

I kissed his nose. "I'll be fine, Bud. But if I don't go now, I'll be late." I left him in the kitchen looking forlorn and concerned, a coffee pot in one hand and a mango in the other.

I kept the engine, and thereby the air conditioning, running when I knocked at Amelia's door, and she emerged immediately. She wore a snowy white starched shirt above a navy skirt that hit her legs mid-calf. Her shoes were navy, as was her handbag. She wore a white straw boater, with a navy band. I suddenly felt underdressed…or overdressed – I wasn't quite sure; I'd pulled on stripy, stretch-cotton, wide-legged pants and a theoretically-loose matching top, in shades of orange and turquoise. It was the closest thing I had to a suit – well, it was a matching two-piece, but not anything I'd imagine wearing to meet a lawyer anywhere other than Jamaica. *It'll have to do*, I thought to myself, though the expression on Amelia's face as she looked me over suggested she didn't approve.

Before she shut her front door she handed me a basket woven from palm fronds, a gaily colored napkin covering its top. "Snacks," she announced. "I'll sit with you in the front. Basket can go on the seat behind for when we need it."

We set off, and I concentrated on getting onto the main road and settling into the rhythm of the traffic before I attempted to engage her in conversation. She didn't seem to mind the silence, and I could tell she was happy enough to take in the scenery as we moved along at a fair pace. I enjoyed seeing the landscape change as we gained elevation, from the palm-fringed coastline to the hardwoods, the wonderful greenery of the breadfruit trees and the lush upland landscape which benefitted from a massive amount of rainfall. The Taíno name for Jamaica had been Xaymaca, which meant land of wood and water in their language, and once you left the seaside there could be no doubt in anyone's mind why they'd chosen it; Jamaica has a ridge of rain-catching, and rain-creating, mountains running along the east-west axis of the island, and, in order for us to make the journey from the north to the south – across the island's narrow "waistline" – we had to get over them somehow. The main road did that with relative ease, though I imagined it must have been hard going in earlier centuries, which was probably why Henry Morgan had favored having his private estate – as opposed to his plantation estates – on the opposite side of the island to Port Royal where his "official" work was done, and which was a place dubbed the wickedest city on earth in the late 1600s.

We were well on our way – a fact marked by Amelia digging into her basket for snacks, which I declined – when I decided I had to make the most of my chance to quiz the woman. "Do you go to Kingston often?" I asked, by way of an easy opener.

"No. 'Tis a terrible place. When I got to go, Tarone take me. Him a good driver."

I wasn't sure if Amelia was implicitly criticizing my comparative abilities as a chauffeur, but I felt I was doing pretty well – under the circumstances – so chose to bolster my confidence by saying, "I'm sure we'll get there in one piece, and on time."

"I pray so," was Amelia's underwhelming reply.

"Do you have any idea why the lawyer wants to see you?" I asked brightly.

"I 'spect him tell me what Mr. Freddie left to me and Tarone." Matter-of-fact tone.

"And do you have any idea what that might be?" I wondered if we were in for a game of twenty questions – or maybe one hundred-and-twenty questions – if I were to discover anything useful.

"Mr. Freddie always say him take care of me and Tarone when him gone."

"Might he make you two being allowed to stay in your bungalow a condition of the estate being sold, do you think?"

I could sense Amelia staring at the side of my head, but didn't dare take my eyes off the road. "Him not gonna do that. Him give the whole place to us. Him said it often enough. Always for us, him said."

I was surprised; it hadn't occurred to me that Freddie might leave the entire estate to Amelia and Tarone. Though I immediately reasoned he had no family that any of us were aware of, so – I supposed – why not? After all, if the estate was sold off, to whom would the money go?

"He had no family?" Best to check.

"Not him."

"Well, you two getting the entire estate would be wonderful," I replied. "Would you live in the big house? Carry on renting out the bungalows?" I imagined the need for some sort of income might come into play.

"I sell half the land, build a new house with the money I get, live in it," said Amelia with certainty. "House with windows with glass in them, and air conditioning, big refrigerators, all the modern things," she said. I glanced across and saw a smile on her face; she'd clearly given the matter a great deal of thought.

She continued, "The big house is old, but not old enough to keep. I like it, but I want everything new. I will have a new house, and I keep my new house private. But Mr. Freddie, him know the tower is important for the island, so I gonna set it up like a museum, I let everyone come see it if they want...and if they pay."

"Clever," I said aloud, and meant it.

"I can be clever," replied Amelia, sounding neither boastful, nor embarrassed. She popped the basket, now empty it seemed, at her feet.

"Have you thought about how you'd like your new house to look?" I asked. Amelia chatted happily for the next hour about all the decorating and furnishing decisions she'd made. She went into the minutia of all the décor she had planned; I began to tune her out after about fifteen minutes, because the eyewatering amount of detail she had worked out was clearly something she wanted to share with me in its entirety.

Eventually I had to interrupt Amelia's flow to ask, "Can you give me some directions now, please?" As we entered the outskirts of Kingston the traffic jammed up, and I had to drive with great care; it was busy – to say the least – and the local interpretation of how to use indicators was lost on me.

We eventually stopped in a large car park, just off Dumfries Road. There, squatting among the banking buildings and restaurants was an edifice that seemed to be constructed entirely of dark glass.

Amelia pointed at it. "They in there." She said it with all the enthusiasm I lavish on making my dental appointments.

"Would you like me to come inside with you?" I offered, not expecting Amelia to agree.

She'd already unbuckled her seatbelt and was opening the door when she stopped, turned, and we made real eye contact for the first time since she'd got into the vehicle. Despite her set jaw, and determined smile, I could see something in her eyes that hinted at a lack of confidence. She was uncertain about something, but trying to cover it up.

"I wouldn't mind popping to the loo," I added hurriedly. "It would save me having to hunt about for one in a coffee shop."

I smiled, hoping I looked like someone needing a bathroom break, then realized that no play-acting was required.

"If you need a toilet, I expect they have one."

"I do hope so," I replied, and got out of the Suburban as quickly as I could before she changed her mind. Despite her seeming certainty about Freddie's wishes, and the amount of time she'd obviously spent planning exactly how she'd use her expected inheritance, all of Amelia's body language was telling me she was apprehensive about this appointment, and I was glad I'd been able to throw her a lifeline she could accept, without losing face.

We managed to cross the road without too long a delay, and finally found ourselves in the reception area of King and Overton, Legal on the third floor of the glass box, where Amelia gave her name, and asked for directions to the washrooms. Once we were there, Amelia tidied herself in front of the mirror. She looked as nervous as a schoolgirl, rather than a woman in her sixties, or possibly her seventies – it was hard to tell.

I decided to make an attempt to achieve my ultimate goal. "If you don't mind me saying so, you look a little apprehensive, Amelia. Would you like me to come into the lawyer's office with you? I'll keep quiet, but I'll be there if you need me."

Amelia wiped her face with a tissue. Her lips pursed. "I leave school when I fifteen. Lawyers are clever. What if I don't understand what him say to me?"

I dared to pat her on the arm. "I'll stay with you, and I won't let him overwhelm you, I promise."

Amelia smiled, and it was agreed. We returned to the tastefully decorated reception area which smelled of something fruity, and accepted water from the receptionist, who was hooked up to a headset, and all-but-hidden behind a bank of computer screens.

She eventually stood and said, "Mr. Cooperman will see you now. I'll show you through."

I stared at Amelia, open-mouthed. I'd expected a lawyer with one of the names of the firm itself: King or Overton.

I spluttered, "Freddie Burkinshaw's lawyer's name is Mr. Cooperman?"

Amelia nodded, and gave me a weird look.

As Amelia and I were shown along a circuitous series of corridors, I texted Bud to let him know the name of the man I was about to meet. I wondered if I'd have a chance to find out if the Cooperman in question knew a certain Wilson Thomas, who was even more recently deceased than Freddie Burkinshaw. I tried to stop my body fizzing with excitement.

## Cooperman, and a Collapse

I wasn't sure what I'd expected Cooperman to look like, but I was surprised when I saw him, nonetheless. He sat behind a large desk carved from gleaming mahogany, and appeared to have been hewn from the same material. His face was deeply wrinkled until it reached what would have been his hairline, then there was a perfectly smooth dome that looked as though someone had polished it. His suit was toffee-colored, his shirt a yellowish cream, and his satin tie gleamed like old gold. His spectacles were large and round, like him. There wasn't an angle, or a sharp edge to be seen about the man. I felt immediately at ease. Then he smiled, and his aura of bonhomie enveloped us as he fussed to get Amelia comfortably seated, offered us refreshments, and adjusted the blinds so we had no sun shining on us.

I wondered if he was treating Amelia as well as he was – and even indulging her wishes for me to remain in the room – because he knew she was about to become a very wealthy woman. But, as he opened a large leather document folder on his desk, I could see that his previously joyous expression had shifted; I also noted that he was repeatedly pushing his glasses up his nose despite the fact they weren't slipping down. I told myself that might be a habit for the man, rather than an indication of any psychological discomfort on his part, but his opening gambit suggested my concerns were warranted.

"As the executor of many estates over the years, it sometimes falls to me to give difficult news to those who are grieving the passing of a loved one." Mellifluous tone; almost-English accent.

Amelia was sitting bolt upright in an elaborately carved chair beside me; she grasped her handbag on her knees. Her only response to Cooperman's words was to slightly tilt her head.

Cooperman took her silence as a sign to continue. "Mr. Burkinshaw was well known on this island, and he lived large, as the saying goes. Of late I know his hospitality has been tempered somewhat by his increasing age, and a natural desire to live a more private life. At least, that is what he would tell those of us who continued to mix with him socially when he wanted to explain his diminished involvement with local charities and so forth."

I had a horrible feeling I knew where this was going.

Amelia still said nothing.

"Mr. Burkinshaw often spoke of you with great warmth and affection, Mrs. LaBadie. You've been more than a loyal employee to him over the past – what is it now, thirty years or so?"

"I been with him over forty-five years, all told. An' you can call me Amelia, everyone does. My mother was Mrs. LaBadie. I ain't her. An' you right, I been more than an employee to Mr. Freddie. Him say this to me many times. Him say he take care of me and Tarone when him gone." She bristled with confidence.

Cooperman nodded and smiled. "Indeed. Indeed. And he has made good on that promise. I can tell you that he has left a considerable percentage of his estate to you and your grandson – by name – in his will. But there's a slight problem I need to make you aware of."

"Tell me what him done," said Amelia.

Cooperman closed the leather folder. "Upon gathering the facts as I have been able, in such a short period of time, it is clear that Mr. Burkinshaw had taken out a good number of loans, using the Captain's Lookout estate as collateral. The nature of my role as his executor behoves me to make good those debts before I can make any bequests to beneficiaries. You, Amelia LaBadie, and your grandson, Tarone Thomas, are due to receive all of Mr. Burkinshaw's estate – with the exception of the Captain's Lookout tower itself, and a small parcel of land upon which it sits. Mr. Burkinshaw legally subdivided that parcel from the rest of the estate some years ago. But it is my duty to tell you that, unfortunately, it is unlikely there will be much residual money, if any, from the sale of the remainder of the estate, once his creditors have been paid."

I noticed Amelia's hands grasp her handbag tighter. I didn't know how she was managing to hold her emotions in check; the detail with which she'd described her dream home during our journey told me she'd been – quite literally – banking on Freddie's bequest to set her up for the rest of her life.

"What will happen to the tower?" she asked simply.

"The tower?" Cooperman seemed surprised. "Ah, well Mr. Burkinshaw has gifted that to the parish. There are a great number of caveats attached to allow them to take ownership, but Mr. Burkinshaw's main aim was to have the tower protected, maintained, and made available to the public. The local authorities will be able to do that."

Amelia nodded. "So, we don't get nothing then. I understand."

Her eyes were glassy. She licked her dry lips. I reached forward to the tray on Cooperman's side table and poured a glass of water, which I handed to her.

As she sipped, I couldn't help but speak. "Does this mean you'll be arranging for the sale of the estate, excluding the tower, Mr. Cooperman?"

The man seemed relieved to be able to turn his attention to me, though he looked at Amelia as he replied. "Indeed. And as soon as possible. The debts Mr. Burkinshaw incurred will continue to grow until they are paid off. It is imperative that I manage to arrange a swift, and fair, sale."

"And how long do you think that might take? It can't be easy to sell such an expensive piece of property." I couldn't imagine there were thousands of people just waiting to snap up a private Jamaican estate – well, there might be thousands who'd like to, but not too many who could.

Cooperman adopted the sort of expression I suspected would be used by kindergarten teachers when a child in their charge isn't yet able to count to five. "It is a prime location, with direct access to an extensive private beach, with no historically protected structures – other than the tower, which will be preserved. It would be an extremely attractive investment for any developer."

I could see that it would be. "But isn't there a movement afoot to prevent large construction projects that might impact the ecology of the island?" I'd been reading as much in the local newspaper during our stay.

"Indeed," replied Cooperman with what I was beginning to feel was an irritatingly indulgent smile. "But I have no doubt that all the appropriate measures will be observed by whomever purchases the property. We have strict guidelines for such reasons."

That was me put in my place.

Amelia was still sipping her water.

"Can Amelia and Tarone continue to live in their bungalow until any sale is finalized?" I asked.

"I have already spoken to a representative of the company I feel will do a good job of presenting the estate to the market, and he assures me this is the case. They would be paid for their services and would be expected to maintain the estate in a way that makes it as appealing as possible to prospective purchasers."

"And have you any sense about how long a sale might take?" *He didn't answer when I first asked him.*

Cooperman looked at Amelia with concern, but capitulated. "I understand there is considerable interest. A sale might be almost immediate. Maybe within weeks. Or days, even."

Amelia put down the glass of water. It was almost empty.

"So, we moving out fast, with not a thing," she said quietly. "No home, no money, no pension, nothing. Soon. Mr. Freddie always say him not pay us much for our work because him see us right. Him not see us right at all." Her voice was thick with emotion.

I started to scrabble in my tiny shoulder bag for a paper tissue, but there wasn't anything lurking in there that was fit to be used. I reached toward the poor woman, and touched her arm. She was shaking. "I'm so sorry, Amelia." I didn't know what else to say.

"All for nothing, then. All for nothing," she said. She pushed herself up out of her seat then stood, swaying slightly.

"Are you okay?" I asked, as the swaying intensified and became a definite wobble.

"I thought I could save my Tarone, you see," she said, staring at me, tears streaming down her face. "It wasn't for me, it was for him. Him a good boy, but the gangs try to get at him. If we have money, him safe. I did it for him."

With that, she went down. I heard the thud of her head hitting the edge of the desk, and she bounced off it, landing in a heap at my feet.

Both Cooperman and I leaped out of our chairs in an instant. "Call the emergency services," I screamed, but Cooperman was already prodding at his cellphone's screen.

There was blood trickling from a wound on Amelia's head. Her eyelids fluttered above her rolling eyes. I moved her into the recovery position, hoping I was doing the right thing. Not daring to look away from her I asked Cooperman, "How long until help arrives?"

"I don't know," he screamed. "This never happen to me before. I don't know how long them take." His smooth lawyer-talk had evaporated, and he'd reverted to his local accent. He ran to the door of his office and ripped it open – for a large man he moved quite nimbly. "I go to reception, so them know where to come when them arrive."

I was alone with Amelia. She was on the edge of consciousness, and unable to speak, but she could groan alright and even kept on crying, in a way. I couldn't tell if that was because she was in pain, or whether it was a continuation of her previous anguish. Not that it mattered.

As I stroked her arm, and said a few "there, there's", I couldn't help but wonder if she'd simply fainted or if she'd maybe suffered a heart attack. I knew nothing of her medical history, and realized I had no idea about how to get hold of Tarone, who might at least know the name of his grandmother's doctor. Then I worried about her head wound, which – if all she'd done was faint – could turn out to be more significant than the original reason for her collapse. I also toyed with the idea of phoning Bud to find out from him if there was anything more I could be doing for the poor woman; he's not trained as a paramedic, of course, but he's had a lot more experience of helping injured people over the years than I have, and I knew he'd received training in what to do in such circumstances, even if he hadn't refreshed that training since his retirement.

The next few minutes felt like an hour, and I was immensely grateful to be able to pass Amelia's care to a professional at that point. It turned out there'd been a false alarm on another floor of the same building, so the EMTs had been able to come to us before even leaving the premises.

Knowing that Amelia was being taken care of, and with Mr. Cooperman hovering behind his desk, I asked if he had any contact information for Tarone. He didn't. I had the bright idea to call Amelia's bungalow at the estate on the off-chance the young man might be there; there was no reply. The EMTs were proposing to take Amelia to the nearest hospital, and all Cooperman and I could do was agree. It was at that point I decided to phone Bud, hoping he might be able to come up with some way for us to reach Tarone.

Bud answered on the third ring. I explained the situation as succinctly as possible, and finally got to the point of saying, "...so I really need to get hold of Tarone..."

"He's with me now. I'll put him on," said Bud.

I heard him give Tarone the briefest of explanations of what was happening, then heard Tarone himself. "She okay? Is Granny okay?"

"The EMTs are going to take her to the local hospital," I said.

"Good, get her seen fast. She got a bad heart. She never say anything to anyone, but I know it." The poor boy sounded distraught.

"Do you know her doctor's name? Any medications she takes?"

Tarone gave me the information I'd asked for, I scribbled it down and handed the note to the hovering EMT, who dashed off with it, following his colleagues who were pushing Amelia along the corridor on a gurney.

When it was finally just me and Cooperman in his office, I plopped down on the chair Amelia had been using and poured myself a glass of water. Cooperman accepted one too. We sat opposite each other quietly for a few moments, both looking a bit dazed, sipping cool water.

"She's in good hands now," observed Cooperman, eventually.

I nodded.

"I feel…I wonder if…I hope it wasn't the news I gave her that caused her to…" His face told me he was grappling with guilt, and deep concern. What I couldn't work out was whether all that concern was for Amelia, or whether some of it might be for himself.

Knowing the best thing I could do was try to somehow achieve my overall goals for Bud, I took my chance.

"Amelia had been expecting to inherit the entire estate, unencumbered by debt. Freddie Burkinshaw had told her that would happen. She'd planned to sell half the land, secure the safety of the tower, and build a private home for herself and her grandson. The news you gave her must have come as a great shock; her dreams were destroyed. Her final words suggest to me she fears for her grandson's safety if they don't have a future at the estate."

Cooperman's face was a picture; his eyes bulged, his chin quivered, and, despite the significant air conditioning in the room, I could see sweat beading along what would have been his hairline. He looked truly panicked. *Interesting.*

I thought through what I'd heard from Lottie about Freddie's potential source of questionable income, the loans the lawyer had mentioned, and racked my brain about the possible reason why a dying man – Wilson Thomas – might throw out Cooperman's name.

"It's a terrible shame that Freddie chose to leave Amelia and Tarone in such a dreadful situation. Do you think he had any intention, or ability, to pay back the loans he'd taken out, had he not died?" I asked.

Cooperman mopped his brow. "I don't know. I don't know."

I knew I had to take my chance to get out of him whatever I could while he was sufficiently flummoxed to not realize he probably shouldn't be telling me anything at all. I took a bit of a flyer, based on what Amelia had told me about Freddie trusting Cooperman.

"You've known Freddie for a long time, and he chose you – of all the lawyers available to him – to be his executor. You must have known the man better than most. Do you think he intended to leave such a mess behind him?"

Cooperman shook his head. "I don't think so, no. He did his best to guide that boy toward his goals. Supported him and his grandmother. He'd have wanted to provide for him, I believe."

*Interesting.*

"And what about Mr. Wilson Thomas?"

Cooperman didn't even look at me. He waved his handkerchief in the air as he replied, "Freddie wouldn't have him anywhere near the estate anymore. Said he'd have him arrested if he ever set foot on his property. Oh no, Freddie was done with him."

"But Wilson Thomas used you for legal services too, didn't he? In fact, I believe he entrusted you with something he sent you in the mail."

Finally, Cooperman lifted his head and looked at me. His eyes narrowed behind his round, friendly-looking glasses. "You know Wilson Thomas?"

I made sure I didn't nod or shake my head, I just tilted it, and raised my multipurpose eyebrow.

Cooperman scratched his chin. "You are a guest at the estate? That's what Amelia said, correct?"

I felt I was losing him. "I'm with a group of guests, some of whom have a significant history on the island." I hoped that might be a nebulous enough statement for him to infer any number of things.

He said nothing for a moment, then snapped his eyes shut, and opened them again. His corporate expression was restored. "I'm afraid I cannot discuss a client's business with anyone but the client in question. Now, since we have no business to conduct, I'll let our receptionist know you'll be on your way to sign out as you leave."

I stood; I dared just one more attempt. "What do you think the estate will sell for? A good price? Millions?"

I'd done what every holidaymaker does, and had taken the odd squint in the windows of the real estate agents on the island, so I knew that the twenty-acre estate, with masses of beachfront, as well as the original house, pool, and bungalows must be worth a pretty penny.

Cooperman gave the matter no more than a second or two of thought. "Hopefully somewhere around the ten-million-dollar mark."

"Jamaican dollars?"

Cooperman finally cracked a smile. "No, most definitely American dollars." He reached across the desk and extended his hand. My terribly polite brush-off was complete.

As I exited the office with thoughts of real estate deals swirling in my mind, I had a sudden flashback to the day Bud and I had enjoyed sucking on the contents of a coconut each, while picking out our dream home in a realtor's window. *That* was where I'd seen Niall Jackson; he'd been leaving the real estate office, whistling. He'd jumped into a red Range Rover parked nearby. The name on the window of the office, and emblazoned on the side of the vehicle, had been Jackson Realty. I recalled how very good the photos had been in the Jackson Realty storefront – not just your average front-on shot of a property, but scenic shots from above, showing how the property sat in the landscape, what the views were like from the decks, and so forth. I felt relieved. It's not like me to have to wait for inspiration to recall something – usually I can do it at will, though I decided to be kind to myself because I'd been a bit preoccupied since I'd seen Niall at the restaurant the night before.

As I plodded along the winding corridors I wondered what on earth Freddie had spent ten million dollars on…because if the repayment of his debts wouldn't leave anything in the pot for Amelia and Tarone, he must have borrowed about that much – allowing for taxes, which I suspected the lawyer would have to sort out too, before anyone else got a penny. And Freddie had spent it all, somehow. Or else…maybe he'd borrowed at an extortionate interest rate? Either way, it was a fascinating question to ponder as I made my way to the Suburban to head back to the estate.

## Hands Free on the Highway

The Jamaican sun had transformed the Suburban into a large oven on wheels. I cranked up the air conditioning, shut all the doors, and waited in the shade of a nearby tree until I felt more confident that sitting on the driver's seat wasn't going to give me third-degree burns.

I phoned Bud to bring him up to date with Amelia's situation. He informed me that Tarone had headed back to his bungalow to make some calls. At Bud's suggestion we then discussed the usefulness of me pairing my phone with the hands-free system in the Suburban; Bud walked me through the process, reading me the instructions off the Internet. Fifteen minutes later I was on the road, nice and cool, and able to chat to Bud as I headed along the A1.

"You first," said Bud. "Sounds like you've had an eventful morning. And it's only just gone eleven."

He was right. But, there again, the pace hadn't really let up since Amelia had stumbled into the dining room and told us that Freddie was dead.

"Okay," I began, and gave detailed accounts of my conversations with Amelia on the way to the lawyer's office, what had happened there, and rounded off with what I'd managed to learn when Cooperman and I were alone.

Bud indulged me. "And how do you interpret this information?" he asked. I could hear him smiling.

"Freddie, Cooperman, and Wilson Thomas are somehow linked. I wouldn't be surprised if Wilson Thomas had some sort of connection with the Captain's Lookout estate, too. And

Cooperman certainly has some sort of client-attorney relationship with Thomas. As for Freddie's debts? That's one heck of a lot of money to have borrowed. He clearly hasn't spent that amount dolling up his property, or anything like that. I think Cooperman would have known about any investments Freddie had made, because they'd be a part of the man's overall assets. What on earth can Freddie have done with it all? I have no bright ideas about that. That's me – what about you? What have you been able to achieve this morning? Were you talking to Tarone about something to do with our inquiries, or did he just happen to be doing an odd job or two at the bungalow when I phoned?"

"He was here trimming back a few shrubs when you first called, then he came back again, after rushing over to his bungalow for a while to get in touch with the hospital. Which means that now, for once, I think I can match your discoveries, and raise you. I found out this morning that the late Wilson Thomas was Tarone's grandfather."

I was genuinely surprised. "Really? I suppose I didn't connect the two men because Thomas is such a common surname on Jamaica, almost as common as it is in Wales, in fact," I began, then added, "so Wilson Thomas and Amelia were married? But her legal name is LaBadie. Cooperman used LaBadie, not Thomas, when referring to Amelia."

"No, they never married, but Wilson was the father of Tarone's mother alright. Tarone told me Wilson had worked on the estate since Freddie bought it, back in 1962. Only sixteen when he started, it seems. When Tarone's mother was born about ten years later, Freddie allowed Wilson to bring his baby daughter – named Grace Thomas, by the way – and her mother, Amelia, to live with him here. Amelia was just seventeen at the time."

"Got it. And what happened to Tarone's mother?"

"Sadly, drugs," said Bud. "She was a beautiful girl, Cait. Tarone showed me some old photographs of her. Went to the local school, did well at athletics, worked with her parents for Freddie, mainly as a waitress at his parties and so forth. But, as the years passed, it seems she began to adopt some pretty wild habits. Too much partying, too much everything, by the sounds of it. She drifted. Wouldn't tell anyone who Tarone's father was. She died of a drug overdose when Tarone was about five years old, so his memories of her are hazy."

"Such a shame," I observed. "Has Amelia raised him since then? When did Wilson leave? And why? Any ideas?"

"Amelia told Tarone – and he's had it confirmed by the parents of school friends of his – that Wilson became persona non grata at the estate about six months after Tarone was born. Now, if you add to that the fact Tarone is most definitely of mixed race, and that no one has ever told him who his father was…"

"We have a situation where we are both wondering if Freddie Burkinshaw fathered Tarone by Wilson's daughter Grace, and if maybe that was the reason Wilson found himself thrown off the estate, while Amelia and Tarone were allowed to stay."

"I love the way your mind works, Wife."

"Thank you." I accepted the compliment graciously. "And Cooperman?" I added. "If he did undertake legal work for Wilson Thomas, could that have tangentially allowed him to discover that Freddie was Tarone's father?" I paused and added, "Cooperman spoke strangely about his assumptions regarding Freddie's wishes for Tarone. Did I mention that?"

"You did not."

"Sorry. Cooperman said 'him' not 'them' when it came to whom he thought Freddie would have wanted to support. I took it that Cooperman inferred Freddie would most certainly have wanted to provide specifically for Tarone. Which would make sense if Freddie knew he was the boy's father."

"It's a working theory," said Bud.

I was just about half an hour away from the estate when I realized something. "In what capacity had you encountered Wilson Thomas before last night, Bud? Why was he wrapped up in the 'thing' you're concerned with?"

"I knew him through a connection I cannot explain. We'd met a few times, and I haven't changed so much over the years that he wouldn't have recognized me. We'd been in a situation where he'd been able to trust me with his life. I can't say more than that. I hadn't let him down on that occasion; I wish I could say the same about last night."

I slowed the Suburban to accommodate the heavier local traffic. "Okay, I suppose you can't tell me everything, but can you tell me this? Did you know before today that Wilson Thomas had once lived at the Captain's Lookout estate?"

"I *can* tell you that, Wife, and the answer is no; by the time I met Wilson he certainly wasn't living on the estate. I knew him as someone who was a bit of a fixer on the island."

"Lottie said Freddie was a man who acquired things for people. Might Wilson have been one of the contacts on the island who made it possible for Freddie to do that, do you think?"

"I believe he could have been, and suspect that to have been the case. You see, Wilson could have given Freddie access to people it would have otherwise been difficult for him to meet – and even if Freddie had managed to connect with them, they might not have trusted him. Wilson's family went back hundreds of years on the island, whereas Freddie was a rich, white incomer. They could have made a good team, if they trusted each other."

"Or had enough dirt on each other for trust not to feature in their business relationship," I observed. "But if Wilson was unhappy about Freddie impregnating his daughter, isn't it more likely that he could have held that over Freddie, and thereby remained on the estate, rather than Freddie having the ability to kick him out?"

"That's an interesting question, Cait, and one we should talk through. We need to stitch all these pieces together."

"Bud, are you thinking that the person who killed Wilson might be the same person who killed Freddie? And do we even know if Freddie was murdered, yet? Any news about his autopsy?"

"Ah, well, Wife, I have to admit I might have buried the lead," said Bud.

I turned off the main road and took my time descending the slip road that led to the estate's gated entry, which was just as well because a gleaming red Range Rover came screaming along the track from the direction of *Caro Mio*, throwing up stones and dust in its wake. If I'd been a few yards further along the track it would have hit me. I slammed on the brakes and swore at the driver; I could see quite clearly that it was Niall Jackson. He didn't acknowledge the presence of either me or the vehicle I was driving; he just sped off.

"I'll be there in a few minutes, Bud," I said, as I waited for the dust to settle. "I'll give the Suburban's keys to Tarone, so he can get himself to Kingston to see Amelia whenever he wants. But tell me before I go, did the autopsy reveal if Freddie was murdered, or if he killed himself?"

"Freddie was shot, that's for sure. Right through the heart. But that's not what's really interesting. What's *really* interesting is that he'd also been poisoned."

# A Lightning Luncheon

I was ready for a big hug by the time I got back to the bungalow, and Bud was only too happy to provide one. I was also ready for lunch, and possibly a drink, but I knew they'd have to wait until Bud had told me everything about Freddie's autopsy; I find that eating while discussing the results of a post-mortem exam doesn't work well for me.

It turned out I didn't have to wait long for food; as I was scrolling through the autopsy documents on Bud's phone, Lottie knocked at our bungalow door and announced that she'd prepared a meal for all six of us. We said we'd be along soon, and I carried on reading.

"Thought you'd be finished with that by now," observed Bud wryly as he looked over my shoulder.

"I read it once, but wanted to go back to the bit about the poison. It says here that they found partially digested ackee in his stomach. It was overripe, poisonous."

"Correct."

"But how can that be? Freddie's lived here for decades. Even I know that overripe ackee will make a person ill, and can prove lethal. Why on earth would he have eaten it?" I gave it a moment's thought. "The report says it was thoroughly masticated, so he chose to eat it, rather than it being forced down his throat in chunks. Why would he do that?"

Bud stood and stretched, gazing toward the ocean. "Maybe it was disguised, somehow?"

I handed him his phone. "Don't be ridiculous. We all ate together that night, and in any case, wouldn't it taste awful?"

Bud slid his phone into the pocket of the palm-frond-emblazoned shorts I'd picked out for him especially for this trip, which I thought made him look quite youthful – for his age. "Does overripe ackee taste different than ripe ackee?"

To be fair, he made a good point.

Bud continued, "I know no more details than you've read for yourself. I could ask some supplementary questions about the stomach contents, but isn't the key point that some time after Freddie left us that evening he must have chosen to ingest the ackee, whatever its specific form?"

"Agreed," I conceded. "And where, when, and how he did that might help us work out who had the chance to give it to him."

"It's on the table!" called Lottie across the pool from the dining room.

I sighed. "I suppose we'd better go. She's made an effort. But listen – how much of all this is she not supposed to know?"

"Nothing about the autopsy, nothing about Tarone's parentage, nothing about Freddie's will, or debts," replied Bud with a forced smile.

"So almost nothing at all about anything?"

"Correct."

"That'll be fun, then."

We entered the dining room together. I was genuinely pleased to see Sheila seated at the table; it looked as though her ankle hadn't swollen to elephantine proportions.

"I won't be running a marathon any time soon," she said when I asked her how she was doing, "but for sure it'll be fine by the time we go home. I'll just keep it strapped up, and elevated when I can."

"No gadding about for you tonight, young lady," I quipped.

"None of us are likely to be doing that, are we? Not with people dropping like flies around us. First it was Freddie, then that poor man on the beach, and now Amelia. It's really quite concerning," said Lottie.

She'd prepared a huge salad to accompany a platter-full of grilled prawns on skewers; we handed the food around the table, helping ourselves with spoons and fingers. The prawns smelled wonderful, and my tummy rumbled before I could get the first one into my mouth. It was delicious – perfectly moist, flavorful, and with just the right amount of charring.

As I ripped off the tail with my fingers and chewed, my quiet "mmmm…" became part of a chorus.

We laughed, and all complimented Lottie on her skills in the kitchen.

"Thanks," she said, almost blushing. "Daddy said I'd never need to cook for myself, but I wanted to know how to, so I took a course at Le Cordon Bleu in Paris. It made such a difference."

I imagined how wonderful it would be to be able to take the time to learn about food preparation from some real professionals. A couple of days making bread, a week or so working through recipes of various types. And getting to eat it all. Bliss.

"Was it fun?" asked Sheila.

"Hard work, really," said Lottie, "but worth it."

"Did you make any preserves?" Sheila seemed genuinely interested.

"Not many," admitted Lottie, "though we tackled the basic techniques. They're very much focused on using seasonal foods. They have a wonderful fruit and vegetable garden on their roof. It's amazing. Bees, too. I enjoyed it very much."

"It sounds like you crammed in a lot," I said, envisioning a hectic weekend. "How long were you there?"

"Nine months."

"Nine months?" I was shocked. "And you had to live in Paris that whole time?"

Lottie smiled. "I loved it. I prefer it to almost anywhere else in the world. Mummy loved it too. Which is why she kept her apartment there. I lived there for a year. It was fun."

John said, "Lottie's an excellent cook. To dine at her home is quite something; she's about the only hostess who actually prepares the food herself. No caterers for Lottie Fortescue, right?"

"Right," replied Lottie, beaming.

I crunched my salad and savored my prawns with two key thoughts in mind – Lottie Fortescue had the culinary training to disguise a dish of deadly ackee, *and* she obviously knew about the dangers of the fruit, her father having been convinced that both she and her mother had been poisoned with it.

The conversation revolved around Amelia's collapse, and the great pity that she'd not been able to pass any information to me about the content of Freddie's will; I'd spun a tale of having to wait in reception while she had her meeting – an account Amelia wasn't available to contradict. I was also pressed about my near-miss at the entrance to the estate, and how it had shaken me up.

"Niall Jackson is as mad as his father," observed Lottie. John patted her hand, which led me to believe he'd forgiven her for having been economical with the truth when it came to her connection with the island. "I dare say he'd been over at Nina Mazzo's place trying to decide a strategy to get their hands on Freddie's strip of land."

I suspected Lottie was right, and said as much.

"Any news on when we can have a poke about up in Freddie's tower room?" asked Lottie.

I was annoyed; having realized that I could get in there because of the necessarily unlocked door, I'd planned to have a private hunt about in the place that afternoon.

"None yet," answered Bud swiftly. "I dare say the police won't bother to tell us about it, on the basis we'd have no real reason to want to invade Freddie's private space."

"But I thought we were investigating his death," bleated Lottie. "And I really would like to see if the crystal skull is up there. It isn't anywhere in this place, and I can imagine he liked to keep it close by. It was very precious to him."

We were interrupted by a knock at the open door. It was Tarone. He looked flustered.

"Come in, Tarone," said Bud, rising. "Is there anything we can do for you? What news of your grandmother?"

Tarone took a few steps into the dining room. He looked younger than his eighteen years. "I just got a call. She not good. They doing tests. Think she have a bleed on her brain. I got to go to the hospital…but…I don't have many friends on this side of the island anymore, they mainly in Kingston, and I don't think I can drive myself. I too upset. Can someone…would anybody…?" His angst and his unasked question hung above the salad bowl.

"I know John was hoping to get to Kingston while he's in Jamaica, and he's a fine driver. You could take Lottie with you, couldn't you, John?" said Bud, staring hard at his colleague.

John smiled. It was a smile that held a bucketful of understanding. "But of course, Tarone. Lottie and I would be only too happy to drive you to Kingston. Do you need to take a bag or something for Amelia? And what about yourself – do you plan to stay there overnight?"

Tarone looked horrified. "I ain't thought of things for Granny. Be good to stay there, yeah man, but where? I got no money, so how can I?"

Lottie stood, and placed her napkin on the table. "I tell you what, why don't I come with you to your bungalow so we can gather together a few bits and pieces for Amelia, and I'll make some calls while we're on the road. I'm sure I can find you a decent place to stay, and it'll be my treat, no questions asked. It's the least we can do, under the circumstances."

Tarone looked shocked. "You do this for me?"

Lottie nodded and beamed. "I was once a girl with nothing much to her name because Daddy would never let me have anything I wanted, ever, after Mummy died. He was so terribly mean to me. I think that might have been because Mummy left everything to me, not him, but that wasn't my fault, was it? Anyway, I had to wait until I got all of Mummy's money for myself before I could do what I wanted, but there was a point when someone was kind to me when I needed it. I like to pay things forward. This is my chance. Now, come along, let's make a move. The sooner we leave, the sooner you can be at your grandmother's side."

Tarone nodded and rushed out. Lottie followed him and said to John in passing, "Could you grab my purple tote, the big one? It's got supplies in it I might need. And bring a couple of things for yourself in case we need to overnight in Kingston. Sorry to rush, folks, but we can do something good for someone who needs it. See you when we see you." And she was gone.

Jack nodded slowly. "Quite a woman."

"She is indeed," replied John. Turning to Bud as he rose he whispered, "I can see you need me to keep her out of your hair. Keep me up to date? And nothing risky without me, understood?"

Bud nodded, looking surprisingly grim. "Thanks, John. Glad you understand. Won't do anything you wouldn't do."

John rolled his eyes, and left.

Lunch had concluded, it seemed, and with Sheila's ankle the way it was, it was a merry band of three that cleared everything away, as rapidly as possible, because we all knew that an uninterrupted afternoon of investigating lay ahead of us. We had the entire estate to ourselves, and we could say whatever we liked, because Lottie wasn't in earshot. Bliss.

# Smoking Hot Sitrep

With the place to ourselves, the four of us felt a lot less tense than we'd been for some time, and we agreed we'd take the chance to sort out exactly what we knew before deciding what needed to be done next. It was a good feeling – we didn't have to whisper, and we didn't have to watch the clock. Even if John turned the vehicle around almost as soon as they arrived in Kingston, we knew we had at least four Lottie-free hours ahead of us, so we were happy to spend twenty minutes or so comparing notes.

Sheila allowed Jack to help her hobble to the lounge chairs that had "attacked" her the night before, and we all put our feet up, enjoying the sea breeze while hiding in the shade of the portico. I lit a cigarette, and we all sipped from chilled bottles of beer – in Sheila's case it was ginger beer, because she was still stuffing painkillers down her throat.

My first question was to Shelia. "Is the ankle really not too bad, or were you making that up? You're limping quite heavily."

"Why would I make that up?" was her surprised reply.

I shook my head. "Honestly, I think I'm losing it – I can't be sure what's real and what's fiction any longer. It's all I can do to keep up with who knows what. I mean I do *know*, it's just so tiring to have to keep it all straight. I don't think I'm cut out for all this cloak and dagger stuff. It's annoying, especially given that I, for one, am not 'allowed' to know everything our husbands do."

Bud and Jack shared a smile. "See?" said Bud. "Every opportunity she sees, she takes it."

"Don't ever give up," said Sheila. "Keep nagging at him, Cait. Half the stuff they don't tell us? When Jack finally folds like a cheap tent and confesses all...well, we both realize he could have told me upfront and it wouldn't have made the slightest difference. I mean, who are we going to tell?"

"Exactly my point. Thank you, Sheila," I replied.

Jack and Bud shook their heads and rolled their eyes in unison.

"Sitrep, please Bud," said Jack.

"I like hearing situation reports," said Sheila happily.

We all gave Bud our full attention. "Working theory is that the deaths of Freddie Burkinshaw and Wilson Thomas are linked. This based upon the fact both knew of the items we're searching for, and knew where they were secreted at some point, even if the items have now been moved. Freddie claimed to have no knowledge of where they are now. We believed him. Wilson's cryptic message at his moment of death mentioned the name of Freddie's lawyer – and possibly Wilson's lawyer too. Another potential link. Also, both shot."

"Two dead men, and a lawyer," I said. "First question: do we think Cooperman's life is in danger because he knows something the dead men also knew? Or, do we think he's 'safe' because he's somehow involved in their deaths? My honest opinion – he didn't look like a killer. Though his air of geniality did dissolve in an instant, so he could be better at hiding his true self than I am at detecting it."

"No Cait, not that again," said Bud. "You were studying him, right? You were on full alert. He wouldn't have been able to prevent you from reading him."

When I'd recounted my morning to Bud, I hadn't mentioned how genuine I'd believed Cooperman's initial bonhomie to be;

I thought I'd keep that to myself, having been disabused of the illusion prior to my abrupt departure from his office.

"If his wasn't the hand that acted, he could have hired a person, or persons, unknown to act on his behalf," said Jack. "He's a lawyer; might know some folks who'd happily do his dirty work for him, if it were needed."

"If you're not sure about exactly how he's involved, shouldn't you be warning him – just in case he really is in danger?" Sheila sounded worried.

Jack sucked the tip of his thumb. "It's a judgement call, alright, but we can't risk tipping him off, in case if he's on the wrong side of this. If he's an innocent player, he'll likely put two and two together for himself."

I asked, "Has Wilson Thomas's name been made public yet?"

Bud nodded. "That's why Tarone and I ended up talking about his grandfather – his name was included in a report on the local radio station this morning, not long after you told Tarone about his grandmother's fall. The boy was in a poor way when I saw him again, and we got talking because of it."

"In that case, Cooperman might not have known about Wilson's death when I was talking to him," I said. "He certainly didn't appear to be a man in fear for his life, but maybe that's changed by now. Do you think we could come up with some way of getting John to see Cooperman when he's in Kingston? If John could get just a few minutes with the man, he might be able to give us some impression of Cooperman's state of mind now that the news about Wilson's death is out."

"I could give John a ring and ask him to wangle it, somehow," offered Bud. We all agreed that would be useful, so Bud made the call, with Jack also stepping away to listen in.

I took the chance to ask Sheila if there was anything I could do to help her.

"No thanks, I'm fine. Just feeling a bit useless, that's all," she replied with a tired smile. "My own stupidity means my body's out of commission, and these painkillers are making me foggy." She leaned toward me as best she could, given her position. "I'm still trying to get over Jack being so close to someone being murdered last night, if I'm honest. I thought all that sort of thing was behind us. I know you and Bud have been married for a little time now, but it's a real grind watching them go off to work every day, not knowing if they'll walk back through the door in one piece."

I knew she was right; the families of people who work in law enforcement really do bear a huge burden of worry. "But you were a Mountie yourself, for a while, Sheila. You know how good the training is, how they're prepared and able to take care of themselves." I didn't mention that I was still grappling with the concept of Sheila having been a cop.

Sheila smiled. "True, but those were different times, Cait. Not that I was in uniform back in the Gold Rush era, or anything, but these days? It feels like a whole new world. There've always been bad people out there, evil ones, too, but nowadays they seem to be more ready to act than to hide."

Sheila had touched a chord for me. "Do you really believe evil exists, Sheila?"

She thought for a moment. "As a religious concept – you know, the devil, and all that sort of thing – no. But people who do evil things certainly exist. I've met some of them, as have you, and our husbands. What's the point of arguing the semantics when the reality is that some people do the most dreadful things?"

I pondered that topic, but didn't say any more, because Bud and Jack rejoined us.

"John will do what he can," said Bud. "What's next for us?"

"The tower," I said. "I want to see inside the room where Freddie was found."

"But we can't get in there," said Sheila.

"If the cops managed to somehow open the door, they're unlikely to have re-locked it, so we should be able to get in. And they've made it clear they don't think of it as a crime scene," I replied.

"Hang on a minute, Cait," said Bud. "That autopsy report might mean they change their minds. I got it fast – we're probably a little ahead of them, because they possibly don't think of this as a case that needs urgent attention yet, but they could come back here at any time and shut the tower down. The poison found in Freddie's system might not have killed him, but it was there, which could cast doubt on their initial interpretation of the scene. And it's highly unusual for a suicide to be found shot in the heart. Of course, they'd have seen the wounds when they initially examined Freddie's body at the scene, but, maybe – when taken with the discovery of the ackee – they might now feel the need to reassess their initial decision."

"All the more reason to not waste any more time," I said, "because you're right, Bud; I hadn't thought of that. Come on, let's save the rest of our discussion for another time – we might be down to the wire in terms of getting into Freddie's lookout room."

I was out of my seat in a second.

"I know you've got a photographic memory, Cait," said Sheila, "but would you do me a favor and film it all for me? I hate the idea of missing out, but I just don't think my ankle's up to it. I don't want to slow you all down. If the cops show up here, I'll stall them – though it's unlikely they'd even bother to come to this part of the property, it'll be the tower they're interested in. Go on now, go!"

Bud and I crunched along the winding pathway, kicking up the seashells. We'd already reached the ground-floor entrance to the building before it dawned on us both that, while the tower room might be accessible, the police had probably locked the main, outer, door. They had.

"The key cupboard in the main house?" I said to Bud, hoping he'd volunteer to return. We were both a bit puffed, and sweaty.

"Hey, need these?" asked Jack as he approached, waggling a bunch of keys. "Sheila suggested I checked the key cupboard before I left, in case the cops had locked the main building."

Bud and I chuckled. "Thank goodness she's got a practical mind," I said. "And she was wrong, those pills aren't making her foggy at all."

"She's a woman with a great deal of common sense," agreed Jack. "Don't know how I'd have managed if she hadn't made it through. We were so lucky."

As Bud tried various keys in the lock, I asked Jack, "What do you mean she 'made it through'? Made it through what?"

In spite of his tan and sweaty brow, I could tell Jack was blushing. "Losing the baby. You know, it came up in conversation?" I nodded. "Sure, we lost the baby, but Sheila nearly didn't make it herself. Worst time of my life; I spent days at her bedside in the hospital. She didn't seem to want to fight. Her sister dead, the baby gone. It was all too much for her. Of course, if her sister hadn't died, she wouldn't have had to come here to Jamaica to sort out repatriating the body, so she wouldn't have been on that flight back home when they experienced some terrible turbulence over Cuba – she never forgave herself for not having kept her seatbelt on…she took a very bad hit and the baby was traumatized. Hence her – us – losing him. We'd have had totally different lives, and at least one son, if Sheila's sister hadn't died."

"There you go," said Bud, as he flung the door wide.

Before I stepped inside I had to check something with Jack. "You're saying that Sheila's pregnancy was compromised because she came to Jamaica, and she came here because her sister was killed in a scooter accident?" Jack nodded. He walked in ahead of me.

I paused on the threshold, wondering if Sheila had any idea who'd been responsible for her sister's death, and if that might have any bearing on the situation we were facing – then I dismissed the idea as being too fanciful, and focussed on getting as much as I could out of what might be my only chance to inspect an extremely puzzling, and no doubt fascinating, crime scene.

## Lookout Room Luxe

"Let's start at the top, in the room we never saw properly, and work our way down," I suggested as I entered the dim, and thankfully cool, interior. It turned out I was talking to thin air; I could hear Bud and Jack slapping their way up the stone staircase ahead of me.

"Lock the door behind you, Cait," shouted Bud. "I left the key in it. If anyone shows up, that'll slow them down. By the way, take a look at the outer lock covering – see if you agree with me that someone might have made a clumsy attempt to open it with something other than the correct key."

"Already done," I replied, trying to sound as though I'd thought of that. I checked the plate surrounding the keyhole. Bud was right; scratch marks suggested it had either been picked open, or someone had made a bad job of trying lots of keys of the wrong sort to open it. I wondered who might have done that, and why. I locked the heavy door and also left the key in place, turned halfway round – thereby preventing anyone with another key from entering. *You can learn a lot from reading children's mysteries.*

I climbed the steps, silently counting them as I did so – for no particular reason other than that my constant internal monologue demanded it; the voice in my head rarely shuts up, and it speaks in fully formed sentences. The only time it stops is when I'm speed reading; it's so keen to be heard there's no chance I'll ever reach the Zen state of having a "quiet mind". It's why I snap at Bud sometimes; he doesn't understand he's interrupted a full-blown conversation going on in my head, poor thing. We've agreed I'll work on that.

"Did you hear me?" called Bud.

I stopped in Freddie's bedroom. "Pardon?"

"I said we're waiting for you, Cait," shouted Bud slowly.

I rounded the final sweep of the staircase. "Here I am," I said as brightly as being slightly out of breath would allow. "Oh dear, that's a mess!" I was taken aback by the sorry state of the once-grand door to the tower room. "When the police said they'd brought someone in to open the door I'd envisaged something less destructive than this."

A massive portion of the door had been sawn away, leaving a gaping square hole where the lock had once been.

"I thought they'd have unscrewed it, for sure," said Jack. "This is a bit much. I guess they'll have to replace the entire door, which is a shame. It looks real old."

"It probably dates to the 1680s, like the tower," I said, feeling sad. "Such a shame. Judging by the size of the planks they used for the door it was a large tree. Oak. Maybe a hundred and fifty years old, or so. This wood was growing, and was a living thing, possibly back in the early 1500s, through the reign of Henry VIII and most certainly when Elizabeth I was on the throne – the only queen with Welsh blood in her."

Jack said, "But there's at least a *Prince* of Wales, right? Isn't he Welsh, like you?"

"Cait, rabbit hole," warned Bud, "we need to get on."

I knew Bud was right, so I answered Jack as quickly as I could. "No, the Prince of Wales isn't Welsh, though I understand he does a lot in Wales, and for Wales and the Welsh. Henry VII was Welsh; came from a Welsh family, going back generations. Elizabeth was his granddaughter. These cells of wood I'm touching were created out of the air, the light, and the nutrients in the soil possibly when Henry VII ruled. I love touching old wood; it brings history to life. I think it's amazing. But Bud's right, we must get on. So, let's have a look at this crime scene, then."

My delivery had been rapid and staccato. Poor Jack looked as though I'd been juggling baby otters in front of him; bemused and somewhat confused, if entranced.

"Before we begin," said Bud, rolling his eyes at me as he held us both in place, "let's set some ground rules. No gloves needed because we have every right to be here. But bear in mind the fact we already believe this to be a crime scene, and the cops will likely want to treat it as such very soon – so, no disturbing it, just noting, photographing, and videoing. If anyone sees something they think is important, shout and hold. We'll each take a look, and discuss if necessary. Touch as little as possible, and watch your step, be mindful of potential evidence on the floor – which is where Freddie was found. Any questions?" We both shook our heads.

The damaged door creaked open; Bud pushed it with his elbow until it lay as flat as it could against the curved wall behind it. The doorway was wide enough to allow the three of us to stand next to each other and take in the scene before we entered.

"I'll film it all, Cait, you don't have to do it," offered Jack. "I know Sheila will be keen to see what we see, and it'll be easier to show her if it's on my phone." Bud and I both thanked him, and Jack started to record.

"For our eyes only, okay?" Bud warned Jack. Jack nodded.

Bud was his old "command and control" self alright, and I had to admit it was great to see him back in action the way he'd been when he'd hired me as a sometime-consultant on his homicide investigation team, back in Vancouver. He was good then, and he was good now. I felt comfortable working with him this way.

"I can smell…vomit," I said, covering my nose to try to stop myself gagging.

"Ackee poisoning is also known as Jamaican vomiting sickness," said Bud. "Freddie had eaten the overripe fruit, so it's not a surprise he'd have thrown up. I'll locate it – it might help us establish a timeline of his movements before he died. Indeed, why don't we divide the responsibilities? Cait, you do your overall thing up here – see what's what, tell us what light it can throw upon Freddie as a person. Jack, you get comprehensive video of the ground floor, the sitting room level, and the bedroom level. I'll focus on this floor alongside Cait, then the walkway outside – close quarters examination, video recordings."

We agreed, and I was grateful I wasn't the one expected to hunt down a pile of sick then work out what it meant. I tried to focus on my surroundings but decided to keep a hand over my nose in any case.

Bud added, "Wide angles of everything, Jack, please, then close-ups. When you're done with the other floors, could you come back here? Thanks."

I'd never seen him and Jack work together this way before, and I was interested in the dynamic; Jack had entered law enforcement earlier than Bud and had become his sort of unofficial mentor in his early years. Then, Bud had been promoted above Jack and had gone on to assume a high-level role in a special task force designed to prevent international drug and gang crime. Jack had only reached the rank of sergeant by the time he'd retired. It was clear to me that Bud and Jack had settled into their old rank roles; I wondered if, maybe, they were their current "secret" rank roles too, because all I knew was that they weren't saying anything to me on that topic.

I tuned them out as best I could, and "did my thing", as Bud likes to call it. For me that means mentally logging not just objects, but their position and relationship to one another, while analysing what they tell me about the victim in question. The first thing I noticed was that what I'd spotted as a brass tube on Freddie's desk was, as I had surmised, a telescope; it was something he clearly used, because it wasn't displayed in a way you'd present something for admiration, it was to hand – smudged with fingerprints and use. I wondered what he watched through it.

The other thing I noticed immediately was the crystal skull that Lottie had been banging on about. It was the "glass paperweight" I'd seen glinting in the sunlight on Freddie's desk when I'd peered through the lock, across his corpse.

I stopped in my tracks. "Something's off here, Bud," I said.

He also froze. "What's up?"

I walked to the door we'd just entered and knelt on the floor outside it. I bobbed my head about the way I had done when I'd been peering through the keyhole at Freddie's body.

"What is it?" Bud sounded puzzled.

I stood and returned to the desk. "A few things. First, there was a bundle of papers on the desk. On the corner, with the crystal skull sitting on top of them like a paperweight. The papers have gone, and the skull is now in a different position. Also missing is a long scroll of paper, tied with a blue string."

Bud bit his lip. "Anyone could have come in here. The door to this room's been wide open since the cops removed the lock. We only know about one key to the outer door downstairs because we're just visitors, but there could be others – it's a pretty standard, if old, type of lock. And there were those clearly visible marks of attempts to open the door, too."

I sighed. "You're right. We can't possibly guess who else might have got in here, so let's just carry on as we planned, okay?"

We did.

I took my time studying the crystal skull; Lottie was right, it was stunning. I walked around the corner of the desk upon which it sat. True, it had been moved, but even when it had been used as a paperweight it would have been within easy reach of anyone sitting in the desk's chair, and it was something Freddie had stroked – I could see smears all over it. It was certainly an object that invited you to touch it. It looked incredibly smooth, even where the eye sockets and teeth had been carved. I wondered at the number of hands that had succumbed to its siren call to fondle it throughout its existence. I pondered Lottie's belief that this was an object that had existed in the 1600s, and knew it was problematic; every crystal skull that's been tested has been proven to have been made at some time during the 1800s, when there was a craze for such "ancient" objects. Similarly, most of the mythologies about the powers of such items cannot be traced back to the times when these skulls were supposed to have originated in Mesoamerica. So this might be a relatively modern creation, like all the rest, or it might be – well, the first ever to be discovered that had a traceable history, and which might show a lack of modern tooling if it were studied. That wasn't something I was going to be able to deduce; it would take expertise and a lot of magnification to achieve that, so all I could do was admire its form, and consider its role in our current situation.

Its original position, acting as a paperweight on Freddie's desk, suggested he had a close affinity for the object, that much was clear, and it being in his possession was certainly public knowledge, so that was what I had to consider. If it was believed by some to be ancient, powerful, and valuable, the truth about it hardly mattered, because even erroneous beliefs can lead to actions that have real and deadly consequences. But if it was still on Freddie's desk, then it seemed unlikely that the desire to possess it had motivated murder. *Interesting.*

Other than the skull itself, there were so many more objects for me to acknowledge and consider, that I dragged myself away from it, and checked the bookcases that curved around the inner wall of Freddie's private sanctum.

The first thing I spotted was a complete collection of all Ian Fleming's novels. I dared to pull the copy of *Casino Royale* off the shelf and opened it. It was a first edition, signed, "To my pal, Freddie. Mine's a large one! Ian". It was in mint condition, with a totally unblemished dust jacket. I reckoned it was worth about fifty thousand dollars. All the others looked to be in the same condition. What a collection.

I was saddened to see that the butterfly in a glass case that I'd spotted when peering through the keyhole was none other than a Queen Alexandra's Birdwing – one of the rarest butterflies in the world. It was magnificent – about ten inches across, its wings were banded with iridescent blue-green and vivid yellow, and it had splashes of scarlet on its body. I'd not long ago read an article about the dwindling population in their only known habitat of Papua New Guinea, and hoped Freddie's specimen was at least decades old, though I feared it wasn't. What a dreadful thing to have on a bookshelf!

He had an impressive collection of volumes about Mesoamerica during both pre- and post-Columbian periods, and a pile of contemporary works from the seventeenth and eighteenth centuries relating to the Caribbean, and Central American locales, all laid on their backs. There was also a boggling array of books about Caribbean beliefs, religions, and mythologies littered on the shelves. These latter books looked pretty ancient, and several were housed in hard, outer cases, for protection. Nonetheless, there they were, the sun beating on them through the open jalousies. *That's odd.*

I could tell from the lack of bleaching that this wasn't normal for the books – they'd have looked quite different if Freddie had kept the shutters open all the time. I stuck up my hand and called out. "Need to discuss a point, please."

Bud gave me his attention. "Yes, what is it?"

"Those shutters were open when we found Freddie, and it looks as though the police didn't close them after they took his body away. It's clear the rain of yesterday and last night has blown in. Agreed?"

Bud looked at the floor, which was still a little damp, and agreed.

"The condition of these books suggests Freddie kept the shutters closed, as a rule. If he'd opened them at, or just after, sunset, the books would have been protected from the glare of the sun. I know it rained on the night Freddie died, because everything was wet when I got up on the morning we discovered his body. I believe Freddie would have closed the shutters if he was here, and alive, when the rain started. Do you know when that was?"

Bud shook his head. "We could find out from some local weather station," he suggested.

I nodded. "That would help to shrink the window of opportunity."

Bud added, "I agree with your theory, though we can't know if it's true, of course. It's something we could have asked Amelia – was Freddie in the habit of keeping the shutters closed at certain times? – but we can't. So, let's find out about the rain when we get out of here, and see if it tells us anything. That all?"

"Yes, thanks. For now."

I returned to my job, surveying the furnishings, and the items displayed on them, around the perimeter of the room. It took a while. It was fascinating.

Eventually, I sat at Freddie's desk, trying to not shift his chair too much. The largest window in the room was directly behind me, but the rest of the tower had smaller windows that allowed for wonderful cross-breezes; the exact position of the chair at the desk seemed to benefit most from the throughflow. *Clever design, and clever positioning of the desk.*

Other than the telescope and the crystal skull, Freddie had a pot of biros and pencils on his desk, and an antique leather blotter, which actually contained blotting paper. By bobbing my head about I could see there were indentations in the blotting paper, though there were no traces of ink. The indentations seemed to be of squiggly lines, rather than words. *Interesting.*

As Jack joined us again on the top floor, I stood up so I could pull open the central drawer in the desk without it hitting my tummy. Inside was a collection of the sort of detritus that seems to grow in such a drawer: rubber bands, a huge number of pencils, and sharpeners, bits of balled-up string, and so forth. However, what caught my attention was a red-lacquered wooden box, fashioned to look like a chest, with a small gold medallion set into the lid. I could feel the excitement in my tummy, but waited, and called out, "Need to open an item I've found in this drawer. I'll use this handkerchief to avoid messing up any prints that might be relevant. Anyone want to watch?"

Bud and Jack stood to my right side, and I placed the box carefully on the desk. I opened it, and my heart went wild. I've always adored the feel of a good fountain pen in my hand – it's what I wrote with at school. These days I resort to a plain old biro for all the grading I have to do, but when I write something I really care about I pull out my beautiful, silky, matt black

Parker pen and allow myself the indulgence of thoughtful, carefully-formed cursive. I admit I have been known to dribble at the thought of some fine writing instruments in my time.

Both Bud and Jack couldn't help but both say, "Wow," when I revealed the contents of the box – a fountain pen with its gleaming black cap and body encapsulated in carved pirate heads, skulls, and seafaring items like ropes, swords, and sirens all intricately created in solid gold, with silver embellishments. It was exquisite.

"That's amazing," said Bud.

"Could you even write with it?" asked Jack.

"A person could," I said, "but I'm not sure I'd dare to. I happen to know that Montegrappa made a limited edition of 399 of these pens in silver, but only ever made nine of this particular type, the gold version. It's worth something in the region of sixty to seventy thousand dollars. American, not Canadian."

"For a pen?" said Bud, stunned.

"How much does the ink cost?" asked Jack with a chuckle.

"If Freddie had managed to run through millions of dollars, buying stuff like that might account for it," said Bud. "That's just ridiculous. All that money…for that? I mean it's a work of art, alright, but it's just sitting there, in a box, in a drawer, with only him ever seeing it. What sort of a man would do that, Cait?"

"Interesting question, and this pen – when taken with the other items I've seen here – suggest Freddie had more than a slight tendency to be what Tarone referred to as being 'gravalicious'. It usually means just plain greedy, but I mean it in terms of Freddie being selfishly acquisitive; avaricious. Freddie liked to own things, yes, but he liked to have them all to himself. Which is quite different, psychologically speaking."

"How do you mean?" asked Jack.

"When we got back from our visit to *Caro Mio*, I told you we'd been treated to a display of wealth; Luca Mazzo had designed the house to quite literally show off his valued, and valuable, possessions. 'I've got it, and I'm going to flaunt it.' That's quite normal. Freddie didn't do that. See that bottle of Remy Martin brandy over there on the armoire?" Bud and Jack nodded.

Bud said, "It's the same as the one he's been serving us in the evenings, right?"

"Well, it's similar," I replied. "The cognac we've all been enjoying is the classic Remy Martin Louis XIII. That costs around three or four thousand dollars a bottle. This one is the Black Pearl version."

"So, more expensive?" asked Jack. A glint in his eye.

"Try something around the one-fifty to two-hundred-thousand-dollar mark. If you can get it," I replied.

The men's mouths fell open.

"Unbelievable," said Bud. "That's such a huge amount of money to spend on something you just drink. It cannot possibly taste that much better than the cognac we've been drinking – which I have to admit is pretty good. But all that money?"

"The Cohiba Esplendidos cigars you've been enjoying after dinner?" Jack and Bud nodded. "About thirty-five dollars each. The ones in Freddie's humidor over there? They're rare. The Arturo Fuente Don AnniverXario comes in at about seven thousand five hundred dollars a box."

"Heck of a way to rip through a bunch of money," said Jack. "Literally setting fire to it."

I continued, "Then there's the crystal skull, a one-off; the fountain pen, a limited edition; that butterfly, extremely rare; the set of first edition Bond novels, valuable. But none of them are on public display; all of them are tucked away here, for his own private pleasure. Even this tower – in its entirety – is something he owned and held close to himself, allowing no one else to enjoy it. Yes, he wanted the public to be allowed to access it after his death, but not while he lived. It's about covetousness, beyond ownership. There are people who want to own something specifically because they cannot. And those who don't care to share, even when they do possess something. You must both know types, and individuals like that, right?"

Bud and Jack nodded. "Do you think that aspect of his personality might have led him to lie to us when he told us he didn't know where the papers we're looking for were located?" asked Bud.

I sighed. "It's hard to be certain, but it could lead him to do that, yes. If he knew you wanted something he had, he might feel the need to cling to it for the pure joy of possession, whatever the implications."

"What's that?" said Jack, hushing us.

"Someone's calling, from down below," said Bud. He moved to the rail of the walkway, and shouted back. "Sure. Give us a minute." He came back into the room. "It's the cops, seeking access. Are we all finished here?"

Jack and I nodded. "Okay then, act all innocent when we leave. We were just curious – wanted to get a look at the place, okay?" We nodded again. "Come on then, let's go." As he reached the door he turned, a glint in his eye. "Fancy bringing that cognac, Jack?"

Jack laughed. "It might be evidence, Bud, so no. But I wouldn't mind having a drop more of the stuff he was happy to share with us back at the big house."

"After dinner, maybe," I said, following the men to the top of the stairs. "Sheila might be grateful if we order in again tonight – she could keep her foot up."

"Let's explain our way out of any difficulties with local law enforcement, first," said Bud, "then we can turn our attention to other things."

We started down the stairs. As we entered the bedroom level I said, "Can you stall them? Just for five minutes or so? I know you've filmed everything, Jack, but I'd just like to have a quick look around every level for myself. Can you manage that?"

"I think we'll be able to cope," replied Bud. "But don't hang about. See you outside, five minutes."

I was as good as my word, and was happy to see that Bud and Jack had convinced Sergeant Swabey, who had returned with Constable Lewis and another officer – to whom I wasn't introduced – that we'd been checking on the well-being of the tower at the request of Amelia, who was not able to do it herself. Bud mentioned that he'd closed the jalousie shutters on the topmost floor to protect the contents of the room from the weather, and we left having displayed what we judged to be just the right amount of curiosity and concern that the police were now going to treat the tower as a potential crime scene.

Swabey's parting shout was: "We'll need to ask some more questions before too long, now that the situation has changed."

Bud called back, "We're not going anywhere this evening. Please come over to the main house whenever you like."

He can be such a sweetie when he needs to be.

## Entertaining an Elephant

Sheila was happy to order food from the same place as a couple of nights earlier. We were all pleased, and I knew it was for the best. Luckily, Bud and I had enjoyed three weeks of swanning around Jamaica hitting all the good food spots, so I didn't mind not having gourmet cuisine every night.

"John phoned," said Sheila after we'd agreed our dinner plans. "He and Lottie should be back here by about seven thirty, traffic allowing. I've ordered food for about that time, so we should be good. And it means we've got time for you guys to bring me up to date, and for us to consider what we know, in detail, before we're under constraint again – not able to talk freely in front of Lottie."

I'd done some intense work at the tower, and felt I needed just a little time to decompress.

"I tell you what," I said, "why don't you look at the video Jack took while I go and have a very, very quick dip in the pool. I'm hot and sweaty, and just floating for a few minutes would do me the world of good." I hoped I wasn't making Sheila jealous of my comparative mobility. "I'm sure you could float about a bit if you wanted to, even with that ankle," I added.

"Don't worry about me – I'm just fine. Go on, have a dip. Think about what you saw while I see it for myself. I dare say Jack and Bud have stuff they need to do, too. Right?"

The men nodded. "Some calls," mumbled Bud. "Want to see if I can get the police report on Freddie so I can understand what they'll be considering at the scene – read it in conjunction with the autopsy. And there are a few things Jack can be getting on with, too. Okay if we leave you girls to it?"

"Divide and conquer," said Sheila, and we all did as we'd said we would.

It turned out that getting into the pool didn't soothe me as much as I'd hoped it would; I don't hate the water, it's just that I can't swim. But I can float on my back, just about, when I know I can put my feet on the bottom of the pool, so I usually find that bobbing about in the shallow end is good for my soul. But, on this occasion, it just made me feel insecure; I kept worrying that I'd float out of my depth, and that Bud wouldn't be there to steer me back to safety.

As I tried to concentrate on relaxing my body, I had to acknowledge that I was feeling a bit out of my depth in terms of what we were facing, too; I hate not knowing everything, I hate not being in control, I hate not being able to fix things, and I hate not being the best and most useful team member. After about ten minutes I gave up, went back to the bungalow and dressed in comfy clothes for dinner.

When I returned to the main house Sheila was sitting on a lounge chair under the portico, where I joined her. "How is it?" I asked, meaning her ankle.

"I think Jack's secretly glad I've had to stop taking an active part in all of this. Sometimes I think he just wants to wrap me in cotton wool."

I hadn't expected Sheila's reply, but decided I'd follow her lead. "Jack mentioned to me earlier that you had a close call when you lost your baby. I want you to know you can talk to me about it, if you ever want to. I've never lost a child, but I've had to work hard to recuperate from what happened to me in Budapest, so maybe I can sympathize with at least part of what you've experienced. Knowing you've cheated death is something that gives a person an entirely different perspective on life."

Sheila's eyes narrowed. She chewed her lip. "It was a close call, you're right. At the time, and for some time afterwards, I wasn't sure that surviving was the best thing for me. I saw no point in being alive if my child was dead. Which I now accept was a result of grief, and hormonal imbalance. I eventually came to understand that Jack and I could enjoy life as a childless couple, and we have. We've had wonderful decades together, and I'm grateful for them. But it was a terrible time. The loss of both my sister and my child overwhelmed me. It frightened me, but maybe strengthened me too; at least, that's how I try to think of it now. I understood why Bud retired after Jan's death; I couldn't cut it when I went back to work. I wasn't focussed, couldn't be relied upon by my colleagues. Bud and I talked about that aspect of his job a great deal during those first few months after he was made a widower, and I hope I helped him work through his feelings."

I knew Bud and Sheila had become closer during that dark period in his life. I reached out and grasped her hand. "Thanks for all you did for him. Friendship is a wonderful thing."

"It sure is. Unfortunately, I'd moved away from all my friends by the time my sister was killed, and then I lost the baby. Jack was as supportive as he knew how to be, but he had to work, and I couldn't. I didn't have anyone I could confide in. No one to share my burden. I couldn't talk to my parents about it – they were destroyed by Wendy's death, and didn't need to be trying to console me, too. I had to muddle through it alone." Sheila began to cry.

I grabbed a hanky from a box in the dining room, and gave it to her.

"Sorry," she said. "I think it's being back here. I can't get her out of my mind. If only she hadn't rented that scooter that day,

I'd still have a sister, and she'd be an aunt to our child, or children."

"Did you ever find out what happened, exactly?" I had to ask.

Sheila wiped her eyes. "The local police did what they could, but it was a hit and run, on a deserted road. There were some rumors, but nothing concrete. They suspected a drunk driver, who fled the scene because of the state they were in. The worst of it was, she lay there for hours before she was found, and even then she was still clinging to life. Can you imagine how much strength that must have taken? How much she must have wanted to live? But she died on the way to the hospital."

"I'm so sorry, Sheila."

The poor woman was sobbing. I felt it best to let her talk it out. "It must be just dreadful for you to know all that, but not know who was responsible for it."

Sheila sniffed. "I understand that knowing who did it wouldn't bring her back, but, yes, I wish someone could have been brought to justice for her killing. It's so unfair. She literally had her whole life ahead of her, and it was taken by a person who probably couldn't say no to just one more drink. He should have been made to understand what he did, but now…it's too late now."

I was puzzled. "He?"

Sheila wiped her nose again. "Probably a man. Maybe a woman, I suppose." *She sounds strangely unconvinced, and unconvincing.*

"All good?" asked Bud warily as he approached us from the far side of the pool.

I nodded. "Just a bit upset."

Sheila pushed the wet hankie into her pocket and smiled brightly. "I'm being a bit silly, is all, Bud. Probably those pills. I hate pills. But Jack's right, they'll help with the inflammation, and I want to be as good as I can be before we sit on a plane for hours in a few days. Now come on, let's talk about Freddie Burkinshaw's murder. That'll cheer me up."

Bud and I managed a sideways glance at each other just as Jack joined us. "I'll sort out some beers, how about that?" I said.

"I'll help you," said Bud.

We gave Jack and Sheila a good five minutes alone; we filled the now-empty fridge as full of beers from the pantry as we could, while I explained to Bud what I was thinking.

His response was what I'd expected. "You're wondering if Sheila knows more than she's saying about who was responsible for her sister's death? You're suggesting she thought Freddie did it, and might have somehow murdered him because of that suspicion? That's not something I'd even contemplate. It's *Sheila* you're talking about. Jack's Sheila. She's no killer."

"The more I think about it, the more it makes some sense," I pressed. "Remember how she was always so odd when Freddie was around? And now she's saying it's 'too late' for whoever killed her sister to understand what they did."

Bud shook his head. "She could just mean so many years have passed it would be a pointless, and fruitless, exercise now."

"She could," I conceded, "but she could also…"

"Are you brewing those beers?" Jack stood in the doorway to the kitchen.

Bud and I laughed. Too loudly. "Just coming," said Bud, wedging one final bottle into an ice bucket. "Couldn't decide what she wanted," he said as he sauntered off. Sometimes he makes me fume when he uses me as an excuse – other times I don't mind so much, like when it saves us from an embarrassing situation.

When we were all settled, I raised a toast. "To the elephant in the room, may he disappear as soon as we address him."

"To the elephant," chorused Bud, Jack, and Sheila, all sounding slightly confused.

"To what are you referring, exactly?" asked Bud, after he'd downed almost half a bottle.

"The fact that there's no way into, or out of, that lookout room except through the door, unless you're Spiderman," I replied.

"Ah, yes, so you spotted that, too, did you?" said Bud, sounding resigned.

"I agree," said Jack. "If Freddie had the key to that door in his pocket – which he did, and if there isn't another one – which we believe is correct, then how did someone get out of the lookout room, through a locked door? Bud, how did the walkway and railing look? Any signs of someone going over them or using them to escape the tower, in any way? We left before I got a good look."

Bud shook his head. "Nothing, and trust me when I say I did my best to spot anything untoward. No scratches, no drag marks, no rope or grappling hook marks – nothing to suggest anyone had used it in any way. There were no strange items out of place outside, or inside, the tower room."

"You mean things that could be used in some sort of Heath Robinson way to get someone out of there – like a zipline made out of bungee cords?" I quipped.

"No bungee cords, no marks of bungee cord hooks," confirmed Bud. He sounded disappointed.

"How the heck did someone manage to shoot Freddie in the heart without being in the room?" said Sheila, sounding completely mystified. "Could they have managed it from the beach, or from somewhere else outside the tower, like in the garden?"

"I believe Freddie would have needed to be outside on the walkway for a shot from the beach, or the grounds, to have hit him, whereas we know he fell dead between the desk and the door to the stairs. Unlikely to make it that far having sustained a shot to the heart. Alternatively, someone might have been on stilts, about forty feet in the air," said Jack, sounding glum. "It seems impossible."

"And yet it happened," said Bud.

"What about one of those James Bond jet pack thingies?" said Sheila, sounding a bit brighter. "The killer could have flown into and out of the tower room using one of those."

We all shared a wry chuckle.

"There was absolutely no gunshot residue found on Freddie's body in the autopsy," I commented.

"None," chorused Bud and Jack in dismal agreement.

"Would the police report, rather than the autopsy, cover whatever they might have found on his clothes, as opposed to the body?" I asked.

Bud nodded. "Yes. But we haven't got the police report yet."

"Tougher to get hold of. Different access required," said Jack, illuminating very little.

"The poison could have been given to him anywhere, by anyone," said Sheila, "so we should concentrate on the shooting. Who might have done it, and how on earth they *could* have done it."

"Well, that's not quite right – about the poison, Sheila," I said. I tried to modulate my voice so she would know I wasn't telling her I thought she was stupid – just wrong. "Ackee makes you sick within hours, and can easily lead to death; we all had dinner with Freddie that night. He was fine when he was with us, so I don't think he can have eaten the fruit until later, closer to the time of his death. Did you find out when it started to rain that night, Bud?"

Jack and Sheila looked confused.

"Local weather people reckon about four in the morning," replied Bud.

"What's the rain got to do with it?' asked Sheila. Jack nodded.

"Cait believes Freddie would have shut the jalousies in his lookout room if he'd been alive when the rain began, and I tend to agree with her. If he was fine when he left us just after midnight, but likely dead by four, therefore – which ties in with the parameters in the autopsy, which are admittedly always a bit vague – then that shrinks the window of opportunity for the poisoner and the shooter to have taken action."

"We're sticking with the two-perp theory?" asked Jack.

"Two? You think two people wanted Freddie dead?" said Sheila, sounding surprised.

"I think a heck of a lot more than two people wanted Freddie dead," called John across the pool.

"Hey, you're back early," replied Bud, checking his watch.

John threw a large, ancient-looking binder onto the table. "Yes, we are that. I put my foot down. Needed you all to see this."

"Photo album?" asked Jack. John nodded.

"Whose is it?" asked Bud.

"It belonged to Wilson Thomas," said Lottie as she joined us. "We went to see that lawyer Cooperman, and made him give it to us." She sounded triumphant.

Bud's eyebrows shot up. "You did what?" He spoke quietly. *Never good.*

John smiled nervously. "That's not exactly what happened, Lottie. But it's a long story, and I am desperate for two things – first the loo, then a beer. And is there any food? I'm starving."

"Me too," said Lottie. "All of the above. This investigating lark really makes one work up an appetite, doesn't it? Excuse me, back in a mo." She rushed off toward the washroom inside the house.

"We need to talk," said Bud to John as soon as we were alone.

"You're right, we do," replied John, looking furtive. "Some of these photos? Not good, Bud, not good at all. We'll have to consider how they change the way we've been looking at things. Freddie's death, and our situation. Take a look at them, then you chaps come and find me in the bungalow. Someone needs to keep Lottie away from us while we have a private confab. Can you manage that Cait, Sheila?" We nodded.

"How did you get your hands on it, really?" asked Bud before John could dash off.

"I took a bit of a flyer, and it paid off. Knowing that Tarone was Wilson Thomas's grandson I got him to ask Cooperman to give him whatever it was that his grandfather had posted to him – sent him in the 'mail', which was what Wilson said to you when he was dying – for safekeeping. Cooperman gave Tarone the album, which Wilson *had* mailed to him, with written instructions to not let anyone but Tarone have it. We've brought it back here for safe keeping on Tarone's behalf. Simple, see? Must dash."

"Thanks John, we'll be over soon," called Bud at John's receding figure.

All four of us licked our lips in anticipation of what we'd see in the album.

## Photos and Phonies

The album creaked when we opened it. It was many decades old, if the first few photos were anything to go by. Black-and-white, and curling at the edges, they'd escaped some of their corner pieces and were a little the worse for wear. But they were crisp, taken with what would have been a good camera in its day. There were gaggles of people in most of the photos; men in dinner jackets and bowties, women in gauzy gowns, with glamorous updos. Everyone had a drink in one hand, and most had a cigarette in the other. Smiles, laughter, glasses raised in joyous conversation, heads bent close to hear a comment or two – all captured on glossy, thick paper.

The location was obvious – exactly where we were sitting, the main house at the Captain's Lookout estate. Some photos showed the pool, some the portico, some the lounge and dining room, which was usually set for a buffet. There were gatherings in evening attire, pool parties on sunny days, casual get-togethers after dark, and small, more intimate dinners. Freddie was in almost all of the photos. And I spotted Nina Mazzo, with a man I just about recognized as her late husband. I also noticed someone who looked like an even skinnier, taller, and more freckled, version of Niall Jackson. I pointed him out. "Could that be Niall's father, Keith?"

"It is," said Lottie, who'd returned from the bathroom. I looked up. She seemed to be a bit pale, but I put that down to her being hungry. She added, "I fancied a stiff one. Anyone else?" She held up a crystal tumbler with a surprising amount of what looked like scotch in it. We all shook our heads and returned our attention to the album.

"Is that who I think it is? And that?" said Bud, pointing.

I looked and nodded. "Freddie's stories about Fleming and Coward might have been true, after all."

Lottie laughed loudly. "Oh my, how Freddie loved those tales."

Her voice was shaking. I wondered if I was seeing her with her first drink.

Some photos were in color, though they had fared less well than the black-and-white ones; they were blurry, and faded.

"Nina and Luca were here a great deal," I said. "I didn't get that impression from her."

"She said they were friends with Freddie back then," replied Sheila. "Maybe this is the sort of activity that used to pass for friendship around here. It looks more like pure hedonism to me."

We all nodded.

"Is this you?" I asked Lottie. We'd reached a photograph that was larger than most of the others, and had been taken from somewhere inside the house, looking toward the pool. Freddie was wearing swimming trunks, lying on a lounge chair; beside him stood a gangly teenaged girl who seemed to be staring straight into the lens. It was one of the crisp black-and-white shots, so it was easy to see the teen's face. Lottie hadn't really changed very much.

Lottie didn't look. "Yes, that's me," she said, and knocked back her entire drink.

"Gosh, that looks idyllic," said Sheila. "Imagine having access to all this when you're growing up. And you said you stayed on the island for years? Did you come here, to this estate, often?"

We all looked at Lottie, waiting for her to answer.

She was visibly trembling. "Yes, Mummy frequently brought me here. I was a very lucky girl."

There was an edge of mocking cruelty in her voice.

"I think I'll change my clothes before dinner. I've been sitting in these for hours," Lottie called, as she swayed away from us.

Remembering our promise to keep Lottie out of her bungalow, to allow John and the others to have a confidential get-together, both Sheila and I said, "No," at the same time.

Lottie placed her glass on the table. "You finish looking at those. I'll be back in a few minutes. Then I'll leave the bungalow clear for you three chaps to get your heads together and work out how what's in there affects your mission."

As Lottie left, Jack said, "He's told her everything, hasn't he?"

"He wouldn't," replied Bud.

"I wish someone would tell me," I said.

"Me too," chimed in Sheila.

Bud stood. "This is no joke. We cannot risk our cover being compromised. They're called 'secret missions' for a reason."

I pulled him back into his seat. "We know that, Husband, just ask John what he's told Lottie, and what he hasn't. She's in a weird mood; maybe she's merely fishing, trying to get you to say something you shouldn't."

Bud nodded. "You're right, we'll ask John. But let's work out why he thinks these photos are so important. I'll be honest, I haven't seen anything that strikes me as significant so far."

I sighed. "Bud, that photo of Lottie and Freddie. The expression on her face? That's a girl who's not 'lucky'. She looks vacant, dead inside."

Bud squinted at the photo. "I can't see what you mean. It's just a snap."

"Bud –" I put my hand on his arm – "that's a moment in time showing us the face of a teenager who's desperately unhappy. Didn't you see how Lottie reacted just now? She's traumatized somehow. That photo acted as some sort of trigger. I'm thinking something bad might have happened to her during the time she spent in Jamaica."

"Other than being poisoned by ackee, you mean?" said Jack.

"Other than being poisoned by ackee," said Sheila. "Even I can see something's off – in that photo, and with her tonight. Though I don't think we should jump to conclusions; there can be a great many causes of emotional trauma: drink, drugs, abuse…any number of things. We need to tread carefully. Respect her boundaries."

Bud stood again. "I get what you're saying, but, whatever the details, how would that change everything for us, in the way John suggested?"

"Let's keep going, there are lots more photos," I said.

We kept turning the pages, and it was clear we were taking a trip through time. Freddie was ageing, the gatherings looked more corporate and less glitzily social. The black-and-white photos stopped; the color ones grew sharper, and were less faded.

"Wait a minute," said Bud, putting out his hand to prevent Sheila from turning the page. "Jack, look at this photo."

Jack looked. "Hang on, I think I saw one of him earlier on, in the black-and-white section." He flicked back several pages. "There he is. It's him, isn't it?"

Sheila and I looked at the two photos in question. In both of them a tall man with grizzled features had his arm around the waist of the glamourous Nina Mazzo. In the earlier photo he looked to be in his fifties – though it was hard to tell because half his face was obscured by a raised martini glass; in the second he was facing directly into the camera and looked truly ancient – white-haired, with a bowed back. He was a man to whom time had not been kind; Nina looked as though she hadn't aged at all, but had bloomed.

"That's Luca Mazzo." Sheila and I spoke in unison, and shared a smile.

"No, it's not," said Bud sounding quite certain.

Shelia and I stared at him. "He's the man whose photographs are all over the place at *Caro Mio*," I replied. "Including wedding photos. Him and Nina."

Bud stared at the photo, then at Jack, then at me. "You're certain?"

I nodded. "Yes."

"That's it, then. That's what John saw. Lottie must have told him this was Luca Mazzo. Come on, Jack, we three need to get our heads together, now. If he's been on-island all these years – or was back then, at least – everything makes so much more sense."

Jack stood.

"No, nothing makes sense at all. What's going on?" Sheila asked.

Jack took her hand in his. "The guy in that photo is a man we know as…um…who went by a different name in the 1940s. Due to information received from Freddie Burkinshaw, it was believed that certain papers smuggled out of post-war America had somehow reached this island by the early 1960s. Freddie never said how they got here, but he did try to get money out of a few governments at that time in return for him gaining possession of those papers, then passing them along. No one was interested back then, now they are, hence us being here. Freddie was our first point of contact, for obvious reasons, but he assured us he no longer knew of the papers' location. Bud hoped Wilson Thomas might be able to help. Both men are dead now, and we are none the wiser. Now that we've seen this guy in these photos, we have another lead. Him."

Bud stood with his mouth open. "*Secret* mission, Jack."

Jack waved an arm at Bud. "They don't know what the papers are, so it's still a secret, right?"

Sheila and I nodded. Vigorously.

Bud stomped about a bit and ran his fingers through his hair several times. "Damn that Freddie Burkinshaw. He must have known about this so-called Mazzo guy all along."

"Are you telling me that Luca Mazzo is linked to these papers you're looking for, somehow?" I asked.

Bud's head-scratching got faster. "There were very few photos of the man you call Luca Mazzo, and those that did exist were of him as a younger man. Military photos. They formed a part of our briefing; his...original name...appeared on the papers we're looking for, you see. I'm sure that's him. It's the eyes, those eyebrows, and those pockmarks on his cheeks."

"It's him alright," confirmed Jack. "Earlobes." Both men nodded.

"And you're also telling us that there's an international kerfuffle about papers relating somehow to the second world war now, in this day and age? Really?" I found it hard to believe.

Bud pounced. "Ah, now that's where we cannot talk, right, Jack?" Jack shrugged, and looked at his wife with apologetic, worried eyes.

Bud continued, "All I can say is that you're both intelligent enough to understand that sometimes things that happen during wartime would not be acceptable outside the theatre of war. When peace comes, and there's a robust rebuilding of bonds between nations in the aftermath, some potential attachments might be better forgotten about."

"Cait's right," agreed Sheila, "and you are, too. We're both capable of understanding all that, Bud, but that war ended a very long time ago. Why are these papers suddenly important again?"

Bud and Jack exchanged a glance.

Jack replied, "The world turns, alliances shift, the balance of power is amended, or upended. Sometimes the world changes rapidly, and that's happening now. In many places. Those papers are more important now than they have been since 1945. And more dangerous. Our orders are to find them and destroy them, with proof of destruction. That's why there are three of us here – a witness for each of the three nations is required."

I was puzzled. "Three, Bud? For Britain – John; for Canada – you and Jack. Who else is involved with all this? What other country?"

Jack didn't look at Bud; he studied his fingernails.

"I'm here representing Sweden, not Canada," replied Bud.

I took a moment to digest that fact. "Hang on, I know you were born in Sweden, and that your parents emigrated to Canada when you were very young. I know you have a Swedish passport as well as your Canadian one. I also know you've been involved with various 'international operations' in the past. But I'm at a loss to understand why Sweden would choose *you* to represent them in this matter when I'm sure they have their own, more than competent, intelligence officers." I was beginning to get that grumbly tummy thing that happens to me when I feel I've been sidelined or let down. And I didn't like it at all. "How could the Swedish government be certain you'd put their interests ahead of Canada's if it came to the point where those two things were in conflict? You're a Canadian, now, Bud; you left Sweden before you were old enough to even know what it means to be Swedish."

"Calm down, Cait," said Bud gently. "I'm here because I had a good 'in' on the island, other than Freddie – Wilson Thomas.

He was known to me because of the work I'd been doing just before I retired. Canadian drug traffickers and gangs, especially those in Ontario, had close links with groups here in Jamaica. They also had links with shipments made through Gothenburg, in Sweden – the biggest of all the Nordic ports. We relied upon a complex network of people on the ground with good local knowledge. Wilson was my liaison here on the island. That's why me. And because of my Swedish citizenship, and a few other reasons I really can't talk about, I am able to represent Sweden, as well as Canada, in the international arena. Indeed, not only am I allowed to – by each country – but they each trust me to act in their interests when the chips are down. That said, had I been sent here to represent Canada rather than Sweden, I'd have done that. And, on this occasion, there's no question of the needs of one of those countries conflicting with the needs of the other. Both need the same outcome – destruction of the papers. I hope, Cait, if there's only one thing that can be said of me with certainty, it's that I am an honorable man. As for *why* Sweden – or Canada, or the United Kingdom – needs a representative here, that I cannot say. Sorry."

I knew he'd never tell me about the "few other reasons", so I didn't bother pressing him about it.

He rested his hands on my shoulders. "Jack and I must go to see John now. We have to discuss this between the three of us, and get in touch with our respective leads on the case. The food should be here soon; give us a shout and we'll come and get something to take to John's bungalow if we can't join you here, okay?"

Sheila and I each got a kiss before Jack and Bud left, but after they'd gone we looked at each other with matching glum expressions.

"I feel as though I've been slapped in the face with a dead fish," I said. "And after a month of some of the best and freshest seafood in the world, I have to admit I'm a bit sick of it."

Sheila hung her head in mock shame. "Sorry. I ordered conch curry tonight – do you think you'll cope?"

"No goat?"

Sheila smiled, "Yes, I saw how much you loved it, so I ordered that too."

"Thanks."

# Girls and Grief

"They threw me out," said Lottie as she plopped herself onto a chair beside me. "I suppose they were quite polite, but I was given the old heave-ho nonetheless." She looked around. "No food yet?"

Sheila checked her watch. "It should have arrived by now. I wonder if one of you could pass me my phone? Or do it for yourself. It's the last number I rang."

Lottie volunteered to call, picked up Sheila's phone and redialled. We watched as she waited. She seemed to not be as wobbly or slurry as when she'd left us a little earlier – which was good.

"Hello there," she said into the phone, "I'm calling from the Captain's Lookout estate. We ordered some food for delivery and we had rather expected it to have arrived by now. Is there a problem? Is someone on the way?" She listened. "Yes, that's right…No, not at all…Oh, you're so sweet…Thanks, that would be lovely…Oh no, thank you, I have a boyfriend." She giggled. "Yes, he is. And yes, he does. Thanks, bye-ee." She replaced Sheila's phone on the side table. "Delay in the kitchen, be here in half an hour. Okay?"

Sheila and I smiled at each other. "Did someone ask you on a date, just because you spoke to them on the phone?" asked Sheila.

Lottie's laughter was throaty. "It happens all the time. It's the accent, you know. Trying to get a bit of posh tottie is quite a sport, for some." Her voice had taken on a cynical edge.

I decided to go for it. "It must be quite a challenge to be beautiful, well-educated, bright, and wealthy."

Lottie looked at me with cold eyes. "Oh really, Cait?" She didn't sound impressed.

"I mean it as a genuine observation," I said calmly. "You are all those things, and more. I'm not, and never have been. I can't imagine what it's like to live your life."

Lottie's dagger-look softened. She smiled, looking tired. "Thanks for asking. It's…it's difficult to moan about being blessed with so much of what others want in life. Though I honestly don't think I'm beautiful, I'm well aware I have more money than most. I was certainly given the chance to benefit from an excellent education, and – no – I'm not as thick as a brick. But when so many want for so much in this world, what right do I have to whine about having it all? It's not proper. Equally, I'm not at all sure I should be so terribly annoyed by the fact it's a rarity for me to have a conversation with a man for more than five minutes without him thinking he can proposition me. But I am. The liberties some of them think they can take, without the slightest encouragement from me!"

"At least, these days, you're less likely to be man-handled," said Sheila. "Trust me, when I joined the RCMP back in the day, almost every man there seemed to think it was his right to pat me, or paw me, wherever and whenever he pleased. And when they weren't being handsy they were making the sort of cracks you'd want to smack them for – and their mothers would have done, I dare say. And the propositioning? Saying no all the blessed time became second nature to me – which meant they had me marked out as 'not liking men' before you knew it. Which didn't stop them trying, of course – made it more exciting for some of them, I guess. Honestly, being a woman in a man's world was a pain in the backside – literally, if they fancied giving you a little pinch or two. Because that's all good, clean, harmless fun, right?"

I watched as Lottie nodded sadly. "You'd think it would be different in this day and age, but it's not," she said quietly. "So many of them don't even know they're doing it, and half of those who do – and have stopped – make out they're so proud of themselves now that you can guess they're just the same as they always were when they're all just men together. It sickens me. Getting through those teen years was tougher, though. I'm glad that's behind me, at least. Now I have a few more tools in my armory. Back then I was so vulnerable – like a turtle out of its shell...utterly defenseless."

"You didn't look very happy in that snap taken of you here when you were a teen," I ventured.

Lottie's chin puckered. "That year was my last on the island. It was pretty awful. I was sick, Mummy was sick, Daddy and she were having the most terrible time of it, and she was around, but not really 'present' for most of that year. She...Mummy had an affair with Freddie, you see. It went on for some time. Daddy thought she was seeing Keith Jackson, Niall's father, but she wasn't. She didn't like Keith at all, but she'd make sure Daddy saw them together whenever she could. I think she was setting up an elaborate smokescreen, to throw Daddy off the scent, so he wouldn't twig about her and Freddie. Daddy's always been terribly clever, but she was better at fooling him than he was at sussing out what she was up to. He's said several things to me recently that tell me he still has no idea about what really went on when he was off on his jaunts and Mummy and I were planted here, twiddling our thumbs."

"Your mother and Freddie?" said Sheila, sounding stunned.

Lottie chuckled. "He wasn't always wrinkly and old, like when you met him. He could be fun. Threw fabulous parties. Well, you saw all those photos. He was a good host because he had lots of practice. Mummy played hostess for years, and then things went on from there between them. That final year they seemed rather serious about each other, but then Daddy came to the island, and there were dreadful rows. Freddie let me hide away here, sometimes for days. He was quite sweet – he'd send Wilson in the Rolls to fetch me. He didn't drive himself, and didn't have to because he had Wilson to chauffeur him. I loved that car. I wonder what happened to it. A burgundy Rolls Royce, of all things. Anyway, then he dumped Mummy. I was fifteen at the time. He told her she was no longer welcome here, and that he'd made a mistake in taking things as far as they'd gone. I thought at the time that Daddy had found out about them and put the fear of God into Freddie, but I've changed my mind about that since then. Mummy…Mummy killed herself about a year later. That photo you saw? That was me just about the time when I was trying to come to terms with Mummy not being happy anymore. She was never happy again."

"A burgundy colored Rolls Royce?" Sheila's tone was sharp.

I was surprised that was her takeaway from Lottie's revelation.

Lottie looked taken aback too. "Yes, he was well known for it," she replied. "It was one of the big, old ones. He'd probably had it since the 1960s. The leather upholstery felt so soft, it was like skin…which it is, of course, but you know what I mean. I used to enjoy being driven around in it."

"And Wilson Thomas was his chauffeur?" pressed Sheila.

This time I could see Lottie was truly puzzled. "Yes," she replied. "Freddie hadn't driven since…well, I don't recall him ever driving. I know he could, because he used to have photos dotted around this place showing him, the car, and his famous chums in various locations all over the island. They would use it to go on picnics. But he stopped driving it. Why, I don't know."

"I damn well do," said Sheila. She pushed herself up out of her chair and hobbled off into the house.

"Something's made her angry," observed Lottie. "I hope it wasn't me."

"Give me a minute? Can I get you anything?"

"Ting, please," Lottie said with a smile and a wink. "I need the sugar rush."

"Back in a minute." I followed Sheila to the kitchen, where she was standing with her feet planted wide, holding onto the edge of the sink with both hands, her head bent, her body wracked with sobs.

I rubbed her back. "Sheila, what's wrong?"

"Freddie bloody Burkinshaw, that's what's wrong. The cops at the time told me paint from the car that hit Wendy was found on her scooter. It was an unusual color. Burgundy. Specialized finish. Now I know how the cops worked out who hit her. And now I understand why they did nothing. He was important, and rich – and above the law, it seems. Freddie Burkinshaw's name was mentioned to me by our family's lawyer – the guy who helped make the arrangements for me to get Wendy's body back to Saskatchewan. It didn't mean anything to me at the time, of course. It did when we got here. But even then I didn't know why his name had been mentioned in connection with Wendy's death. Now, I do. I'm as certain as I can be that Freddie killed my sister. And here we've been worrying about who murdered him. Well, I for one couldn't care less who did it, or why, or how. I'd like to shake them by the hand, that's what I'd like to do."

"This is the first time you've mentioned having heard Freddie's name before you arrived here last week," I said. "Is that why you came to Jamaica with Jack? Because you'd heard

Freddie's name all those years ago, and then Jack mentioned it when you managed to get him to tell you about this covert operation the men are caught up with? You wanted to meet the man who might have killed your sister? I mean, I know it fits your personality – you're a direct person, who likes to face problems head on, and I bet you were electrified by the coincidence that Jack was coming here, to Freddie's estate, but…" I paused as Sheila turned and looked at me. Her face was mottled, her eyes streaming, her mouth a thin line. *Not her normal self, then.*

"Cait Morgan, you can't help yourself, can you?"

"What?" I was puzzled.

"*What?* Analysing, that's what. Jack was saying to me last night that you seemed surprised you didn't know about Wendy, or my time in the RCMP, or about the loss of our child; I told him that's because you've never had a real chat with me before – that we've never engaged in what most people would think of as a normal conversation. He doesn't understand that you just don't care about people, Cait. But you don't, do you? What happened to you, Cait, to make you such an island? You're disconnected from the rest of the world. Except Bud, of course. And Marty, I guess. With them you seem to come alive. But why just them? What's wrong with the rest of humanity? Are we not clever enough to keep up with your amazing brain? Is that it? Always have to be the smartest in the room, don't you? Jack's told me Bud talks about you as though you're so special. Well, you're special alright, but you'll probably die alone and lonely, because once Bud's gone, no one else is going to take you under their wing like some sort of project. So make the most of it."

I was gobsmacked. I said nothing. Which spoke volumes in itself.

"Are you two alright in here?" said Lottie from the doorway. She looked at me, then Sheila. She didn't move.

"No, we're not alright, Lottie," wailed Sheila. She pulled a sheet off the roll of kitchen paper on the counter and wiped her eyes and nose. "I've just worked out that Freddie probably killed my sister, and all this one can do is find that to be an 'interesting' fact'." The way she stabbed her thumb at me suggested she wished it wasn't just a thumb doing the stabbing. She sobbed, then continued, "I lost my sister because of that man. And my baby. And my chance to have any other children. And my career. I'm angry with him. Flaming angry. If he wasn't dead already, I'd like to throttle him with my bare hands."

"Oh, I say!" said Lottie.

I couldn't help myself – my mind flashed back to our receiving the news of Freddie's death, when Lottie had said exactly the same thing. Sheila had reacted in that moment with anger. I knew in my gut that Sheila had believed back then that Freddie had been responsible for her sister's death. So why was she putting on this show about having just put two and two together? I didn't like what I thought it could mean. But, for the second time that evening, I said nothing.

# Frying Pan, Fire

I left Lottie to console Sheila in the kitchen, and walked over to our bungalow. I needed time to think, and knew I'd have the place to myself. I sat on the little wooden deck that was surrounded by greenery, shut the doors, and lit a cigarette. The tree frogs were peeping away like nobody's business, and the crickets were singing too. The cacophony allowed me to focus on my thoughts, which was good…and bad, in a way, because my thoughts were dark and troubling.

Sheila's outburst had caused me to reconsider a few things: she'd seen through my veil of pretence of being interested in other people's lives, and that was a concern, because the pretence is all I have, and it seemed it wasn't good enough to fool at least her. I dwelt on that for a moment, but decided to set aside that subject because I knew there was nothing I could do about it in the short term.

I went inside the bungalow and grabbed a pen, and a little notepad I like to carry with me. I've needed to make lists more and more frequently in the past months; I've always liked lists, but now I find I need them. It's strange – since the incident in Budapest, I've noticed that while the eidetic nature of my memory hasn't changed, I am even more scattered than usual when it comes to remembering things I need to do, or mention to, or ask, people. I've opened the fridge and not remembered why I did it more frequently of late, and have found myself in a room for no apparent reason more often that I used to. I know that turning fifty is the average time in women's lives when we start to get peri-menopausal signs and symptoms, but

I'd only had my birthday a few weeks earlier; was my body clock that accurate? I couldn't imagine it knew I'd just celebrated the Big Five O, as so many people like to call it, or that I'd hit the age when the horrendous term "bucket list" starts to appear on birthday cards.

I retook my seat outside, opened the pad, and began to organize my thinking.

The first thing I decided to do was ignore how Freddie was killed, because whomever might have done it, I still couldn't understand how they'd managed to shoot him or get him to eat poisoned ackee. I'd given both problems a great deal of thought, but just ended up going in circles, so I set aside those issues, and told myself to focus on who might have wanted to do it, and to come back to how they could have done it later on. I'm a psychologist; I think it always makes sense to start with the "why".

I focussed on what Sheila had just said about Freddie, and how she'd said it. I also recalled a few key facts about Sheila from the past week or so: her coolness toward Freddie since her arrival; her reaction at the news of his death; her seeming relief that Bud had put his hands all over the door of the tower room when we first visited it; and her hesitant responses the first time I asked her if she thought Freddie might have been murdered. If she'd been anyone other than Sheila, she'd have been at the top of my list of people who might have wanted to kill Freddie, especially given what I'd just learned. I asked myself whether I believed Sheila could have wanted to kill Freddie, and I answered myself in the affirmative. Then I wriggled around to how she might have done it, and was back at a locked door – literally. *No Cait, stop thinking about how, think about who, and why.*

Of course, there was also Lottie to consider as a suspect. She, too, had good cause to hate Freddie – he might not have been directly responsible for the death of a loved one as in Sheila's case, but he'd dumped Lottie's mother and that had possibly contributed to her committing suicide. Lottie had been a highly impressionable teen when Freddie broke her mother's heart – those wounds can run deep and might never heal. She'd also been incredibly secretive about her past life on the island, and her familiarity with Freddie. Indeed, her story kept changing all the time, revealing deeper and deeper connections with Freddie and the Captain's Lookout estate; I realized I wouldn't be surprised if she still wasn't telling the entire truth. And I wondered if she'd been going on and on about that possibly mythical treasure just to throw us off the scent.

Amelia and Tarone had millions of reasons to want Freddie out of the way; despite the fact they now faced ending up with nothing, I had witnessed Amelia's utter confidence that she and her grandson would inherit the entire estate. When she'd been in Cooperman's office, just before she collapsed, she'd said that it had all been for nothing. What could she have meant? She might have wanted to kill Freddie…or…

I saw the ground floor of Freddie's tower in my mind's eye, and immediately worked out how she could have done it. Then I realized that Tarone could have done it the same way. I congratulated myself on having come up with at least one concrete idea about how the poisoning might have taken place, but was still completely at sea about the shooting.

At sea? Maybe someone in a boat could have shot Freddie through the open window of the tower, thereby allowing Freddie to have been standing where he was when he was shot? I made a note to ask Bud about guns, distances, and trajectories, when I saw him; not my area of specialism.

I told myself off for allowing my thoughts to wander into the realm of considering the how rather than the why, and got back to my notes.

What about Wilson Thomas? Okay, we'd been working on the basis that Wilson and Freddie had been shot by the same person – possibly someone who was somehow connected with Bud's "case". But what if Wilson had killed Freddie? He and Amelia had been a couple, but he'd been ejected from his home by Freddie, so…what if he had also believed that Amelia and Tarone would inherit the Captain's Lookout estate after Freddie's death? He might well have shared the reason Amelia and her grandson had for wishing Freddie dead – the inheritance angle. And if, as Bud had told us, Wilson was a man with good connections on the island – good enough to be able to furnish Bud with information about gangs and drug-running over the years – might he also know someone with the ability to have shot Freddie and somehow escaped the tower after doing so? I made a note to ask Bud about that too.

That led me to another thought; Wilson had spent years on the estate, as had Amelia and Tarone. What if there was another way out of that tower room? A secret exit? I liked that idea…those walls were incredibly thick, and ancient. Might Henry Morgan have been the sort of man to have an escape route built into his tower? If he'd had it built for a mistress, he might have wanted a way to get into or out of the place without being seen.

I was on a roll, and feeling rather pleased with myself. There'd been so much activity over the past couple of days, I hadn't had a chance to think through things properly, with clarity. Nor to talk things through with Bud. I do better when I have quiet time to focus.

Next, I decided to consider other possible players.

There was Nina Mazzo. She was too frail to gain access to the tower by athletic means, but if she knew of a secret entrance, she could have done it. As could Niall Jackson…though in the case of both of them I couldn't think why they'd have wanted to. Nina seemed convinced that the new evidence Niall had gathered on her behalf would win her case in the courts to gain possession of the land she wanted. So why on earth would she want Freddie dead? Unless her case was much weaker than she'd said, and Freddie's death would benefit her claim. There was only her word to go on about the new evidence, after all. I needed to know more about Nina Mazzo; her husband's connection with Bud's case could also provide another reason she might have wanted Freddie dead. If her precious Luca's "true identity" were about to be revealed, might that cause her to take deadly action? I needed to know more about her, and her late husband, whatever his real name. I made a note.

Niall Jackson was another person I noted I wanted to know more about. Having realized that the first time I saw him was in the office of a realtor, and recalling that was how Lottie had originally referred to him – as Nina's realtor, though Nina herself had spoken of him as her lawyer – I knew I had to find out just how many jobs the man had on the island. Restaurateur, lawyer, realtor…what else? Might he be the realtor Cooperman was planning to use for the deal to sell Freddie's estate? Yes, I needed to know a lot more about Niall, because he might be the sort of man who'd take drastic action to gain an advantage for a client…or maybe just to get a potential sale with a huge commission attached.

With an eye to being thorough, I then did the unthinkable – I forced myself to focus on Jack and John as possible suspects.

I sadly noted that Jack was so devoted to Sheila he might be prepared to get rid of Freddie if he shared Sheila's belief about him killing her sister. But would Jack be capable of murder, even so? My academic knowledge battled with my personal insights into the man, then I admitted to myself I didn't know Jack any better than I knew Sheila – possibly even less well, because he was in the same position as Bud when it came to being a professional deceiver, on occasion. *Oh dear.*

I also noted that I still didn't understand exactly how John Silver's first wife Emily, with whom he had honeymooned in Montego Bay and who had killed herself, fitted in to the whole picture. Might there be some reason for John wanting Freddie dead? He didn't know Lottie well enough to take action on her behalf, I didn't believe, but what about his own reasons? I had to find out more about his connections to the island, and the whole Emily situation.

And what about Bud? I chuckled to myself. *No, not Bud.*

I was awash with suspects, and potential suspects, all with motives to kill Freddie, but no closer to any solution for how such an impossible murder could have taken place. My only idea was straight out of the pages of an Enid Blyton adventure and involved secret doors, stairs, and tunnels. Not good.

I was almost relieved when there was a knock at the bungalow's door.

"The food's arrived," shouted Lottie, without waiting for me to even get inside. "The men are all in our place, Sheila's gone back to hers, and you're here. I'm not sure what to do."

I got up, sighed, padded into the bedroom to tuck my notebook under my pillow, and strode out to get things sorted; if I didn't do it, no one would.

# Surf and Turf

I knocked at the door of John and Lottie's bungalow. "I know you're all huddled in there, boys, but I need Jack to come to talk to Sheila because she's in a right old state, someone needs to give Lottie a hug, and all of us need to get some decent food into us, or we'll be worse than useless. Come on, chaps, you need to break it up for just a little while."

Bud opened the door and stuck his head out. "Not a good time, Cait. John's on the phone to London. Can't this wait?" He sounded annoyed.

I gave him my measured response. "Sheila's just announced that she's convinced Freddie killed her sister; Lottie's admitted that Freddie dumping her mother after an affair they had contributed to her suicide; I've been doing some laser thinking about why everyone connected with the case might have wanted to murder Freddie, and they *all* have a reason. So, no, Bud, it cannot wait."

Bud's eyes popped. "Sheila's sister? Really?" I nodded. "Lottie's mother, and Freddie?" I nodded again. He sucked in air, the way a plumber does just before they tell you how much it's going to cost to fix something. "Hang on." He disappeared into the bungalow, shutting the door.

A minute later Jack ripped the door open. "What's happened? Where's Sheila?"

"In your bungalow. She needs you." I kept my reply factual. He could sort out the rest for himself. He dashed off, looking more than a little concerned.

Bud was the next to emerge. "John has to keep going with his call. He'll be out when he can. Let's go get some food. Jack and Sheila will...well, let's play that by ear, okay?"

I nodded, but there must have been something a bit off about how I did it because Bud whispered, "Are you okay?"

I flung my arms around him and hugged him, hard. "I'm sorry I don't connect with people better than I do," I said.

He looked, and sounded, confused, "You connect with me just fine, and that's all that matters."

"All this spy nonsense has given me the jitters," I said quietly. "Even if you are *The Spy Who Loved Me*."

Bud sighed, and we pulled apart so he could look at me as he said, "Bond titles? You're fine, really, aren't you?"

I flashed him a smile. "Sorry, inappropriate levity on my part again, I suppose. Defense mechanism. You know."

"Come on, food," he said. And we headed for the kitchen.

Lottie was pulling foil containers from the oven. "I kept it warm," she announced. "I fear the conch curry might not have liked that too much, but we can try it."

The three of us sat at the vast dining table taking spoonsful of food from the restaurant's containers and plopping them onto our plates. We had no idea how long John – or Jack and Sheila – would be, so we decided to make the best of a bad situation.

I tried to sound almost disinterested as I asked, "What's all that about John, his first wife Emily, and Montego Bay, then, Lottie? What happened there? And why is the place such a sore point for you? You mentioned you might be able to face it again *now*...why is it difficult for you to face?"

Lottie stopped heaping food onto her plate. "Montego Bay?" Her micro-expressions were telling; the mere name of the place stressed her – she was reliving something in milliseconds that was an unpleasant experience. I wondered what she'd say.

She stared at the serving spoon in her hand. "When I was in school here, I had a boyfriend. A few years above me. Desperately attractive, I thought. Just a little on the wild side, you know? His parents owned a large resort on Montego Bay. I was madly in love with him, of course, and I would visit him there; we were both in the drama club at school together, you see, so I'd tell Mummy I was rehearsing, and I wasn't really lying. Much. He and I…he was my first. And I don't mean just my first boyfriend, I mean my first everything." Her downcast eyelids fluttered as she added, "Let's just say that losing my virginity wasn't quite what I'd expected. The entire school knew about it by the next day – and this was in pre-social media days. He dumped me shortly thereafter. I was devastated."

"The first cut really can be the deepest. He wasn't the person you believed him to be," I said. I was tempted to tell her about how utterly devastated I'd been by the treatment I'd received from Angus, my late ex-boyfriend, but I knew it wasn't the time, nor the place, and didn't want to get sidetracked. "Sorry that happened to you," was all I said aloud.

Lottie nodded, then started to eat the food on her plate as though someone was about to steal it from her.

I pressed on with: "And it doesn't sound as though John's experiences of Montego Bay are much happier than yours. Do you know what happened there between him and Emily?" I couldn't lose this chance to find out all I could.

Lottie eventually took a break between mouthfuls and said, "She only went and had sex with someone else, while they were still on their honeymoon, if you can believe it."

"Really?" Bud and I spoke in unison, and exchanged a look of shock.

"I know, it's dreadful, isn't it?" said Lottie, picking up a round of bammy and ripping it to pieces. "John only told me about it because much the same thing happened to an old schoolfriend of mine quite recently – though that was in Thailand, and it was the husband who strayed. Those ladyboys can be very appealing, it seems. Anyway, I was bemoaning my chum's problems, when John told me about Emily. They were young, he said – her a good bit younger than him even – and she wasn't a very worldly girl. Allowed herself to be seduced by an older man, it seems. John found them on the beach. *In flagrante delicto.* Not being at all discreet. Terrible."

"And was this many years ago?" I asked, sounding as innocent as possible.

Lottie paused, with a forkful of rice hovering in front of her face. She shook her head. "I don't know, but not long after Prince Charles married Diana, I shouldn't think; John mentioned how much Emily had spent on her wedding dress, because she'd wanted to look just like Princess Di. That fad didn't last very long, I don't believe, and with good reason. Diana's frock looked like it was made out of a crumpled old parachute. I've seen it in photos."

I had no idea how long said fad might have lasted, but it allowed me to anchor John's first marriage to the early 1980s, which I realized was before Lottie had even been born. I allowed myself five seconds to feel very, very old.

"John and Emily married in 1984," said Bud. His tone told me he didn't understand why I was pursuing this conversation.

"Of course, you know him well, don't you, Bud?" said Lottie. "See, you could have asked your husband all this."

Bud's nothing if not quick on the uptake, and supportive of me, so he helpfully said, "I know when he was married, and to whom, but I don't know much about his personal life really – just key dates, names, places, that sort of thing."

"You chaps don't give much away, not even to each other, do you?" observed Lottie. "Daddy's always been the same, too. It must be the job."

"I expect so." Bud sounded resigned.

"And that was the beginning of the end for them, then?" I queried. "John and Emily."

Lottie waved a hand. "I believe so. He told me about her, and what happened, but not a lot more than that. She was dead about a year later, I know that much. Shot herself. In the heart, of all things. One always imagines that a person shooting themself would do it in the head – the logistics, if nothing else, would dictate that, you'd think. But, no, she shot herself through the heart. John took it rather badly, of course. It was a message to him, you see, that he'd broken her heart by rejecting her. Said so in the note, apparently. Anyone want a drink?" Lottie waggled her empty glass.

Bud and I declined, and Lottie headed out to the kitchen.

I couldn't believe Lottie was able to speak of a woman's death in such a matter of fact way. I wondered if she'd have used the same tone if John had been in the room with us. Of course, I'd raised the topic for the very reason that he wasn't there, and reckoned the best way I could get information from her was if she felt she could speak freely. But that level of dismissiveness? I wondered how much she really felt for John; I could never speak about Bud's late wife's death that coolly. I could even hear her singing *Montego Bay* to herself as she rattled about in the fridge.

As soon as Lottie was out of earshot I whispered, "Someone else shot in the heart? Did you know about this, Bud? What if the man John's wife had a fling with was Freddie? What if John knew that, and therefore had a really good reason to want Freddie dead? What if he chose to kill him exactly the way his ex-wife had killed herself?"

Bud sat back in his chair and scratched his hand through his hair. "Come off it, Cait. That's stretching the concept of coincidence way past breaking point. What would John's young bride be doing having a fling with someone like Freddie? It's inconceivable. And I can tell by that eyebrow of yours that you're about to try to argue with me about it but don't. Just don't. John? Emily? Freddie? No, Cait. You cannot possibly imagine that John's wife's suicide was also precipitated by Freddie Burkinshaw…that's just…ridiculous!"

I hovered on the edge of telling Bud that the current set of circumstances under which I found myself living was forcing me to reassess my previous understanding of the word "ridiculous", but I was prevented from debating the point with him because we were interrupted.

"Sorry about being a bit late," said John as he entered the dining room from the lounge.

I wondered how long he'd been close by, and what he might have heard. "I had to finish the call," he added.

Taking a seat beside Lottie's empty chair he leaned in to whisper to Bud, "By the way, the police reports have arrived. We've managed to get a copy of the entire thing. Pre-bedtime reading, I think. I emailed the file to you, and Jack." He looked around the room. "Where is he, and Sheila?"

Lottie returned smiling, carrying a can of Ting.

Bud replied, quickly. "Sheila might have needed to get her leg up. Jack went to check on her."

"Fair enough. More for us then, eh? I'm starving. What's left?" John poked at the dishes and mounded food onto his plate.

My goat curry was starting to congeal, and the conch tasted like lumps of rubber in curry sauce; it was good curry sauce – but not good conch, so I worked around it and scooped up the sauce with my bammy and rice.

"I put some into another dish, in the oven," announced Lottie as we finally cleared the plates and dishes. "What do you think – should I take it over to Jack and Sheila's bungalow?"

Knowing how angry Sheila had been with me I answered, "I think that's a good idea, Lottie. Maybe we can put together a tray with everything they might want, then knock, and leave it outside their door?"

Everyone agreed my idea was sound, so we did just that; I was a wimp and let John take the tray across. Then I wondered what we should all do next. There wasn't even the remotest possibility I could relax, but it was only just gone nine. I also really wanted to read the police reports the men had managed – who knew how – to get hold of. I suspected Bud felt the same.

"Fancy a swim?" Lottie asked John when he returned.

"So soon after dinner?" I said.

Lottie laughed. "Yes, so soon. Mummy and Daddy would never let me swim for an hour after I'd eaten – they convinced me when I was a small child that to do such a thing would inevitably lead to cramps and immediate drowning."

"There's a lot of truth in that," said John.

"Not in a pool, with you," said Lottie. "Come on, John, I'm desperate to do something fun. Please?"

I could see that – whatever her feelings for John – Lottie had the poor man wrapped around her little finger.

He capitulated. "Just half an hour, then I do need to get some reading done. Just a quick little something for work, okay?"

Lottie smiled playfully. "Half an hour. Deal. Night, night folks," she waved and ran toward their bungalow.

"Come on," I said to Bud, "let's get reading. I don't think I can bear to see her in yet another tiny bikini, especially not when I'm feeling as stuffed as I am right now. Fancy taking one of those sinfully expensive brandies with us, though?"

Bud chuckled, "Now that I know how much it costs, I'll probably never be able to bring myself to have another sip."

John smiled. "Freddie poured us good brandy, so what? Have you seen how much of it he has in the back of the pantry out there? Go for it, Bud. Take a whole bottle. He's gone, drink it in his memory."

"What do you mean?" asked Bud. "There isn't any more brandy in the pantry."

John looked puzzled. "There is. Ten bottles. Saw them when I was out there the other day. Day we got here. I was being introduced to Amelia in the kitchen. Couldn't help but notice it. It's excellent cognac."

"Hang on a minute," said Bud, walking toward the kitchen. "When Amelia showed me and Cait around the kitchen – after Freddie had died – I know we had a good search around the pantry, and I certainly would have noticed ten of those fancy bottles. Let's have a look."

All three of us checked the pantry, but there were no more bottles.

"Hand on my heart, Bud," said John, "there was a row of those bottles on that shelf, right at the back, behind the vegetable racks. I specifically noticed them because I adore Remy Martin Louis XIII, but rarely, if ever, have the chance to drink it. When Freddie started splashing it about after dinner for us, I assumed we were helping him work his way through his extraordinary stock. Where can it all have gone?"

"I don't know. That's a puzzler," said Bud. "In any case, it's not something I should acquire a taste for, so I'm happy to grab a few beers to take to the fridge in our room, and sip through what might be a long and interesting night of reading. Now you'd better go and get into your world-famous Speedos for that gal of yours, hadn't you, John?"

"Hardy-har-har," said John, as he left us to join Lottie.

"That's about thirty- to forty-thousand-dollars-worth of brandy that's disappeared from this pantry," I noted. "If John's telling the truth."

"Why on earth would he lie about that?" asked Bud.

"Maybe he's pathologically incapable of telling the truth, or maybe he's learned how to lie about everything as part of his training and trade craft. Maybe he likes to throw out improbable lies just to keep his hand in, I don't know."

"Cait, that's not fair."

"Look, Bud, I'm up to here with all this secrecy stuff. Every time we face a problem in life, we face it head on, together. This time? This time I feel like you're not one hundred percent on my side. As though you're not 'all in'. It's unsettling, and I'm off-kilter enough with everything else at the moment. I'm even *forgetting* things, and what good am I if I can't remember everything?"

Bud sighed. "Come on, Cait, not this again. What have you remembered that you'd forgotten this time?"

I had a quiet word with myself before I spoke. "I forgot to tell you that I love you often enough today." I flashed my winning smile at my husband, who hugged me.

"Police reports," he said, and off we went with half a dozen beers and a spring in our step.

## Reports and Refreshments

"I'm going to take advantage of this cool night air and sit outside to read. Coming?" I was so pleased to not be a sweaty mess that I wanted to enjoy as much of the less humid nighttime as possible. "But I might just jump into the shower first, then I'll be nice and fresh to start with. These past couple of weeks I've felt sticky all the time."

"Thanks for sharing, and if that's the case it sounds like a shower's a real good idea," replied Bud. "I'll email the reports to you too so we can each read them on our own devices, at our own pace. When you've finished in the shower, I know you'll be easily able to catch up with me."

When I rejoined Bud I was delightfully un-sweaty, had left my hair to dry naturally, and was ready for a beer and some reading. Bud had already finished his studies, which surprised me.

"Don't panic," he said. "It'll take you about five minutes. Their reports are woefully lacking. There's the lab report, and the police report that was filed immediately after they found Freddie, when they believed it was a suicide. It's pretty thin."

He was right. "Oh dear. They really didn't expect that autopsy to go the way it did, did they?" I said.

"Nope, and I can see why not. To be honest, even the ackee wouldn't necessarily make them immediately think there was a killer to track down, but put the bullet wounds and the ackee together, and that's why they're back at the tower now, with the entire building taped off."

"True. That said, these photos are interesting. At least we can see now what we couldn't see through the keyhole, and what had been removed by the time we carried out our examination of the room," I said. "Look here." I pointed to the photographs of the body, in situ. Bud scrolled to his own copies. "See how the wound on Freddie's chest is high? I'm no anatomy specialist, but I would say that suggests a shot that went in above his heart, then tracked downwards to hit it – which the autopsy said it did. And that's odd. Also, I can't see any scorching that would suggest the gun was in contact with his shirt. What do you make of those two points?"

Bud scrolled. "You're right, I can't see any scorching either, but there's a lot of blood, so we might not be able to notice it if there were any. The already knew the report from the autopsy said there were no signs of gunshot residue anywhere on the body, and this subsequent report from the lab – scroll to the end, it's there – says there was none found on Freddie's clothes either. I'm putting money on *that* being one of the main reasons for the police now treating this case as murder. There's no way for someone to shoot themselves and not have some sort of residue somewhere on their person. Also, the gun on the floor beside the body is a Walther PPK with a suppressor attached––"

"I spotted that in the report," I interrupted. "It's like the one people always say is 'James Bond's gun' – even though it isn't. Well, not always. Not until the later books when he'd been forced to give up his Beretta."

"If you say so, Wife," said Bud, using his patient voice.

"Having had the benefit of seeing what types of items he hid away up in his tower, I would suggest that might turn out to be Freddie's own gun; one of his 'rare and collectible' possessions, maybe."

"Fine," said Bud, sounding less patient, "but let's put aside the whole Bond thing for one moment, and think about the logistics. That suppressor makes the barrel of the gun too long for someone to use it to shoot themselves in the chest with any degree of comfort, especially with a downward, rather than an upward, trajectory."

"Comfort?"

"You know what I mean. Look." Bud stood, and demonstrated how far from Freddie's body the trigger would have been if he'd used the gun in the photo to kill himself. "He'd have had to have pressed the muzzle against his upper pectoral, pointing down toward his heart, then pulled the trigger with his left thumb, or both of his thumbs, with his elbow way up here in the air. I realize we're trying to imagine the mindset of someone about to end their life, but that seems incredibly awkward to me. And why the suppressor in the first place? The gun would be much shorter and more manageable without it, so why bother? If Freddie had really shot himself, why worry about anyone hearing the shot – not that a suppressor makes that much difference to the noise a gun makes in any case. No idea why they call them 'silencers' – they certainly don't make a shot 'silent'."

I smiled. "I knew you'd be good on the gun stuff, Husband."

Bud shrugged, and sat. "So, we're convinced he didn't shoot himself. The next question is, why the elaborate set-up to suggest he might have done so?"

"If it hadn't been for the ackee, do you think the police would have really considered murder?"

Bud took a glug from his beer. "Reading this initial report, written by Sergeant Swabey, he made it quite clear that his determination of the scene as that of a suicide accounted for all the facts. Which, to be fair, isn't a bad assessment. Upon receipt of the autopsy, however, showing the presence of overripe ackee in the victim's stomach contents and the lack of gunshot residue on the body, plus the subsequent lab report about the lack of gunshot residue on the clothing, Swabey's original assertions were – again quite rightly – thrown into question. It's clear those reports would have been prepared whether foul play had been suspected or not, as we can see…because they were, and it wasn't. The local authorities were thorough, and really fast – considering how long this sort of report can take to get hold of back home."

"Okay, then, maybe a killer with an understanding of local police procedures would know that a suspicion of foul play would eventually transpire. So…maybe the killer wanted Freddie's death to be initially ruled a suicide, to give them a chance to…do something they couldn't do if it was immediately suspected as a murder?"

"Like what?" asked Bud.

I searched my mind. "There were at least two sets of papers missing from Freddie's desk in that tower room. I couldn't see the entire room through the keyhole, but I did see them. But now the papers have gone. Between the time the police left the tower with Freddie's body, and our entering it, the room was open for anyone to gain access. The main entry to the building was locked, as we agreed, though with more of a chance of someone having been able to gain entry via what was a more 'normal' locked door than the one to the tower room itself."

"Good points, Wife. None of them lost on me. You couldn't see exactly what the papers were, could you?" His tone was plaintive.

"No, I'd have told you if I had. I merely saw a bundle of what looked to be much-thumbed loose sheets, judging by their edges, secured under what I now know to have been the crystal skull, and a roll of several large sheets of paper, tied with a blue ribbon."

"Maybe the killer wanted those papers, specifically. Maybe Freddie wouldn't give them up. They were in his tower room, after all, and that's where you said he kept his private treasures. I hate to say this aloud, but I have to because it's crawling around inside my head – what if the papers that were in a bundle on Freddie's desk were the very ones we're after? That would be terrifying. I was that close to them, but now they're gone."

"I know, Bud. Of course that's crossed my mind too. But we could speculate all night about what the bundle, or the scroll, might have been, so I think that's a pretty fruitless task," I said. "There is, however, the critical question of why the killer didn't take the papers with them immediately after killing Freddie. Which might suggest…"

"…the killer didn't want the papers at all, and someone else did…or the killer only realized later on that they wanted, or needed them," added Bud. He began to scratch his head. *Not good.*

"I tell you what, instead of dwelling on that, let's consider the other information in this initial police report. They noted the vomit, they noted the gun and the body, but they also noted the lack of obvious signs of ingress or egress by anyone other than Freddie, as they should. They took a photo of the key to the tower room, which they removed from Freddie's trouser pocket. I still think it's weird that Freddie had it in his pocket…but, taking that thought, why *might* he have had it in his pocket? Do we think someone was inside the room with Freddie, they shot him, put the key in his pocket to consolidate the idea that Freddie had locked himself in, then they somehow got out by some so far impossible-to-determine means?"

"Could be," said Bud. "Or else Freddie really did usually keep the key in his pocket when he was inside the tower room. Some sort of weird possessiveness on his part? You said he was that type."

I pondered that issue for a moment. "Having seen what I've seen, and having built up a better picture of Freddie's psyche, I have to say I now believe that putting that key into his pocket, even when he'd locked himself into the tower room, could well be consistent with his personality. Moving on, let's discuss the next critical point I picked up from these reports."

"And that is?" asked Bud, placing his empty bottle on the floor beside him.

"The note about the vomit. See how they just noted it, plain and simple. It doesn't say they took samples for testing."

Bud shook his head. "Maybe it's not standard procedure here? It would be back home. But, again, this is the report written when they thought he'd shot himself. I bet they'll test it now."

"I bet they will, and the remains of that gloop I saw in a glass."

We sat in silence for a moment or two, then I said, "Look, Bud, we both know there's no such thing as an impossible murder – there's only a puzzle that hasn't been solved yet. A secret entrance could allow for someone to come into, or at least get out of, the locked tower room, so I've been thinking about secret passages, and wondered if the walls of the tower are thick enough to accommodate a way in and out that wasn't apparent when we searched the place. I believe we should go back to the tower room and do what we didn't do before – which is to pull all that beautifully constructed furniture away from the walls and see if there's anything hidden behind it…like a door, for example."

Bud looked surprised. "Get into the tower again? Move all that stuff? It's under police guard, Cait."

"Yes, it's under guard, but I bet they won't have anyone posted there overnight. And no, not all the furniture, just some of it. I've been picturing it in my mind's eye, and the bookshelves could easily slide somehow to allow you to access a doorway. It's a great idea to build curved furniture for a round tower, but I think it's been done with more than esthetics in mind."

Bud sighed. "You're not Nancy Drew, Cait."

"And you and your chums aren't the Hardy Boys, but we are trying to find out who could have killed Freddie, aren't we?"

Bud stood, and stretched. "Indeed we are, but is finding a secret entrance to the lookout room going to help us? I thought you'd naturally gravitate toward the why, not the how."

"You know me so well, Husband," I said, then I talked him through the notes I'd made earlier that evening. Bud sagged a little when I spoke about Sheila, more when I spoke about Jack and John, but perked up a bit when I got to Lottie, and the others who were not our friends and confidants.

"Not Sheila, Cait. She's Sheila. She wouldn't kill anyone."

"An ex-Mountie, trained in firearms? Suffering all that loss because of Freddie? She might have, and she possibly could have. But, if the killer used a secret doorway to access the tower, then it's a lot less likely to have been Sheila, right? Because how could she possibly know about any secret entrances?"

Bud smiled. "You're sharp. You want to go to the tower tonight to see what we can find out, and you're dangling the possibility of clearing Sheila like some sort of carrot, aren't you?"

"You see straight through me, Husband. And don't drink any more of that beer."

"But we'd be entering a police-secured crime scene. It's not something we can do lightly, Cait."

"If this killing were connected to your mission, and it helped you achieve what you called 'a positive outcome' to that mission, would you do it then? Would you see it as a situation where it's best to break the rules first, and ask for forgiveness afterwards? Could your oh-so-high-up contacts in three countries get us off any associated charges? You know, the same way the original privateers like Henry Morgan were able to break the law with the support of their governments?"

Bud groaned. "It's a good thing I love you as much as I do."

"I'll change my shoes. Flip-flops won't work," I said, and I dashed off.

# A Privateer's Private Places

I knew from previous visits that walking along the crushed-shell path to the tower was going to be too noisy; we could see the top of the tower from our bungalow, but not the building at its base, so we had no idea if there was any police presence, and we couldn't take the chance of being overheard if there was.

Before Bud and I set off, we agreed on our basic plan. "I have the key to the main building," I told Bud. "If we skirt the edge of the estate, along the shoreline, we can get to the tower without making too much noise. We'll also be able to wait there to see if there's a guard of some sort."

"You do realize I know all this, don't you?" said Bud wryly.

"You've liked it when Lottie has shown she can take the initiative, Husband, so allow me to do the same, eh?"

"You and that Lottie. You know she's not nearly as bright, or beautiful, as you, don't you?"

"Aww, thanks," I mugged. "You've got your mini-binoculars, right?"

"They won't be much use in the dark."

"No night vision paraphernalia hidden in the heel of your shoe, then?"

"Cait…" warned Bud.

I squeezed his hand. "I love the way you keep me so…"

"Grounded?"

"Tethered."

"If we're doing this, let's do it," said Bud, looking serious. "We both have our phones. And I've left a note for Jack and John, in case anything goes awry."

I took a breath. "We're going to be fine, Bud. If there's a guard we'll have to come up with a different plan, because we cannot go hauling about pieces of furniture if there's someone on duty there. The coast will either be clear, or we won't be doing anything at all."

"True, but we have an operating procedure I need to follow. Jack and John know to check in with me. We have a system."

I couldn't help but roll my eyes. "Don't tell me, let me guess...all three of you have access to an email account where you save drafts of emails you never send, so you can all keep in touch but there's no email trail to follow, right?"

"An oldie, but a goodie." Bud shrugged.

We made our way out of our back door, through a gap in the greenery, to the beach, and hugged the line of the tropical plants as we made our way toward the edge of the property, where the tower was located. In the more than three weeks we'd been at the estate it was only my third trip onto the beach itself; I grew up on the beaches around Swansea, and haven't liked sand between my toes ever since...something to do with the way Mum rubbed it off my feet when we got back to the car, I think. And the sea around Jamaica isn't a place for someone who's afraid of getting out of their depth in the water, like me. According to Ian Fleming, it's packed with angry barracuda, poisonous lionfish, fearful octopus, and jellyfish that prefer to sting you rather than just glide past – so why on earth anyone would want to venture into it is beyond me. I know the man was a fiction author, but seriously? All those things that want to kill you, and can? Hence my preference for the pool. This journey onto the sand was for a different reason though, so I stuck my feet into its yielding embrace and plodded on.

When we reached the part of the beach closest to the tower we pushed our way into the undergrowth as far as we could without making too much noise. It was a bit painful, but I managed alright. I was glad I'd put on deck shoes, because my flip-flops would have been a nightmare.

We kept as still and quiet as possible. The nocturnal chorus was loud, especially as we were now sharing the habitat of the noisemakers. It was difficult to hear anything above the clattering of the crickets, the peeping of the tree frogs, and the breaking waves behind us, but we both strained our ears in any case. By bobbing my head about I could see the building below the tower. In the moonlight I could make out the yellow and black crime scene tape; there was enough of a breeze to make the tape move, but not flutter. We waited. And waited.

"There's no one doing rounds, that's one thing," whispered Bud. "But they could have a static guard, somewhere out of sight."

"Wouldn't the guard be keeping an eye on the door?"

Bud shrugged.

"What about if I walked up to the tower looking all innocent, to try to flush out anyone stationed there?"

Bud shook his head.

"But…"

Bud shook his head again and grabbed my arm.

"Tethered," I whispered.

He glared at me.

We waited another five minutes, then he pulled gently at my arm, and nodded in the direction of the beach.

I was already feeling stiff, having been immobile for all of ten minutes or so, and was glad to move. We padded along the sand, a little closer to the surf line than on our outward journey.

I still felt the need for secrecy so whispered, "What about a frontal approach now? Both of us, on a moonlit stroll?"

Bud didn't answer at first, then he leaned in and said, "Okay, let's do that. Along the path, cuddling."

I perked up. "Lovely idea."

By the time we reached the tower, this time via the crunchy pathway, we realized the reason we hadn't seen anyone was that no one was there. We walked around the entire building; not a soul.

We both felt a bit foolish, but we also agreed we'd done the right thing by taking the approach we had.

"You can't be too careful," observed Bud. "And, speaking of being careful, we're now entering a crime scene, so pop these on, okay?"

He handed me a pair of latex gloves, and I wrestled them onto my hands. "These just happened to be in your pocket?" I asked.

Bud chuckled.

We slipped through the main entrance, and I locked the door behind us.

We waited for our eyes to adjust to the complete darkness. "Shall we risk using the lights on our phones?" I whispered.

"Yes, but just the regular light from the screen, not the flashlight app, for now. It'll be good enough to begin with," replied Bud. When he swiped his phone I could see what he meant; in the darkness just the screen itself gave a good amount of illumination.

"Let's start at the top," I said.

"Why not the bottom?"

We hadn't discussed our plan of action once we were inside the tower, which seemed like a serious omission.

"There might be doors, or tunnels and so forth on this level that don't go to the lookout room, and that's the room we're interested in, not this room, or the other floors. The only door barring access to the lookout room is at the top, so let's start there," I said.

Bud grunted, and we mounted the stone staircase, more slowly than we had done in daylight.

The police had chosen to not try to close up the door they'd damaged, instead, it stood open, inviting us inside. The windows were all shuttered.

"Would it be better to open the shutters and let the moonlight in, rather than use our flashlights?" I asked.

Bud looked around, moved to the windows facing the moon, and opened two shutters. "That's the best it'll get, and no one giving the place a casual glance would see our flashlights bobbing about."

Luckily the moon was large and bright, but, even so, the room was washed with only a partially helpful amount of light.

"Let's start with the walls over here," I suggested, indicating the bookshelves. "Let's see if these move at all."

"Wouldn't they open? You know, by pulling a book, or pushing a secret button in the carved bits?" whispered Bud.

"Okay, let's try that first."

Each of us started at one end and Bud – who is a few inches taller than me – pulled a stool from the other side of the room to stand on, so he could check the tops of the units, while I checked the bottoms. We slid our fingers across every inch of the wood used to construct the frames of the shelves, and we each pressed on anything that felt raised, or indented. I felt as though I was trying to play a piece of music on a completely uncooperative instrument. It seemed to take forever, but we were probably only at it for about half an hour before we both admitted defeat. There didn't seem to be anything that shifted beneath our touch even a little bit. We tried pushing the boards at the back of the bookshelves; they were wide, and ancient, but also totally unyielding. Finally, we began to lift and replace every item on the shelves themselves, wondering if there might be some sort of weighted trigger. Nothing.

We stood back, glowering at the bookshelves. We then tried to move them in their entirety, hoping they might slide, or magically swing open. Nothing. They didn't budge. They were extremely heavy.

"Stonework next," said Bud, sounding unfazed.

We took the same approach, feeling the knobbly stones, high and low, pressing and pushing as we went. Nothing. I sighed with exasperation. It had always been much easier to find a secret door in all the books I'd read, and films I'd seen, than this task was proving.

"Ssh," said Bud.

"I can't help it, the floor creaks," I snapped.

"Well don't stand right there then, it's only creaky there," he snapped back.

We both froze. Then we sank to our knees and started the now-familiar process on the floorboards. The only squeaky area was a few feet away from the shelves, close to where the desk was located.

"Let's see if we can move this lump," said Bud, nodding at the desk.

It took some doing; even though the feet of the desk slid easily, it was the weight of the thing that proved problematic. However, as we were shifting it a few inches at a time, it occurred to me that beneath the desk would be an excellent place to hide a trapdoor. Surely only the owner of the desk would ever go to such lengths to clear the floor it was protecting? Brilliant.

Eventually we had completely removed the desk from the footprint it had once created, and we could see the floor that had been beneath it quite clearly. There was a noticeable set of scratches where the desk had been dragged across the wooden planks of the floor, but only one...made by us.

"I'll close the shutters," I said. Bud nodded. It was obvious we'd need more than moonlight to examine the floor as closely as we needed to.

Using both our flashlight apps it was easy to see that there wasn't a straight line cut across any section of the floorboards, though there was a sort of vague area where the staggering between the ends of the boards was a little less pronounced than elsewhere.

"There's nothing here to prise open," said Bud, kneeling. We switched off our lights, I gave Bud a hand up, and we stood looking at each other in the darkness, thinking as hard as we could.

"Push?" I suggested.

Bud nodded, and we began to push the edges of the squeaky boards, in turn, with our toes, then we put more weight into it. As we pushed in one spot, a plank groaned, then started to move. The far end of it lifted a little. The end we were pushing had a metal rod threaded through it that was acting as a pivot. Once we'd got it started, Bud was able to get his fingers under one end to lift it up. Once it was raised a few inches, we had an edge of the rest of the floor to lift, and we pulled with all our might. The movement was less than easy, but we persisted, and eventually we had a large section of the floor standing up at right angles. The trap door had an irregular edge, where the planks had been set into the general pattern of the floorboards; it was an extremely clever way to disguise its presence.

Our flashlights showed us what looked like a wooden cavity below, probably about four feet deep.

"There must be a much bigger space between the ceiling of the room below, and this floor, than we imagined," I said.

"That might be why the climb to this top floor seems so great. Are we going in?"

"Me first," said Bud. "I'll lower myself down, and have a look around. See what we've got. If it's worth investigating, then you come down. Can you pass me that stool, please?"

"Why the stool?"

"How are we going to get out again without it? I just don't have the upper body strength to haul myself up out of there. Best I know my limitations and act to accommodate them rather than pretend I can do what I could twenty years ago."

I squeezed his arm, then watched him lower himself. I could see him flashing his light around. "Okay," he said. I passed him the stool.

"Be careful when you come down, Cait, these edges aren't smooth."

I took my time, and was finally standing beside Bud. We both had to duck down to see exactly what was there. It seemed as though the entire floor area of the lookout room had a cavity beneath it. I couldn't imagine that was merely an architectural decision. I also began to feel my claustrophobia set in; it's not severe, but I really appreciate being able to get out of a small space if, and when, I want to. Bud understood, bent more deeply than I had to and said, "Let me explore the edges, you stay there with your head poking up out of the hole, like a meerkat."

"Ha, ha," I replied gratefully.

Bud shuffled and grunted, and kept on shuffling and grunting for a few minutes.

"This runs to the outer walls, and that's that. I'll go this way now."

More shuffling, more grunting. "Cait, I need help."

My tummy clenched and I ducked down. "What is it?"

"I need more than two hands here. There's a sort of doorway in the wall, but I can't hold the light and try to open it. Do you feel able to come here?"

I shone my light toward him, and could see he was hunched against a door alright, but it was even smaller than the space we were in – the planks were about three feet square, set into the stone wall.

"Hang on a second," I said, and poked my head up above the floor, then back down again. "That little door is in the part of the wall that's beneath the bookcase," I said, "along from the door into the room, by a few feet. I'm coming."

I took a deep breath, hunched down, and went for it. Bud put his phone away, and I held my phone's flashlight as steady as I could so that he could use both hands to turn the large iron ring set into the wooden planks. The door finally creaked open, swinging into the space we were occupying. Bud took his phone out again and shone it into the opening.

"What is it?" I asked. I felt both physically and psychologically uncomfortable, but really wanted to know what we'd found.

Bud turned to me. "There's a ladder hanging down, a rope ladder."

I peered in, over his shoulder. "It's called a Jacob's ladder," I said. "They had them on the old ships. Just the sort of thing Henry Morgan would have used during his time at sea. I wonder if it's as old as the tower. And, in case you were considering climbing down, I have to say I don't think you should trust it to hold you."

Bud leaned further into the opening. "I can't see beyond the first few rung-things on it. They look a bit sketchy – not wooden slats, but sort of dangly rope loops."

"It's the style of ladder. The rope would get wet at sea, then dry out again. They made the rope rungs longer than they really needed to be to accommodate them shrinking. It seems it hasn't shrunk here, so the rungs will be a bit saggy."

"Good to know, Cait, but not helping," said Bud, sounding patient.

As the light flashed about inside the shaft – that descended between an inner and an outer wall of the tower – I realized I wasn't feeling at all well.

"We could do with some glow sticks, something I could throw down, to provide some more light at the bottom," said Bud. "I think I can see a tunnel leading away from the shaft, but I can't be sure. It's too deep."

"I have to get out of here," I said abruptly, and shuffled back to the opening in the floor. I was relieved to stand upright and see something other than walls close around me. I was sweating profusely and feeling more than a bit wobbly. I hate having irrational fears – heights, and enclosed spaces, and getting my face splashed, and not being able to put my feet down on something solid when I'm in the water. All really annoying. But all possibly life saving fears, I always tell myself. "Please come up for air too, Bud," I pleaded.

"I just want to take a look…"

"No, we're not doing this alone. It's too dangerous. We need back up of some sort."

Bud shuffled toward me, then we both stood with our heads poking up out of the cavity, above the floorboards. A heated conversation ensued about what we might have found, its implications, and our next move.

It took me a good quarter of an hour to talk Bud into leaving, and then it took us another fifteen minutes to get everything back to where it had been when we'd first arrived. By the time we crept down the stone staircase it was getting close to two in the morning, we were both exhausted and covered in dust. We shared the feeling that we'd achieved something, but were annoyed that we really weren't well enough placed to be able to capitalize upon it.

I had yet another shower when I got back to the bungalow – my fourth of the day – and collapsed into bed. Bud was already snoring; I closed my eyes as tight as I could and hoped for sleep.

## Addictions and Predilections

To say that I didn't feel like getting out of bed when someone knocked at our door at seven the next morning would be understating things. I could have happily throttled them, whomever they might be. Bud kindly went to see who it was, and I managed to snuggle down again, because he was also kind enough to close the bedroom door when he left.

I thought I'd closed my eyes for no more than a moment, then felt awful when I realized I'd drifted back to sleep for nearly an hour. When I peeled myself out of the sheets, Bud was nowhere to be seen, his phone was gone, and I panicked. I pulled on some clothes and ran across to the big house. No one there.

I hit Bud's number on my phone and heard his ringtone in the distance. I kept the call open as I followed the sound, and discovered him at John and Lottie's bungalow; he, Jack, and John were huddled on the little verandah.

"What's up?" I asked. I didn't dare say that the thought had crossed my mind that he might be crawling along some ancient secret passage.

"I've reported back about our nocturnal activities. We've agreed that we three will plan a sortie tonight. We'll keep an eye on the place to establish when the coast is clear, then get into that tunnel as early as we can."

I knew there was no point arguing. "Okay. All three of you?" They all nodded. "And between now and then?"

"Follow up on Wilson Thomas's autopsy report, which we've just received. Shot through the chest, twice. One shot nicked the aorta. Which is interesting," said Bud.

I nodded. "If he was able to speak to you at all, with an aorta that had been damaged, you must have arrived just after he was shot."

"Correct," said John.

"But we didn't see anyone," said Jack. "All three of us were watching the shack at what would have been the time of the shooting. None of us heard anything – though we all agree the rain was real heavy and the surf roaring – but none of us saw anything either."

"Another impossible murder," I observed, probably sounding as tired as I felt. "No overripe ackee in his stomach too, was there?" I quipped.

"No," said Jack, sounding puzzled.

Bud rolled his eyes at me. I flashed him a cheeky smile.

"I need coffee," I groaned.

"I made some," said John. All three men raised coffee mugs, and grinned. "There should be some in the pot, over in the big house."

"Let me know what your plans are." I headed to the kitchen, and coffee.

"Good morning," said Lottie brightly as I staggered into the dining room. "Tarone just phoned from Kingston. Amelia is doing much better. It's not a bleed on the brain as they'd feared, and she hasn't got a concussion either. Tarone hopes she'll be able to come home later today."

I was surprised. "That's quite a turnaround."

"You say that as though it's a bad thing," snapped Lottie. "I'd say it's rather good news for Tarone, *and Amelia.*"

I sighed. "Sorry, I didn't mean it to sound that way. It just seems odd that a hospital would call Tarone to rush there as though Amelia's at death's door, then we hear she's able to come home a day or so later. It doesn't say much for the diagnostic abilities of the doctors at the hospital, does it?"

"Sounds as though they were doing the best they could for their patient, to me," said Lottie, then she shoved a piece of mango into her mouth and chewed. I headed to the kitchen where I was tempted to drink straight from the coffee pot, but I poured myself a giant mug of the stuff and shuffled back to the dining table instead.

"Did someone get out of the wrong side of the bed this morning?" inquired Lottie, somewhat sarcastically.

"*Someone* wishes they were still in bed," I replied. "I'm taking this outside, I need caffeine and nicotine, then I'll be almost like a normal human being."

I could hear Lottie muttering something about "addicts" as I left, but chose to not bite off her head as a pre-coffee treat. All things considered, I thought I'd comported myself rather well.

I was allowed five minutes of peace and quiet before Lottie stood beside me. "Have you seen Sheila?"

I shook my head, and realized my headache wasn't going away without some help. Caffeine, nicotine, acetaminophen; the trinity worshipped by the hungover, and the plain dog-tired, as I was. "She'll be having a lie-in, if she's got any sense," I said.

Lottie was about to leave, when I had a silent word with myself, then added, "I need to find out all I can about Niall Jackson. Can you help at all?" I didn't have the patience to be sneaky, or even subtle, about my request.

She put her hands on her hips and scowled at me. "After what I've told you about him, you want me to talk about him even more?"

I was confused. "You've hardly talked to me about him at all."

Lottie's mouth dropped open. "I poured my heart out to you yesterday. Told you about how he took my virginity, made a fool of me, and broke my heart. Weren't you even listening?"

"That was Niall Jackson? You were talking about him? But you said the boy in question had parents who owned a resort in Montego Bay."

"I did. They did."

"*And* they owned the restaurant we went to the other evening near Negril?"

"Yes."

I took stock. "Sorry, I didn't realize. Umm…okay then, I'm also sorry I asked. But…"

I must have looked as pathetic and flummoxed as I felt, because Lottie flopped into a chair beside me. "Go on, what do you want to know?"

I smiled as brightly as I could manage. "Niall seems to have fingers in a lot of pies. Do you know which pies, exactly?"

"No, I haven't kept up with his many undertakings. I know he's a lawyer, a realtor, runs the restaurant, and possibly runs the resort the family owned. His father also had a number of boats that took tourists on trips around the island, that sort of thing. I have no idea if Niall does that too, but he was always on the water, I recall that much. Loved his boats, he did."

"What about photography?" I asked. "Was he ever into photography?"

Lottie gave me a look that was almost disdainful. "Do you mean dirty photos? That sort of thing?"

"No, I mean photography of anything…birds, views, buildings, just normal stuff."

"I don't recall him being particularly interested in photography, though he did have a camera, I recall, which I suppose not everyone did at the time. And a Walkman. And his was one of the first iPods I ever saw, too. He liked that sort of thing. Fiddly electronic gadgets. And, with his parents' money, he got anything and everything new he ever wanted. He also enjoyed pulling them apart to see how they worked, and liked to try to improve them."

"I wonder if you could talk to him – I have a few questions I'd like to get answers to; maybe we could also have another get together with Nina Mazzo." It was worth a try.

Lottie shook her head. "No, I won't approach Niall for you. But Nina would have us back at her place again if we asked. She seemed to be pleased to have all the inside info about Freddie. If you like, I could phone her and suggest we might have more to tell her. Do you think Sheila might want to come too? Or the men? Funnily enough, John was saying he wouldn't mind meeting Nina; he said she sounds as though she'd be highly entertaining."

I thought back to what Bud had told me about the man I knew as Luca Mazzo, and I wasn't at all surprised that John had said he'd like to meet the man's widow. I was a bit surprised Bud hadn't said the same thing, but then realized he'd been somewhat consumed with other leads since seeing the photo of Mazzo in the album, and might not have had the chance to mention any interest he had in Nina to Lottie, or even to me.

"I tell you what, we could invite her here. Do you think she'd come?" I spoke in as effervescent a manner as possible – believing I had to make some sort of effort.

"I don't know. I suppose all we can do is ask. Why don't I phone her now?" Lottie pulled her phone from her pocket and hit the screen.

I watched and waited. Eventually it was clear that Lottie was speaking to Nina herself, because Lottie spoke to her in fluent Italian. Luckily, I know enough of the language to get by, so I was able to listen to at least Lottie's side of the conversation, while feigning ignorance – which meant slapping an idiotic grin on my face when Lottie had finished.

"She's invited us there for lunch," announced Lottie, as she pushed the phone back into her pocket. "All six of us. It will be a party, she said. I suppose that suggests a certain type of dress code, which is nice; I brought several little frocks with me, so at least I'll have the chance to wear one of them. Pick up at twelve thirty for one. She'll send a car, to save any of us from having to drive – which suggests drinks, I think. I have to say, it sounds lovely."

Lottie all but skipped off shouting she was, "Going to tell the boys."

I called back that I'd tell Sheila. I hauled myself out of my chair and plodded around the pool to do just that, then changed my mind, and nipped into our bungalow to get some painkillers inside me, hoping to shake off my headache – though I knew the humidity meant it was going to be an uphill battle for two little tablets.

I finally stood outside the Whites' bungalow and steeled myself. I knocked. And waited. Nothing. I knocked again. "Sheila, it's only Cait."

*Only Cait? Only the woman she clearly cannot stand,* I thought.

The door opened, and a red-eyed Sheila greeted me with a hoarse voice. "Come in," she said, and stood back, opening the door a little wider.

The room was as dishevelled as she was; I'm not the tidiest person in the world, but it looked as though someone had thrown all the clothes she and Jack had brought with them onto the floor of the siting room. She kicked a few floral tops out of the way to allow the door to open fully. I walked in and waited; there wasn't an empty chair to sit on.

"I'm sorry…" I began, just as she said, "I wanted to apologize…"

We shared half-smiles.

"Sorry," I said.

"Sorry too," she replied.

She looked around the room. "I know you can't ignore the mess. I decided to pack to leave last night, then, when I realized how stupid I was being…well, you can see what I resorted to. Clothes don't make a noise when you throw them, and they don't smash. So that's a bonus, right?"

"I can give you a hand to pick everything up, if you like," I offered.

Sheila shook her head. "My penance, and I can sort everything as I do it. So, what did you want?"

"Nina Mazzo has invited all six of us for lunch. She's sending a car. Twelve thirty for one. Lottie believes it's an event that will require a frock of some sort, so you'll be fine, because you have several lovely ones, but I'll have to make do with something featuring trousers."

"Why don't you ever wear a dress?" asked Sheila.

I thought it an odd but harmless question and decided to give her an honest answer. "Because the tops of my thighs rub together when I walk, and I find it uncomfortable. Trousers solve that problem."

"Oh, I see."

"And I don't care for my calves, nor my knees."

"Right."

"And I'm too short for dresses that would fit my girth; and they never look right when they're shortened."

"Got it." Sheila was backing away from me, eyeing the mounds that surrounded her.

"See you in the big house ready to leave at twelve thirty, okay?" I said.

She nodded, and I walked out through the still-open door. She shut it behind me. I thought I heard her sigh.

I headed to the dining room to try to find something to eat. If we weren't going to be lunching until one, I'd never make it. I'd just found some not-quite-stale banana bread when I heard Bud calling my name.

"In the pantry," I called back. He appeared. "Still no brandy," I quipped, waving my free hand at the shelves.

"The cops are on their way here, to ask more questions. You clear about what you do and don't know?"

I paused, mid-chew, gave it some thought, nodded, and swallowed. "Are Jack and John briefing Sheila and Lottie?" Bud nodded. "And Lottie told you about our luncheon invitation to *Caro Mio*?"

"Yep. That'll be an excellent opportunity for us to try to dig up something about Nina's late husband, thanks for that, Cait. Lottie told us it was your idea. Good thinking."

I'll admit I glowed in the moment of flattery. "When will the police be here?"

"They've asked us to congregate in the lounge at ten. You okay with that?" I said I would be. "And, Cait...just follow my lead during questioning – I hope to draw some facts out of them rather than have to wait until there's an updated police report on Freddie, or something on Wilson Thomas beyond his autopsy."

I checked my watch. "Okay. I'll just run back to the bungalow to freshen up a bit."

"It's just some cops, and some questions," called Bud as I left, my banana bread in hand.

"I know," I replied, wondering if there was any way the word "just" should ever be applied to such a situation.

# Cops and Questions

When compared with their first visit, there was a totally different atmosphere in the lounge when Sergeant Swabey and Constable Lewis entered it on this occasion. It might have been because they were accompanied by an inspector from the criminal investigation bureau. He introduced himself in even more formal language than the lawyer Cooperman had used, and it was clear from the outset that Inspector Ewan Charles was a man with a mission.

He opened with, "Mr. Freddie Burkinshaw was a respected member of the community, with many years of charitable works behind him. He had enjoyed a full life, and was an elderly gentleman, but it is our duty to uncover the identity of the person who robbed him of however many years he still had ahead of him. We will act as speedily as possible, and I wish to assure you that our intent is to reach a favorable conclusion to this case."

I could feel myself twitching at the injustice that Wilson Thomas didn't even warrant a mention in this introduction, but gave the inspector the benefit of the doubt; maybe he was simply playing to his audience? How could he know we weren't just a group of wealthy tourists? We'd rented an entire estate for a month, after all, and he wasn't to know it had been done on the cheap because of some shady dealings between three governments' secret service agencies and a long-time informer – the man he was so keen to portray as a pillar of the local community.

"I understand you all gave statements to my uniformed colleagues when Mr. Burkinshaw was first found to be deceased. I have read those statements. It is now my sorrowful task to inform you that we no longer believe that Mr. Burkinshaw died by his own hand, but, rather, that he was killed by a person, or persons, unknown. Our investigation must, therefore, be reinvigorated with this fact in mind."

"He didn't shoot himself, inspector?" asked Bud. I was impressed by how innocent he made his question sound.

"We suspect that might not be the case, sir," replied the inspector.

"Should we be concerned for our safety?" asked Jack, looking almost paternalistically protective as he placed his hand on Sheila's shoulder.

"It is unlikely, sir, though, of course, one can never be too careful. As I am sure you are aware, this beautiful island of ours has its burden to bear. Some people are determined to not live by the rule of law, and our officers are constantly fighting the good fight to deter those who would endanger life and property on the island. We also seek to apprehend those who have already taken the wrong path. It is our duty, and our pleasure, to protect those who live here, as well as those who visit."

I felt we were in for the long-haul with this Inspector Charles. He was clearly a practiced professional communicator; I wondered if he was also an accomplished detective, or whether he'd been given this case purely because of the public relations angles. Personally, I was happy for him to be able to detect anything except that there was a lot of underhandedness going on right in front of him, courtesy of the three men he was addressing.

Bud raised his hand, like a schoolboy. "Excuse me, inspector. We've heard some rather worrying rumors that Freddie Burkinshaw's death is linked to another killing – that of a man who lived on the beach not far from here. Can you confirm that?"

Inspector Ewan Charles looked shocked, but before he could reply, another hand shot up.

"Yes," said Jack, "we also heard it was the same gun that shot each of them. Is there someone running about the island killing old men? If so, I think we should be told, because both murders were committed very close by, and we're none of us spring chickens anymore."

The inspector glared at Swabey and Lewis.

John spoke as he waggled a hand in the general direction of the officers. "Should we be hiring some security guards to make sure we're safe in our beds at night? We all knew that Jamaica has one of the highest murder rates per capita in the world before we chose it for our hols, but we really thought we'd be safe, here." John had added a cut-glass edge to his accent.

Lottie seemed keen to join in, even as the inspector opened his mouth to reply. "I'm so terribly frightened now, inspector," she said breathlessly. "Should we all be getting guns for ourselves? I realize we Brits aren't used to such things, but I'm sure one could cope in a pinch. I've shot a little with Daddy, at home."

The inspector was beginning to sweat.

"Don't worry, Lottie," said Sheila, "I'm used to handling firearms. I can shoot a snake out of a tree at a hundred paces, if I need to."

The image was disturbing, and I couldn't fathom why Sheila might ever need to do such a thing back home, in British Columbia.

The inspector was about to raise his hands in defeat when I finally chipped in with: "If Freddie Burkinshaw and Wilson Thomas were both killed, within a day of each other, within a mile of here, and with the same gun, I think you should be entirely open with us about all the findings you have to date, or else we might find it necessary to represent our concerns to the Canadian and British embassies."

The man snapped. Waving his hands about, and almost panting, Inspector Ewan Charles, of the Jamaican criminal investigation bureau, proved to be a bit of a wimp. "Please, stop, all of you," he all-but shouted. His voice was high, almost a strangled cry. Each of us had stood as we'd asked our questions, so he patted the air in front of himself to suggest we should all take our seats again. We did.

After gathering himself for a moment he said, "I understand your concerns, of course I do. But I am at the very beginning of my investigation. Still at the stage of gathering basic information – hence my presence here. Does anyone have anything they want to add to their original statement pertaining to the death of Mr. Burkinshaw?"

We all shook our heads and looked as stupid as possible.

"Also, you all told Constable Lewis," he nodded toward her, "at the time that none of you saw anyone or anything out of the ordinary on the night of the second shooting? Is that correct?"

More heads shaking, and nodding.

"Was it the same gun, inspector, that killed both men? Was neither man shot with the gun we saw beside Freddie's body?" asked Bud.

"You are correct on both counts, sir, but you have no need to worry, I assure you. We do not believe these were random killings." Charles smiled in an attempt to convey reassurance.

"You think they're connected? How? In what way? Did the men know each other?" I asked.

Charles half-nodded his head. "Mr. Thomas used to live here, at the estate. He was employed by Mr. Burkinshaw."

"I told you we were in the danger zone," exclaimed Lottie, sounding horrified." She flung herself at John, who coped with her lunging pretty well.

"No, that is not what I said," replied the exasperated officer. "This estate is not the epicenter of a crime spree, it's just where two men who are now deceased once happened to live at the same time."

"But what if the killer comes back here?" I cried.

I could imagine the inspector being delighted by the idea, especially if it were to shut us up once and for all. He smiled and said, "Not going to happen. No need to worry at all. You're telling me that nothing has given you concern since the time of the second killing, on or about the estate, so I have no worries about your safety. You will need no guns. No guards."

"We saw that your people were over at the tower yesterday," said Bud. "Are they there again now? Will they be there forever? It's a part of the estate some of us have hardly been able to enjoy at all."

Bud sounded like exactly the sort of unfeeling twit we both hate. The look on the inspector's face suggested he was stifling his annoyance – as best he could.

"It is most unfortunate that your time with us in Jamaica has been impacted by this tragedy, but we do need to keep the tower closed to the public for some time."

"But we're not the public, old chap," said John, "we're guests here. That's what Freddie said, wasn't it, Lottie old bean? Treat the place as your own, he said. But we can't, can we? Not with your lot galloping about all over the place. Some of us haven't had a chance to poke our noses into the tower yet – and that was where Freddie said he kept all his historically interesting knick-knacks."

I half suspected John had considered closing his little speech with "Pip, pip," just for good measure.

Inspector Charles turned to Sergeant Swabey and they exchanged a few whispered phrases. Swabey then spoke to Lewis, who left us, and bustled off toward the tower.

"I'm just about to ascertain when we'll be able to release the tower from its designation as a crime scene," said Charles.

"They say you got a phone call alerting you to the presence of a body on the beach," said Jack. "Who phoned it in? Who found the body?"

The inspector looked a little fazed. "Er…it was an anonymous call," he said, sounding flustered.

"It couldn't have been the killer," I shouted, making everyone jump. "Imagine a killer telling the police they'd shot someone. Why on earth would they do that? Wouldn't they want the body to remain undiscovered, allowing for the passage of time to erase any forensic evidence? That's what I'd do. If I'd shot someone. Not that I would, of course. But you must know who phoned you – can't you trace the phone they used?" I tried to sound as annoyingly batty as possible.

Charles settled his shoulders. "We have traced the call. It came from a pay-as-you-go telephone. No, we do not know who it was who reported the body. But, as you know, figures were seen departing the crime scene. They were pursued as far as this estate. Maybe one of you knows more than you're saying? Indeed, I have to tell you that your presence here gives me cause for concern, though maybe not it the way you might imagine."

It was interesting to note that Charles was able to withstand our irritating onslaught and still make his key point – that we were six strangers on the island, and two deaths had occurred within a mile of our location, since our arrival.

Sheila went for it. She stood, as best she could, and flung her arms about. "Surely you don't suspect any of us, Inspector

Charles? We are simply here to enjoy a vacation." She managed to look deeply wounded at the thought.

Charles set his jaw; I could see the muscles twitching. "We are facing an exceedingly unusual set of circumstances," he said, then he listened as the returning Constable Lewis whispered in his ear. He nodded. "You'll be able to enjoy as much access as you wish to the tower after approximately four this afternoon," he said. "By sunset, at the latest, we'll have removed any items we want to examine further."

"Oh, goodie," said Lottie, clapping her hands. "I get to see Freddie's famous crystal skull, at last. You're not taking that away with you, are you, inspector?" She pouted. Like a sweet little girl. She was good at this.

Charles smiled, more genuinely this time. "Indeed not. It can stay exactly where it is. Though I would mention that object has a certain...reputation, miss, so I wouldn't go handling it too much."

"Do you mean the curse of the crystal skull?" said Lottie, sounding gleefully ghoulish.

"There are many things we do not understand," said Charles. "Mr. Burkinshaw was a most generous supporter of many charities on this island, so it seems he was immune to the power of the skull, but it has been said it can make a man focus on the temptations of Mammon, rather than on the gifts of God."

"Praise the Lord," said Constable Lewis. Sergeant Swabey looked confused.

Charles smiled at the constable, returned his gaze to us, and said, "I'm a lay preacher at my church; Constable Lewis is one of our congregants." They shared a smile. Swabey looked irked.

"If there's nothing else, then, inspector, we have a lunch date at the *Caro Mio* estate, so we could all do with having a little time to prepare," said John.

The inspector looked impressed. "Ah, the wonderful Signora Mazzo has invited you? You're honoured. She tends to not mix with society any longer. She's one of our long-term residents, you know. Starred in films, back when they were good."

"We had drinks with her," gushed Lottie, "and now we're going back for lunch. Such a wonderful house, it's like a little palace."

"Indeed, and she was fortunate to not lose it in the last big earthquake. When the land cracked along more or less the line between these two properties, her home could have fared poorly – as could the Captain's Lookout tower. But both were spared. Thanks be to God."

"Thanks be," echoed the constable.

"Cheerio, then," said John, standing.

Fortunately the officers all left, and we were able to share sighs of relief and all scuttle back to our bungalows for a quick wash and brush up, having managed to obtain the information that Freddie and Wilson were, indeed, shot with the same gun – obviously not the one found beside Freddie's body – and that someone had been possessed of enough foresight to report Wilson's killing from an unregistered phone.

## Bubbles and a Breakthrough

The "car" that was sent for us wasn't a stretch limo, but it was a stretch Jeep, and a luxuriously appointed one, at that. The white leather interior belied the theoretical ruggedness of the exterior design, and told me it was the choice of a woman who wanted to travel in style, but whose every journey began with a tortuous drive over a dismal track, which I could tell – as we traversed it – had been washed out again in the recent downpours. I couldn't imagine what sort of mess it must be in by the end of the rainy season.

We all grabbed whatever we could to try to stop bouncing around in the vehicle, and I was glad I wasn't wearing a skirt after all, because both Lottie – in pale coral linen, and Sheila – in orange floral on white, managed to show a fair bit of thigh as they slithered about on their seats. I realized, too late, that Bud and I looked as though we'd dressed to match each other; he was wearing his smartest cream, lightweight chambray pants, topped with a pale turquoise linen shirt, and I was in a bouncy, cream two-piece with a turquoise over-thingy. Still, at least we both looked clean and fresh, which was good.

The men were all as horrified as we'd been when we'd first encountered what was something more akin to a dried-out riverbed than a road. By the time they got to enjoy the bougainvillea-lined vista, then the vision of the fabulous sea beyond the gleaming white stucco of *Caro Mio*, they were convinced none of we three women had been lying about the road; it really was that bad.

Stretching of necks and backs accomplished, we all followed Nina's impeccably dressed butler, Arnold, as he led us into the palatial sitting room. There was our hostess, waiting for us, sitting very upright on a couch, surrounded by pillows. She was wearing an emerald green, chiffon dress and what I suspected was a real emerald necklace; it had stones the size of loonies and toonies, surrounded by diamonds. She didn't rise to greet us, but held up her hand, which John leaned down to kiss; Jack and Bud seemed to feel they had to follow suit. Nina looked most gratified and nodded her head to indicate we should sit. I imagined she saw herself as a queen and we her courtiers. It felt weird, but unusual enough to be quite fun.

"You will all take champagne?" She smiled at the men, and almost acknowledged we women. Six heads nodded, and Arnold magically appeared with a tray of fine crystal flutes. The woman we'd seen on our previous visit carried in an ice bucket that she placed on one of the many marble-topped tables, then she left.

Once we all had a glass of bubbles, Nina raised hers and said, "A toast; to the making of new friends, and the death of old enemies."

We all chose to focus on the "new friends" part of the toast, and I was glad to bury my face in my glass for a slightly awkward moment. I couldn't help but notice that Nina drained hers, gave a satisfied sigh, then nodded at Arnold, who immediately replaced the empty bottle with a full one, which he opened. Seeing him recharge Nina's glass meant none of us felt embarrassed to also drink our glasses dry and accept another. I wondered just how boozy lunch was going to be, and was grateful my headache had gone before I started to drink on an essentially empty stomach. However, I suspected that if Bud and the boys were going to go scrabbling along tunnels later in the day, when the police had abandoned the tower, they'd have to come up with some way to avoid getting tipsy.

Before we'd left the Captain's Lookout estate, Bud and I had agreed on a plan of action for our lunch date: I was to be on full alert in terms of reading everyone in the room, and he was going to do his best to find out all he could about Luca Mazzo, thereby hopefully making some headway regarding the papers he was hunting down. Jack and John would be following his lead in that matter, but we both agreed I'd be essentially on my own in terms of digging about for anything that might lead to an understanding about who'd killed Freddie and Wilson.

However, it seemed Lottie had her own agenda, and she managed to hijack the conversation before anyone else had a chance to get a word in edgeways.

"You have such stunning taste in décor, Nina," she began. "I have to admit I came to the island somewhat interested in finding out all I could about pirate treasure, but it seems you didn't hang about to find any treasure, you went out and acquired your own. Some of these pieces must have wonderful tales attached to them. Those illuminated song sheets, for example. They're beautiful. Must be old. What, thirteenth- or fourteenth-century Italian? Stunning."

Nina looked proud and wriggled a little in her sumptuous seat. "They are, indeed, exquisite. Luca knew of my love of old things and spared no expense to please me, but he preferred big, solid things. I prefer more delicacy. These were a birthday gift, to myself."

As I took in the items displayed around the room I could see there was a definite difference in taste on display; I mentally logged the larger, more grandiose artefacts as likely to have been selected by Luca, whereas there was no shortage of more decorative and brilliantly hued objects I assumed had been chosen by Nina.

"That's an ancient Roman vase, isn't it?" Lottie stood. "May I?" Nina nodded and Lottie walked across the room to the large round marble table where the vase stood. She skirted the table, sighing. "So beautifully decorated. Apulian red-figure pottery – probably from about four hundred BCE, am I right?"

Nina shook her head. "Of this I am not so certain. That was Luca's choice. It does not appeal to me. Too heavy. Lumpen. I prefer delicate things."

Lottie rejoined us, and I allowed myself to take my eyes off Nina for a moment to scan the lounge again. I totted up the sort of expenditure represented by just this one room. It ran to millions of dollars. Luca Mazzo – or whatever his name really was – must have been an extremely wealthy man to have built the place from the ground up, and then filled it with such fine artefacts. And they weren't just fine artefacts, they were rare. Most of them should have been in a museum, not sitting in niches and on tables to possibly catch the eye of an ageing Italian starlet when she flitted through on her way from the pool. I couldn't help but wonder what her insurance premiums must cost.

Possibly because he saw I was distracted, Bud picked up the conversation. "Your late husband must have been an extraordinary man, Nina. Is that a photograph of your wedding?" It was his turn to stand and he picked up a silver-framed photograph that sat atop a Steinway grand piano; at Nina's bidding he brought it across the room to her.

She took it from him, and gazed at it with a sad smile. "Such a man. Yes, my Luca." She returned the photo to Bud, who showed it to John and Jack. "He was older than me, of course, but good for me. I never wanted for anything with him. I was always his first thought. My life ended when he died."

*Posh mausoleum*, I thought.

We all nodded sympathetically. "How did you meet?" asked Bud, using his most charming tone.

Nina replied, "You do not want to hear this story." Her sparkling eyes and coquettish smile screamed that she was desperate to tell it.

We all encouraged her, and her body language told me she was loving every moment of attention. Arnold refilled her glass, and moved among us, topping up ours as he passed. Nina settled herself and launched into what I expected would be a much-told tale.

"It was 1956, and I was sixteen, just a girl, really. I was walking along the road from the village to my home when a large car stopped and a man in a silk suit got out. He asked for directions, then asked my name. He then enquired where I was going, and invited me to ride to my house in his car. I accepted." She paused and cocked her head. "I was a simple village girl, you see, I did not know that I shouldn't get into a car with a man in a silk suit. This was not something my parents had ever told me to not do." She smiled impishly.

We all laughed politely. I had a feeling this was an even more well-worn account than I'd initially imagined.

She continued, "The man spoke with my parents, and it was agreed that I was to travel to Roma with him to work in the movies. He knew everyone, he said, and I would become a great star." She shrugged. "This is not how things went, of course. My parents and I were naïve. I had to endure much when I arrived in Roma. But that is not of any importance. What is important is that I managed, by doing what I had to do, to get myself into movies, in small parts. I knew that once I could show people how I looked on screen that they would want to put me there more and more. And so it went. I worked a good deal, and I became popular at parties, too, because all of us who worked at the Cinecittà Studios lived this way – work and fun. We were young, we were beautiful; it was before Fellini made *La Dolce Vita* by a few years, but his movie was certainly inspired by the lives we were all leading at that time. It captured the spirit of those days very well. It was at one of the parties we girls would be invited to attend that I met Luca. He stood away from the crowd, and I found that interesting. He found me interesting too. We clicked. It was love! We began to see each other from then on – just each other, no other people – and he spoiled me with so many wonderful gifts. When he asked me to marry him a few months later I agreed, and I also agreed that I would give up my acting career to be his wife. We would build a home together, and live happily with many, many children. But the children never arrived, so we decided to enjoy a different type of life. As you see, we did just that."

We all acknowledged how wonderful the story was, and how marvellous it must be to experience love at first sight.

"Why here?" asked Jack. "I mean, of course, Jamaica's a beautiful place, but how did you come to choose this island, and this spot?"

Nina was in her element. "We rented apartments in Rome, then Paris, then Zurich. We moved about, always with Luca working, working. He traded goods everywhere, and constantly flew all over the world. But I was bored; I knew we had enough money for him to not work as much, but I did not know how to get him away from all his business contacts. Then we came here to stay with some people Luca had met on one of his many trips to Washington, in America. They had built a new house just along the coast, on the hillside. They liked the view, and the winds, and did not care for the beach, you see. I adore the beach, and the sea, and quickly discovered I did not care for them, but they had wonderful neighbors, and the parties were very enjoyable. There was a great deal of freedom here, more than in Europe. People could be themselves – their *true* selves – in Jamaica, so they were happier all the time. I convinced Luca we should buy land and build our home here. This parcel became available, and we began our Great Project. I still love this place, though I am happier when I have guests than when I am alone."

"It's a wonderful house, sure enough," said Sheila. "You should see the pool outside, Jack. I've never seen anything like it."

"I bet the inside's pretty special too," said Jack. "I guess there's no chance of a sort of a tour, is there? I hope it's not impolite to ask, but we live in a little old house on a hillside in Canada – this isn't the sort of thing we get to see very often." He played the country hick quite convincingly.

Nina glowed. "It would be my pleasure. Arnold." Arnold raced to her side and offered his arm. It was a duty he performed with grace, and a warm smile. She took it and rose from the sofa.

Her green chiffon gown floated around her tiny body, and it was only once she stood that I realized she was wearing one of those outfits you see in 1960s films – where there's a pair of pants beneath a skirt that's open at the front. I've always loved those things, though I know I could never wear one myself. I wondered if it had been made for her back then, and that she'd kept it. I had no way of knowing, but I could tell the chiffon was silk, and that the outfit must have cost a great deal of money whenever it had been made. The satin of her shoes matched the gown perfectly. I sighed inwardly.

Nina led us to what I thought would be an anteroom to the main salon, but it turned out to be a library, of gigantic proportions. "This is where the men would retire with their brandy and cigars," said Nina airily. "Talked a lot of nonsense in here, most of the time. We girls would have to come in to break up the conversation if they became too boring."

"There are a lot of old-looking documents in here," said Bud, pointing to a glass-fronted cabinet, filled with scrolls and bundles of papers. "Look, Cait, this is the sort of stuff you love, isn't it?"

I tried to hide my surprise and gushed, "Oh yes, I do. Was Luca a collector, Nina?"

She shrugged. "Not so much. He preferred things that looked interesting, rather than things that were interesting. He did not read many books." She waved an arm at the hundreds that lined the room. "I do not know what most of these books are about. Or where they came from. They just arrived, in boxes, and the shelves were filled."

"Could I have a look at some of these?" I asked, still trying to be bubbly. "That scroll there, with the blue ribbon, looks especially enticing."

Nina appeared to be surprised by my enthusiasm, but opened the cabinet door and handed me the scroll nonetheless. "Be my guest," she said. "There are many tables where you can open this to see what it contains. I have no idea."

I examined the blue ribbon as I untied it. It really did seem to be the same as that which I'd seen on Freddie's desk when I'd peered through the keyhole. The scroll comprised several sheets, all of which were protecting one aged map of Jamaica. The paper was extremely old; the lettering wasn't modern script, but the words were nonetheless legible. The map was dated 1690; I could make out the Laughlands River and the Cistern River. I pointed out an area to Bud. "There's a place just there now called Llandovery, named after the original town in Wales. Famous for rum at one time, but now derelict." I scanned the map more closely. "Look, there's the Captain's

Lookout tower, clearly marked. This map shows the location of all Henry Morgan's lands on this part of the island. See?"

Nina came closer. "This is our home – at least, it is where our home is now." She smiled. "I did not know I had this map, and I did not know there had been a building here before our home."

We all huddled closer.

"Look Bud," I said, "you can make out just how much land fell into the sea in the 1692 earthquake. And Nina's right, there was something built generally where this house now stands, and it has a Welsh name. *Ty Gwerthfawr*. If that's what it says – and I admit the writing's a bit small and squiggly – that would mean Precious House."

"Maybe that's where Henry Morgan's lover lived then, not at the tower at all. Maybe the tower was just for him to sit in, and look at the sea, and this was where his precious lover lived," said Bud. "Look, there's even a dotted line connecting the two – maybe a path the lovers used for their daily trysts?"

"No, Morgan had a proper house out on his plantation lands," said Lottie. "That's where he lived, there, not here. The tower was just his hidey-hole by the sea." She sounded unreasonably annoyed.

"I think it's a lovely map," said Nina. "It should be on display, how much fun that would be. I shall have it framed."

"Where is everybody? Nina, Nina my darling, we got it for less than ten million. Break open the bubbly, we did it!"

We all turned as Niall Jackson entered the room.

# An Illuminating Luncheon

"Luncheon is served," announced Arnold, entering the room silently behind Niall Jackson, who almost jumped out of his skin when the butler spoke.

Niall cleared his throat, too dramatically. "It seems I'm just in time. Room for one more, Nina?"

Nina smiled and tottered over to Niall; he bent down to allow her to kiss him on the check. I realized I didn't have to wonder any longer about why such an elderly woman was still indulging in Botox and the odd bit of plumping. To be fair, Niall wasn't a bad-looking bloke – in fact, he was a startling-looking man. He had blue eyes and red hair, a million freckles were visible though his tan, and he was lanky, rather than overly tall; a bit weedy looking for a man in his late thirties. But the age difference between him and Nina was stark; despite her fabulous wardrobe, jewels, and the efforts of possibly several beauticians, Nina looked her age – well, maybe she looked ten years younger, but there comes a point where that hardly matters.

"Has my clever boy managed to strike a deal?" Nina gushed.

Niall shifted from one foot to another. "Maybe this isn't the right place, Nina?"

"Nonsense," replied the octogenarian, "these are the lovely people I was telling you about, the ones who rented Freddie's bungalows for a month. They won't care, but they can help us celebrate. So, what did they agree to?"

A less enthusiastic Niall said, "Nine and a half million. Immediate possession. I have the papers for you to see. I signed them on your behalf, as you agreed I should. But you'll have to sign the final transfer yourself."

"Isn't he marvellous," said Nina, beaming. "I have just bought the Captain's Lookout estate. It's so strange that we were looking at that map when Niall arrived. It is as though I will be putting back together what was taken apart. The land will all be mine, now, as it was Henry Morgan's."

"Except the land immediately around the tower, Nina," said Niall.

"Ah, the tower. It does not matter. At least Freddie is no longer singing from it every day – ha! Singing? This is not the correct word at all. Howling. This is more accurate. I do not miss this at all."

"What will you do with it all?" asked Bud.

Nina looked surprised. "Do with it? Nothing. I just have it, this is enough. I do not want anyone else to do anything with it, this is why I want it. Now I have it, I can enjoy my home without anyone else spoiling it. Freddie's wicked plans will not happen, I can remain here in peace, until I die."

"Was Freddie planning to develop his estate?" asked John, sounding as innocent as a baby. "He didn't mention anything to us. We said we might all come back again next year, make this a sort of annual jaunt. I even discussed dates with him, the evening he died." He lied quite convincingly.

Nina waved her hand as if swatting a fly. "You would never have had the chance to stay at that estate again, unless you wanted to be overrun by people. Freddie had decided. And he had powerful contacts everywhere on this island. They might stop other people from doing what they want – like poor Niall, who wants very much to make changes at his resort in Montego Bay – but no one would have stopped Freddie. I had nightmares about what might rise up beside me. All those people? All that noise? Horrific." She waved her hand in front of her face as if brushing aside the vision. "Now, luncheon. We must celebrate. Come."

We walked across the great room, and into the magnificent dining room that was the mirror image of the library. The gleaming mahogany table was set with silver and crystal, and three servers, all in dove gray dresses, stood at attention alongside Arnold. Lottie, Sheila, and I were helped into our seats by a server each, with Arnold attending to Nina. He fussed over her, shifting her seat an inch at a time, until she was perfectly positioned. It was all incredibly swish, and I had no doubt the food would be phenomenal. However, the profusion of glasses on the table did give me pause – I suspected the champagne we'd already drunk was just the start of what could be a problematically boozy meal.

The first course was served, and more champagne was poured. I looked sadly at the light, bright salad in front of me, dotted with slivers of grapefruit and pomegranate seeds – neither of which I care for; I pretended to eat it, like the polite guest I was. As I pushed food around in the tantalizingly speckled dressing, I reckoned that if the map I'd just examined in Nina's library had been on Freddie's desk when he died, somebody had really had a very bright idea to hide it in plain sight. That person must have had access to Freddie's tower, and Nina's home, aa well as a knowledge of Nina's lack of interest in papers, to allow them to come up with the idea.

Niall Jackson was the obvious candidate, and I made it my mission to study both Nina and Niall throughout lunch. Nina was the perfect hostess, and Niall and she seemed comfortable together, even when Bud returned to his mission, aided by his tag-team of Jack and John, of trying to find out more about Nina's late husband.

"You said you met Luca in Rome, and it all sounds so romantic, Nina. You were in the movies at the time, and you said Luca traded things? Was that what he did? He was...what? Into import and export?" Bud managed to sound both interested and befuddled.

Nina was doing the same as me, moving bits of food around her plate, but eating almost nothing. At Bud's question, she cocked her head, continued to play with her food, but gave her attention to him. "I shall be honest, Luca's business never interested me. He did not speak of it. I was his escape from business. But I know he was well respected, because wherever we lived we always socialized with good people. People with taste and refinement. People who knew how to enjoy life."

"Then you chose the right island to settle on," I said, keen to support my husband. "Jamaica's always been a place of trade; sometimes it's been questionable trade, sometimes downright illegal trade, but it's always been a busy port, used by nations and peoples from around the world. Luca must have felt at home here, with so many people trading so many things. It must have been good for him to be able to mix with people who understood that way of life."

"We did not mix very much with business people here; they came to dine, of course, but they were not fun. I preferred the actors and actresses who visited. They were *great* fun. We tried to mix the two groups sometimes, but the business people seemed to be so easily shocked. I don't know why. A great many of them made a show of attending church, maybe that was why they were so straight-laced. But the others? We had some wonderful times. People would stay at our guest houses, and we'd swim under the moonlight. I was beautiful then, and young. Now? I keep my old body covered. I am not beautiful anymore."

She was fishing for a compliment or two, and got plenty. Niall was most effusive, to the point of becoming a leering mess. It wasn't a pretty sight, but Nina lapped it up.

Jack was next up to bat for the team, it seemed. "Did Luca manage to have any get-togethers with old war buddies during his time here? I know so many people of my father's generation – which your husband must have been, not you, of course, Nina – they all liked to meet up and discuss the old days. My father gained a great deal of comfort from it. I can only imagine the Italian war experience must have been difficult."

Nina dramatically clutched at her breast, "But yes, it was a terrible time. I was very young when the war ended, of course, but even afterwards life was difficult in Italy. Outside the cities maybe we had a better recovery, because we could grow our own food, raise our own animals. Rural life always returns to normal more quickly after a war, it seems. But Luca was in the city. It was hard for him. He spoke of it rarely. I never met anyone he served with. Of course, the Italians had to do some terrible things in those dark days. I think he felt happier to not remember such times."

"Did you spend a lot of time with Freddie when you first moved here?" Obviously, John had decided to adopt a different approach.

"We did." Nina's tone was brittle. "We thought he was good company. A generous man. But it seems we did not know him properly at that time; he managed to hide his true nature from us quite successfully."

Nina scanned the table and nodded at Arnold. The servers cleared our plates and filled our water glasses. Then they presented us with small plates of ceviche, which glistened in the sunlight filtering through the voile-covered windows. The slivers of white fish on the plate were translucent, drenched in zesty lime juice, and lightly dusted with black pepper. There wasn't much of it, but it was delicious; succulent, and truly mouth-watering.

As I ate, I watched Niall like a hawk; he seemed to be preoccupied, which didn't surprise me. I needed to come up with some way to get him to talk, but Lottie beat me to it.

"You're still getting involved with other people's business, then Niall," she said. "Still got the restaurant, what about the resort, and the boats? Still got them?"

Nina replied faster than Niall could. "He's such a good sailor. So confident on the water. I do not think they have invented the vessel he couldn't sail. It was a great shame for me that Luca was never interested in boats. I should have enjoyed a yacht. Niall keeps a boat here, don't you? A special little one I gave him as a gift." Niall nodded. "He takes me out in it sometimes. I enjoy seeing my home from the sea. It is very beautiful from the sea." I imagined it would look stunning. Nina giggled. "Sometimes we would sail past Freddie's tower at sunset, when he was screaming out his song about his queen. He hated it, because we would make the engines roar, wouldn't we, Niall?"

Niall nodded. "He did. And, yes, I still run the resort, and the boat business, much as Dad did." He sounded glum.

"And how *is* business?" asked Lottie.

"Tourism's down, generally, but we're doing okay. Good reputation, regular guests, that sort of thing." He talked as he chewed. Not a pleasant sight.

"Nina mentioned you'd like to develop the old place," continued Lottie. "That would cost a pretty penny, so your lawyering and real estate business must be flourishing."

"Niall is an excellent lawyer, and realtor," said Nina. "Look at what he has achieved for me. Arnold, more champagne." Arnold approached, wearing a surprisingly sour expression.

"It's all going well, thank you for asking, Lottie." Niall was certainly subdued in Lottie's company, so much so that I noticed Nina giving him a quizzical look. I spotted a flash of…jealousy? Yes, that was it. So, Lottie's focus on her man was starting to irritate Nina as much as it had annoyed me when Lottie had been batting her eyelids at Bud. I wondered if Nina knew about the history between Lottie and Niall. I suspected not, because she wasn't the sort of woman who would have let it pass without comment.

"This deal for Nina must be good for you too," said Lottie. "You're bound to be making almost a million dollars from it yourself. Or did Niall cut you a deal on the legal fees, Nina? Payment in kind maybe?"

I was taken aback by the sharpness of Lottie's comments. The collective intake of breath around the table told me I wasn't alone. I watched Nina and Niall. Nina's eyes sparkled, her lips pressed into a thin line. Niall slumped.

Lottie drained her glass. "Niall was very good at letting the girls pay for things in kind, back in the old days. Used to swap ganja for all sorts of favors at school, didn't you Niall?"

*This could get messy*, I thought to myself.

Bud reached over and pressed his hand onto my leg. I swear he'd have whispered, "Down, girl," if he could have got away with it.

Nina looked surprised. "You and Niall were in school together?"

"We were a few years apart," said Niall. His voice quivered.

"Ah, but so much closer than that in other ways, right, Niall?" Lottie's voice dripped with sarcasm. "Did he ever tell you just how close we got, Nina? No? That's a surprise, because he couldn't wait to tell everyone at school about it. It must have made you feel so special, Niall, joking with your chums about my inexperience. Not much fun for me, of course. Indeed, it was why I became rather depressed and had to leave. First school, then the island. So, when Mummy needed me most, I wasn't of any use to her; I was too wrapped up in my own dismal little world, full of therapists, and pills. And all because I agreed to Niall's seemingly 'good deal'. I do hope he hasn't done the same sort of thing to you, Nina."

Nina thrust her chin in Arnold's general direction, who marched across the room. He pulled back her chair, and she rose. "Call for the transport, Arnold. My guests are leaving." She turned and walked out of the dining room – head held high, heels clicking on the marble floor, chiffon skirt swirling.

Niall pushed back his chair, threw down his napkin, stood, and drained his glass. "You always were a stuck-up little bitch, Charlotte," he snarled. "And I know you think you've messed up things for me here, but you haven't. You'll run back to Daddy any day now, like you always used to, but you can't get him to do your dirty work anymore." His Jamaican accent strengthened as he grew redder in the face. "This is the grown-up world, not school. And if you think a few poisonous words are going to spoil things for me with Nina, you're very much mistaken. She and I understand the world as it really is. You? You're still in the playground." He stomped out of the room, leaving us all stunned, and the serving staff studying their toes.

Arnold reappeared. "Your transport is ready. Allow me to escort you off the premises." His tone was anything but warm.

We could do nothing but accept the help offered to the ladies to leave their seats, and walk in a straggling line through the great room toward the entrance hall. I didn't think we'd ever be seeing it again.

# Tension and Talk

We rode back to the estate in silence, except for the odd "Ow" as we bumped along. As I pulled on my swimming two-piece back at our bungalow I called to Bud, "I'm having a dip in the pool. Back in half an hour." I had to move my body about a bit, or I felt I might explode; I'm not good with tension.

I relished being alone in the cool water, and sadly realized I wouldn't have many more chances to enjoy the sensation. It had been okay having Jack and Sheila around for a week – not that we'd been joined at the hip, because they'd wanted to explore the island without us. Indeed, Sheila had spent hours being entertained by the macho types at Ocho Rios who were convinced they'd easily master the water jet packs that sent them shooting up from the sea, only to come crashing down – unceremoniously – back into it. When she told us about that at dinner one night she'd laughed so much she'd given herself hiccups.

But my favorite memories of our visit were of the times when it was just me and Bud, the pool, the sun, a couple of good books, and a cold beer when we wanted it. The simple pleasures in life. In a few days we'd be back at home, coping with all the reality we could handle, so I allowed my mind to wander as I made cycling motions underwater while holding onto edge of the pool. It was almost exercise. Maybe I could work out what had happened to Freddie just by waggling my legs about?

"Penny for them."

I squinted, and saw John's silhouette against the achingly blue sky. He lowered himself into the water beside me.

"Honestly, nothing, at that moment," I lied. "How are you doing?" *You're opening a can of extremely wriggly worms, Cait,* I told myself.

"I made a mistake bringing Lottie with me," he said bluntly. "A dreadful mistake. I don't know how I allowed her to talk me into doing it, in all honesty."

"Maybe you weren't making decisions all that rationally."

"Wrong part of me doing the thinking, more like."

"It happens. Is it over now?" I knew there was no point beating about the bush with John, and after all he'd done for me and Bud, I owed him at least some directness and honesty.

He dunked himself under the water; when he emerged, he shook his head like Marty does – I missed Marty, for a longing moment – then he let out a hollow chuckle. "You could say that. She's off to a hotel for the next couple of nights. Packing now. I have to stay here, of course. But I can't tell her why I'm not doing the gentlemanly thing and allowing her to stay with all of you. Not that she wants to. I don't think she wants to face any of us, ever again. Not difficult when it comes to the four of you, who live in Canada, but she and I might find it a challenge to not trip over each other within our circles in London."

"Sorry, John," was all I thought it wise to say.

"It's alright," he replied heavily. He leaned closer to me. "I just hope she hasn't endangered the mission."

"I don't see how her attempt to get her revenge on Niall can have done that," I replied. "It might have been a somewhat fruitless exercise, but I reckon she's been storing up that vitriol for years. It sounds like Niall wounded her much more deeply than I'd imagined."

"I was shocked, to be honest," said John. "I hadn't noticed anything in her character that would suggest she could hold such a grudge. She's only ever appeared to be a surprisingly well-balanced woman, considering her family background. Though it turns out there's quite a lot about her I didn't know. Like her long-term connection with this place, for starters. I mean, what are the odds of that?"

I struggled with how to respond, then decided to speak my mind. "Really John, for someone in your line of work I find it remarkable that you're as surprised as you are. Having discovered what we have about Lottie over the past few days, don't you think it's quite likely she targeted you, in order to wangle a way to be exactly where we are now? For example, how far in advance of this mission did you know about it? If you became involved with Lottie a couple of months ago, could the start of your relationship have somehow been connected to this very mission? Bud and I knew we were coming here three weeks before we arrived, and we've been here almost a month…a window of seven weeks, at least. Would her father, Tarquin, have known about this? Could he have said something to her? Could Roger Rustingham have told Tarquin about Freddie? When did you realize Freddie was involved? Let's be honest, Lottie had a couple of very good reasons to want to be here – to try to find out about what she believed was Freddie Burkinshaw's discovery of a treasure trove she seems obsessed with, and to have a chance to reconnect with Niall and put him in his place. It all suggests a set up, to me."

John's darting eyes, then his horrified stare, told me he hadn't considered any of these possibilities. The way his brow furrowed further informed me he realized my points made sense. He squeezed his eyes shut. "Dear God, Cait, there's no fool like an old fool, is there? I didn't see it at all. I thought she wanted to be with me. Really believed it. All my training, all those years in the field, they just didn't come into play. I'd have done almost anything for her, you know. Am I that desperate to feel attractive? Wanted? Am I really just a lonely old man? Or, worse, a man of an age where he'll allow himself to be exploited by someone who makes him feel reinvigorated?"

He lay back, allowing himself to sink beneath the surface. When he came up for air, I could sense a change in his attitude; he'd arrived at the pool feeling sorry for himself, now he was angry.

He swam toward the ladder and hauled himself out. He shook his entire body, grabbed a towel, and dried himself off. Before he left, he looked down at me and said, "Thanks, Cait. That helped. And Lottie's not going anywhere until I've had this out with her. If her father's been in the know about this thing from the off, there could be implications. Just don't say anything to Bud or Jack for now. I'll…I'll fill them in when I have better intel."

"I felt it best to say what I really thought," I replied.

"And I appreciate that, Cait. See you later. We have a plan for after sunset, regarding the tower. My time is my own until then, and I'll make the best possible use of it."

I, too, got out of the pool – not with as much ease as John had done – and towelled myself dry. I was just about to head back to the bungalow when I heard Tarone's voice.

"Mrs. Cait, my granny come home, and she ask if she can talk with you." I thought his face might crack, his smile was so wide.

I was surprised. "You're both back? How did you get here?" I knew the Suburban hadn't left the estate since John and Lottie had returned in it the evening before.

"Miss Lottie, she give us a number to call for a car. Pay for it too. She a good woman."

*If only you knew*, was what I thought. "How is your grandmother?" was what I said.

"She doing good, but she keen to talk to you. She say, can you come over?"

"I'd be delighted to, Tarone. Just let me get into some dry clothes? Give me maybe ten minutes."

"Good, we see you then. She bakin' already, you know. Banana bread. She feelin' good, I can tell."

I interrupted a telephone conversation Bud was having when I got back to the bungalow. He was pacing, and his body language told me he wasn't just having a happy chat. I scuttled off and got myself dressed, then wrote a note telling him where I was going and waggled it under his nose. I got a thumbs-up, and I headed over to Amelia's home. I wished I had something to take her, by way of a welcome home gift, but the only thing I could think of was to pick some flowers along the way, and that seemed a bit silly; I'm not keen on cut flowers as a gift – it's like handing someone a bunch of things that are already dying. I told myself I'd offer to help her in any way I could instead of bringing something, and knocked on her door, looking forward to seeing her.

The dressing taped to Amelia's forehead took me aback. "Oh, that looks nasty," I said. I'd meant my first words to her to be more supportive, but they were already out, so I added, "But you're looking great otherwise."

Her kind smile broadened. "I look like the old woman I am." She stood back and invited me in.

I hadn't been inside her home before and was surprised that it was no bigger than the space Bud and I had been sharing. Our bungalow was perfect for a couple staying for a short period, but the small sitting room, with a bedroom and bathroom attached, just didn't seem sufficient to accommodate both Amelia and Tarone. A sofa bed in the sitting room, a double hotplate and toaster oven in the corner, and a slightly larger fridge than Bud and I used for chilling beers and water were the only differences between our accommodations. The décor made the place feel even smaller – happier, but smaller. Our bungalow was all white, with pale blue accents; Amelia's home was decked out in every colour of the rainbow, plus a few more, and the mixture of patterns was almost overwhelming.

The other thing I noticed was the smell of baking. My tummy rumbled. Amelia must have heard it because she immediately said, "Warm banana bread ain't good for you – it taste good, but it not good for the body. You have to wait a while, then you can have some." She moved a few things off the sofa bed, and I perched on the edge.

"How are you feeling?" I asked.

"I been worse, and the doctor say I be fine."

"You give us all a fright, Granny," said Tarone, who'd entered from the back of the house. "She got to be quiet, the doctor say. I say to him she don't know how to be that. Him say she must try. You hear him, don't you, Granny? You have to be quiet." He looked tired, worn out by concern, and older than his years.

"You can keep an eye on her now," I said.

"Him got to go back to Kingston tomorrow. Selection races. Him got to go, you tell him." Amelia's eyes pleaded with me.

*Why would he listen to me, not you?* I thought.

"You should listen to your grandmother, she's a wise woman, Tarone. How long will you be in Kingston?"

"Supposed to be until Sunday afternoon." He looked grim.

"We're here until Sunday lunchtime, we'll keep an eye on her for you."

Tarone sucked his teeth. "It not right. She just come home from hospital. I can't go back there tomorrow."

"The bus is at nine in the morning. You gone buy all new kit. Put it out back there in the shed. I seen it. I don't know how you got the money for that lot, but them special shoes gonna make you run like the wind. You be on that bus tomorrow," said Amelia. "We all be good here, right, Mrs. Cait?"

"Right, Amelia."

"Now you go to the market and get them things I tell you," she said to her grandson. She looked at me. "Him make me promise I don't be doing your stuff for you, but I can make sure you got what you need to be able to do it for yourself. And I can bake. It like a hobby for me, no work at all. I can't be sitting about all day like a queen, doing nothing. Him agree, so this is what we do. Now off you go, Tarone. I give you that list and there be no good things left before long. Go!"

Tarone kissed his grandmother's cheek and left.

Amelia and I sat smiling at each other as we heard the Suburban's engine roar into life.

Amelia patted the space next to her on the small settee. I sat where she indicated.

"Thank you for saving me," she whispered. "I don't know what happen in that lawyer's office, but you save me, I know it." She squeezed my hand.

"You're welcome, of course, but it seems you just fainted and bumped your head. It could have been worse. You were lucky."

"Ain't no luck, it the will of the Lord," said Amelia quietly, "and I know what him have in mind, too. I done something awful wicked, and him punish me. But my real punishment is that I must confess my sin, and I going to end up spending the rest of my life in prison."

*Not what I was expecting.* "What on earth do you mean?"

"Covetousness is a sin," said Amelia, her eyes downcast, her chin quivering. "I been laying in that bed in that hospital and I can see now I been a bad woman. I make plans, I think of just myself. I covet what was Mr. Freddie's and I ain't got no right to do it. It be in the Bible – I's wrong to make plans for something that ain't mine. And the Lord went and struck me down for it. He kept it from me, and he struck me down. I am a sinner, Mrs. Cait. I should be in prison."

My heart went out to the woman. I put my arm around her shoulders and held her as she sobbed. "There, there," I said. Amelia produced a large handkerchief from the pocket in her apron. "It's alright," I added. "It's perfectly natural to dream of what might be, one day. And if Freddie had told you he was going to leave the estate to you and Tarone, then I think it's perfectly reasonable to give some thought to what you might do when that day comes. It's not a sin, it's just being human."

"But we gotta try to be more like God, and him Son. Human beings is bad. We's sinful creatures. We must be like Jesus, not like animals. Mr. Freddie, him like an animal. Him want Tarone to do this and do that – him not want Tarone to be all him can be, but just to be him servant…like him slave. They say we ain't slaves no more, but you show me the jobs for my Tarone that ain't under a white man, somewhere, somehow. Them clever black 'entrepreneurs' works hard, but if a boy ain't good at school, they don't want him. Now Tarone? Him not good in the classroom, but him have a gift, a God-given gift, and him must use it. I don't want him working no tough-life job. Or worse, them gangs get him. They at him all the time. All the time, everywhere. But Tarone, him a good boy. Him take care of his granny, and him look after Mr. Freddie."

I didn't want to wade in on the topic of God-given anything – I've learned it's impossible for two people to agree one hundred percent on either religion or politics, so I avoid them both like the plague; I enjoy the process of debate too much to let a point go when I want it to be heard, and I know it's best to keep my mouth shut on some topics. I released my hug so Amelia could better attend to her tears.

"Would you like a cup of tea?" I didn't know what else to suggest.

"I don't deserve tea, I's a wicked woman."

I sighed inwardly. "No, you're not wicked, Amelia. You had some hopes and dreams, and you want the best for your grandson. These are not wicked things."

Amelia looked at me with bloodshot eyes. She sniffed, and giant tears welled. "Thank you, Mrs. Cait. You's kind alright. And maybe you right, maybe you not. But…but…there's more…"

She broke down to such an extent she couldn't speak for a few moments. I could see she was beyond consolation, so I just let her sob it out. I felt dreadful for the poor woman.

When Amelia finally managed to compose herself, her expression had changed – hardened. "I owe it to you, Mrs. Cait, or you not understand. I got to tell you. Killing a man is wicked, see? And I kill Mr. Freddie. So I *am* a wicked, wicked woman. I know I will go to Hell. It where I belong, after prison."

## Killer Confession

I felt my heart thumping in my chest. I even heard it in my ears. Amelia had killed Freddie? How could that be? I'd been working my way through everything I knew when I was in the pool, before John's arrival, and I'd thought I was at least partway to a solution. I'd even decided what I needed to look for to prove my theory. But Amelia shooting Freddie hadn't been anywhere on my list of possibilities.

"What do you mean?" I asked. *Stupid question, Cait, she means she killed Freddie!*

"Mr. Freddie always easier on Tarone when him feel not so well, so I make Mr. Freddie sick." She wiped her eyes. "I…I make him sick sometimes before, too, then him not going around the place telling Tarone to do this and do that. I know Tarone have these selection races. Him must go, then him get picked for the team for sure. But Mr. Freddie him start up angry with Tarone again. Him start to find big jobs for Tarone to do, and I think him not going to let Tarone go to Kingston this time. I need Mr. Freddie to be sick, in bed. I swear on my Bible I not want him to die. But him dead. And now I go to prison, and Tarone not be able to run for the team anyway. Him have to get a job, full-time, so him can't go to the gym, or to training camp no more. I make this happen, I am a wicked woman, but it not fair that God punish Tarone too. Him should take just me."

Amelia was sobbing again, and I had to try to get her to calm down; she was only just out of hospital, after all. I found a glass, filled it with water, and brought it to her. I recalled her words as she stood swaying beside the lawyer's desk. "Is this what you were thinking about, in Cooperman's office, when you said it had all been for nothing, Amelia?"

She nodded. "Without the estate it don't really matter if Tarone don't go this weekend, because him going to have to get another job soon, and then him won't be able to run no more, but *him* must not know that. At least if him make the team this weekend, then him know him good enough. Him must know how good him is. Him need confidence. To grow. To do other things good too."

I understood the logic of what Amelia was saying; from a psychological point of view it was true – a person who succeeds at one thing can often perform better when presented with other, novel challenges, because they know how success feels, and understand that it's worth striving for.

"Explain to me exactly what happened, Amelia." I was fascinated to know how she'd managed to shoot Freddie and escape the lookout room; I couldn't see her shimmying down that Jacob's ladder we'd found. Maybe she did have a spare key for the lookout room, after all, and that was all she'd needed. *Was it that simple all along? Just the existence of a second key?* I thought.

"I poison Mr. Freddie with ackee. Bad ackee. It supposed to put him into bed. Just in bed. Sick, you know? But Mr. Freddie, him always like a baby when him sick. Him get very afraid when him sick. I know this from before, but I don't think him do nothing because of it. Honest I don't. Then I see him shot on the floor, and I know him feel so sick, so bad, that him kill himself. It all my fault. Mine. I go to the police now. To start, I think I can still go on, like usual, knowing I kill him. But I can't. It too much for me. My soul hurts. It burns. I am a bad woman. I got to go to the police. Be punished."

I allowed my mind to run through all the evidence, as I knew it. "You used to make Freddie smoothies, didn't you?"

Amelia nodded. "Him old, him not like food much. I make him smoothies every day, over at him tower. Morning and night. Lots of that protein powder in them. It good for him."

"You'd chargrill fruits and vegetables on a wood fire you'd build in the little fireplace on the ground floor there – things like peppers, pineapples and so forth – then cut up the fruits and veggies, and use the blenders kept in the little kitchenette, beside the bathroom, to make the smoothies, right there at the tower. You'd take the drink to him, with the glass standing in a dish full of ice, and he'd drink it when he wanted."

Amelia stared at me. "You know all this? How? I never tell you. Did Tarone tell you, or Mr. Freddie?"

"No, but I observed all the clues that allowed me to work it out. You put overripe ackee into the drink you gave Freddie after our dinner that evening. He'd hardly eaten – though he'd drunk a fair amount and smoked a couple of cigars. He must have drunk the smoothie over the next couple of hours and, you're right, it made him sick. His autopsy suggested he'd chewed up the ackee, but the blender had done the work for him. He vomited in the lookout room, though he didn't manage to completely clear his system of the poison, and I dare say he was feeling pretty rotten. But you didn't shoot him, did you? And he certainly didn't shoot himself, so you didn't kill him, Amelia. You will not go to prison, and you will not burn in Hell."

Amelia's eyes grew round. "But the police, they say Mr. Freddie kill himself. Them tell us that, after they see him body."

I realized Amelia had no idea of the revised police opinion – she'd been in hospital as the case had progressed. I explained it all to her. She gradually stopped crying, and I began to see the light of hope in her eyes.

"So, I did not kill him, because he did not kill himself?"

I nodded. Amelia started to weep again, but these were different tears; they were an expression of relief.

Sadly, I knew I had to be the bearer of bad tidings, and decided I'd better get on with it. "There's something else I have to tell you, too, Amelia. The gun that was used to shoot Freddie was used again, the next night. Wilson Thomas was killed with it."

I watched her face. A look of resignation set in. "I know this. Tarone tell me." A half-smile crinkled the corners of her lips. "Tarone is happy. Him think I hate Wilson." Amelia shuddered, then began to cry again, silently.

I could tell that the poor woman needed a moment, but she deserved the facts. "Wilson had been homeless, camping out in a shack not far from here. Just along the beach, in fact. I'm sorry."

Amelia let out a long sigh. "Him a good man, Mrs. Cait. A good man. But you must let Tarone think I hate him. Don't say nothing, please."

I was puzzled. "Why do you want Tarone to believe you hated Wilson?"

Amelia wiped her eyes and stared deep into mine. "I love him from the first time I see him. Wilson Thomas was always a gentle man, and him work hard him whole life. I's just a girl when I see him first, and him love me like I love him, right off. Our beautiful girl come along, by the grace of God – so we call her Grace – and Mr. Freddie let me and Grace come live here with Wilson. It a good life. We all work hard, but we's a happy family. As Grace come along her get to be very friendly with the folk who come to Mr. Freddie's parties. Her a good-looking girl, but her not so good at schoolwork. Wilson always big on schoolwork. We done our best for her, showed her the right ways of things. Him and me know it make a difference if you good at schoolwork, but Grace? Her don't see it this way. Her get very angry with her father, and with me too. Her think her all growed up – but her just a child."

"Then she became pregnant with Tarone?"

Amelia nodded. "Her a wild child, and now with a child of her own. Me and her father try to get her to see how bad her behavin', but her fight with us, and go off. Leave the baby for me to look after. One day when her come back askin' for money, Wilson hit her. Not so hard, but her riled him up real bad. Her wanted money for drugs; Wilson found her with them filthy things so many times. But Mr. Freddie see Wilson hit Grace, and him get angry with Wilson. They have a fight, a big one, then Wilson have to go. I want to beg Mr. Freddie to let Wilson stay, but Wilson tell me I must not say this because Mr. Freddie say if Wilson go quiet then me, Grace, and Tarone can stay. So, Wilson go, and we all stay. But Mr. Freddie make it hard for Wilson to get good work anywhere else, so him have to take bad jobs, and him make money best way him can. But always straight ways, not crooked."

Amelia looked around the bungalow, leaned toward me and whispered, "Wilson and me? We have a message tree. We talk through messages we write and hide there. I meet him sometimes, and him give me money when him can. And him watch out for Grace, and her boy, too. But Grace – my baby Grace – she never pick up on the good life. For her? It like her want to shine bright, but short. And her done just that. Her die. Too young. Too many drugs. Then it just me and Tarone, and I raise him, and I don't want him to think him granddaddy go leave him, and I don't want him to be angry with Mr. Freddie neither, so I tell him stories about Wilson that ain't true. Tarone think him mother an angel and him granddaddy a devil, but it the other way about."

"Did you know that Wilson slept on the beach, so close to you?" I suspected I knew the answer.

Amelia nodded. "Sometimes I go to him there, still. We got history. Him a good man."

She blew her nose, and – once again – my heart went out to her. "I'm so sorry," was all I could say.

"It my fault. Even if I don't kill Mr. Freddie, I still done a bad thing, and now I be paid back. It all be my fault. Poor Tarone, soon him have no one."

I begged Amelia to not say anything to the police about what she'd done.

"But I done wrong," she wailed.

"Maybe pray about it for a couple of days, before saying anything then," I suggested. It was the best I could do.

She was still crying when Tarone came home.

"All the things are in the big house," he announced as he entered. "Granny, what the matter? Why she upset?" he asked me. His tone suggested he thought it might be my fault.

"Your grandmother's just glad to be home, and she's really pleased you'll be trying out for the team this weekend after all. She was just telling me how very proud she is of your athletic talent, and she got a bit overwhelmed. She might be a bit tearful for a little while to come," I said, standing. "But we'll keep an eye on her. You go tomorrow, and we'll all be just fine."

Tarone nodded. "Mebbe. I get her to talk about what her gonna do with her new house, later on," said Tarone as he opened the door for me to leave. "Her always enjoy that."

"Okay," was all I could muster.

As I walked away, I realized that meant Amelia hadn't told Tarone about the debts Freddie had incurred, requiring the sale of the estate. And I hadn't told either of them that Nina Mazzo had already snapped it up. That news could wait, I decided.

# *A Liar Laments their Lies?*

I got back to the bungalow as fast as I could, bursting to tell Bud about Amelia. But he wasn't there. I checked everywhere, then decided I'd look for him at the big house; it was late in the afternoon, so maybe he, John, and Jack were making plans for exactly what'd they'd do when the police had left the tower.

I walked into the lounge to discover Jack and Sheila sitting on one sofa, Lottie on another, John on a chair beside her, and Bud pacing about. "There you are," he said. "What happened to you? I thought you'd only be gone for five minutes."

I considered telling everyone about Amelia, but the expressions greeting me told me that something was up. I sat beside Bud, and waited.

"Lottie has something she'd like to say to you all," announced John. It reminded me of the way a parent spoke about their errant child. "Lottie."

We all gave her our full attention. She sat up, squared her shoulders and said, "Daddy sent me here. He knows about the papers you're all looking for, and he wanted me to be on the spot, because he wants them for himself. Or else he wants me to tell him that I have seen with my own eyes that they have been destroyed. I'm sorry, I've been lying to you all the entire time I've been here. And I've been lying to John since he and I first met."

I was the least shocked person in the room – except for John and Lottie, of course.

Sheila laughed. "What do you mean? You've been sleeping with John just so you can get hold of these papers? And your father made you do this? I don't believe it. No parent would ask that of their child. No decent parent, in any case. That's disgusting."

When she put it that way, Sheila had a point. I had to admit to myself I hadn't taken my analysis that far.

John's jaw clenched, his nostrils flared. He was seething. I wondered how much of his anger was reserved for himself, and his naivety.

"Tarquin Fortescue, Lottie's father, is caught up in all this?" asked Jack, looking at John, not Lottie.

John nodded. "Looks that way. Been onto us since the start, maybe since before we even knew about it. Tell them, Lottie, tell them everything you've told me. Let them hear the whole story. Trust me, folks, you're in for a treat." I could see a vein pulse at his temple.

Lottie's neck was becoming increasingly mottled. Despite her duplicitousness, I felt sorry for her. I even decided to reserve judgement until she'd spoken, which is unusual for me.

"Daddy approached me a couple of months ago; told me he was in a bit of a pickle. Some documents my grandfather had signed on behalf of Her Majesty's government, back in the war, had gone missing donkey's years ago, and hadn't mattered too much at the time. But now they could reflect badly on the political leanings of our family, at that time. Daddy's terribly concerned about his reputation. And mine, of course. But...but especially his. And, to be fair, I know he's always put country first, but the standing of the family name? Well, that comes before first, if you know what I mean. He was in a right old tizzy about it. Please believe me when I tell you I don't know any more about what the documents are, or what they say, or why they are so important now. He said I'd know them when I saw them. Lists. Names. Dates. My grandfather's name. That's all I know. I realize you have no reason to believe me, given that I've told so many lies, but it's the truth. I don't know more."

Sheila's voice vibrated with anger when she spoke. "These papers have already cost lives – now, as well as who knows how many more in the past – and the whole point of this mission is to destroy them so no one will ever know what they say. This whole thing is so insane that knowing what they say will probably just enrage all of us anyway. It might be the guest list for a party given in 1943 and that's all – but who cares, eh? All anyone wants is for them to never be seen by anyone ever again. So you men all go running around the world to make sure that's what happens, right?"

"How do you know that?" snapped Jack.

"Know what?" replied Sheila, equally snappishly.

"That we're looking for guest lists for dinner parties held in the 1940s?"

Sheila, Lottie, and I looked confused. The men didn't; they all swallowed, in unison, which spoke volumes.

"I don't *know* anything," said Sheila. "I just made that up. It's as ridiculous an idea as I could come up with. What do they call it on TV these days? A 'nothingburger', that's it. I just invented a silly nothingburger." She paused, then added, "You're not telling me that's what this is all about, are you? A list of people who were invited to some dinner or other? Jack, tell me that's not true."

The expression on Jack's face made me wonder how he'd ever survived any missions at all.

"That's it?" exploded Lottie. "Some ancient guest list? Daddy got me to do all this, for *that*? Tell me that's not right, John."

I glanced at Bud's white knuckles; I didn't have to ask him anything, instead I said, "Some context might be useful."

Bud sighed. Heavily. "The back end of 1941; Washington, DC. A number of informal dinners. The documents in question list persons present at those dinners, and show that the guest lists were officially approved, signed off at the highest level, by various governments. The Americans somehow managed to lose those lists. They were rumored to be in several places after the war, and were last heard of in Jamaica. Freddie Burkinshaw tried to broker a deal for them back in the 1960s. It fell through. The man we now know to have been using the name Luca Mazzo was believed to have been in possession of them at some point in time, though we had knowledge of him under a different name, and couldn't – until now – connect that name to this island. That's all I can say."

"My bloody father," spat Lottie. "I'll never forgive him for this. Guest lists? I'll give him bloody guest lists."

"I thought we had something, Lottie, I really did," said John. His face was slack, his eyes empty. He was not himself. At all. "These friends of mine will now always see me as a foolish man. Something I have never believed myself to be. I totally trust these people; I know they'll never speak of this. But you? I saw how you acted toward Niall today, and have no doubt that, at some point – maybe after a few tipples with your chums at the local gin palace one night – you'll be only too happy to tell people what a complete idiot I made of myself over you. I might as well resign after this mission and retire to the countryside. Or maybe to Jamaica, eh? I know a particularly slippery real estate agent if I need one. Maybe Nina will let me live in one of these bungalows – she'll take title to this place soon, and she could probably cope with one Englishman who's well past his prime doddering about the place. Maybe she'll retain Amelia and Tarone to look after me and the old place."

Lottie threw a cushion in his direction. "Shut up, John. Thought all your Christmases had come at once when I took an interest in you, didn't you? Don't they teach you chaps anything at spy school? Like if it seems too good to be true, it usually is."

"There's a little of the preying mantis about you, Lottie." John looked grim. "Like to eat your mates, don't you?"

"This isn't getting us anywhere," said Bud forcefully. "Given your lack of transparency with all of us, Lottie, you can see why we're not too keen to take you at your word at this stage, but I have to ask you this, and it's vital you tell the truth. Did you kill Freddie Burkinshaw, or Wilson Thomas?"

Lottie threw back her head and laughed. "Listen to yourself, Bud. You're such a bloody Boy Scout. No, I didn't kill either of them. I wanted them alive as much as you three did. Daddy was quite clear that Freddie was my first point of contact here. Oh yes, you didn't know Freddie was dealing behind your backs, did you? Had a direct line of contact to Daddy. Desperate for cash, apparently. But he kept upping the price. Daddy began to suspect he didn't have the papers after all, only 'knew how he could lay his hands on them'. Daddy told me all about it. He even mentioned Wilson Thomas to me as an alternative contact. But I couldn't get John-boy here to come to Jamaica any earlier than we did, or I'd have got to Wilson before you lot messed it all up."

"Boy Scout?" I was livid, and I wasn't going to put up with Lottie any longer. "You say that like it's the worst insult imaginable – but at least Bud has a moral compass. You? You have nothing but an abnormally developed desire to please your father. You began this little performance by saying you were sorry. Well, you're clearly only sorry that you got caught out, because you're not at all sorry for what you did."

"Cait," said Bud quietly.

"Yes, keep your little Welsh corgi under control, Bud," sniped Lottie, "or she might bite."

My heart was pounding. I had offered Lottie a shoulder to cry on when I thought she'd needed one. And now this? This was just another example of why it's such a bad idea to let people into your life, to show an interest in them, and allow them to find your soft parts and wound you there.

I could hear roaring, felt bile creeping up my throat; anger is a physical force, and I had to get out of the room or I might have said or done something that would have changed the way those people thought of me for ever, Bud included.

I strode off, out into the darkness, the no-longer-soothing racket being made by the blessed tree frogs annoying me even more. Every inch of me was fizzing with anger at the injustice of it all. It burned in my eyes. By the time I flung myself onto the bed I was crying. Bud found me there moments later, and held me as I sobbed.

# Panamanian Plunder

"What's the plan, Bud?" I asked, about half an hour later. I'd recovered my composure, and washed my face. I knew we had to push on, whatever my feelings about Lottie Fortescue might be, and I owed it to Bud to be as helpful to him as possible. I'd already told him about Amelia poisoning Freddie, and we agreed to put that on the back burner for a while.

"Lottie's gone off to a hotel in a cab," said Bud, "Jack's established the cops have left the tower, and we've agreed all three of us will get down into that shaft we discovered as soon as we can. Given we don't know exactly what we might find there, we'll go as well prepared as possible. You and Sheila can wait here, or come with us to the tower if you want, but we really don't want either of you to do the underground exploring with us. And there's no discussion on that matter, Cait. None."

"I'm fine with that; I felt as though I was choking just being under the floor of the lookout room, so I'm pretty sure I wouldn't fare too well in any sort of tunnel that's actually underground. But I would like to be in the tower, at least. I could have a bit more of a dig about at the place. Remember, I haven't given any of the other floors a good going over, yet. Sheila and I could do that."

"Thanks. We're off soon."

"One thing, Bud."

"Yes."

"What are you looking for down there?"

Bud sighed. "Whatever we might find. Hearing Lottie's claim – and it's just a claim, we've no way of knowing if she was lying or not – about Freddie not being prepared, or able, to supply the papers he said he could to her father, then maybe this is a totally pointless exercise. If Freddie didn't have them, then they weren't on his desk, they weren't stolen, and we can't possibly find them."

"If Luca Mazzo had them in the first place, and Freddie offered to sell them thinking he could get them off Luca, might they not still be at *Caro Mio*? Given the interest Nina has in anything made of paper – that's not money – they could be sitting on her bedside table and she probably wouldn't notice them," I offered.

"We guys discussed that, but gaining access to *Caro Mio* is not something we're equipped to do. There are conversations taking place in various offices around the world about whether a special team should be dispatched to supply services on that front."

I laughed. "You mean a secret burglary team? Those things exist?"

"Cait, don't go there," warned Bud. He smiled too brightly as he said it.

Ten minutes later, all five of us trooped off toward the tower; Jack and Bud helped Sheila cope with her ankle, and I managed to give John a hug as we walked together. We could have been five tourists looking a little sad because the end of their wonderful vacation was in sight, and if anyone had seen us and thought that, it would have been a good thing – because that's not at all what we were.

We all climbed to the top of the tower; the men made quick work of moving Freddie's desk and opening up the floor, then Sheila and I sat about while they decided exactly who would fill what role in their descent. It was finally agreed that Jack should go down the Jacob's ladder first, as we all reckoned he was the lightest and slimmest, so there was less chance of it collapsing under his weight. He was to scout the tunnel; John and Bud would join him – one at a time – or not, depending upon what he found.

Sheila and Jack hugged before he dropped down into the floor cavity, followed by John. Bud stayed with us, and we three worked out where best to secure a rope that the men could use to get back up the shaft, in case of the rope ladder failing. That done, Bud joined John under the floor to be able to hear whatever Jack reported.

"I'm off to have a good search of Freddie's bedroom," I said.

"I could do the sitting room," volunteered Sheila, "But what am I looking for?"

I chuckled, "Exactly what I asked Bud when we searched this room, and we agreed 'whatever we found'. So that. Anything odd, out of the ordinary. Something that stands out – or something that's a secret door, or cavity. That sort of thing."

Sheila scanned the lookout room. "Out of the ordinary? In this place? Oh yes, that'll be easy to spot. The whole thing looks like a charity shop – for a charity that no one likes."

I hugged her. "I'm sorry we had that run in, Sheila. I've never been known for my ability to connect. I'll try harder, I promise. You're a wonderful person – with hidden depths, I must say."

"And quite a mouth on me when I want." She shrugged. "I was cruel to you, Cait. I'd take it all back if I could, but I can't, so we'll just have to heal, with time. Now let's get on."

We did.

Freddie's bedroom was just that, a room with a bed in it, and the sort of basic bedroom furnishings you'd expect. I'd established that much on my first visit, and I'd walked through it on my way to the top of the tower more than once. As I stood beside the bed I noted a stool that acted as a bedside table, with an old oil lamp on top of it. I looked around, visualizing where the shaft was that the men were now exploring. I calculated it was close to the foot of the stone staircase, so that was where the wall must be a double wall, with a space in between. I went to the other side of the staircase. Maybe there was a gap between the walls there, too. I examined the stones, then the floor. I wondered if there was a cavity beneath my feet that matched the one upstairs, which might give access to another shaft. I repeated the process Bud and I had been through the night before, but one look at the bed told me I'd never be able to shift it; if a door in the floor was hidden under there it was gong to have to stay hidden until all five of us could tackle the monstrosity.

With the idea of another cavity in my head, I nipped upstairs and shouted to Bud. "When you checked under this floor, you were sure there wasn't another opening in the wall anywhere?"

"I'm sure," he replied. He sounded as though he had his head in a bucket.

"Any news from Jack yet?"

"Not yet."

"Okay, going back down again."

I bounced down the stone steps and into the bedroom. I opened every door in every piece of furniture. The wardrobes were full of Freddie's clothes, all freshly pressed and washed. I knocked the back of everything, tried to move everything, and removed every drawer I could – and carefully replaced them. I ended up having a staring match with the bed. I walked around it, taking in the depth of the mattress, the richness of the brocade that adorned the posts and the awning above it. The base was essentially a box standing on four flattened balls. I knocked it. It was hollow.

*Of course, Cait, why would it be solid?*

I bent down and pointed my phone's flashlight at it. I took my time, and I finally found a crack that shouldn't be there. Then I found another. I ran to the stairs and called for Sheila to come to help me. When she arrived, panting and looking panicked, she found me sitting on the floor, my legs poked under the side of the bed.

"Can you help at the other end?" I asked.

Sheila positioned herself and we both pulled at what was, essentially, the entire base of the bed. The framework didn't budge, but the base did a little. Something was holding it in place.

I could feel the excitement at the nape of my neck. "There's got to be a catch somewhere around here that's holding this in. It's got a tiny bit of movement in it; if we can find the catch I think the entire thing might open, like a drawer."

"Got it," she said. "Drawers under beds, very Ikea."

We each worked our way from the end where we were sitting, shuffling toward each other on our bottoms. Nothing.

"You try the top end, I'll try the bottom," I said.

We did.

"Got it," said Sheila. "At least I think I have."

I joined her at the top of the bed. Sure enough there was a button of wood, that looked like the head of a large wooden peg. "Go on, push it," I said.

It popped in.

"Let's try this again," I said, and we pulled at the base of the bed. It slid out without a sound.

"Oh, my word," said Sheila.

"Oh, my word, indeed," I said, glowing. "Hang on, I'll be right back. Don't touch anything." I ran up the stairs and stuck my head into the cavity in the floor. "Bud?"

"Yes, love?" he sounded a bit exasperated.

"I have some news."

"Good, because all that Jack found was about thirty feet of a dirt tunnel heading east, that ended in a pile of rubble. No way through to anywhere. A dead end. He's on his way up. Ah, there he is. Okay, we're coming out now."

I tried to keep my breathing even, steady. I waited with more patience than I ever imagined I possessed as all three men hauled themselves out of the hole in the floor.

"Come with me. Sheila's standing guard. We found something."

Bud patted me on the bum as I led the way down the staircase. When I entered the bedroom, I turned – I wanted to watch the men's faces as they saw what we'd found.

Sheila gave a loud, "Ta-daa!" and three mouths fell open. "Gentlemen, say hello to Henry Morgan's Panamanian plunder."

# *Nonsense*

Five faces glowed gold, reflected off the treasure Freddie Burkinshaw had slept on every night. It was the purest Enid Blyton moment of my life – I wouldn't have been surprised if Amelia had materialized with a plate of fish-paste sandwiches and lashings of ginger beer at that exact moment. We'd found treasure. Henry Morgan's treasure. For all her lies, Lottie had been right – Freddie had somehow discovered the treasure. It was thrilling.

We were all caught up in the moment, and we allowed ourselves to soak it in. We were truly agog. There were golden platters, heavy chains with massive stones embedded in them, goblets, dishes filled with coins…and everything was gold. It was staggering.

"It must weigh a lot," said Sheila.

"It must be worth a lot," said Jack.

"It's priceless," said Bud.

"It's beautiful," said John.

"It's all wrong," I said. Everyone tore their eyes from the treasure and looked at me. I bent down and picked up a chalice. It was gold, weighed about five pounds, and was covered in ruby cabochons. "See this?" Everyone nodded. "Lottie told me this was an item she'd seen sold in an online auction, one of the items that made her believe that Freddie had found the treasure. She said it was unique. Despite all her lies, I believe she was speaking the truth about that."

"He found it then; this is proof that it's Morgan's treasure," said Sheila, flapping her hands about with excitement.

"But this chalice was *sold*. So why is it here?" I asked. "Indeed, if Freddie was selling off this treasure a bit at a time, why was he millions of dollars in debt?"

Silence.

Eventually Bud said, "Maybe he just couldn't let any of it go? You said yourself, Cait, that his psychological profile suggested he was extremely avaricious. He might have offered it for sale, then just couldn't part with it."

I replaced the chalice, shaking my head. "Lottie mentioned several of the specific sorts of items we're looking at here as being 'sold', not just 'for sale'," I replied. "I had an idea when we were at Nina's, earlier, that seemed a bit far-fetched at the time, but now it makes more sense...making the engines of a boat roar when Freddie was singing 'God Save the Queen'..."

"But what does that..." began Sheila.

Bud raised his hand. "Let her think."

"What time is it?" I asked.

"Just coming up to seven," replied John.

"We have to get hold of Amelia, Tarone, and Lottie, and we have to get over to Nina Mazzo's house. We need Niall there too. How can we make that happen?" I looked at the four faces staring at me.

Bud scratched his chin. "If you don't mind Inspector Charles being there too, I think I could make that happen quite easily."

"No one's supposed to know he's working with us," snapped Jack.

Sheila slowly shook her head. "Now we all do, Jack."

"I wondered why he was so patient with us, when we were being so obnoxious to him," I said. "All those copies of autopsies and police reports? The speed with which everything's been orchestrated? Inspector Charles on your team? Handy. Of course he can be there; if he's okay with you, he's okay with me, because we'll need him," I replied. "And I could do with talking to him before we get going. Can you get that sorted for me, please Bud?" He nodded. "Okay then, let's hide this away again, and get out of here."

Bud moved aside and pulled out his phone.

"We're going to leave it all here?" asked Sheila. She sounded horrified. "What if someone steals it? Shouldn't we tell someone about it?" She stopped and gave the matter some thought. "Who does it even belong to? If Freddie found Morgan's treasure hidden on land he owned, does that mean it was his? Or is it the government's for some reason?"

"I don't know the Jamaican laws regarding the discovery of buried treasure, but we can certainly find someone who does," replied Jack. "And it looks like it's been safe here for a long time. The cops didn't find it, for sure. I reckon we can risk it."

I left as Jack, Sheila, and John were taking photos of the treasure, and Bud was on the phone. I knew they'd all be a while, because they had to put the tower room back the way they'd found it, and I had to get back to the bungalow to do a few things to be ready for our trip to *Caro Mio*.

Dressing up to impress Nina Mazzo wasn't on my list.

# Day Dreaming

When I got back to the bungalow, I grabbed the DO NOT DISTURB sign off our front door and put it on the handle of the bathroom, then locked myself in. I sat on the little basket-weave chair in the corner of the room; I needed somewhere I could be alone so that I could take just a little while to wrap my head around the entire case. This time I didn't try to recollect what I'd seen and heard; I needed to allow all my recent experiences to mix and meld without my learned attitudes and expectations intervening.

I manage that by using a process called wakeful dreaming, where I allow my mind to wander as it chooses along the pathways of my memories, and put things I've seen, heard, tasted, smelled, and felt into a new perspective – where the relationships between them are not being commandeered by my conscious self.

To be able to do it properly I prefer to be calm, quiet, and alone, if possible. The bathroom allowed me to be all three, so I held onto the armrests of the little chair – which was really meant to have robes and towels tossed onto it, rather than a person of my girth sitting in it for any length of time – and allowed my mind to swirl.

Unsurprisingly, the first thing I see is the crystal skull; and it's laughing at me, its suddenly articulated jaw showing me how hilarious it thinks I am. It hangs in the air against a backdrop of fluttering hummingbirds, their iridescent plumage flashing blues, greens, oranges, and reds at me as I look though the crystal itself. The birds have been our constant companions since our arrival, but not in the extraordinary numbers in which they now appear. They disintegrate and become a flock of hovering black witch moths, all with the faces of Freddie Burkinshaw, all screaming at me. As I watch, the moths become smaller, and smaller, until they are invisible, but still noisy – they have started to sound like tree frogs, and give off flashes like fireflies. Then the darkness bursts into light, and I am surrounded by gold falling from the sky, like heavy rain. It hurts when it hits me, and I bleed all over, then I realize I am sweating. Bud appears through the rain and offers me platters and platters of cakes; the platters are gold, the cakes keep coming, and he keeps saying, "Look Cait – fifty cakes, fifty candles…blow hard, blow hard." I turn away, but I can smell the candles after they've been extinguished. The smell follows me as I scale a wall that's appeared in front of me. It's Freddie's tower, and I hop over the rail into his lookout room, which is stuffed with artifacts and maps and gold coins. Sheila's sister welcomes me inside; I don't know her face, but I know who she is, and she smiles as she invites me to sit on a throne made of burgundy velvet.

I decline, because I have to see what is making the noise I can hear outside the tower. Is it a giant dragonfly, or a million hummingbirds? No, it's Freddie moving across the surface of the sea on one of those water jet packs, the columns of water shooting from his feet, then, below him, Wilson Thomas appears, rising from the waves like Venus, holding an infant in his hands and crying, wailing. Freddie shoots at him with a massive gun with a silencer attached – the noise is deafening. I clap my hands against my ears, but the noise rings inside my head, like church bells, which morph into Freddie's voice singing "God Save The Queen".

I look over the parapet to the beach below, which comes rushing up to meet me, but I can't get over the railing to escape before the top of the tower disappears into the sand, which starts to rain on my head as the gold had done. I know I mustn't get buried...a Jacob's ladder falls from the sky, and I cling to it. The sand that had been threatening to overwhelm me dissolves beneath my feet and I fly high in the sky looking down at the Captain's Lookout estate. I can see Bud, Sheila and Jack, and Lottie and John as tiny figures lying on beds beside the pool, and I see Nina and Niall doing the same beside her pool, the water of which is in turmoil, rent by violent waves. The ringing in my ears is replaced by the snapping of a camera's shutter, which changes to the sound of picks hitting rock, and shovels hitting sand. I see Lottie, still tiny beneath me, and she shoots at me with a bow and arrow. I am hit, and I fall; from far, far below I feel many hands reach to save me, and I allow myself to be safe within their grasp. They set me down on a crystalline beach where an amethyst palm tree shades me from an emerald sun, and I hear the flutter of wings again, but now the birds are made of white paper, their wings are sheets and their bodies scrolls. They all have blue feet.

Amelia appears from beneath the palm trees and tries to shoo the birds away. She throws ackee at them, the fruits bursting open as they hit, their seeds scattering, and the birds disappear into puffs of gray cloud. Tarone tries to take the ackee from his grandmother, but she sits on him. He screams like a baby, but she doesn't hear when I tell her to let him get up, instead, she bounces on him, and I start to bounce too. I am jumping from the sand to the stars, then descending again. Each time I rise, and fall, I have a clear line of vision into first Freddie's lookout room, then Wilson's shack...bounce, bounce, bounce...bang, bang, bang. They are both dead. Blood mists my eyes and I am...

I opened my eyes and released my grip on the chair's arms. My palms bore the indentation of the basket weave, but I didn't mind. There were still a few things I had to do, but I knew how two men had died, and who'd made it happen, and why they'd done it. I even thought I might have a line on where Bud might find the papers he needed. But the next steps wouldn't be easy.

## Delivering the Denouement

The "formal" request to attend a meeting at *Caro Mio* came via a call from Inspector Charles to Amelia's home. Tarone found us seemingly relaxing at the big house and gave us the message. He was a bit flustered that he and his grandmother had also been asked to attend.

"I know you have an early start in the morning, but it probably won't take too long," said Bud as reassuringly as possible. "We'll all go together. I'll drive, if you like, the road out there is pretty bad, and it's dark."

"I be fine, Mr. Bud. No problem, man."

I wondered how Lottie was taking the news about our little get-together – my money was on "not well". Bud had managed to get Inspector Charles to agree to get everyone together at *Caro Mio* under cover of a police briefing of some note, and one for which we all had to congregate. Lottie was to be brought forcibly if she declined to join us, and the inspector was going to act the same way regarding Niall, and Nina – should she not want to host the gathering.

I recognized how lucky I was that none of that was my problem to solve, and felt a surge of warmth when I realized how utterly reliable Bud is in every aspect of our lives. As we all walked to the Suburban, I hugged him. He looked surprised, and hugged me back.

"You're going to be great," he said.

"So are you," I replied.

Tarone collected Amelia as we passed their house; we all insisted she took the front seat beside her grandson, and none of us moaned about being squished in the back. If anything, at least being tightly packed meant we didn't jiggle about as much as usual as Tarone navigated the track to Nina's house.

He made such a good job of the journey that I asked him, "How did you manage that, Tarone? We've been shaken to bits coming along this road before."

"You got to know the land, Mrs. Cait. I run along this way when I don't go to the track. I got to keep movin', me. Sure, it change here every time it rain, but not in big ways. The land is always where the land is – until it ain't, of course." He chuckled to himself.

Upon our arrival at *Caro Mio*, Arnold looked far from pleased to receive us. His facial expression was set to "grim but polite" as he led us into the main salon, where Lottie stood scowling in a corner and Niall was seated on a brocade chair, tapping his foot impatiently. Nina was once again ensconced on a sofa, but this time she sat with her back very upright, and her get-up was a matching set of gauzy garments and jewels that were all sapphire-hued, rather than emerald.

Inspector Charles stood in the corner opposite Lottie, and there was an officer positioned at the front entrance and one at the back – both out of earshot, I noticed.

Nina, via Arnold, provided the least possible amount of hospitality, by ensuring a glass of water was offered to each of us. No one accepted. The greetings were muted, to say the least.

"Thank you all for coming," opened the inspector as he walked to the centre of the room.

"Thank you for not giving us any choice in the matter," said Lottie sulkily.

"You are all welcome to my hospitality, though I do not care to be told who I must invite to my home," said Nina imperiously. "Nor do I care to have the police running about all over the place searching my home and my guest houses – however many official papers you wave underneath my nose."

"Your hospitality is noted," said the inspector, sounding grim, "as is your compliance with our legally approved right to search your premises. You all know we have been investigating the murders of Mr. Freddie Burkinshaw and Mr. Wilson Thomas. Now I can tell you that our investigations are close to a conclusion."

"This could have been done over the telephone," said Nina, "there is no need for all of this." She waved her hand around airily.

"But there is," continued Inspector Charles. "New information has come to light that means I now know that the person who killed Mr. Burkinshaw is in this room."

I glanced across at Amelia and saw her entire body become rigid. On our way up the steps to the portico I'd managed to whisper to her that she should keep quiet unless she was asked a direct question, and to then answer it truthfully. I hoped she'd do exactly what I'd asked, because I knew how she acted was going to be important.

The looks of suspicion flashing around the room were just what I'd hoped the inspector's words would generate; I was watching, and judging, and knew immediately that my assessment of the situation had been right. I didn't want the inspector to drag things out longer than needed, so I cleared my throat – our agreed sign that I was ready to take over.

The inspector said, "Professor Cait Morgan would like to say something. Professor Morgan, the floor is yours."

Nina and Niall looked confused, as did Amelia and Tarone. None of them had any idea what I did for a living; why would they?

I stood and made my way to a spot where I could see everyone's face, and where no one had to make a special effort to be able to look at me. As it happened, this meant I was standing next to the grand piano – a photograph taken at that moment might have suggested a genteel soirée, but the event was going to be anything but a jolly evening filled with music…unless a suspect or two decided to sing.

"Thank you, Inspector Charles," I began, "I appreciate the opportunity to speak, and promise I won't keep you all too long. We're here because two men are dead, and now we know who did this dreadful thing, and why. Being a professor of criminal psychology, my interest tends to lie in answering the question, 'Who would want to kill Freddie and – or – Wilson, and why?' We'll come to the how shortly, but let's start with that initial question. The answer is, surprisingly, almost anyone here."

I took a moment to watch the faces in the room; there were looks of feigned disinterest, rapt attention, and – yes – a slight nervousness. *Good.*

I continued, "It didn't take me long to discover that Freddie Burkinshaw was a man it was more than possible to hate. He was vain, greedy – rapacious, even – and had probably managed to make himself unpopular with many individuals over the years. Did he have enemies? Most certainly. Some of whom he'd never even met – and that takes some doing." I allowed my words to sink in, then – with regret – I pushed ahead. "Let's start with Sheila."

Sheila gasped, and her eyes widened; I saw the pain and horror in them, but I had to press on. "Some personal tragedies resulting from actions by Freddie many years ago might have meant Sheila White was someone who wanted to see him out of the way, and Jack – you love your wife so much – you have to admit that if she'd been up to it, so would you."

Jack puffed out his cheeks, and we both knew I spoke the truth. "He had a lot to answer for, had we but known it," he said slowly.

"But I believe Sheila *did* know it, Jack, and before you arrived in Jamaica, too. The police mentioned Freddie's name to her when her sister died, but it took until her arrival here for her to put two and two together, she *said*. But you're bright, Sheila, and we all know you'd have made that connection immediately upon Jack telling you the name of the man who owned the estate you were coming to visit, which I'm sure he did. So, when you acted out your shock at 'discovering' it was Freddie's Rolls Royce that had tragically taken your sister's life, and changed yours forever, it was just that – an act. And I wondered why you'd do that. Then I realized it was because you wanted to throw me off what you believed was a trail I was following to discovering Freddie's killer…leading to Jack."

Sheila's face reddened, and she looked at her fingernails.

"Sheila – you thought I killed Freddie? And Wilson?" Jack stared at the side of his wife's reddening face, then at me.

I felt my multipurpose eyebrow arch. "Jack, without going into any details, over the past couple of days I have seen you act in ways that mean you'd never have survived very long in your chosen profession, and I have to believe it's all been put on for my sake. You and Bud are friends, you were his mentor. That wouldn't be the case if you were a buffoon; Bud doesn't tolerate idiocy, or incompetence. So, I had to ask myself why you were doing it. And I had the answer to that one, too. You were doing it to try to distract me from what you believed was my line of inquiry into Sheila. You were both defending each other."

Sheila's head turned, and she looked at her husband with wide eyes. They exchanged smiles of relief, and grasped each others' hands.

"How sweet," said Lottie. "Excuse me a moment, I might have to throw up."

Nina's response to Lottie's exclamation was to shudder, and rearrange her shoulders to turn away from the young Englishwoman.

"And what about you, Lottie?" I said. "Your connections to this island, to Freddie – your mother's ex-lover – and to Niall…they all put you in my sights. You had an excellent reason to want Freddie dead; I believe that in your eyes he was responsible for your mother's suicide because he dumped her so terribly coldly, and for your own depression too, though I suspect Niall's treatment of you had a more to do with that."

"Well, if you're so clever, why would I want that old Wilson Thomas chap dead too?" Lottie sounded petulant.

"He might have seen you kill Freddie," I replied calmly, "indeed, Wilson might have seen anyone here kill Freddie. Don't forget, he lived on the beach not far from the tower – he could easily have been a witness to Freddie's murder."

"You think that's why Wilson was killed?" asked Bud. He leaned forward in his seat.

"I'll cover it all, I promise," I replied, trying to tell him with my eyes to be patient.

"He could have killed Freddie," said Nina, pointing at Bud. "He's your husband, but he looks like he could kill. Or is that not something you think is possible." She dug her nails into her dress as she spoke.

I made sure I smiled when I answered. "I happen to know that my husband is, indeed, capable of killing, though only in self defense, or in the defense of his country, but that's not what happened here. This is a tale of greed, not glory. I haven't discounted Bud as a suspect because he couldn't have done it – he could – but he had no reason to do it. Nor did John."

John's head snapped up. "I'm assuming Freddie was not the

man with whom your late first wife Emily had a fling, during your honeymoon, John?"

"Freddie and Emily?" John sounded puzzled. "No. It was some idiot from Slough who was here on a golfing jolly with some mates. Why would you think it was Freddie?"

I shrugged it off, and said, "Thanks for that." Then I turned to face Amelia and her grandson.

"Of course, Amelia might have had a reason to kill Freddie; Tarone, too. After all, they both believed that they would inherit a valuable estate when Freddie died. With that in mind, I have a question for you, Tarone."

All eyes turned toward the young man, who looked terrified. "Yes?"

"Has your grandmother told you yet that Freddie Burkinshaw died with many unpaid loans? That his lawyer had no choice but to offer the Captain's Lookout estate for sale? And that she was made aware it was unlikely there would be any money left over after Freddie's debts had been repaid to allow you and her any real compensation for your years of service?"

Tarone's mouth hung open. He said nothing, but shook his head, staring at his grandmother.

"Well, you know now. You need to understand that your grandmother is quite well, really – other than a bump on the head. Amelia collapsed in the lawyer's office immediately after receiving the news I've just told you, which is hardly surprising, given that Freddie had told her on many occasions that she and you would inherit the estate to do with as you pleased."

Tarone nodded dumbly. He was still taking in the news.

I returned my attention to the group in general. "Until she met Freddie's lawyer, Mr. Cooperman, Amelia was unaware of this, and Tarone didn't know until I just told him, now. So, as you see, folks, they both *believed* they stood to gain mightily if

Freddie was killed, but I happen to have proof that neither of them killed him – because I believe I have proof of who did."

I'd spotted Constable Cassandra Lewis entering the door from the pool area outside the house. She caught Inspector Charles's eye and nodded at him, smiling. He in turn looked toward me and gave me a none-too-subtle thumbs-up. I was relieved.

Nina shifted in her seat as she frowned at this little pantomime; Niall's foot-tapping paused for a beat or two, then continued at an increased pace.

"But this is all wrong…what you say about these people inheriting the estate one day as it is now…this is wrong. Freddie was going to develop his estate," said Nina. "I know this." She certainly sounded as though she was stating a fact.

It was the turn of Amelia and Tarone to look shocked, and puzzled. "Him never going to change nothing there," said Amelia with equal certainty, then she shut her mouth tight, and looked at me, her eyes wide. "Sorry, Mrs. Cait. I don't speak no more."

I asked Nina, "Who told you Freddie was going to develop his estate?"

"I believe it must have been Niall," she replied, not making eye contact with him.

"Do you get most of your news about the outside world from Niall?" I made sure to tilt my head as I spoke, it helps put people at ease – a "genuine" signal of enquiry.

Nina waved a hand vaguely. "I suppose so. I do not leave my home very often anymore. Niall is my connection with the world beyond my walls." She cast a coy glance at the redhead, who was studying his nails.

I continued, "When we were here earlier today, we were all enjoying looking at a map that showed how extensive Henry Morgan's lands used to be along the coast here. The map was dated 1690. I knew that a part of his property had sunk into the sea as a result of the earthquake in 1692 but, until I saw that map, I hadn't realized exactly how much had been lost. If you consider the Captain's Lookout estate and the *Caro Mio* estate as one piece of land, it looks as though the tower was built almost in the middle of Morgan's property – because it's quite close to the current boundary between the two – and just a small distance away from the sea. But when Morgan built the tower was set off to one side of the much larger, original property, and a good deal further back from where the beach would have been at the time. As he drove us here tonight Tarone said the land is always where it is, until it isn't – and that's what happened here; the position of the tower relative to the sea has changed significantly since the 1680s, when it was built, because the land around it has changed."

Nina plumped up her skirt. "So?" she said. "This is not very interesting."

"But it is," I replied. "Because there was another big earthquake in 1993, when the shape of the land changed again. That's when your access road disappeared, Nina, as you know."

"And this is when my problems began," she said, throwing up her hands as if in utter despair.

I managed a chuckle. "And those problems merely concerned access to a good entry road, right, Nina?" Nina nodded. "Well, I think it was rather more than that. You have chased Freddie through the courts to get that land for decades. Why? Just so you don't have to make a ten-minute journey that's a bit uncomfortable? Rubbish. It had to be more than that."

"It's about quality of life," piped up Niall, sounding like a whining child. "Nina deserves it."

I snapped, "Would she kill for it, Niall? Would you kill for her to have that quality of life?"

Nina and Niall responded quite differently; Nina flung an arm at me as if to discount my theory as worthless, while Niall's neck started to change color…it became red, beneath his tan and his freckles.

"I did not want him dead," said Nina. "The truth is I preferred to torture him, to make him miserable. Spending money on lawyers and papers and courts…this was sport for me. For Freddie? He hated it. It made people look at him and think him a mean man. Which is what he was. I made him come to the court all the time, and I gave interviews to the newspapers, so more and more people could see Freddie for what he was – a spiteful man." Nina tossed her head; if there'd been a bit less hairspray holding it in place her hair might have moved, but it didn't.

"I sense an affair gone sour, Nina," I said. "Your beloved Luca was dead, Freddie was nearby, and a good friend at that time. We know he wasn't averse to having relationships with women, despite his never marrying. Were you two an item before, or after, he broke Lottie's mother's heart?"

Nina wilted within her magnificent dress. Her chin quivered, she rubbed her fingers together, then her small hands. "He was a snake," she hissed. "He treated me badly. I was desolate when my Luca died, and I thought Freddie truly loved me. He made me believe he loved me. Then I find out he is also making love to another woman. Until now I did not know it was her mother."

She gestured toward Lottie with a thumb. Lottie's eyes grew round.

Nina continued. "I tell Freddie it is this 'other woman', or me – and he chooses me. This is good. I know it is real love. Then, after about a year, Freddie tells me it is over for us, that he will never speak to me again…that I have made him hurt someone so badly that she has taken her own life. She has written to him to tell him so before she kills herself. He never spoke to me again – except in court, when he had to face me. This is why I have fought him in court for so long; he *has* to speak to me there, the court *makes* him speak to me. Makes him look at me. Really see me."

"*That's* why you did it all?" said Niall. He sounded genuinely shocked. "I thought it was…I had no idea that was how you felt." I could see he was processing this new information, and not liking it. His eyes darted back and forth from one of his knees, to the other. His breathing became more labored. I began to wonder if my assessment of his attraction for Nina was accurate. I watched as the woman sitting beside him failed to rally, following her confession, and wondered how this would change Niall's actions going forward.

"But you tortured Freddie in other ways, too, didn't you, Nina?" I knew I had to capitalize upon the moment.

Everyone's eyes turned to the diminished figure on the sofa, including Arnold's, whose usually implacable demeanor was cracking, just a little. *At last.*

"I don't know what you mean," replied Nina, who sat a little straighter, and had a glimmer of a glint in her eye again.

"1993 wasn't just the start of your problems with your access road, was it? It was also when you discovered Henry Morgan's treasure and started to sell it off," I replied.

*I love it when everyone in a room looks shocked by something I say. Most gratifying.*

"But…what we saw…in Freddie's tower…" said Sheila.

"No, no, you're wrong. *Nina* didn't find the treasure, *Freddie* found it," shouted Lottie contemptuously. "*He* had the crystal skull. I saw it all those years ago. You said you saw it, too. How stupid are you, Cait?"

I tried to not show my annoyance as I replied, "I may be incredibly stupid, Lottie, but I am not wrong. Freddie had the crystal skull because he bought it, not because he found it. He didn't know who he'd bought it from, but he most certainly bought it."

Lottie looked confused. "But…but the other items I saw being sold, and going up for sale, online. Freddie was selling them, I'm certain of it." She nibbled her lip.

"No. Not Freddie, Nina," I said. "That's right, isn't it, Nina? It was you, with Niall's help, eventually. And, I believe, Arnold's before that?"

Nina's eyes flitted from Niall, to Arnold, to Inspector Charles, then to me. "I say nothing." She sat on her hands, as though that might help.

Unfortunately for Nina, Arnold's expression told me all I needed to know; the mask had slipped, and I saw the man behind it clearly for the first time. His eyes shone with love, and regret. His chin puckered.

"So, hang on, Cait…all that treasure we found in Freddie's tower…he *bought* that?" John sounded incredulous.

I nodded.

"Freddie had more treasure in his tower? More than just the crystal skull?" shouted Lottie. "Where? When did you find it? Why didn't anyone tell me?" Her entire body was rigid, she'd even dared to take a few steps out of her corner.

Throwing a withering look in Lottie's direction, Jack asked, "Where did Freddie get the money to buy it all? That stuff couldn't have come cheap." Then he answered himself. "Of course, the loans against the collateral in the estate. You're saying Freddie borrowed millions to be able to buy the treasure Nina was selling?" Jack's tone was filled with awe.

I nodded. "Look around you – there's a clear difference between the pieces here that Nina has chosen, and those purchased by her husband. Luca bought big, showy things, whereas the delicate, museum-quality rarities were Nina's choices. And what Freddie managed to buy from her wasn't everything she sold. He couldn't have afforded everything, could he, Nina?"

Nina stared at me with her mouth closed tight, her eyes flashing, nostrils flared.

Sheila spoke, "But…but if Nina was selling some of Henry Morgan's treasure to Freddie, that means Nina *wouldn't* have wanted him dead – that would be like killing the goose that lays the golden egg, right?" She seemed rather pleased with herself.

"That would make sense, yes, Sheila, except for a couple of things." I tried to not sound as though I believed I was the cleverest person in the room. "First of all, the goose had stopped laying; Freddie had taken out loans to the full extent of his creditworthiness – he was desperate for cash. We know this from several sources. Indeed, he was trying to put together deals to raise more money right up to the end of his life. For example, Nina's certainty that she was about to be able to get her hands on that strip of land she wanted so much? Yes, Niall might have been able to gather new evidence to support her claim, but I bet there was still going to be money involved, wasn't there? How wonderful for you, Nina – you'd have paid for your bit of extra land, then Freddie would have given you back your own money in exchange for another piece of the treasure. Perfect."

"Wait. Please stop. Where *was* the treasure? Did you *really* find it, Nina? Where was it hidden?" Lottie sounded desperate to know.

Nina said nothing.

"I believe it was buried by Morgan just about where the infinity edge of Nina's pool is now located," I said. "At least, around that spot, and toward the beach a little."

Lottie looked at me as though I'd grown a second head. "But that pool's been there since the 1960s, Nina told us so when we visited. If that's where Morgan buried it, they'd have discovered it when they first dug out the area for the pool."

"I know she told us that," I replied, "and I'm sure the pool was designed, and first installed, in the 1960s, as she said, but the entire thing had to be rebuilt after the big earthquake of 1993, didn't it, Nina? The liner it has now, with the attractive tile-pattern printed into the vinyl, that couldn't have been installed until some time around the mid-nineties, because the material didn't even exist in that form until about then." I couldn't help myself – I looked directly at Lottie and said, "I read a lot, and remember it all, that's how I know that little nugget of information."

I returned my attention to Nina. "My money's on you making the discovery of the treasure as a result of that pool collapsing, and having to be re-dug and re-built, in 1993. Remember that house on the map we all looked at before lunch…the one you were so surprised once sat pretty much where we are right now? Well, given the change in topography due to the earthquake back in the seventeenth century, it wouldn't have been where this house now stands, but closer to the current shoreline; between your pool and the sea, in fact. If you recall, it was called *Ty Gwerthfawr*, the 'Precious House' – or maybe the 'Treasure House'? There wouldn't have been a lot of people who spoke Welsh on the island back in the 1680s, and those who did – like Morgan's wife, and even his Welsh manservant – could have read the name literally, whereas maybe Morgan might have meant it more figuratively. What I'm interested to know is where you keep it now, Nina. The remainder of Morgan's treasure, I mean."

Nina didn't speak. Lottie glowered at her as she sunk back into her corner.

"Ah well, we can return to that topic later. For now, let me talk about Niall. Yes, you."

Niall looked as though he were about to be led to face a firing squad. "What do you want with me? I know nothing," he whined.

"That's such a lie, Niall. You know everything," I replied. "You know who shot Freddie, and who shot Wilson. You know why, and you know how. Of course, what I'm really interested in is the why – and that's complex, but it all hinges on you having messed up in some way. Am I right?"

His micro-expressions were screaming that I had hit the mark, despite the fact he was furiously shaking his head. "I didn't mess up, I didn't. I mean…I mean, I don't know what you're talking about."

I sighed, "Lottie told us she'd been following the sales of items she believed came from Morgan's Panamanian haul for some years. The world we live in demands that most transactions now take place via the Internet, and Lottie confirmed that was where the agent acting on her behalf discovered the items. That was a great way to sell them – even though Freddie lived right next door, he'd never know exactly who he was dealing with. He'd have known it was someone on the island, of course, because he believed that to be where the treasure was located. He must have put every bit of himself into trying to find out who was selling, but – for years, it seems – to no avail. And I believe that was because Arnold was good at doing his job."

We all looked at Arnold, who didn't move a muscle – which was impressive, and rather proved my point that he had a cool head and could probably keep it under pressure. It was Nina's stolen glance at him, and the pitiful expression on her face as she did it that spoke volumes; she was embarrassed.

I continued, "Now I admit I cannot be sure *exactly* what happened, but I think it went something like this…you usurped Arnold's place in Nina's affections, Niall, and you also replaced him as her 'treasure disposal and dispersion manager'. Let's not beat about the bush here, folks, it's clear to anyone with eyes that Arnold feels more affection for Nina than any butler would for someone who was merely his employer – it's visible not just in everything he does for her, but how he does it."

Arnold dared a sideways glance at me, then he and Nina finally exchanged a sad smile.

I continued, "I don't think Arnold would have hesitated to act as Nina's right hand man when it came to ensuring that the treasure was safely stowed away, and I suspect he used his not-inconsiderable organizational skills to set up the system whereby sales of the objects were undertaken in the first place. When you managed to get Arnold 'demoted' from that role, Niall, I'm sure you managed to do things well enough for a while, and Freddie still didn't suspect who had the treasure. But something changed; I believe Freddie worked out where the treasure items were being shipped from, and maybe by whom, and that meant you needed Freddie out of the way – before Freddie confronted Nina about being the source. What happened, Niall? When you got involved with the shipping of a piece, did it somehow turn up at Freddie's home with a 'Return to sender' label? Was it a simple paperwork issue? Something trivial like having been seen by Freddie when you were taking a recognisable package to have it 'shipped'? You're an incredibly busy man; stretching yourself thin across so many responsibilities, it must have been easy to slip up."

Niall looked at his feet, and finally stopped tapping them. He didn't speak. Nina's tongue darted from side to side along the edge of her gleaming teeth, like a snake sniffing the air.

"Once Freddie knew about Nina having the treasure, or at least suspected her of having it – because, let's be honest, Niall, you and Nina are certainly closely linked in so many ways – he became a problem. I don't think you hesitated, Niall, but you had to embellish, didn't you? By which I mean you had to plant that gun beside Freddie's body...not something it would have been easy for Freddie to have shot himself with; a Walther PPK with a silencer attached, making it almost impossible for the angle of entry of the bullet that killed him to have been achieved by someone shooting themselves."

"But how did Niall do it?" pleaded Sheila.

"I worked it out thanks to something you said," I replied.

Sheila's brow furrowed. "What did I say that helped?"

"You told me it sounded as though there was a giant dragonfly – or maybe a black witch moth – trapped in your bathroom, or outside it, in the small hours of the night Freddie was shot."

Sheila shrugged. "And?"

"It was the noise you heard that helped me come up with the solution; drones are wonderful gizmos, aren't they, Niall? Toys for adults, you might say, just the sort of thing a gadget freak like you would love. And when you pair a drone with a realtor you get great overhead photographs of properties to display in your sales window, and you get a clever way to get aerial shots of an estate to try to prove exactly where property lines fall."

Niall still wouldn't look up at me, so I turned my attention to the rest of the people in the room, most especially Inspector Charles. "Niall did all that with his drone, but he did more with it, too. Much more. He's always been good with his hands, as Lottie told us, and it wouldn't be beyond him to manage to fit up a drone to allow it to shoot a gun. Trust me – a quick trawl online will show you that people have been altering drones to make them capable of firing semi-automatic pistols for years, so it can be done, and that's what I believe Niall did. Using his skill as a sailor he took out the boat Nina gifted him, sent up the drone, flew it right into Freddie's tower through the open window and fired a gun at him. Not from the perfect angle, but it worked. Freddie went down, and Niall recalled the drone. Then he attached the 'James Bond' weapon – from which he'd probably already fired a couple of shots into the sea – and sent the drone back to drop it beside the body, hoping anyone finding said gun would imagine it was just the sort of thing Freddie might own. A ridiculous flourish. Pointless. As was killing Freddie."

"It wasn't pointless," screamed Nina, "Freddie was going to ruin my life, take away my peace. He was going to build a resort, right next to me. Probably with nightclubs. Niall told me. He showed me plans drawn on a big, overhead photograph of the Captain's Lookout estate. I didn't want Freddie to die, really, but Niall said it was the only certain way to stop him."

"Shut up, Nina," hissed Niall.

"And what about Wilson Thomas, Niall?" I continued. "You didn't expect a witness, did you? And you certainly didn't expect to be recognized. You must have been concentrating on the drone; my guess is that you ran it off a tablet, with a video feed from a camera you'd mounted on it. That's how most folks do it, it seems. No time to notice an old guy rambling along the beach, watching you on your boat, until it was too late. He might not have realized the significance of what he'd seen until the news of Freddie's death was made public the next day."

"I don't know any Wilson Thomas," said Niall.

"Oh, come off it, Niall, of course you knew him. You've lived here your entire life – Wilson Thomas was a local character. I've learned from Inspector Charles that Wilson's reputation as a decent, honest man was well known, too. I bet he could have described everything you'd done the night you killed Freddie, and you knew he was just the sort of person who'd be prepared to speak to the police about what he'd witnessed. So, you decided to get rid of him too. And why change the MO? It had worked so well, you decided to repeat the performance. You waited until Wilson was inside his shack, with his lamp lit – allowing for an easier shot for you – then you sent in the drone from your boat. This time you were more careful; the way the arms of the cove curl near where the shack is located meant you could pretty much hide your boat around the corner from the shack and yet still steer the drone using the camera mounted on it. Almost invisible, and certainly quiet enough for the sound to be drowned out by the pounding of the surf and the heavy rain that night, your drone got the job done again. Even better, you'd spotted someone hanging around the beach, hadn't you? You didn't know who it was, but thought you'd use them as a scapegoat – hence the call to the police. I bet the police will find a pay-as-you-go phone when they search your belongings – or maybe you were bright enough to dispose of it. I doubt it; you strike me as the sort of man who'd find a phone like that to be useful, especially if you wanted to keep some of your more interesting calls completely private."

I didn't want anyone to know that Wilson had lived long enough to utter some last words to Bud, so I left it at that.

"It's all rubbish," said Niall petulantly. His ears glowed red.

I continued, "The killer not taking items they clearly wanted when they killed Freddie, but coming back to do so at a later time, was puzzling. But the drone wasn't able to do that for you, was it? Amelia told me you'd recently visited Freddie in his tower, and I bet that's when he showed you the map he'd found of the original Henry Morgan property lines. It would have been easy enough for you to get in through the door at the base of the tower – it was a pretty standard lock, and I bet a bit of lock-picking isn't past you, is it? Bud and I saw the scratches you left with your handiwork. You wanted the map Freddie had located, because if anyone else had found it after Freddie's death they might have put two and two together, guessing Morgan's treasure had been buried on this estate, because the map showed the existence of a secret tunnel running from the tower to where the 'Precious House' sat. It's just a dotted line that could be a pathway, as Bud suggested when we all saw it, but, once you know where the tunnel is – running due east from the base of the tower – it's clear that's what's marked on the map. We've found the tunnel, by the way – it's blocked, but it's still there alright. The funny thing is that I don't think Freddie ever knew it existed. When we shifted his desk to gain access to it we scratched the floor, but there were no other signs of damage to the planks. None of the mechanisms worked as easily, and the dust alone suggested the cavity beneath the floor hadn't been entered in many, many years. But you couldn't take the chance that Freddie didn't know about the tunnel, could you? You didn't want Freddie to *know* the treasure was here, on this property. All he did was *suspect*, but how would he ever prove it? The map with the tunnel on it would help him do that – and then the game would be up, because there'd be an almighty fight for ownership of that treasure once it was known it had been found."

Niall squirmed, but didn't speak.

I pressed on, "And let's not forget that you'd already convinced Nina that she should buy up Freddie's entire estate after his death, so she could protect her precious peace and quiet. How much did you make on that deal, Niall? A million? Acting for both the seller and the buyer would net you about that much, I should think. Nice. And a clever move on your part; you planted the seed of horror into Nina's mind about what might happen on that land if it were to be developed. You convinced her Freddie was about to develop it, and further convinced her that killing Freddie would stop it. You got her to allow you to make the deal with Cooperman on her behalf, and it's all coming up roses for Niall. Thanks to Nina's bank balance…which is stuffed with the money Freddie borrowed to pay for the treasure, which is what put him in debt and meant the estate had to be sold. Absolutely neat, and practical, and perfect – for Niall."

Nina shifted, and started to shrink into herself again.

At a nod from Inspector Charles, I continued, "So, Freddie was dead, you could take what you wanted from his tower room – but what *did* you want, Niall? You wanted that map, yes, but did you also grab up a bundle of old papers that had been sitting on his desk beneath the crystal skull?"

"This is all rubbish," said Niall again – his ability to think creatively seemed to have deserted him. His voice quivered.

"No, not rubbish." I nodded at Inspector Charles, and he nodded at Constable Lewis. She walked into the sitting room with a large plastic evidence bag containing a matt-black drone, about two feet wide. "The police found that in one of the guest villas here, where you've been staying, Niall. I'm going to assume it's covered in your fingerprints, and yours alone."

Nina and Niall exchanged a significant glance. Nina's chin quivered, and she began to cry. Arnold reached forward and gently handed her a handkerchief. She smiled at the elderly man as she took it, and he smiled back. It was a warm exchange, loaded with sorrow, and regret.

Niall's shoulders slumped. His entire body sagged. He knew we had him. Eventually he shrugged, and spoke, "There was a copy of a part of the map on top of the pile," he said flatly. "It looked old, but it turned out it was just something I think Freddie himself had copied out using an ordinary fountain pen – you know, with real ink. That's why it looked old, I guess. I thought it might be useful, but all it showed were the places where the land had slipped in the 1993 quake. It didn't help me at all, but I didn't know that until later. When I saw it on his desk I was in a hurry, so I just picked up the whole bunch of papers. I realised I didn't need the sketch, so I just chucked the entire pile away; the rest of the papers were just useless old lists of names."

"Chucked?" Bud's tone was harsh.

Niall's head snapped up. "Yeah, chucked. Out. In the garbage."

"When?" Bud's entire body tensed; he wasn't messing about.

Niall shrugged. "Yesterday? I don't know."

Bud leaped to his feet. "Here's a chance to be helpful, Arnold. Where would Niall's garbage, from yesterday, be right now?"

Arnold sized up the situation in an instant. "Sir will find it in our recycling sorting shed. Would sir care to follow me?"

Bud glanced at Inspector Charles, who nodded, then Bud, Jack, John, and Lottie all left the sitting room with Arnold, and headed toward the pool.

Niall and Nina looked genuinely confused, if cowed. "Lot of fuss over nothing," muttered Niall.

I'd had enough. "Nothing? Freddie Burkinshaw might not have been a trustworthy, pleasant or popular man, but he was a human being. Wilson Thomas was a good man who'd fallen on hardship, and who happened to be in the wrong place at the wrong time. They are both dead. That is not 'nothing', Niall. That's a double murder, with greed – pure and simple – as the underlying reason. I understand that Nina didn't pull the trigger, but she's got to be accountable too. It's up to the police, and the courts, to decide how you're both charged…and to decide if anyone else needs to face charges too, like Arnold, for example. In a way, it was maybe a very fortunate error you made that night, Amelia…by mistakenly putting some overripe ackee into Mr. Freddie's smoothie. That accident raised questions about the initial decision the police had reached about his death being a suicide. True serendipity."

Amelia stared at me open-mouthed, as did Tarone; Inspector Charles merely nodded, sagely.

I pressed on, "I also think it's going to be an incredibly complicated process for the courts to sort out who now really owns what. If Niall has signed legal papers on Nina's behalf, undertaking to purchase Freddie's estate with money paid to her for treasure she never had the right to sell, then maybe she hasn't bought the estate at all…I don't know. Do you, inspector?"

Inspector Charles shook his head. "I'm glad to say that's not my decision, though I'll be interested to find out where the rest of that treasure is at the moment, to be able to arrange to have it placed somewhere for safekeeping. We have already taken everything that was stored beneath Mr. Burkinshaw's bed."

Nina threw her hands into the air. "Freddie *slept* on it? That is so like Freddie. His possessions had to be close to him at all times…things, and people. What an odious man. As for the rest of it? Yes, I shall tell you everything. The inner wall of the library is false. It leads to another room; originally my Luca played high stakes card games with his special friends in there. It was his private place, dark, no windows. No one knew what time it was, or whether it was even day or night. He would sit in there for days, sometimes, and the money that changed hands also changed lives. Those were heady days, when the stakes were high in so many ways. As they still are today, it seems. I understand everything now. I have been a fool. A blind, old fool. I should have learned by this time in my life that there are people upon whom one can rely, and those one should not trust. I made the wrong decision. I was flattered because a young man showed an interest in me. I hurt Arnold deeply; all he ever did was support me. I can show you where the door to the secret room is, inspector, and how to open it." She looked around, obviously expecting to be helped to her feet by Arnold, who wasn't there. "Niall," she said, and stuck out her hand.

Niall pushed her arm away. "Get up yourself, you old crone."

Inspector Charles did the gentlemanly thing and strode over to help Nina from the sofa. He also indicated – with a swift flick of the wrist – that Niall Jackson should be handcuffed. Sheila and I knew we could leave, and we also both knew we wanted to; when we got the nod from Charles, I told Amelia and Tarone to wait for us. As Sheila darted out into the night heading in the general direction we'd seen the others take, I hung back for just a moment, and leaned in toward Tarone.

"I know you believed the entire estate would be yours after Freddie's death, and that – in your mind – you probably felt that everything on the estate was yours to do with as you pleased. The ten bottles of cognac in the pantry? I know you've sold at least one of them to raise money to be able to buy an entire new kit, and running shoes, and so forth, but have you still got any of the other bottles left?"

Amelia's mouth dropped open, and Tarone nodded sullenly. "I only sold one. Got good money for it, too. I got the others at home, in the shed. I can easy put them back into the pantry." He sounded contrite.

"Good idea," I said. "That cognac's worth about three thousand, five hundred dollars – American – a bottle."

"How much?" chorused Amelia and her grandson.

"I kill that Ronnie. Him robbed me, yeah man," said Tarone, his eyes wide.

"You selling stuff you been stealin' to that Ronnie Hangar? Him a wicked, wicked man, Tarone…"

I left Amelia giving Tarone a good telling off as I headed toward the pool, calling Bud's name.

## Fiery Finale

As I passed the gleaming turquoise pool, which sounded even better at night with its fountains and jets, I could see a flame flickering just beyond the far end of the guest annex. I walked as fast as I could and crossed paths with Arnold, who was returning to the house. He seemed to have aged a decade or so. We exchanged a sad smile.

When I reached the group I was a bit out of breath. They'd found a metal waste-paper basket; there were just a few sheets of paper still burning inside it, among ashes.

"Did you find what you were looking for?" I asked.

Bud nodded. "All of us saw the lists, all of us witnessed their destruction. Our mission is successfully completed. Thanks to you."

"So, now they don't exist anymore, can you tell us exactly what the papers were?" asked Sheila of Jack. I didn't say a word, because I suspected Jack was much more likely to spill the beans than Bud.

Jack looked at his colleagues, who both shrugged. When Jack spoke, it was with gravity. "First of January, 1942: the Big Four nations – the USA, Great Britain, China, and Russia – signed the papers that became the foundation for the United Nations. The next day a host more countries followed. More and more signed up as the months, then the years, went by. Prior to that, during the last few months of 1941, Washington, DC was a hotbed of negotiation. Of course, it being Washington, not much was *truly* secret because everyone had their nose in everyone else's business. But there was a series of private dinners, hosted by various individuals, that were deemed truly confidential, because they were 'informal'. The names of the guests invited to those dinners, who represented their countries, was a matter that was closely guarded at the time. Today, there are those who might want to point at the way in which such 'informal' negotiations were undertaken as a means to cause friction within the UN; those guest lists could have become inflammatory. Now, they no longer exist."

Sheila shook her head. "Guest lists? Secret dinners? The UN? You might be getting a bit long in the tooth for all this, Jack. But, well done; I'm glad it's all over, now."

I was at the end of my tether; I decided this was the time to break free. "Nope, sorry Jack, that's just not good enough. I've led you to those papers, and I think I deserve to really know why they are so important. Lottie, you said you were here on behalf of your family's reputation – at your father's insistence. What on earth could your grandfather have signed that would bring your family's name into disrepute now, almost eighty years after the events the lists recorded? And Bud, what's all this about Sweden needing you here?" I looked at every face; no one made eye contact with me.

I'd had enough. "I won't give up, I'll just keep asking. So tell me now, and you'll be glad of the peace and quiet later on." I realized Bud, at least, would know this to be the truth.

Bud shrugged. "Sweden managed to remain neutral throughout the war, but it occasionally made 'concessions' to its neutrality. If the guest lists for dinners where Sweden was represented were to become known, it might be inferred that Sweden favored a world view that today would be seen as...damaging to Sweden's current position within it. There might have been certain persons close to the Swedish royal family named in those lists. Possibly."

Jack jumped in. "Canada did some things in the war she's far from proud of. All nations did. Though that's no excuse. Sending specific people to attend private dinners, where said individuals mixed with those present, could be read as Canada at least contemplating some terrible options. And the fact that one of the Canadians in question was the grandfather-in-law of a current minister doesn't help."

"And the Brits?" added John. "Well, we were in a terrible position in 1941, of course, but couldn't allow it to appear that way. Nowadays, the list of people at some of the dinners held would allow for a revisionist's free-for-all when it came to whom Britain was prepared to consider her friends and allies." He looked at Jack with a shake of the head. "And there's a minister of state whose reputation could be irreparably damaged by the knowledge that a member of his family was an attendee at a dinner where certain…elements…were hosts. It's one of those things – wars make strange bedfellows, and those jumping enthusiastically into said bed at the time can find their children, and their children's children, ruing the day they did."

Lottie was the most forthright and illuminating of anyone when she said simply, "My grandfather was dining with people who later became rather well known as much more terrifyingly left wing, and right wing, than he might have believed at the time. Imagine Daddy living that one down; his father dining with closet commies and Nazis. Daddy was horrified; there was evidence of his father breaking bread and clinking glasses with a list of Who's Who in dodgy politicking. He'd managed to hush up the fact that my grandfather had once roomed with the infamous Philby for months on end, then he found out about these guest lists and went potty. I *had* to help him out. *Whatever* it meant. After all, it's my family name too, you know."

I gave some thought to what the men, and Lottie, had said. The world of politics is not my forte; the types of personalities drawn to that particular arena have some of the most fascinating, yet worrying, profiles – often sharing many traits with those who commit terrible crimes. Risk takers, narcissists, those who truly believe only they know the "right" answer, and those who act purely for personal, venal reasons. Yes, it's an area ripe for psychological investigation alright, but I'd long ago decided to focus my efforts on the legally defined criminal element, which keeps me busy enough. But it seemed as though my life with Bud might still draw me close to the place where the crimes were on a global scale, and where many saw those acts not as being at all criminal, but as necessities…imperatives, even.

I absolutely understood that liaisons during a time of war, and recorded in the papers in question, might have meant that current parties in, or out, of power could be viewed by their supporters as having a history not quite as they had presented it. Or that individuals closely associated with, or even personally related to, those currently active in global politics might be viewed as having a questionable background, based upon their attendance at one documented dinner, as recorded in these lists…and I wondered about that. Should someone be Twitter-trolled, or worse, because a grandparent was instructed to attend a "social" event eighty years earlier? I grappled with wondering what my husband might do – or possibly had already done, at some point – on behalf of his country, without having any possible chance of understanding the potential implications of his actions decades later. I understood why three governments, and a family, would want the lists destroyed. No one likes to be reminded of their mistakes. But the price that had been paid? Terrible.

I simply said, "Thank you for telling me," then I hugged Bud.

"I'm so proud of you, Wife," he said. "I'd never have worked it all out like you did." I glowed. "And s for working out where the papers were? Thank you."

Jack and John also congratulated and thanked me, then Sheila and Jack hugged each other in the light of the dying flames, and the moon.

Lottie was bouncing from foot to foot. "I'm off," she said. "I want to see whatever treasure Nina has hidden here. This is my only chance. Ever. I'll get a taxi back to my hotel."

John's expression of joy faded a little. "You can stay at the estate with us tonight, if you like." He seemed to want her to say yes.

"You're joking, aren't you?" Lottie snapped. "Insane, the lot of you. You knew how much I wanted to touch the skull again, to see Henry Morgan's treasure, and not one of you let me have that satisfaction, did you? May you all rot in hell, and the sooner the better. Good bloody bye." Lottie stomped off toward the sitting room.

"And good bloody riddance," shouted Sheila after her.

The rest of us mumbled our agreement.

"So, you did what you needed to do, Cait, and we did what we needed to do, and tomorrow's our penultimate full day here," said Bud. "Anyone want to make any plans?"

"Have a lie in?" I said.

"Nap beside the pool," suggested John.

"Wimp," said Jack.

Sheila laughed. "We can all do exactly as we please, until we have to get ourselves to the airport just after lunchtime on Sunday. When's your flight, John?"

John swore. "No idea, Lottie has the details. I'll have to somehow get her to share that information with me. Maybe she'll hate the idea of sitting next to me all the way back to

London so much that she'll sort out an alternative flight for herself. One can but hope."

We began to walk back toward the main house.

"I wouldn't mind a quick look at whatever Nina still has left of that treasure, too, but then let's get back to the estate and get our heads down, for tonight," I said. "I expect Amelia and Tarone will be glad to get home; Tarone is due to head off to Kingston tomorrow morning. Big weekend for him; trials for his running team," I said. "I do hope they'll be alright. There's still no certainty about their situation, is there?"

Bud hugged me. "Cait, there's only so much we can do. Sheila told me how you covered with the police for Amelia, regarding her feeding overripe ackee to Freddie. Well done. Of course we can all hope for the best for them, but – short of John's brilliant plan for him to retire to the place, and them being kept on to care for him as he becomes more and more decrepit – I don't know what to say."

"Hey, that's my idea, and I'm going to stick with it," quipped John.

"Are you really going to call it a day?" Bud asked him.

"Don't know, old friend. Really don't know," replied John, patting Bud on the back as we walked.

"None of you ever really give up, completely, do you?" said Sheila.

"I'm sorry to say I think you're right about that," I said.

"You're acknowledging someone else is right about something, Wife?" said Bud, squeezing my waist. "That's unusual."

"Wonders will never cease, Husband," I said.

"Now that's something you're definitely right about, Wife. Come on, let's go and see that treasure."

# *Acknowledgements*

May, 2020

This book has been written during "unprecedented" times (my money's on that word being recognized as one of "the" words of 2020). I don't know when you're reading this, of course, but I'm sure you'll have your own recollections of what was happening in the world between mid-January and May 2020, which was when this book was written. If nothing else, what I *have* learned is that there's no way to predict the course of the COVID-19 virus, nor the way nations will respond to its challenges. What I can be certain of, however, is that you'll be reading this in a world that differs from the one in which I am living today.

All of that being said, the people who helped me get this book finished and out into the world will not have changed, and I want to acknowledge their contributions.

Unusually for me, I didn't write this entire book at my desk. I fell behind (not so unusual) and had to finish writing it on a cruise ship. I was lucky – I was sharing the ship not only with my beloved husband, but also with a crew who did everything they could to ensure that our month-long trip was as safe, and delightful, as possible. With that in mind, there are a few people I want to thank here: the stalwart and delightful Ansel Williams, ably assisted by Double A and Sandip – without their constant attention I don't think I'd have been able to finish this book; they helped keep me sane, and refreshed! Ansel and his fellow-countryman Nicholas also allowed me to double-check many facts with them, despite their longing to be back in Jamaica, rather than just talking about their home. One day I'll be able to return to that lovely island, I hope, and to – somewhere, sometime – reconnect with that wonderful quartet of men who were our daily companions at sea.

I'd like to thank Nina Mazzo – yes, there is a *real* person named Nina Mazzo who bid at an auction held at Left Coast Crime in Vancouver, in March 2019, to have her name appear in one of my books. I was honoured to be the Toastmaster at the convention, and Nina's generosity benefitted the charity One to One, a children's literacy program that provides one-to-one tutoring to children in elementary schools during regular school hours. You can find out more about their wonderful work at: www.one-to-one.ca

When Nina placed the winning bid, I wasn't sure which book I'd be writing next, but Nina was delighted that her name would be given to a character in a Cait Morgan Mystery. I hope she enjoys her "other life" in this book. Thanks for bidding, Nina.

My editor, Anna Harrisson, was grappling with homeschooling her children, as well as meeting deadlines, when she worked on this book – my thanks to Anna, and to her family, whose support meant she could keep going.

My copy editor, Sue Vincent, was also juggling new responsibilities, as well as working from home for her various clients, and she didn't let one of us down! Thanks, Sue.

My thanks, too, to Janice Dumas, who gave me valuable insights and bolstered my confidence just when I needed it.

As ever, my husband's support has allowed me to work on this book without losing my mind, and my sister and mother have both been incredibly patient as I have talked through the intricate details of plot and characters during our daily, lengthy, telephone calls. Also, I must thank Gemma and Kevin, to whom this book is dedicated; I am not stretching the truth at all when

I say that, without their help, my husband and I would have lacked the necessities of life, which they have delivered to our front door, during lockdown, on a weekly basis. Trust me when I say the very least I can do is dedicate a book to them by way of thanks.

Then there are the people who are working within the seismically-shifting world of publishing at this time. I know bloggers, reviewers, librarians, and booksellers are all facing a slew of probably long-lasting challenges, with impacts none of us can imagine as I write. My gratitude is overflowing for those who have helped this reader find this book, somehow. Thank you.

Finally, thank YOU. As I said when I began, I have no idea when you're reading this, but I hope you enjoy/enjoyed your trip to Jamaica with Cait, Bud, and the "gang", and I hope you consider reading about all her other adventures. Thank you, and happy reading.

*Cathy Ace*

## ABOUT THE AUTHOR

Author CATHY ACE was born and raised in Swansea, Wales, and now lives in British Columbia, Canada. She is the author of The Cait Morgan Mysteries, The WISE Enquiries Agency Mysteries, The Wrong Boy, and collections of short stories and novellas. As well as being passionate about writing crime fiction, she's also a keen gardener.

You can find out more about Cathy and her work at:
www.cathyace.com

Lightning Source UK Ltd.
Milton Keynes UK
UKHW011413250920
370518UK00003B/896

9 78